Flashman and the Zulus

Robert Brightwell

Published in 2020 by FeedARead.com Publishing

First Edition

A CIP catalogue record for this title is available from the British
Library.

Introduction

While many people have heard of the battle at Rorke's Drift, (featured in the film *Zulu*) and the one at Isandlwana that preceded it, few outside of South Africa know of an earlier and equally bloody conflict. Under a tyrannical king, the Zulu nation defended its territory with ruthless efficiency against white settlers. Only a naïve English vicar, with his family and some translators are permitted to live in the king's capital. It is into this cleric's household that Thomas Flashman finds himself, as a most reluctant guest.

Listening to sermons of peace and tolerance against a background of executions and slaughter, Thomas is soon fleeing for his life, barely a spearpoint ahead of regiments of fearsome warriors. He is to learn that there is a fate even worse than his own death before being pitched in with Boers and British settlers as they fight a cunning and relentless foe. Thomas strives for his own salvation, before discovering that chance has not finished with him yet.

As always, if you have not already read the memoirs of Thomas' more famous nephew, edited by George MacDonald Fraser, they are strongly recommended.

Robert Brightwell

Chapter 1

It looked like a grey, watery porridge with black seeds sprinkled over the top. I wasn't hungry and every part of my body was in pain. It hurt to breathe and when I tried to move my left arm there was a sharp stabbing pain below the elbow, where I suspected there was a broken bone. I felt like I had been thrown down a mountain. I was cold, even though I had a blanket around my shoulders under the warm sunshine. I still was not sure what was going on or even where I was. Minutes before I had been in a dark space. I was awoken by shouting and then carried on a stretcher out into a very bright day. As my eyes adjusted to the glare, my attention was taken by two black men in front of me. They were big, powerful brutes, with oiled skin like polished ebony. Taller and darker than other Africans I had seen, they glared down at me with barely disguised contempt.

I cannot have been an impressive sight; my clothes were dirty and torn, my head throbbed and as I looked down my body, I saw that my right ankle had swollen to twice its normal size. I had just cried out in pain as a white man and a boy hoisted me up by the shoulders into a sitting position.

The lad was holding out a wooden bowl containing the porridge. "You 'ave to drink it, sir," he encouraged. I stared at him and he seemed familiar. Dressed in little more than rags, he too was filthy and I guessed no more than twelve years old.

"But what is it?" I gasped, confused. "And where am I? What is going on?"

"This 'ere is the king's physic," announced the urchin, gesturing at the bowl. "Made by the king's doctors and given only on his order. It is a great honour to 'ave it."

"And it will make me better?" I pressed, staring suspiciously at the contents.

"God be praised it will," announced the man at my other shoulder. I looked around and was sure I had not seen him before. Weak eyes surveyed me through small spectacles and beneath his smile, a starched white parson's collar looked incongruous over a darned blue shirt. "Put your faith in the Lord," he encouraged.

I groaned. The last thing I needed was an overly enthusiastic God-botherer. Turning back to the boy I repeated my question, "Will it make me better?"

4

The lad could have worked on his bedside manner, for he answered with alarming honesty. "No, it will probably make you worse," he announced. "It might even kill you."

"Then I don't want it." I pushed the bowl away to a growl of disapproval from the two watching Africans.

"You don't understand, sir," whispered the urchin. "If you refuse it, these two messengers," he gestured to the men standing in front of me, "will tell the king, who will be insulted. He will then send his guards to get you and they will take you to the top of that hill opposite. Then they will put your head on a rock and dash out your brains with their clubs."

"What?" I croaked, astounded. "You mean I will die if I refuse it and I might still die if I drink the damn stuff?" Fear and indignation battled their way to the front of my consciousness. Had they confused me with some vagrant who could be threatened? It was understandable, given my appearance, but before it was too late I needed to show them I was not a man to be trifled with. "Who the bloody hell is this king?" I glared angrily at his messengers and then winced in pain as I took a breath to continue, "Doesn't he know who I am? I am a personal friend of the British governor, who will have his ruddy hide for britches if he hurts me."

My raving was brought to an end by the urchin, who to my surprise took charge of the situation. Ordering the parson to hold my arms, he grabbed my nose, and as I gasped for air he started to tip the vile filth from the bowl down my throat. I tried to struggle and throw them off, yet found I was as weak as a kitten. My chest was in agony as the cleric pressed my arm against it. The damn brat nearly broke my nose as he held my head firmly in the crook of his arm. I tried to spit out as much as I could, but I had to swallow some.

"You're spilling it," warned the parson as I thrashed about between them.

"'Course I am," grunted the urchin as he held my head steady. "He would be dead for certain if he had it all." I remember that exchange vividly, for it was both alarming and comforting at the same time – at least they were not trying to kill me.

Eventually, the bowl was empty. As I was released and lowered back down on my stretcher, I heard the Africans shouting angrily. They were pointing to the mess down the front of my shirt. While I could not understand what they were saying, it was clear that they thought I had spilt too much. At that moment I felt a sharp stabbing

5

pain in my stomach and I was soon doubled over in a new agony. I heard the boy arguing with the Africans in their own tongue, but I was far too distracted to pay any attention. It was like my guts were on fire. I was panting in pain – at that moment, having my brains bludgeoned out on a rock would almost have been a blessed relief.

God knows what the boy told the Africans. They went away still shouting and waving their arms in the air, while the parson kept asking the lad what was happening. "Quick, get him inside," ordered the boy, ignoring the repeated questions. Without a moment's delay, my stretcher was hoisted up and then I was back inside the dark hut.

"Help me," I gasped, looking around the gloomy interior. To my surprise, I saw a white woman with her arm around a young girl, staring at me in wide-eyed horror.

"What did they say, William? What did they say?" The reverend was wringing his hands and staring out of the hut door at the retreating backs of the two Africans.

The boy who, despite his youth, I was quickly realising was the person to rely on, ignored the cleric. "Mrs Owen, could I trouble you for a cup of water with three spoonfuls of salt stirred in it?" The cup was swiftly provided while I writhed around, more confused than ever as my bowels continued to convulse. "Here," the boy I now knew as William passed me the cup. "Drink this as quickly as you can. Your life might depend on it." I knew that salt water would make me vomit and I wanted to get that poison out of my body as quickly as possible. I downed the cup in three gulps and then felt fresh spasms wrack my guts.

I will spare you the details of what happened over the next half an hour. Suffice to say that the wooden bowl was refilled again and then some, as I retched and heaved while crouched over it. Unable to speak, I could still listen and what I learned only added to my sense of alarm. William explained to the parson that he had told the king's messengers that I had drunk enough of the physic that I was bound to be cured. "I agreed he would seek an audience with the king before the next full moon to personally thank him," he continued.

"But what if he can't?" wailed the cleric. "He has been ill with a fever these past two days."

"He has to," insisted the lad stubbornly, "or they will see it as proof he has rejected the physic. You know what will happen then."

The hut was soon filled with the acrid stench of vomit, but the parson, who kept regularly peering out of the door for any sign of the king's guards, would not let them take the full bowls outside. I learned that the king often watched the priest's hut with a telescope from his compound at the bottom of the hill we were on. Eventually, the young girl was sent out to get a pail. My bowls were placed in the bottom and another larger one with grain set on the top. The girl was then instructed to feed the chickens the grain, with orders to leave the pail behind the hut, out of sight of the curious king. By then my guts had settled a little and while I was sure it was nothing to do with the physic, I was beginning to feel a little better.

"I know you, don't I?" I gasped to the lad called William as I took more interest in my surroundings.

He grinned. "Yes, I found you in a hippo trap. Well, some villagers told me you were there," he corrected himself. "But I got them to get you out and when you got ill, to bring you here."

It was coming back to me now. A deep steep-sided pit with stakes hammered into the bottom that had done for my horse and nearly skewered me. I remembered seeing the vultures circling in the patch of sky above and hearing the bark of wild dogs that must have smelt the horse's blood. There had been faces too, timid black ones that had peered over the edge, but ignored my pleas for help. I couldn't stand on my ankle and had tried to hack at the mud sides with my good arm and my knife, but it was a hopeless task. I fell back twice, nearly impaling myself on a stake the second time. The vultures were getting braver, gathering at the edge of my pit, gimlet eyes in ugly bald heads surveying my pitiful efforts to escape. At night I heard the sound of other unknown animals. I sat hunched in one corner of the pit with my rifle, ready to make a last stand against tearing claws and teeth. I must have been there close to two days before William's face appeared over the edge of the pit. Ropes and poles had been produced then and soon I was being hauled out, screaming in agony as my ankle was knocked against the side. I was taken to a small native village, but that was the last thing I clearly remembered before this rude awakening.

"How did you get in the pit?" asked William.

I wracked my disordered wits to think. "I was hunting with the Dutch, the Boers. They had found some elephants and wanted the ivory." Fragments of memory came back; the Boers laughing at me when I suggested capturing one to put to harness. I told them that one elephant could do the work of a dozen oxen and how I had seen them used in India. They had mocked the idea and ridden off while I had hung back. I did not want to take part in the hunt. I recalled the

7

elephant I had ridden from Madras and how its mahout had left the animal in charge of his infant son. I was just recalling the gentle intelligence of the creature when there was the sound of splintering wood from the trees nearby. Smashing its way into view was a massive elephant, twice the size of any I had known in India. Seeing me, it raised its mighty tusks in a challenge, its huge ears flapping and making it look even bigger. Man and mount were frozen in shock and awe at the creature's appearance. Then it raised its trunk and trumpeted its call louder than any angel. My horse did not wait to feel my heels; its ears were back and we were racing, not that I was trying to slow it down. We were hurtling down a shallow slope towards a distant river, the elephant briefly in pursuit. As the huge creature turned back towards the stand of trees it had emerged from, I was just thinking of hauling the horse up when the ground literally disappeared from under us.

"You said you knew the governor?" The parson interrupted my train of thought.

"Yes, I am only in this damn country because he invited us... Oh hell, Louisa. She will probably think I am dead." God knew how long ago it was when I fell in that pit, but the Boers would have searched for me and then gone back to their camp to tell Louisa I was missing. Would she think that my luck had finally run out? I doubted it. If I knew my girl, she would have bands of them out searching again where I was last seen. She would not give up until they found a body. "I need to get back." I winced as pain in my chest reminded me that I was in no state to travel, "or at least get a message to the Boers to let them know where I am." I frowned and added, "Er, where the hell am I?"

"You are in Umgungundlovu," the cleric informed me. "It is the capital of the Zulu nation." He stiffened slightly with pride as he added, "I am the Reverend Francis Owen and this is my mission station. We are newly arrived here to convert the Zulus to Christianity. The governor was kind enough to agree to be president of my mission."

"Zulus," I whispered with a growing sense of horror. I had heard a lot about this people and their king just recently and very little of it was good. A greater urge to get far away from this hut built within me, restrained only by my continued shivering and a variety of throbbing pains. "Can you get a message to the Boers for me? I need to reassure

8

my wife I am still alive. Then I am going to need a cart or a horse to get me back to Port Natal, but not for a day or two."

"The king regularly sends messages to Port Natal and the Boers," Owen gave me what he probably hoped was a reassuring smile. "I write most of them and I can easily add in a message for your wife. But the Zulus do not have any horses, you would need to travel by ox cart."

"And you cannot leave until you have seen the king," added William. "You need his permission to go and he will want to see that his physic has worked."

Even the mention of that vile potion made me feel ill again. I lay back on the cot they had put me on to rest. I shut my eyes, but sleep would not come. My mind was too busy piecing things together. Louisa and I had come to South Africa at the invitation of its governor, General Sir Benjamin D'Urban. He and I had been comrades fighting in Spain over twenty years earlier and had remained friends thereafter. Readers of my previous memoirs will know that he invited us while we were in the United States, avoiding some legal troubles at home. It had taken a year to get here, not least because my former business partner in New York had developed a taste for gunrunning. As a result, we had been briefly involved with that fanatic Garibaldi and his Ragamuffin War in Brazil.

When we had finally arrived in Cape Town, the colony was in a state of great unrest. Colonists were complaining bitterly that the government gave them no protection against raids by the Xhosa people. The Xhosa had recently rampaged through the eastern half of the territory, killing hundreds, burning farms and stealing livestock. Another old peninsular comrade, Colonel Harry Smith, had helped D'Urban drive them back. They had captured a large tract of land between two rivers, driving the Xhosa further north. D'Urban had planned to populate this with tribes the Xhosa incursions had displaced, who were friendly to the British. This would have created a defensive area between the settlers and the Xhosa and helped ensure peace, but he had been stopped by the missionaries. Those hand-wringing liberals had written to London with tales of British oppression of the noble savage. The London Missionary Society had also been in full cry in the press. As a result, the politicians had taken fright and ordered D'Urban to hand back the captured land to the Xhosa. When we arrived, he had just learned that he was also to be replaced as governor. To say he was furious about the actions of the colonial secretary in London would be something of an understatement.

"They have no idea what they are doing!" he had raged. "It will be war again for certain, that is if the colony does not fall apart first." He explained that the Boers were so frustrated at the lack of protection from Xhosa raids on their farms, that they were resolved to move out of the colony entirely. They had sent expeditions to lands northeast and north of the colony looking for new territory to settle, where they would protect themselves without British interference. D'Urban had wanted the Boers to stay. He told me that they were brave, industrious people and a mainstay to the welfare and economy of the colony. "Their mounted patrols were vital in repelling the Xhosa incursion the last time," he had said. "Without them we will need more troops from Britain, or we could be pushed into the sea."

I confess that I did not care a fig for D'Urban's problems at the time and paid little attention. I just planned to stay for a month or two and then I vowed we would never darken that shore again. Louisa and I enjoyed a pleasant few weeks touring the country, with various trips organised by the governor and his staff. We saw the strange flightless black and white birds that live in the sea. Then we went touring inland with a guide and an escort of Khoi-khoi soldiers, who are the tribe local to the Cape Town area. We saw bison, cheetahs, ostriches, wild dogs and various other creatures. I was not sorry that we failed to encounter lions. On our return to the governor I was ready to go home and asked D'Urban about getting passage on a ship to Britain. That was when he asked his favour.

He explained that a while back he had been visited by a former naval captain called Gardiner, who lived in a region northeast of the colony called Natal. This man informed him that the local tribe had gifted to Britain a vast tract of land. Furthermore, the British citizens living in the main port in Natal, had just renamed their town as D'Urban in his honour. The governor had never been there and was far too engrossed in local politics to leave Cape Town then. He asked if Louisa and I could visit this town of D'Urban as his special emissaries, to thank its citizens for this singular honour. It was a hard request to refuse, especially given his hospitality. Yet no sooner had we agreed, than he was telling us that this Natal land was also of interest to the Boers. He wanted us to take a private message to their leaders, reassuring them of his personal support and encouraging them to settle back within the colony. It did not seem an onerous task: giving a couple of speeches of thanks, perhaps attending a civic dinner and then delivering D'Urban's letter to the Boers. How wrong I was!

The first thing we discovered on reaching the port, was that hardly anyone there knew about the change in name. Most still called the place Port Natal. It was a miserable fly-blown settlement with fewer than fifty Europeans in it. There was a general store, two lodging houses and a handful of shacks along what was grandly referred to as Main Street. It would have flattered the place to be named after D'Urban's dog, never mind the man himself. It was obvious that Captain Gardiner had vastly oversold the importance of the town when speaking with the governor. No one was surprised at this news and I soon learned that Gardiner was a slippery devil, who no one liked or trusted.

It was then that I first heard details of the powerful African people who were their near neighbours. The Zulus had been growing their territory, pushing the Xhosa people south so that they came into conflict with the British. Gardiner had been one of the few people in Port Natal to visit the Zulu king, who had a ruthless reputation. In exchange for giving Gardiner the grant of land, he had demanded a treaty whereby the citizens of Port Natal return any Zulu fugitives who sought shelter there. A number of Zulus had fled the king's justice to the town and this treaty did not sit comfortably with the white settlers. They were more resentful when Gardiner insisted that the land grant was for him personally. He pointed out to the people of the port that they really did not have a choice but to agree to the treaty. If they were to anger the king by refusing, then they risked the vast Zulu army razing their community to the ground.

Soon afterwards, a demand for the return of the first fugitives was made and reluctantly, they were handed over. Then came more requests, not just for the accused, but also their wives and families. They were all put to death. When Gardiner tried to intervene for one group and got an assurance from the king that they would not be executed, the poor devils were just starved to death instead. It was a most unsavoury business. I was glad that Gardiner was not in town when I arrived as I wanted no part of it. Instead, I asked for directions to the Boer encampments. I was pleased to see that these were to the south of the territory, while the Zulu capital and its king were northwest of Port Natal.

My reverie in the vicar's hut was interrupted by the sound of a woman screaming nearby. Somebody with a drum was trying to drown out the noise, but it was a shrill shriek of terror that sent a chill down my spine.

"Don't worry, we will pray for her," the woman I now knew as Mrs Owen murmured, hurrying her young daughter back into the hut. Together, they knelt in front of a small cross on a table on the other side of the room.

"What on earth is going on?" I demanded above the continued screeching.

"It is nothing to worry about," replied Mrs Owen, looking at me over her shoulder and then glancing down meaningfully at the still bowed head of her daughter.

Sitting up, I found that a roughly made crutch had been left by the side of my cot. The drumming was coming closer. If some new horror was approaching, I wanted to see what it was. With difficulty I managed to stand, keeping my injured ankle off the ground. The room span for a while as I got vertical, but settled after a few moments until I had my balance well enough to hobble outside. Once again I blinked in the sunlight, but unlike before when I was lying on a stretcher, this time I was able to take more notice of my surroundings. Owen's hut and several other buildings were on top of a hill. Below us to my right was what I took to be the Zulu capital. It was a huge place that must have been the home to several thousand people. It was surrounded by a high rampart of cut thorn bush and cattle pens. Inside were concentric rings of tightly packed, dome-shaped huts. Another ring of thorn bushes encircled the centre of this hive of humanity that I guessed was the palace of the king. I only gave the place a cursory glance before looking to my left at the source of the commotion. A woman was being dragged up the opposite hill. There was a band of warriors about her, along with the man beating the drum. The group was nearing the top and still the woman continued her screeching. Owen was nearby, down on his knees, holding the crucifix around his neck and muttering a prayer.

"What on earth is going on?" I repeated my question.

"That poor wretch is to be executed," called out the cleric over the din. I stared across the valley at the group climbing up the slope. It was a strange hill, its top covered with something white like snow around a black rock at its summit. Then as two vultures flew off at the approach of the execution party, I realised what the 'snow' really was.

"My God, they are bones, that hill is covered with bones." I was astounded. There must have been the remains of hundreds of people on that hillside, all picked clean by animals and then bleached in the sun.

Owen frowned, probably at my taking the Lord's name in vain, although given the sight before me, a plea to the Almighty seemed entirely justified. "They hold life cheaply here, Mr Flashman," he replied. "I am praying for her, but these people do not understand that they have souls. They cannot be saved and go to heaven. They are damned by their ignorance of the Lord."

There was a struggle at the hilltop as the condemned prisoner fought desperately against her captors, who were trying to prostrate her across the flat top of the black rock. "I doubt theology is her prime concern at the moment," I muttered. "Do we know what she is accused of?"

"It is witchcraft." I turned and saw William walking around the hut. He grinned and added, "You found the crutch, then. Best practise with it as we will need to see the king soon." Compared to the frightened girl inside the hut, this young boy was remarkably unconcerned about the view. I could not help but wonder at what horrors he had already witnessed.

"Witchcraft," I repeated, feeling as though I had gone back in time two hundred years. "What has she done?"

"An old man claimed she stopped his favourite hen laying eggs," William explained. "The king commanded her to lift the spell, but she couldn't. The hen had probably just got old." As he spoke an awful crack sounded from the opposite hill and the screaming abruptly stopped. There was a second of horrible silence and then the drumming restarted, this time accompanied by chanting, as the guards started to make their way back down the slope.

I turned back to Owen, who was still down on his knees and crossing himself as he finished his prayer. Such Christian piety in the face of the savagery opposite seemed absurd. "What on earth possessed you to bring your wife and child to this godforsaken kingdom?" I demanded.

He got to his feet brushing the earth from his knees and looked slightly embarrassed. "I was a rector in Normanton, Yorkshire when I went to a lecture given by Captain Gardiner. He talked about his travels in Africa. Then he asked for someone to help him bring the Zulu people to the embrace of the lamb of God."

13

My dislike of Gardiner grew. He had evidently fooled this poor sap into abandoning his safe English life and entering the lion's den. "I take it Gardiner does not live near the capital, then?" I probed.

"Oh no, he lives near the coast, but he has been very good to me," assured Owen. "He has not visited for a while now, but he sends letters and he organised this hut for me with the king." At this Mrs Owen stepped out from their abode and from the look she gave her husband, I suspected that I was not the only one with misgivings over the benevolence of the good captain.

"So how goes the embracing of the lamb of God?" I asked. I suspected I knew the answer to that one. There was no sign of a church, or one being built. Just a few huts isolated on a bare hilltop opposite the execution site, which already had an alert vulture circling overhead.

"Well I confess that it has been much harder than I expected," admitted Owen. "I have tried to teach them about good and evil, but they question everything. Their way of life is so different to ours. There is another mission run by two American preachers, but they are not making much progress either." He went on to describe their journey to Natal. Instead of travelling by ship, the former naval man Gardiner had recommended coming overland from Cape Town. The trip had been a series of disasters: wagons had overturned and been smashed; others had been lost fording rivers and those left had repeatedly got stuck in bogs or up mountains, requiring whole teams of men and animals to pull and dig them free. Many of their remaining possessions had been stolen by curious natives. Their guides also relieved them of valuables before abandoning them to find their own way. It was a miracle that they had made it to the capital at all, and on their arrival they were not to get a warm welcome from their new host. The king had been deeply suspicious of the Christian messages that Owen preached. He challenged the parson on nearly every point and kept a remarkably close eye on what he was doing.

If they had not had the good fortune to come across young William Wood, then I suspect that the Owens would have been broken with despair. The lad had grown up in Port Natal and had an ear for languages, learning Zulu from the children of those who had fled from the capital. When the king learned that there was a white boy who spoke his tongue, William was invited to be one of his interpreters. His parents had little choice but to accept if they wanted to stay in Natal.

14

I liked young William, there was a natural street cunning to him. It was just as well, for soon, our lives were all going to depend on him.

Chapter 2

I did not sleep much that first night in Owen's hut. It was not just because I could hear rats scurrying about and gnawing fresh holes in the walls. I was to learn that Zulu huts are infested with rodents at night, probably due to the grain stored in jars inside. It was not even the pain that kept me awake; if I lay perfectly still and breathed lightly it was bearable. That afternoon Mrs Owen had confirmed that a bone in my arm was broken by squeezing it and nearly causing me to leap through the hut roof. She found splints and bandaged it as tightly as I would allow, warning that she would have to tighten the binding further to ensure the bone healed straight. She also bandaged my ribs that she thought were cracked. In all, a whole petticoat was ripped into strips and wrapped around parts of my body that showed violent hues of purple bruising. My ankle she pronounced was merely sprained and the swelling would go down if I could keep off it.

Mrs Owen was a brisk and practical woman, a typical vicar's wife who looked after worldly affairs while her husband attended to the more spiritual. Having heard from the reverend the trials of their journey to get here, I did not doubt that she was the one who worked out how to overcome each obstacle. In between dressing my wounds that afternoon, she gave a school lesson to her daughter, William and another white boy who also lived on the hillside. She also oversaw a maid called Jane, who had come with them from Yorkshire. The girl was roasting a joint of meat over the fire and soon tempting smells filled the hut, reminding me that I had not eaten properly for days.

I sat down for dinner that evening with the Owen household, including William. We were joined by a Mr and Mrs Hulley, along with their son, who had been in the school lesson earlier. The reverend opened the meal with a rambling grace, including a plea to the Almighty for the repair of my battered carcass. I am bound to admit that by then I was feeling a little better. The fever was receding and was being replaced by a hearty appetite. I must have devoured at least a pound of beef, which my stomach appreciated much more than the king's physic.

Talked turned to affairs in the Zulu court and I learned that Richard Hulley was another interpreter and courier. The king had recently instructed Owen to draft a letter for Gardiner, asking the captain to visit his capital. Hulley was to take it and would also travel to Port Natal. He undertook to pass back details of my whereabouts. If Louisa had not returned to that settlement, a messenger could be sent on to the Boer camps to find her there. When I predicted that Louisa would have the Dutch combing the land from dawn to dusk to find me, William thought that they would have found the village who had reported my presence to the Zulu court. From them the Boers would learn where I had been taken. I was not sure how much comfort Louisa would take from that.

"When we were with the Boers," I remembered, "there was a man called Retief who was gathering cattle for the Zulus in exchange for a grant of land. Do you think that the king will let me return with him and his men?"

There was a pause of several seconds before anyone replied. The other adults around the table and young William exchanged meaningful glances. They seemed to be prompting each other to answer my enquiry. Eventually, Mr Hulley cleared his throat, "Yes, yes that is entirely possible." Yet I got the distinct impression that such a thing was not advisable at all. I must have furrowed my brow in puzzlement. "Perhaps you will join the reverend and I outside after dinner," he suggested, glancing down at where his young son was giggling with Owen's daughter. "Now, sir," he continued, "we have not had any new stories around this table for a while. Perhaps you would be kind enough to tell us how you come to be in Africa."

I told them some creditable tales of my time in Texas and South America, as well as how I came to know the governor. They exclaimed appreciatively, but my heart was not in it. I was getting increasingly anxious about what they would tell me when the meal was over, for I was certain that it would not be good news. Eventually, the women rose to clear the table and get their children to bed. The rest of us got up and headed outside. I was not surprised to see William join us men, for the lad appeared to know as much of what was happening as anyone else. We sat down on some log seats around the embers of a fire and as the flames were rekindled, I began to understand a little more of their precarious existence.

They started by telling me a little about the king. His name was Dingane and he was a brother of a great Zulu king called Shaka. This fearsome ruler had done much to make the tribe a powerful nation in the region. Shaka went mad after his mother died, executing thousands of his people for being insufficiently grief-stricken at his loss. He ordered no crops to be planted and any woman who became pregnant to be killed with her husband. Even cows were slaughtered so that their calves would know what losing a mother felt like. He was set to destroy everything he had built up. Dingane soon found support for a revolt and literally stabbed his brother in the back.

That had all taken place some ten years before. Given the means of his own accession to power, you could understand why Dingane was distrustful of those about him. He ruthlessly killed any who might defy him, but it was not just his own people he was suspicious of, it was his white neighbours too.

"He has heard how the Boers with their horses and guns crushed the Matabele people to the south," explained Hulley. "The Zulus have fought the Matabele too, but they have not been able to destroy them like that. The king worries that the Boers or the British might come after his land next."

"But has he not given Gardiner a huge tract of land? And does he not allow Port Natal to exist on his territory?" I asked, puzzled.

"It was Shaka who granted land at Port Natal to settlers there after their medicine saved him from an assassination attempt," explained Owen. "I fear Dingane would not be as generous, for his soul is black with sin, Mr Flashman."

"As for Gardiner's land," continued Hulley, "that was given to just one man. Dingane knows he can take it back whenever he wants."

"Some of the elders," interrupted William, "do not accept that the land has been given to Gardiner. They say Zulu land is sacred and cannot be given away."

"Yet this is the same territory that Dingane has also promised to the Boers," continued Owen. "I tried to warn them when they came before, but they just thought I was protecting Captain Gardiner's interests."

"So Dingane is trying to use the Boers to recover stolen cattle from his enemies," I concluded, "but he has no intention of giving them their land." I was not entirely surprised at this, for any African king would be a fool to invite a powerful neighbour to take half of his territory. More Boers would pour over the mountains to the south to join them and it would only be a matter of time before they came after the rest of his land. Many of the other Boer leaders had seen this for themselves. While Louisa and I had been in their camp they had claimed that Retief was a fool to trust the Zulu king. For others, though, the new land was the answer to their prayers and they allowed hope to outweigh caution. Many had lost their farms to Xhosa raids. They had, as they saw it, been betrayed by the British, fought the

Matabele, endured hardships crossing the mountains to the south and now a vast and fertile land lay before them. They had nowhere else to go and few wanted to return south. The Boer leaders I had met had received me civilly enough. They respected D'Urban, but they took little comfort from his letter. It was the government in London that had little idea of the ways of their world that they did not trust. News had reached them that D'Urban was to be replaced and they were sure that the government would appoint a new man that was hostile to their interests. From what D'Urban himself had told me, I could not disagree.

"Well," I continued, "Retief will only do the king's bidding for so long, then he will realise he is being played. I would not like to be in the king's shoes then, for the Boers are tough fighters, they have proved that."

Owen looked over his shoulder to check that none of their African servants were within earshot before saying quietly, "The king knows that too, which is why he is likely to strike first."

"What do you mean?" I felt the hair on the back of my neck start to prickle in alarm.

"After Retief visited Dingane the first time," replied Owen, "I got a letter from Captain Gardiner."

"The king demands that we read to him all the letters between us and Port Natal," interjected Hulley, "but I hid this one in my boot."

"Yes," continued Owen, frowning in irritation at the interruption. "Gardiner told us that Dingane had ordered one of his chiefs to intercept Retief and his men on the way back to the Boer camps. This man, Isiguabani, was to invite Retief and his men to his village and offer them hospitality. Then, when their guard was down, he was to murder them all."

"But they weren't killed," I countered. "They were away recovering Dingane's cattle for him when I visited the Boer camp."

"No," replied Owen. "That is because Isiguabani refused to do the king's bidding and his village paid a terrible cost for his disobedience. Isiguabani knew that the king would never forgive him and so he tried to take his people away. But when Dingane learned of his treason he sent his army after them. They were caught by a river and over six hundred of them were killed or drowned." He gestured at the opposite hill and added, "Well over a hundred more ended their days on that rock."

"Good heavens." I was astonished. "So he did not really care about the stolen cattle at all, that was just to trick Retief into thinking there was hope for a deal."

"Now he has sent Tom and some of his advisors after Retief," added Hulley, "so that they can see how the Boers fight and report back to him." Tom, I learned, was Thomas Halstead, another interpreter who lived in the buildings of Owen's mission.

I had heard in Port Natal that Dingane jealously guarded his power, killing all who challenged him, but I had not appreciated just how cunning and ruthless he could be. He must have assumed that Retief was the only Boer leader and that once he had been murdered, the rest would be intimidated and go away. I thought he might well be right on that, for I had heard that the Zulu army had thousands of men, well organised into disciplined regiments. Now while his first attempt at dispatching a potential invader had failed, he still had the man doing his bidding. In a few weeks Retief was expected back at Umgungundlovu and probably completely oblivious to how close he had come to being killed on his last visit. Joining his men for their return journey now did not look so appealing. Which raised a rather important question.

"How the hell am I to get away, then? Damn it, why don't we all get away from here? You men have families, you know that you are all living at the whim of this despot. Why do you stay here?"

"We have no choice," replied Owen grimly. "Zulu soldiers guard all of the main trails and they would only let us pass with an escort of the king's guards. Even if somehow we made it to Port Natal, under the treaty they might be obliged to hand us back if a Zulu army was hot on our heels. We need Dingane's permission to leave and he would never grant it, at least not now. He is not a fool, Mr Flashman. I read or write all of his letters to the outside world and," he gestured at the other two around the fire, "Richard and William speak to many of his men in their own tongue. He can guess that we know much of his plans. If we were to suddenly ask to leave, he would assume we were going to betray him."

"But he is letting Hulley leave tomorrow," I objected.

"Only because he has my wife and son as hostage here," the man explained. "He knows I must come back for them."

Once again it was young William, with his direct approach, who put his finger on a more important issue. "Instead of worrying about how you get away, we need to work out how we can keep you alive."

"What, surely even Dingane would not dare harm a friend of the British governor?" I had thought that my friendship with D'Urban would give me some form of protection, but even as I spoke the words, I began to see that the reverse might be the case. A king willing to wipe out the man he thought was the Boer leader and all his supporters would not hesitate to kill the lone representative of a more distant enemy.

"He does not know you are a friend of the governor," asserted young William. "I have not told his messengers that. If I had, he would have thought you were a British spy in his lands."

"Dingane does not trust any white people," Owen confirmed. "He is sure that they will try to take his land. He has heard that the British have pushed the Xhosa back and he would like to get some guns for his people. When I first arrived, he tried to trick me into getting him gunpowder."

"But then what do we tell him about why I am here?" I looked up at the moon and continued, "I will have to see him in the next three days to thank him for his physic. He is bound to ask what I am doing on these shores. From the sound of things, my answer had better be a good one."

There were a few seconds of silence as we all stared into the flames seeking inspiration and then Hulley straightened up. "You could tell him that you are a friend of the reverend and that you are visiting on your way back to England. No, wait," he held up his hand to stall any interruption, clearly pleased with some new refinement to his plan. "Tell him that you are from England and the reverend's mother is ill and wants him and his family to come home." He turned to Owen, "This could be *your* chance to get away too."

The cleric licked his lips and gave a slight sigh. He must have been picturing himself back in the benign setting of the Yorkshire Dales, but then his sense of duty caused him to sadly shake his head. "No, Richard. I only have a small Christian flock on this hilltop, but I will not abandon it. When we go, we will go together."

After much debate it was decided that I was a humble clerk in the East India Company returning home. I had decided to visit my cousin, the Reverend Owen, when my ship called into Port Natal. My guide had abandoned me, I had got lost and then was injured falling into the pit.

As we talked, our faces flickering in the light of the fire in front of us, for once my first concern was not myself. I was exhausted after what had been an awfully long day and still feeling a little feverish, yet my thoughts kept straying to Louisa. What would she do when she found that I was 'enjoying' the hospitality of the Zulu king? There were plenty in the Boer camp who did not trust him and who would fill her ears with tales of his tyranny. I half feared that she would ride to Umgungundlovu herself and demand my release. That would rather put paid to any lies we had planned, but surely the Boers would stop her before she reached the king. While they had not heard of Isiguabani when I had been with them, many thought that Retief would be sent on a series of errands until he finally realised that he would never get his land. As I sat there in the darkness, I silently prayed that she would stay away. The alternative did not bear thinking about. During any pause in our conversation we could hear noises from the hill opposite. Wild dogs were there now, their barks, snarls and howls clearly audible as they fought over the remains at the summit. It was a stark reminder of our fate if things went wrong.

Chapter 3

Standing in front of a small mirror that Mrs Owen held for me, I had to admit that I looked quite respectable. More importantly, I appeared to have made a full recovery. William had explained that I must look as healthy as possible so that the king could be assured that his physic had worked. If I was still ill, he would be insulted. Ironically, he might then have me executed or given another dose of his medicine, which would likely have the same result.

Fortunately, the fever had now completely subsided. Mrs Owen had re-splinted my arm, ensuring that the bandages did not show beneath the cuff of one of her husband's shirts that I now wore. This also hid the bandaging around my ribs. My ankle was still a little swollen, but much better than it had been. I had rested it as much as I could and now walked with a stick rather than a crutch. I was fortunate it was not on the same side as my injured arm. Mrs Hulley had lent me a pair of her husband's boots as his feet were bigger than mine, so I could at least walk comfortably. Mr Hulley was now on his way to Port Natal with a message summoning Gardiner to Umgungundlovu. The king was accusing him of breaching their agreement by providing refuge to some of Isiguabani's people. I was eagerly awaiting his arrival, relishing the chance to meet the villain whose lies and deceits had landed me in this mess.

As I looked at myself, I ran my hand over my newly shaved chin, courtesy of Owen's razor, and had to concede that I was as ready as I could be to meet Dingane. Not that the prospect filled me with joy, indeed as the time approached, I felt increasing trepidation. William and Owen had used the days since that first meal to advise on how I should behave when meeting the king. I had to look grateful when I was thanking him for saving my life. It was my appearance that was important, the words did not matter, for William would take care of that. He would also apologise on my behalf for entering the king's lands without permission. I had to appear contrite then, but not timid, for the king despised weakness. Most importantly, I was not to look the king in the eye or appear to challenge him in any way. I was to remember that I was a humble East India Company clerk and not a proud English gentleman.

Well, I have played a few parts in my time and this one did not seem too much of a challenge. I had spent time in India and could add detail from there if required. I had even lived there for a while disguised as an Indian cavalry trooper. Compared to that, this deception looked to be a breeze. Yet if ever I felt overconfident, I would be brought back down to earth most afternoons, when the beating of a drum heralded a fresh tragic procession up the hill opposite. The children would be ushered out of sight, but I found a horrible fascination in watching proceedings, and I stood with Owen as he kneeled in fervent prayer. The hill was several hundred yards away and so mercifully we could not see the features of the poor devils dragged up it. Sometimes I could not help but imagine myself on that hideous track, which was a very real possibility if I did not play my cards right. As a man who has faced death more times than I care to remember, I know that I would be kicking and screaming every step of the way. The majority we saw behaved in exactly that manner and I did not blame them. Yet on the day before I met the king, we saw something different. It was a man and a woman. This time as the drum banged, we watched as the couple walked quietly between the soldiers up the hill. The condemned had their heads down, resigned to their fate. The only resistance they showed was when they tried to hold hands and the soldiers pulled them apart. They had a resolute dignity that I knew I could never match in those circumstances. For a hoary old cynic like me to be moved takes something, but I felt a lump in my throat as I watched them. Their silence made the subsequent cracks of club on skull even more awful. While my ankle precluded me from falling to my knees, for once I did join Owen in a silent prayer. We sent young Woods to make enquiries as to their crime. It turned out that they had committed adultery. The couple had certainly paid a terrible price for their love.

I had a bad dream that night and desperately hoped it was not a premonition. In it, Louisa had come to the Zulu capital to rescue me and been captured. My lies had been revealed and we had both been sentenced to death like the couple the previous day. I woke up sweating in the darkened hut and could not get back to sleep. I just lay there listening to the gentle snores of the Owens, the gnaw of rats and the howl of dogs on the opposite hill. It was not the best preparation for an encounter on which my life depended.

The following morning I was reminded again how resourceful young William was. I had expected to have to gingerly walk down the path to the capital. That was only half a mile away, but afterwards I would have to walk at least that distance again to get into the king's palace at its centre. I feared I would be limping badly by then. Instead,

William led me down the slope away from the city and there I found an ox with a blanket over its back.

"The king watches us through his telescope," the boy explained, pointing to a trail at the bottom of the hill. "He won't be able to see us take this path." I had never ridden cattle before, but the beast took me slowly and steadily down the hill and then along a track towards the capital without my ankle hurting at all. Owen explained that the Zulus had heard about how the Boers had used horses to defeat the Matabele people. While the Zulus had no horses, they had plenty of cattle and had been trying to train them for war. The beasts might have horns, but I doubted that they would charge the guns of an enemy. All the same, I was grateful that they had trained my beast for a rider.

As we descended the slope, I felt a growing sense of apprehension. I would have preferred to avoid meeting the king at all, but that was impossible. I was already committed to thank him for my recovery and if I ever wanted to leave this brutal land, I would need his permission for that too. Having regaled my companions with tales of my military valour, I tried to look unconcerned at my imminent audience with royalty. In contrast, Owen did not bother to hide his own anxiety. As he knew Dingane well, this did not help calm my nerves.

"Much will depend on what mood he is in," he warned. "He can change from good humour to dark suspicion in the blink of an eye and often on the slightest cause." He admitted that every time they met, Dingane would question him on Christian tenets and the cleric never felt he got the better of the encounter. "He refuses to believe our Lord's resurrection," Owen complained. "I explained to him about the crucifixion and how a Roman soldier speared Jesus' body, but Dingane insisted that meant nothing. The king boasted he knew several people who had lived for three days and more after being speared in the chest."

As we rounded a bend, I got my first close-up view of Umgungundlovu. From the hilltop I had been able to study its layout, with its concentric rings of thick hedges, cattle pens and huts around the king's enclosure, called a kraal, at its heart. Close to, I could see that the hedges were thick, high thorn bush ramparts. They would make a formidable obstacle to any invader. There were the sights, sounds and smells of a city too. A group of women were chanting some song as they washed clothes in the river while their children played nearby. I could hear the distant clang of a smith working metal, while my nostrils were assailed by cooking smoke, the stench of latrines and more than a whiff of cow dung. Most of the people we saw were old men, women and children; the army was elsewhere apart from a few soldiers guarding the palace's main entrance. They paid little attention to us. Owen and William were clearly well known to them. Even another Englishman riding on the back of several hundred pounds of old beef was of little interest. William kept them at their ease, exchanging a few words with the sentries in their strange tongue. The lad then pointed at me and said something which made them laugh, before they waved us into the city.

"I told them that you think Zulu cattle are so comfortable, you want to ride one all the way to the sea," he said quietly, as he led us down a street with towering thorn bushes on either side. Through gaps I could see into the side streets, tightly packed with round huts. The place was filled with a sea of humanity. "You will have to get off that steer at the entrance to the royal kraal," William warned. "The king will want to see you walking." The boy tried to give me a smile of encouragement, but even he looked tense. I was all too aware of the responsibility on his young shoulders. All I had to do was look sufficiently grateful. It was William who had to listen to the king's questions and judge what answers would keep us safe. One mistake and this capricious monarch could order our imprisonment – or worse.

As we got closer to the centre of this metropolis, we found more soldiers. These were tougher veterans than those on the outer gates and there were more of them guarding each entrance we passed. They glared at us with suspicion if not outright hostility. It was not hard to imagine them dragging us pitilessly up the execution hill. Even Owen, who had chatted nervously all the way down from his hilltop, now fell silent under their gaze. I too felt increasingly uncomfortable riding my steer. Perhaps I imagined the looks of contempt on those hard faces, but I doubted it. I was glad when an old man stepped forward to grab the animal's rope bridle and William indicated that I should dismount. He handed me my cane and as half a dozen warriors closed in about us, we progressed into the royal compound itself.

The inner wall was thickly lined with yet more huts, but staring ahead we could see a large clearing and beyond that, several much grander dwellings.

"Those are the king's huts," whispered Owen as we progressed through the last of the smaller buildings. "He holds his entertainments in this space in front."

Finally, we stepped into the courtyard and I looked about. It was a large round area, with plenty of room for whatever 'entertainments' the king enjoyed. I estimated that you could fit the Drury Lane Theatre in there with room to spare. We were halfway across when a growl from the guards indicated that we should stop. No one went ahead to announce us, but I suspected that a runner had taken news of our arrival long before. As Owen twitched apprehensively, I forced myself to at least look relaxed. Kings, whatever their hue, like to keep the commoners waiting. It reinforces their sense of power. I well remembered waiting nearly a day with Marshal Ney for an audience with Louis XVIII. From what I had been told of how suspicious this king was, I strongly suspected that he would be studying us from somewhere before he appeared. I resolved to play my part from the outset. The kind of man who sauntered hundreds of miles into Africa to visit a cousin, would not be intimidated now. I strolled around the small square of space allowed by our guards and whistled a jaunty tune. The nearest sentinel growled his disapproval, but I responded with a cheery smile and, "Good morning to you too, my fine fellow."

I studied the brute with interest. He was taller and broader than I and there was not an ounce of fat on him either. In his left hand he held a large wood-framed ox-hide shield and two long spears. In his right was a much shorter spear, with a thicker shaft like a sword hilt and a long, broad metal point. The hide on the shield was pure white and glancing at the other guards I saw theirs was the same. "Look, Francis," I called. "They have two kinds of spear." Owen was appalled as I reached out to try and examine the shorter weapon, only for the guard to bark something at me and push me back into the centre of our space.

"Best leave them alone, sir," warned William. "The long ones are for throwing and the short ones are for stabbing," he explained. Then the lad turned to the guard and began apologising for any offence I had caused. The man appeared slightly mollified and even answered a question that William asked as he pointed to the stabbing spear.

"The shorter one is called an *iklwa*, sir." The boy grinned as he added, "He says it is named after the sound it makes when it is pulled out of your innards."

"Oh dear God," murmured Owen, going pale. "Please, Mr Flashman, do not antagonise them any more."

"Call me Thomas, I am your cousin, remember." I could feel my heart beating in my chest but I forced myself to laugh, and felt my ribs

27

protest at the movement. The chuckle sounded as false as a politician's promise, yet I beamed at William and asked, "What do they call the long ones?"

"They are *assegais*. All the tribes have those, but only the Zulus have the *iklwa*. They were introduced by King Shaka to help him conquer new lands." Any further discussion was interrupted by the appearance of a group of men coming out of the entrance of the largest hut. I did not need Owen and young William bowing to tell me that Dingane was among them. I dropped down into a hasty bow myself before studying the man leading the group. He was huge, perhaps a foot taller than most of the other warriors we had seen. The broad shoulders and the chest we could see under a blanket toga were heavily muscled, although he had run to fat a little around the belly. He was around forty years old, his hair having a hint of grey to the temples, but most importantly he was smiling. I had been fearing some mercurial encounter, but he genially invited us to join him on some stools outside the royal residence.

As we sat down, the rest of his entourage took their places standing behind him. Most were older and must have been some of his advisors. One was muttering incantations and waving what looked to be a human bone in front of him. When I looked over my shoulder, I saw that our guards now stood impassively in a line behind us, shield and spears in their hands. They did not make me feel any more comfortable.

The king beamed at us and opened his arms expansively as his deep voice boomed what I thought must be some greeting. Then he pointed at me and gestured for me to stand again.

We were on low stools, but I left my cane lying on the ground. I fixed a grin on my features and gritted my teeth to hide a sharp twinge of pain that shot up from my ankle as I launched myself up. "Tell His Majesty," I instructed William, "that I am most grateful for his physic, which has affected a full recovery. Tell him that I am deeply honoured by his hospitality, but now I would like to leave his kingdom and return home. I will be sure to tell all I meet that he is a most gracious and generous ruler."

William started to pass on my message in the strange Zulu tongue. I could not understand a word of their language, but beamed back like the grateful fool I was supposed to be. Dingane watched me closely, his dark eyes glittering with interest. He gestured for me to resume my seat and as I did so I forced my wounded arm to rest on my lap in a more natural pose. Then I heard the king's rumbling tones again.

"The king wants to know," translated William, "what you were doing on his lands."

This was the question that we had expected and rehearsed for. I did not need to give William my answer for the boy knew it by heart, yet Dingane would expect me to say something. "Tell him that I am on my way from India," I proclaimed pointing to the east, "returning to England." I moved my arm north in the direction of home and then clapped a hand on Owen's shoulder, which caused the man to jump slightly in alarm. "As my ship stopped in Port Natal, I thought I would take the opportunity to visit my cousin here, who I have not seen in many years, but who has often written to me praising Your Majesty."

"I will not say that last bit," warned William. "The king makes Owen read his letters and so he would know it is untrue." The lad then gave my explanation to the king, who continued to study me closely.

"He wants to know how you got hurt," the boy asked after another booming royal retort. Keeping as close to the truth as possible, we explained that while riding to see Owen my horse had been startled by an elephant and had fallen into the trap. The king nodded; I suspected that he already knew much of the answer from his own spies.

"He wants to know if it was a bull or a cow elephant," pressed William. "The bulls are more likely to charge," he added.

"Tell him I confess that I did not stop long enough to look," I answered. "If it will make him happy, you can say that the elephants in his lands are much bigger than those in India. Now has he confirmed I can leave?"

A look of wry amusement crossed the king's features as he listened to the young translator. His gaze flickered between Owen's anxious expression and my own. I strongly suspected that he did not believe more than half of what he was told. He was still smiling though. Perhaps he thought me a too amiable fool to be a threat, for he slapped his knee and then pointed to Owen as he answered. "He says," announced William, "that having come all this way, you surely do not want to leave your cousin so soon. He will talk about you leaving another day. He also wants to know if you are a missionary too."

By chance I had played the part of a missionary some ten years before on the west coast of Africa. "Tell him no. I tried it once for a day and things did not go well." I smiled at the memory, which had seen me turn a devout Christian settlement into a den of debauchery within a few hours. "I am just a humble clerk for the East India Company," I lied, thinking that would sound far less of a threat than the truth.

William looked thoughtful for a moment and then started to translate. Whatever he said was considerably shorter than my message and it made the king laugh. To my relief he then turned his attention to Owen. "The king says he saw you praying for the witch a few days ago," William informed the cleric, nodding to the brass telescope that I now noticed on a stand near the corner of the king's hut. "He wants to know why you would pray to the Christian God for a witch."

"I pray for the salvation of all, that they may know God's grace," intoned Owen. He must have thought that was a safe answer, but he still looked guarded under the king's close inspection.

William frowned for a moment as he decided how to translate such piety into Zulu and then passed a version of the message on. The king's eyes narrowed in suspicion on hearing the answer and he immediately asked another question. "The king wants to know if you disapprove of the killing of witches." The boy licked his lips nervously and added, "Be careful, sir, he will not want his decisions challenged."

Owen nodded in acknowledgement. "Tell the king that I would not presume to question his judgement. I know nothing of the trial."

Dingane looked only slightly assuaged by the answer and probed again. William asked, "He wants to know how Christians punish witches."

The cleric paused in thought. Perhaps he did not want to admit that until a hundred and fifty years before we burned them at the stake. Giving this king a new means of execution was probably not a good idea. Eventually, he announced, "Tell him that we leave it to God to decide if they are a witch. If they walk with the Devil then they will surely go to hell, but if they have a Christian soul then they will be saved and go to heaven."

Dingane was most dissatisfied with this answer and angrily replied at some length through William. "He says that witches must be punished or they will continue to cast spells." The lad paused as the king continued his tirade and then went on. "He asks if you leave God to judge murderers or cattle thieves? I think he knows we don't, as a man was hanged in Port Natal for murder last year. He wants to know what is so special about witches that they alone are judged by God."

"Oh dear, oh dear," Owen wrung his hands together in anguish as he searched his memory of the scriptures for an explanation that would

30

serve. "What do you think, Mr Flashman? We can hardly admit that we do not believe in witchcraft or he will be most offended."

I could not think of a good answer either, but before I could reply, young William brightened and announced, "I have it. A powerful witch could make another person look guilty by casting a spell on them. Only God will be able to see their true heart."

"Excellent," agreed Owen beaming with delight and not a little relief. "Judge not, that ye be not judged, Matthew Chapter 7, yes indeed."

William quickly passed on his own answer to the question and the furrow in the king's brow lifted, to be replaced by another look of amusement. He had been watching our discussion closely. He must have realised that Owen had been stumped by his enquiry and the answer had been thought up by the interpreter. He laughed and said something to the boy which brought a smile in return. The king was clearly pleased at being able to outwit a missionary on a religious point. He glanced up at Owen's cluster of huts on the hillside and asked another question, translated by William.

"Do many of my people come for your Christian teaching?" the king enquired.

Owen admitted that since he had run out of gifts for his congregation, the numbers attending his services had dropped off considerably. The king grinned, I suspected that he already knew this from the use of his telescope. To my surprise he announced he would send more parishioners. He would command some boys to attend, he told Owen, as boys learn things quicker than men. The cleric beamed in delight, or perhaps it was relief, as the king was standing to signal an end to the encounter. As I picked up my cane to get back on my feet, the king turned his attention back to me and frowned. He spoke sharply to William, who suddenly looked worried as he translated for me. "The king says that if his physic had worked properly, you would not need that stick. He questions whether you are truly healed."

In a matter of seconds his cheery *bonhomie* had been replaced by a dark, brooding suspicion. The guards, sensing the changing mood, took a step forward, ready to seize us if ordered. I stared back at the king with dismay. He returned my inspection with a cool look of appraisal, a smirk twitching around his lips. The villain was no fool. He must have known the lethal potency of his physic and I am sure he was enjoying watching a white man realise that he had no power or influence in this palace. Several of his advisors were grinning at seeing a European humbled. Dingane glanced at them and was clearly enjoying playing to this gallery to demonstrate his power.

As Owen started to feverishly mutter some prayer beside me, I remembered all too well my last time in the court of an African king. The Ashanti had no fear of the British either and for good reason – they nearly swept us into the sea. The only British the Zulu knew were those living around Port Natal. Those settlers had no defence against a Zulu army. To object would likely see me poisoned to death. Even if I survived, I doubted that D'Urban would thank me for having the town he thought named after him razed to the ground by a new enemy.

There was nothing for it but to grit my teeth, smile graciously at the spiteful swine and let the cane drop from my fingers. "Tell His Majesty that a cane is an item of fashion where I come from, but I will happily stop using it, for I am quite recovered." As William passed on my reply, I gave a gracious bow to prove the point, ignoring the pain from waving my injured arm and the pressure on my ribs. As I rose, I glanced back at the king, who was still staring at me impassively. Too late I realised that I was looking him in the eye, something that William had warned me not to do. This man, who had stabbed his own brother in the back, returned my inspection impassively as he decided whether I should live or die. I felt a trickle of sweat run down my back and was reminded of tales of Roman gladiators waiting for the emperor to decide their fate. I was sure that he had seen through my tale of being cured and he must have doubted that I was Owen's cousin. With one gesture to his guards, in a moment I could be dragged up the hill to have my brains dashed out. The thought of those vultures tearing into my flesh gave me an involuntary shudder and perhaps that saved me, for the king suddenly smiled again. I think he sensed my fear. This despot ruled through intimidation and the fact that I was frightened of him must have given him comfort that I was not a threat. He might not know who I truly was, but he was sufficiently curious to let me live… for now.

Chapter 4

Having been in the royal presence I was keener than ever to leave this domain, yet there was no alternative but to wait a little longer. It was a hundred and fifty miles to Port Natal and there was no way I could make a run for it. The king would soon realise I was missing and have his soldiers on my trail. I would not stand a chance and yet I did not relish another audience with this tyrant to ask permission to depart. We would have to leave it another week or two before we raised the matter again. In the meantime, I certainly did not lack for entertainment. Dingane was as good as his word and sent twenty young boys from the capital, as well as two grizzled old warriors, who would normally be teaching them the ways of the Zulu. Poor Reverend Owen soon found his faith tested to the limit.

On the first day he read the *Te Deum* and then gave a short analysis on the first three chapters of *Genesis*. When William had finished translating, Owen foolishly invited questions. First, they wanted to know where the Garden of Eden was. Before he could answer one of the veterans spoke angrily. William informed us that the man was asserting that the Garden of Eden must be in the lands of the Ndebele people, as keeping it secret was just the kind of thing those devious worms would do. Then they fell to arguing over whether God could make Adam and animals out of the earth. One fellow had to be stopped from going to the execution hill to find a man's rib, so that Owen could make a woman out of it. They left still debating what kind of snake had tempted Eve with the apple.

On the second day, when his class returned, Owen decided that something from the New Testament might be safer. He tried to teach them the parable of the lost sheep and sparked even more controversy. One of the boys stood up, his fists clenched in anger. "If he abandoned ninety-nine sheep to go searching for one lost animal, he would be whipped for stupidity, and rightly so. This man Jesus," he asserted through William's translation, "clearly knows nothing about herding animals, so why should we listen to anything else he says?" Poor Owen tried to explain that the story was really about men and sinners and the boys furrowed their brows in confusion, evidently wondering why he had talked about sheep. Then Owen prattled on about us all being sinners, but they threw their hands up again at that. "Who says that any of us have stolen cattle?" demanded one, which it turned out was the only sin that they recognised.

I was trying hard not to chuckle now as Owen just dug himself deeper into problems. He endeavoured to explain that there were other sins and gave the example of turning the other cheek when struck. To Zulus such timidity was incomprehensible; and just when he had really begun to struggle, the grizzled old veteran spoke again. I suspected that the man had been sent by the king to cause trouble in the class and now he destroyed Owen's case. The British, he pointed out, had not turned the other cheek when the Xhosa had invaded their lands. Instead they had driven them out and over two rivers, capturing more territory. Was Owen saying that all the British and their governor and king were going to the place full of fire?

Owen just gaped and then glanced across to see if I was listening. I smiled and cocked an eyebrow to show I was interested in his answer before adding, "Didn't you say D'Urban is the president of your mission? I don't think my friend Ben will be happy to hear that you are preaching he is bound for hell."

"No, no, of course not." Owen turned back to William, "Tell them that the British were fighting with God's blessing to defend the lives of saved Christian souls."

"I would not say that, sir," replied William quietly. "They may think this means that the British will attack the Zulus too."

"Oh yes, you are quite right," a harassed Owen agreed. "I think it might be best to end the class now." He gave a weary sigh and added, "And perhaps tell them that they do not need to come back tomorrow."

Having the opportunity to do some preaching did not seem to have done Owen much good. He was, I think, finally beginning to appreciate the hopelessness of his task. One morning he even asked me about my faith and whether I had any doubts. When a man of the cloth comes to Flashy for moral reassurance, you surely know that things are in a perilous state.

I am only prone to think of the Almighty when a meeting with Him seems imminent. Normally, I am indifferent to religion; I have seen far too many villains do unspeakable things in the name of their God. I well remember a Portuguese priest killing and torturing French soldiers as well as their women and children. Yet I could not resist a little mischief with Owen. I told him that as he had asked, I had to confess that I had doubts about the Resurrection too. I wondered if the disciples had only seen Jesus in dreams and later scholars had misunderstood their testaments. He looked appalled at the idea and went off into the hut to pray at their private altar.

While the Reverend Owen considered matters of divinity, it was his wife who ran his mission with a calm efficiency. They had hens for meat and eggs and most days she would take William with her to the village market to barter for food. In the afternoons she would give the children lessons and often include some of the other servants to help them learn to read and write. She seemed to cope with whatever life threw at her. The only time I heard her raise her voice was when her husband had left a new candle on the table overnight. They only had a few left; it was not something you could buy in the market and a rat had eaten it.

We had celebrated Christmas shortly after my arrival and a grand feast had been prepared for all those living on Owen's mission hilltop. It was in fact my second Christmas in Africa. The first had been ten years before on the Gold Coast and spent with some slave traders eating roast monkey. This time the roast beef was far more palatable, although Owen would insist on interrupting the festivities with his preaching.

Over the following few weeks we settled into a routine of sorts. Owen would spend time writing in his journal, holding a daily service that we were obliged to attend and visiting the few Zulus that he thought showed some interest in Christianity. Occasionally, he would be summoned with William to attend on the king. This would involve him in reading or writing letters for Dingane or helping the king learn to read and write for himself. Owen confided that he sometimes did not read all of the letters the king received to avoid angering him. This was becoming harder as Dingane sometimes recognised words and was becoming suspicious of the cleric's work.

I was happy to stay as far away from this volatile monarch as possible but pressed Owen to raise again the need for me to leave during these lessons. "Teach him F is for Flashman and G is for going home," I encouraged. Owen did suggest my leaving once, but reported that his pupil's mood immediately turned sour. "No one leaves now," the king had grumpily responded.

The one bit of good news I received came with the return of Hulley. He reported that Louisa had not yet returned to Port Natal from the Boer camp, but he had arranged for another courier to get a message to her about my whereabouts. He had told her rather optimistically that I should be released shortly, but on no account was she to try and visit me in the Zulu capital. That was a great relief, for since my nightmare I had been afraid that Louisa might be planning to do precisely that. I

35

had been fearful that she would arrive with their leader Retief, who was due in the capital in less than a month's time.

One person definitely not coming to the capital, though, was Captain Gardiner. He had written a letter for Dingane that Owen had to read for him. It explained that the captain was ill and unable to travel. Gardiner promised the king he would visit as soon as he was able. Privately, Gardiner had sent another verbal message via Hulley. He was not ill at all, but did not trust the king. It had been Gardiner who had told us of Isiguabani's orders to kill Retief. Now he claimed he was fearful that the king might serve the same fate to him. Gardiner was going to wait to see what happened after Retief's second visit. He was not going to risk getting his brains dashed out on the execution rock.

Having looked into the king's dark eyes, I was all too aware that our fates depended on his capricious whim. Even so, I confess that I thought that the colour of our skin might save us. As far as we knew, no white man had ever been executed by the Zulus. I did not trust Gardiner an inch and William had not been able to confirm the stories about why Isiguabani's people had been killed. The Zulus he had spoken to knew only that the king had been angry with the chief, who had then tried to run away. I wondered if Gardiner was playing some game, with us as vulnerable pawns right in the middle of it. Even if the story were true, Dingane had been careful to distance himself from the murder of Retief, so that he could blame someone else if necessary.

I comforted myself that all of those he publicly ordered executed were his own subjects, whereas we were visitors to his realm. Mind you, as a precaution I persuaded Owen to drop into his conversations with the king just how powerful the British monarch was. A Zulu regiment or impi had roughly a thousand men. Dingane soon understood that the British had a thousand regiments, each armed with guns and horses as well as huge cannon. I thought such information could do us no harm. I naively believed that he would have to let me go eventually and unless we did something to grossly offend him, we would be safe.

Gradually, my injuries were improving. I took daily walks once my ankle allowed, in part to avoid Owen's sermons. I now also preferred to be away from the mission buildings in the afternoons, when the gruesome processions went up the opposite hill. That helped to avoid any more nightmares. In the evenings we would settle in the cleric's hut as the ladies sewed red jackets from a bolt of cloth that Dingane

36

had given them. Zulu women, it appeared, had poor needlework skills and he wanted the jackets for his courtiers. Mrs Hulley joined in the work even after her husband had returned, as did Jane the maid. Soon they had thirty red jackets to present to the court. Life was gloriously uneventful. It was the following morning, however, the tenth of January 1838 according to Owen's journal, that we had a reminder of our knife-edge existence.

Jane had left the hut to collect eggs for breakfast, but returned moments later screaming hysterically that we were all to be killed. While Mrs Owen tried to calm the girl so she could explain herself more coherently, Owen and I cautiously stepped outside to see what had alarmed her – and immediately wished we hadn't. All around the bottom of our hill was a solid line of Zulu soldiers. There were hundreds of them, perhaps a whole impi, and they had come prepared for war, with at least two throwing spears protruding over the tops of their hide shields and their shorter stabbing spears in their other hands. They had been standing silently, a black sinister line surrounding us. When they saw they had been spotted, they began a slow rhythmic knock of their *iklwas* against the wooden edge of their shields. It was like the heartbeat of a single serpent surrounding us. Then one of their officers shouted something and the whole mass answered in a rumbling roar, taking a step forward as they did so.

"Oh Jesus," I muttered in horror, "they *are* coming to kill us." But as I spoke the words, the warriors stepped back to their original positions. Yet the chanting continued to grow louder all around us, as I realised that they were beginning some sort of threatening dance. "What the hell have you done to upset them?" I demanded of Owen, who looked as appalled as I must have done.

"Nothing, I have not seen the king for two days." Owen turned to William, who had now followed us out of the hut. "What are they singing about?" he demanded.

The boy listened for a moment and for the first time I saw fear in those young eyes. "It is nothing, just a marching song," he answered. I was sure he was lying, which made me even more afraid. Then we saw the line part and up the path from the capital came a new line of soldiers, around fifty of them, led by two of the king's advisors. The procession climbed the hill towards us and twice I saw one of the advisors glancing over his shoulder towards the palace. I stared in that direction too and, perhaps it was my imagination, but I thought I saw a glint of sunlight on metal. Dingane must have ordered these soldiers here and right then I would have bet a guinea to a farthing that the bastard was watching proceedings through his glass.

"It must be a misunderstanding," asserted Owen. "I am sure it will be resolved." As he finished speaking one of the king's advisors pointed at us and began to shout, then the soldiers with him charged. There was nowhere to run; I just had to hope that Owen was right as we were quickly surrounded by sharp stabbing spears and driven to a clear space ten yards from the huts. More soldiers were going inside the buildings and driving out the occupants to join us. Women were screaming, children crying and some of the African servants begging for mercy, but all were forced to sit on the ground beside us.

"They are shouting that the king thinks we have betrayed him," muttered William, but he could not understand what we had done. The soldiers were searching for something. We watched them drag all the trunks and bags of possessions in the buildings outside. Then everything was tipped onto the ground and the warriors used their long *assegais* to rummage about among the Owens' clothes. Even the children's things were not spared and I even saw one warrior staring suspiciously into Owen's inkwell. Eventually, after half an hour we finally discovered what they were looking for. Dingane was convinced that the cloth he had provided would make more than the thirty red jackets the women had made. He suspected that they had kept some of the cloth for themselves. That was enough for him to threaten our lives and turn the mission upside down. Mrs Owen pointed out the few red trimmings that the soldiers had already found. Through William, she explained that there was barely enough left to make a hat, never mind a jacket and at last the advisors were satisfied. We watched as a soldier ran back to the palace with the news.

"Surely he would not kill us over some missing jackets?" I protested as we continued to sit in the dirt.

"Certainly not now that he has seen we did not keep any cloth," agreed Owen, but I noticed that William had stayed silent. I decided that I did not want to know what the warriors had been singing about earlier. Eventually, another messenger from the king arrived and in a moment the search party were all marching back to their barracks. We were left sitting there, still frightened and vulnerable, surrounded by strewn clothes that were flapping gently in the wind. Mrs Owen was the first to rise and soon organised the servants to tidy up their belongings. As I got to my feet, a glance down the hillside revealed that not all the soldiers had gone. Around a hundred remained, stood around the bottom of the hill. I was not sure if Dingane was a mad despot or trying to intimidate us. It was hard to know which was worse.

For nearly a week the warriors guarded our hilltop, leaving us in trepidation as to what Dingane would do next. Only our Zulu servants were allowed to pass through this cordon to bring us fresh supplies from the market. Then as suddenly as he had turned against our little settlement, his mood changed again. The guards disappeared to be replaced by another advisor offering the king's apologies for the misunderstanding, and the gift of another ox. Just as we began to relax, the advisor announced that Owen, Hulley, William and I were all invited to the palace later that day to join Dingane for a celebration. Our first thought was that it was some trick or a trap, but we knew that we had little choice but to accept. If he meant us ill, he could seize us at any time he pleased. On the other hand, if we were to refuse to attend, he was bound to take offence and heaven knew what he might do then.

January in South Africa has long summer days and there was still plenty of light that evening as we made our way down to the palace. The women had taken fond farewells from their husbands. Hulley's wife was distraught, but Mrs Owen tried to calm her and avoid spreading alarm to the children. We were in our best clothes, or in my case, Owen's second best, less any clerical collar. The reverend tried to keep our spirits up too, asserting that Dingane was a shrewd ruler who must have realised that he had made a mistake. It sounded like he was trying to convince himself as much as anyone. Strangely, it was young William's opinion I valued most. He could understand the Zulu and could hear whispers and rumours that gave a better indication of their true feelings. Worryingly, though, he kept his thoughts to himself.

The guards at the gate to the capital were clearly expecting us and waved us straight through. The streets were much the same as before, with perhaps a few more cooking fires burning. Soon we were approaching the central kraal and once more guards appeared to escort us across the palace courtyard. There was no waiting for our host this time, though, for we were no more than halfway across when Dingane strolled out to welcome us. To our relief he was smiling. In fact, his show of good humour was a little too effusive to be genuine and I am sure we all remained on our guard. Stools were brought out from the royal hut and then a gourd of some local cloudy beer. Perhaps sensing our lingering suspicions, the king was quick to drink a deep draught himself to show that the brew was a lot less lethal than his physic. We sipped politely as, through William, the king offered his apologies for the 'misunderstanding' of the week before. He then assured us, ominously, that the advisor who had misled him had been severely punished. I could not help but wonder if he was one of three poor devils we had seen executed over the last few days.

"You must forgive me," the king announced, "for that is the Christian way, is it not?" Dingane beamed happily at Owen as William translated his question.

"God will know your true feelings," responded Owen, I thought a touch recklessly. Whether William translated this fully I am not sure, but the king suddenly frowned and asked the cleric another question.

"The king is asking about the Day of Judgement," William informed Owen, who looked slightly appalled at the prospect of another theological debate with Dingane. "He wants to know, if the dead are going to come back to life, why do they have to wait for this day?"

The next five minutes were filled with a barrage of questions for the Bible-thumper, who grew increasingly flustered as he fended off the royal interrogation. If the dead were currently in heaven and hell, where exactly were these places? When the hapless Owen gestured upwards for heaven, the king demanded to know why he could not see the saved souls floating above his head. What about those who had been burned or executed, would they come back to life with those injuries? Would the people in hell come back as well as the people in heaven? As a man who had stabbed his own powerful brother in the back to seize the throne, not to mention the hundreds he had ordered executed, you could certainly understand Dingane's concern that they could all rise again to take issue with him. He was particularly interested in whether one could die again *after* the Day of Judgement and where you would go in those circumstances. Owen's biblical training had failed him on that point and he floundered around trying to produce convincing answers. I did not need William's translation to see the that the king was far from convinced.

After a while, Dingane gave up on his inquisition and sat brooding at us for a minute or two in silence. We stared between us, unsure what to do or say. There was a sudden chill in the air now and I was not sure if it was due to the sun going down or the king's changing demeanour.

He suddenly looked up and glared at Hulley. "How ill is Captain Gardiner?" he demanded through William.

"Er, very ill, he has the fever." Hulley had started nervously at the question and now shifted uncomfortably. He was not a good liar.

"Was his tongue black?" the king pressed, his eyes narrowing in suspicion.

Hulley glanced briefly at Owen, unsure how to answer. After a pause he admitted that he had not noticed, but added as an afterthought that Gardiner had not mentioned his tongue.

Dingane grunted an acknowledgement but did not take his eyes off the hapless courier. I wondered if the king had sent some of his own warriors to the captain's house to see if he really was unable to travel. He certainly seemed to have his doubts and the royal voice rumbled out once more from that huge chest.

"The kings says that he is sending you back to Gardiner," William passed the message on, his voice high in comparison. "You are to tell the captain that he is to present himself in ten days when Retief and his men visit. Then we will sort out the land once and for all."

Hulley nodded in agreement, yet all of the white people present knew that there was not a chance in hell that Gardiner would obey this demand. I feared what would happen to the rest of us when Gardiner refused again. Then I was struck with a moment of reckless inspiration as I blurted out, "Perhaps I could ride with Mr Hulley and help him bring Captain Gardiner back to you?" As soon as the words were out of my mouth, I was sure that the king would see my request for the obvious falsehood it was. Once I was out of this cursed city a whole herd of their giant elephants would not drag me back. William looked at me in alarm but with Dingane watching expectantly, he had little choice but to pass on my idea.

The king's initial goodwill had long since disappeared. There was a malevolence to him now, which deepened as he heard my suggestion. The black eyes bored into mine. I was now certain he had sensed my real intentions. There was a shuffle behind us as the guards stepped closer in anticipation of being required. I felt a trickle of sweat run down my spine as my mind filled with images of being dragged up to the execution rock. I was on the cusp of adding that I would of course be happy to stay if he preferred, when that deep voice rumbled again.

"He says you can leave with the Boers," William announced. I felt my guts clench in alarm. We were by no means certain that Dingane planned to let the Boers survive the journey back to their camp. Had I

41

just exchanged captivity for a death sentence? I opened my mouth to say that I wanted to go back to Port Natal rather than the Boer camp, but under that continuing glare I shut it again. At least I was alive for now and I got the distinct impression that any further protest would risk that status. The king's face had twisted into an angry scowl. A volcanic rage was only a reckless comment away and heaven knew what would happen to us then. Perhaps his courtiers sensed the same, for now one of his counsellors stepped forward. He whispered something in the king's ear, which caused the royal shoulders to relax and once more a smile appeared on those volatile features. The counsellor stepped back and gestured to someone hidden inside the royal hut. Immediately, a horn sounded to herald one of the finest processions I ever saw.

The king turned to face this new spectacle. He clearly considered his dealings with us completed, although glancing behind, I saw his guards had remained to prevent us from leaving. For once I did not mind as my attention was taken by a line of figures emerging from between the royal huts. There were at least a hundred of them, tall slim women with high cheekbones and expressions as proud as Lucifer. But it was not their faces that grabbed your attention, for they were all naked but for a grass skirt – some of which were rather sparsely thatched. I stared agog for a moment at this vision of mass womanhood. When I tore my gaze away, I saw that Hulley and young William were similarly distracted. Owen had fixed his eyes on the dirt between his feet, as though the sight of so many bare tits could send him to eternal damnation.

Despite the scene before us, my nerves were still reeling from what could well have been a death sentence passed down on me. It says something of my anxiety that a hundred near-naked stunners dancing in front of me failed to distract me entirely from worrying about my fate. Then half a dozen other women appeared to obscure the view; the contrast between them and the beauties beyond could not have been starker. Years before in New Orleans I had seen something called a sea cow. It was a vast, blubbery creature that lived in the marshes and it was the closest thing I had seen to these new arrivals. Each must have been close to three hundred pounds of human flesh; there were rolls of fat around their faces but mercifully their bodies were more demurely draped. The king shouted a command and these bloated creatures began to sing, some with deep voices, others high. The overall effect was of a droning dirge.

42

The performance was to go on for over an hour, during which time Owen minutely examined every grain of dirt around his boots. The noise soon became an irritating din and the performers must have tired simply from standing, never mind singing. Dingane, though, ignored their discomfort and kept shouting out requests as though they were the band at the Vauxhall Pleasure Gardens. I soon managed to block out the noise, for there were ample compensations. At length I even began to relax a little. The king was happy again and laughing in delight at the performance; the immediate danger had passed. As for the rest, I would worry about that nearer the time. Perhaps I could persuade the Boers to lend me a horse to ride for Port Natal, so that I missed any ambush intended for them on their journey. I had been in far tighter fixes before and wriggled out.

It was, I reflected, a strange day. I had spent half of it with a reasonable expectation of hideous execution and even then, I might be a condemned man. Yet much to my surprise, I had ended it swaying in time with two hundred pert black breasts dancing before my eyes.

Chapter 5

Once in India I saw a priest or fakir lie in a hessian sack up to his neck, into which a live cobra was placed. We watched the coils of the snake move under the rough cloth as the serpent roamed inside the sack, but the man later emerged unscathed from the experience. Those weeks in Umgungundlovu reminded me of that holy man: lying close to a dangerous creature and knowing one false move could result in your death. By the end of January, I had been in Owen's settlement for six weeks. The Boers were due in early February. At least this incarceration would not last much longer for me, but what would follow was causing increasing alarm.

Dingane had instructed Owen to write to Retief requesting that he bring all of his settlers with him, including the women and children. Now that the king had mastered a few of his words and letters, he would get Owen to read the letter back to him while he studied the writing. The cleric dared not add a warning to the note, for the king was bound to notice the extra words, even if he could not understand them. The only reason I could imagine for Dingane to summon all of Retief's people to his capital, was to kill them. I could not think of a better explanation. William told me that he had interpreted for Retief on his earlier visit. Dingane had asked how many people the Boer leader had. Retief had answered that his wagon train numbered at least a hundred and fifty settlers. Perhaps Dingane thought that this was all the Boers as Retief was negotiating for their whole group. Yet I knew that there were three other Boer leaders already in Dingane's territory, each with a similar number of followers.

I reassured Owen that Retief was unlikely to bring the women and children. Even when I had been with the Boers there was much distrust over the Zulu offer, which sounded far too good to be true. Surely, he would not take such a risk? Still, I began to have a horrible nagging fear that he might, and that Louisa would come with them. That night I woke up in a lather again with the same nightmare as before: Louisa and I being dragged up the hill, with me making a lot more fuss than the adulterous couple. In the end I got up and went outside to avoid disturbing the others. It was a quiet night, even the top of the execution hill seemed peaceful. Thinking back, I could not recall any processions to its summit for a couple of days. Just a slight odour of rot and decay on the wind gave any clue as to its purpose. The capital lay down to my right, only a handful of flickering fires to give away its presence in the dark. I stared into the blackness towards the palace and quietly cursed the tyrant inside it.

What was going on in Dingane's mind, I wondered. He knew that the British and Boers had dominated the Khoi-khoi people on the southern tip of the continent and then pushed the Xhosa tribes north. He had heard that the Boers had defeated the Matabele people, who he had long tried to conquer. Dingane must know that with their firearms and horses, the white men would make formidable enemies. His brother Shaka had invited British settlers to stay at Port Natal, but Dingane had offered a vast tract of land to Gardiner and now this same territory to the Boers. The more I considered it, the more I agreed with Owen: the king had no intention of giving his land away. The gift to Gardiner was meaningless. It could be snatched back in a moment and there was nothing that Gardiner or the few British souls in Port Natal could do to stop it, even if they were minded to help the unpopular captain.

The Boers, though, were another matter. Dingane must have assumed that they would try to take some of his land whether he gave them permission or not. He could have gone to war with this powerful enemy, but instead the wily devil seemed to be trying another approach. He could draw them in with the promise of a treaty and then when their guard was down, perhaps on their journey home, when they were planning the farms they would build, he would strike. I doubted Retief and his riders would stand much of a chance, for Dingane was bound to send more reliable men this time who would get the job done. I shuddered at the memory of those black eyes boring into mine and then his casual 'suggestion' that I could join this doomed band.

If I was right, he was happy to kill the Boers and equally content to murder a British visitor. I half turned as a soft snore came from the hut behind me. What about the rest of them? Would they be seen as inconvenient witnesses to his treachery? I had already decided that it would be fatal to ride back with the Boers, but I had a nasty feeling that even if I managed to stay with Owen, my fate would be little better. My only hope was to get back to Port Natal and even then, I might not be safe. But how the hell was I to get away? There were no horses, only lumbering cows. I was fifty-five, for heaven's sake. There was no way I could outrun the fit, young Zulu soldiers who would be sent in pursuit when I was discovered missing. My best chance was with a horse and for that I would have to wait for Retief and his men to arrive.

The next morning our suspicions deepened as some of the army began to arrive in Umgungundlovu. The first regiment all had shields covered in pure white hides; there were over a thousand of them. They came past our hill at a slow run, one of their commanders calling out chants as they went, to which the whole mass responded in a deep roar. They stopped at the city gates and continued their singing, clearly not tired from their journey. Stepping back and then forward, raising their spears, which glinted in the early-morning sun, they were clearly making a mock attack. Their war cry made the hair on the back of my neck stand up in alarm even from half a mile away. There were certainly enough of them to wipe every white man from the territory, but that afternoon they were joined by the black shield regiment, who gave an identical display before following the white shields into the city. Umgungundlovu must have already been packed with soldiery by then, but, incredibly, a third regiment arrived that evening. There was no more room amongst the huts in the city and so they made their camp on one of the hills outside. We watched them swarming around like ants as they made their bivouacs. Then as night fell, their fires lit the night sky in the same profusion as the stars above.

There was not a lot of conversation around the Owen dinner table that evening. I suspect that I was not the only one wondering if we had just seen our executioners. Owen gave another interminable grace prayer about the righteous entering heaven, which gave away his own sense of foreboding. Even his redoubtable wife struggled to stay resolute; I noticed her hand was trembling slightly as she poured me some water. Mrs Hulley had joined us and the two women exchanged silent looks, which spoke volumes as their children chattered carelessly beside them.

None of the adults slept well that night. I could hear the Owens whispering in their bed and I am sure at least one of them sobbed for a while. In the morning I even thought of joining their morning prayer session, for I was increasingly of the opinion that we would need Divine assistance to get out of this mess. Instead, I stepped outside to see what the regiment on the nearby hill was up to, only to find that around a hundred of them were in a pitched battle. The rest of the regiment were cheering on their fellows as they darted backwards and forwards with weapons raised. To my surprise while several took vicious stabs, they appeared to suffer no harm from their injuries and got up and fought on. I was just reaching for Owen's glass for a closer look when young William arrived.

46

"What on earth is going on?" I asked. "Are they using blunted spears?"

"They are not spears at all," he told me. "They are fighting sticks. They use them for games and ceremonial dances."

"What is the gossip from town?" I asked, gesturing at the direction from which he had come.

"They think that the Boers will arrive today," William announced. He looked disappointed that I showed no great reaction, but it was what I had expected. Dingane would not have moved his army any sooner than he had to, for the capital had to be bursting with soldiers by now. I had roughly counted each regiment and thought that in total there must have been around three and a half thousand men in or around the town, perhaps as many as four thousand. I was about to ask if William had any more news when we heard the sound of distant gunfire coming from behind us. It had to be the Boers; they were the only ones with guns.

"Owen, they are here," I shouted through the door of his hut, before walking around it to stare in the direction of the noise. At first all I could see was a cloud of red dust rising between two hills. Then the dark line of a column of men emerged, followed by the hundreds of cattle that Retief had retrieved for the Zulu king. I was using Owen's glass to study them when its owner arrived at my shoulder.

"How many are there?" he asked anxiously. "Have they brought their women and children?"

"Less than a hundred," I told him. It was a group roughly the size of a squadron of British cavalry. "I doubt they have any women or children as they have not brought their wagons with them. They would not have abandoned those – they contain most of their possessions."

"Oh, the Lord be praised," Owen breathed. "I feared that my last message for the king might have persuaded some to come and then they might be… well… you know." There were some things that were best left unsaid, and the possible fate of the Boers was one of them, not that the Dutchmen themselves seemed to have any concerns. As they got closer, we could see them waving happily to the growing crowd of Zulus who had come out of the city to welcome them. The Africans were fascinated by the horses; many would not have seen such riders before. The Boers were happy to show off their skills, some making their mounts dance sideways, while others got their steeds to rear up on their hind legs. The Zulus applauded every trick and even the regiment on the far hill had come down and were beating their fighting

47

sticks together in approval. There was a happy carnival atmosphere. I remember Owen and I looking at each other and wondering if we had misjudged things after all.

While Zulu herdsmen drove the cattle off to pens, the rest of the Boers passed on through the gate towards the centre of Umgungundlovu. "We should go after them," suggested Owen. "We need to warn them to be on their guard and you need to speak to Retief about leaving with them."

"Are you mad?" I protested. "I am not going anywhere near that lion's den until we know it is safe. There are still two Zulu regiments hiding in there, remember. There is a good chance those Boers will not survive the next hour." At my insistence we stayed on Owen's hilltop where, with his glass, we could look down into the central kraal. It was hard to see any detail at that distance, but at first it appeared that my worst fears were confirmed. There were crashes of more gunfire and we could see the horsemen riding backwards and forwards as though attacking. Then the shooting stopped and the smoke cleared to reveal all the Boers mounted on one side of the courtyard. Now the distant chant of a thousand Zulu voices reached us on the wind as a black line of humanity crossed the courtyard, white shields raised, and while we knew we could not hear their footsteps at that distance, there was a strange thudding as though we could. Owen and I stared at each other, perplexed as to what was happening. Two grown men, whose lives might hang in the balance wondered what to do next. Then we came to our senses and sent a twelve-year-old boy to find out.

In our defence, William Woods Junior was far better equipped for the task. The king seemed to genuinely like him for a start, which was more than could be said for us. William had many friends he could talk to in the capital and if one of us had gone, we would have had to bring him with us anyway. He was also as keen as mustard to go, wanting to know what was happening to the Boers. He raced off down the hill and was back in just over an hour. He explained that the king had wanted to see how the Boers fought and so he and Retief had arranged a mock battle in his huge central courtyard. The Dutch had charged, firing their guns in the air. Then the white shields regiment had responded but with fighting sticks instead of spears, which they had beaten on the sides of their shields making the noise we had heard. William reported that the mood in the central kraal was very friendly. The king, using Thomas Halstead, the interpreter he had sent with the Zulus who had joined the Dutchmen, was laughing and joking with Retief. By the

48

time William had arrived the king was treating his guests to the sight of lines of dancing titties – mercifully, he had spared them his singers.

The encounter was going surprisingly well, although I could not help but wonder why Dingane was so keen to see how the Boers fought. Was it so that he could plan how to beat them? The Dutch finally left the palace to set up their camp for the night. They were led to a hill near ours and were followed by hundreds of still-curious Zulus, particularly children. As they passed by, one of the riders turned and galloped up towards our settlement. It was Halstead, who normally lived in Owen's mission, but for now was staying with the Boers. He was laughing as he hugged the children who rushed up to greet him and then he assured us that all was well. The king had been effusive in his greeting to his Dutch guests and was all set to negotiate on the land the following morning. Indeed, one of the reasons for Halstead's visit was to pass on Dingane's request for Owen and William to come to the palace on the morrow to help draw up the treaty. Retief had been concerned that the Zulu leader would try to delay or prevaricate agreeing to the land grant once the cattle he had demanded had been delivered. The Dutchman had insisted that the contract be drawn up the very next day, yet Dingane had raised no objection at all. Owen was required to write the agreement while William would help with the translation.

The next morning they both set off for the palace, while I strolled down to the Boer encampment. Most of the Dutch were still there as Retief had only taken a handful of his people with him to witness the discussions. Many were older men although there were two boys amongst the group, one of whom I discovered was Retief's son. Almost all had been away in the band recovering Dingane's cattle when I had been in the Boer camp, but I found one I knew, who had joined for the ride to Umgungundlovu. I eagerly asked him for news of Louisa. He told me that when he had last seen her, she was well, but worried about me. He confirmed that she had got my message and so knew where I was. As I had feared, she had even tried to join Retief's band, but they would not allow any women to come. "She is a brave *dame*, that one," he had laughed. "She wanted to tell the king that he had to let you go. She even had some jewellery to use to pay a ransom."

"She is bloody stubborn," I countered, smiling indulgently. "Coming here was the one thing I told her *not* to do." I gave a silent prayer that the Boers had stopped her, for the last thing I needed was her falling into Dingane's clutches. I tried to banish from my mind the memory of my recent nightmare. It caused me to glance up at the nearby execution hill, which had been unused since the Dutch had arrived. "I say, are you sure you can trust this king?" I asked. "We have heard rumours that he tried to have Retief killed after his last visit and now he has ordered thousands of soldiers into the capital. You need to be on your guard."

The man nodded and admitted that when they had left the Boer encampments, many there had thought that they were riding to their deaths. "But we have to try," he explained. "We need land and Dingane is the only one offering it. He may want us to fight for him against his enemies, but that will be a small price to pay if there is good pasture here and we can raise our families in peace."

"That is if he does not change his mind and butcher them first," I warned.

My companion nodded grimly that such a thing was a possibility. "Let us see how the negotiations go," he suggested. "For if he gives us everything we want and makes no demands, that will be a sign that he plans to play us false."

I explained that Dingane had agreed I could leave with the Boers, and asked if I could borrow a horse. This was no problem as they had brought several spare animals. I was still undecided if I would ride with them all the way back to their camp in the hope that the Zulus would not ambush the party, or to break away and go to Port Natal. If I was not murdered first, I would see Louisa sooner if I rode with the Boers, yet I could easily travel on to her from the coast. I too would await the outcome of the negotiations, but having looked into Dingane's black eyes, I would take some convincing not to ride first for the sea.

I was introduced to others among the Boers and they all displayed the same guarded optimism of the first. One remembered me as D'Urban's messenger. I pointed out that he at least would welcome them back into British territory. Compared to Dingane, I knew who I would rather have governing me, but to my surprise the suggestion was treated with scorn.

"You British forget that we Dutch fought first for this land," railed one greybeard. "We beat the bushmen and the Khoi-khoi, we built farms and prosperous communities and when the tribes rose against us, we dealt with them too. Now you British are here, you think you know better." He spat in disgust before adding, "You fight to take land and then you give it back. The Xhosa think you are weak to do such a thing. There is no protection for us; our farms are raided and burned time and time again. There is no point building again on our old land. We will be better off starting somewhere new and protecting ourselves."

"D'Urban did not want to give that land back," I protested. "That decision was made in London."

"My cattle's shit has more brains than your London colonial people," the old-timer roared. "Let them come out here and farm so that they see for themselves. And one of the first things your D'Urban did," he added jabbing a finger at me, "was to cancel the vagrancy act so that we had thieves roaming our farms."

There was little sense in arguing with him further and he probably had a point about the colonial office. I asked Halstead about the vagrancy act and he confirmed that D'Urban had indeed put a stop to it. The act had allowed any itinerant Khoi-khoi to be declared a vagrant. They could then be drafted into forced public labour or contracted to a farmer. Essentially, it allowed farmers to seize whoever they wanted who was not already employed and put them to work.

Owen had previously told me that another reason the Boers had moved north was to hang on to their slaves. All slaves had been freed in the territory back in 1834, although they had then been required to complete a four-year apprenticeship that finished at the end of the year. If the Boers had their own land, then British laws would not apply to them.

I stayed with the Boers for much of that day and while most were friendly and hospitable, the fact that I was British made me only marginally more trustworthy to them than the Zulu king. When I tried to suggest that they should be on their guard, they would grin and nod before often suggesting that I was just trying to persuade them to go back to their old land.

In the end I gave up and returned to Owen's hilltop, where I waited another two hours for the cleric and William to return from the palace. They had spent all day drawing up the agreement, which had been a tortuous process. Retief and Dingane had negotiated their terms through William and when each clause had been agreed the boy would advise Owen what to write down. Then Owen slowly read out the agreement, Retief listening to him carefully, then waiting for William to translate again for the king. Between them amendments were made as the principals agreed more details. Finally, both sides were happy and Retief signed next to where Dingane had made his mark. Then the leaders who had come with Retief were also invited to sign as were two of Dingane's generals and several of his counsellors. The deal was done: the Boers had been given their new home.

Chapter 6

The Dutch had been given the same land that had been granted to
Captain Gardiner. Retief and his followers were permanently granted
all the territory west of the Tugela River up to and until the
Umzimvubu River, to include Port Natal. The Boers took the news that
an agreement had been reached back to the camp and I could soon hear
cheering and the firing of their guns in celebration. Owen and William
arrived back in the mission a short while later, far less jubilant. They
were both still convinced that Dingane was planning some form of
treachery. While the king had negotiated hard and insisted on various
points in the agreement as though it was something he intended to
observe, he had still conceded a huge amount of land. William had
overheard the two Zulu generals, who had signed the document
reluctantly. Both had been furious as William had translated the
agreement.

"I have tried to warn Retief before," insisted Owen. "I have even
got the king to admit to him that this is the same land that he has
already granted Gardiner, but he says that he cannot afford to let this
opportunity pass. He is on his guard. The king sent the Boers a
messenger asking them to hand over their weapons, but Retief tells me
that he pointed to his grey hair and asked if Dingane thought he was a
child. They have, however, agreed to leave their guns with their
servants."

Certainly, the Boers were not mindless of the danger they were in,
for that evening as the sounds of celebration continued from their
camp, I noticed that a few of them patrolled with their guns around
their tents. A group, exercising their mounts, even rode as far as our
hill and doffed their hats to us as they rode past. With the deal signed,
I thought that they might leave the next day. This meant that my
departure was imminent too. Despite Owen's misgivings, I began to
entertain the hope that I would soon be in Port Natal and reunited with
Louisa. Then we would leave this shore and never darken it again.

The next morning, however, I strolled over to the Boer camp only
to discover that they were not leaving until the following day. They
laughed at my eagerness to depart and promised not to go without me,
but Dingane had suggested a day of celebration to cement their new
alliance. He had sent a bullock to be killed and asked for more displays
of their weapons and horsemanship. Owen and William acted like
Jeremiahs when I gave them this news, convinced that some treachery

was afoot, but they could not have been more wrong. The only weapons that the Zulu warriors carried were their fighting sticks as they showed off their skills. Several Boers were persuaded to have a go and there was much laughter when they failed. The Dutch gave demonstrations of their marksmanship, although I noticed that they politely declined when one Zulu asked to try their weapon. The muskets were then returned to the camp where they remained under guard as the Boers rode their horses up and down the impromptu fairground that had formed outside the capital. Some of the Zulus even tried to race the horses. These were fit young men and were victorious over shorter distances, before the animals got into their stride. When Dingane joined the festivities, Halstead explained to him that the Boers wanted to toast their agreement. Some Zulu beer was brought out and a slightly puzzled king raised his cup with Retief, to cheers from the masses. I was starting to wonder if I might be safe riding back to their camp with the Boers after all.

By the end of the day even Owen was starting to question if Dingane was genuine in his agreement. He had been delighted to see Zulus and Boers mixing so freely and had begun to wonder if the devoutly Christian Dutch would aid him in his mission to convert lost souls. However, long experience of dealings with Dingane, and warnings from his wife reminded him to be cautious. He spent much of that evening on his knees praying that this peaceful union might continue.

Young William, though, was as resolute as ever that the Boers' days were numbered. He had wandered through the capital and amongst the Zulus at the fair, eavesdropping on their conversations. He reported that those who knew what was in the agreement were deeply unhappy about it. Once the Boers had taken up their new lands then everyone would know how much Dingane had ceded and the resentment against him would be even greater.

"The king has spies who will tell him what the people are saying," William warned. "I am sure that the Boers will not be alive by the end of tomorrow."

"You said that this morning about today," Owen reminded him from his private altar. "We must pray that you are wrong," he continued, as he proceeded to do just that.

The next morning two of the Boers joined us for breakfast. They had come to let me know that we would be leaving that day. But before we departed, they were to attend a farewell ceremony of singing and dancing in the palace. As one of their group now, I too was invited. It was an offer I instantly declined. I could tell you that it was William vigorously shaking his head behind them that persuaded me, but if I am honest there were other factors. Chief among them was the wish to avoid that awful dirge of singing from the fat trollops. The last time I had heard them I concluded that even bagpipes might be more bearable; at least the piper would run out of puff sooner or later. The promise of two hundred pert black breasts swaying in unison was not a sufficient inducement to suffer that noise again. I also had no wish to see Dingane again, or more specifically, I did not wish those black eyes to see me. They contained fathomless cruelty and I feared that if he glimpsed me, then my escape might be snatched away once more.

Again, Owen tried to persuade the Boers to be on their guard, but our guests took such warnings lightly. They reminded us that they had wandered unarmed around the capital for the last two days and come to no harm. Quite the reverse, the king had shown them every courtesy. He had also kept his side of the bargain by signing over their land and now he was inviting them for a send-off celebration. By then even a notorious poltroon like myself was beginning to wonder if my caution and fear were misplaced. Only William remained completely adamant that treachery was afoot, but he had been warning of that since the moment the Boers had arrived. By now the calls of this twelve-year-old doom-monger were wearing thin. I well remember Jane telling him off. "Don't be silly," she snapped. "You are always saying things like that. You told me a long time ago that the king would kill *you* because you talk too much."

Our guests left and soon we saw Retief leading the Boers to the city gate for their farewell ceremony. They were laughing and joking, waving to us as they went past, apparently without a care in the world. Halstead was with them, doubtless hoping that the dancing girls would make another appearance as there was one in particular that he was quite keen on. Only the native servants were left in the Boer camp to guard the weapons and the horses. Most of them were taking down the remaining shelters and packing away pots and pans in preparation for their departure. It reminded me that I should get ready to leave myself. Owen had leant me some spare clothes – I had been wearing his duds since I arrived as my own clothes had been little more than torn rags when I was found. His wife was just showing me some bread and dried meat that she had wrapped and placed in my sack of belongings when the cleric called me back outside.

"Mr Flashman," he never would call me Thomas, "come and look. Tell me what you think." I went back out onto the hilltop and found him hunched behind a tree. He had wedged his glass in the branches to keep it steady and was now squinting through the lens. "Look," he called as he heard me approach. "How many men do you think he has in that courtyard?"

I bent down to look and had to adjust the tubes a little before the centre of the palace swam into view. It was black with men, I guessed that all three of the regiments Dingane had summoned to his capital were there. As I watched some signal must have been given, for they all began to move to the sides, presumably to allow the Boers to enter, so that they lined the space in ranks that must have been ten men deep. A space was thus cleared in the centre except for a few men who remained standing there as the lines parted. It was hard to tell from such a distance, but I guessed that one of the figures in the middle was Dingane, for he was welcoming the Boers and inviting them to sit on the ground in the centre of the space, while others brought out what looked to be cauldrons of their beer.

"There are far more of them than when they showed off their stick fighting before," murmured Owen.

"I told you," piped up William. "He is going to kill them all." But no sooner were the words out of the boy's mouth than singing erupted from the mouths of the massed warriors. Even from that distance, the sound coming from three or four thousand throats was clearly audible. I watched as they took a couple of steps towards the Boers before stepping back. Then we distinctly heard the clack of thousands of fighting sticks being clashed together.

"They are just dancing," I confirmed, watching as the movement and clacking settled into some rhythm. To William's visible annoyance, it was a false alarm. Owen went and sat in the shade to read his Bible while I returned to the hut to find a cord to secure my sack to a saddle. I had just got the bag tied with a good loop ready for use when William called out again.

"Messenger coming," he yelled and so I stepped outside once more. The Boers' servants had finished their packing too. The sun was shining and if we left by noon, I thought we might well travel thirty miles before making camp. It would give me plenty of time to decide whether to strike out for Port Natal on my own. My heart quickened at the prospect of finally leaving; it promised to be an excellent day. I remember frowning as I heard dogs barking in the capital. The noise

56

seemed to be coming from the palace and so I went over to the glass, still wedged in the tree, for another look. The dancing warriors had closed in around the Boers until they were no more than twenty feet away. They were still lunging forward with their fighting sticks and clacking them together. Some of the Boers had brought their dogs to the gathering and the animals were feeling threatened, barking at the Zulus that surrounded them. The Dutch were still sitting on the ground in the middle of the circle. If I were among them, I would not be feeling that comfortable either. Dingane's men seemed to be deliberately intimidating their guests.

"I knew I was right!" William shouted accusingly at Owen and I. He was standing by the messenger, who was still puffing from the exertion of running up the hill. "I bloody told you, but you would not listen."

"What on earth are you talking about?" demanded Owen.

"The king is going to kill the Boers," announced the boy jabbing a finger at the messenger. "He has just sent us a message to say that we will be spared the slaughter as we are subjects of King George."

"What? But he can't. No, surely you are mistaken." Owen's now ashen features stared at me in disbelief. Together, we faced the sudden realisation that we had been horribly wrong in giving Dingane the benefit of the doubt. Our optimism, led by self-interest in my case, had blinded us to the fact that we both knew the king was more than capable of such an act. This was after all the same ruler who had murdered hundreds of his own people for failing to do precisely what he now proposed to do himself. I ran over to the telescope. The Boers were still in the centre of the palace, like cattle in the slaughterhouse yard. Perhaps they were still ignorant of their fate, but some were standing now, others holding tight to the leashes of angry hounds that strained at the closing noose of warriors about them. I cocked an ear and beyond the barking dogs and clacking of spears, the strains of the Zulu song were familiar. I did not understand the words and perhaps it was my imagination, but it sounded suspiciously like the threatening ditty they had sung when they had surrounded our hill a few weeks before.

As I watched, the figure I took to be Dingane stood and waved his arms in the air. He must have shouted some command, for the black tide, which had until now been rising and falling, now broke over the hapless Boers like a wave. Some of the poor devils could not even have got to their feet before the fighting sticks rained down blows on

57

them. Elsewhere knots of fighting broke out as men and dogs tried to defend themselves. They did not have their guns, but I dare say a fair few at least had knives, which must have flashed out. They were hopelessly outnumbered, though, and will have known that they did not stand a chance of surviving. I watched in horror as prone white bodies were dragged away from the melee and yet more black soldiers pressed into the gaps created. I was damn glad that I could not see any more detail from the distance we were. When I turned to Owen he was down on his knees, his eyes tightly closed and his ever-present Bible gripped in his fists as he fervently muttered, "Tell me it isn't so, tell me it isn't so."

Whether he was talking to me or the Almighty, it was hard to say and so I did not reply. William was still truculently triumphant, with his hands in his pockets and chin tilted up defiantly. I gestured for him to take his turn observing through the glass. I thought that the gruesome sight of his prediction coming true might take some of the wind out of his sails. It had shaken me and would leave most twelve-year-olds horror-struck. Yet I suspected this one would take it in his stride. As I looked away, my eyes met those of Mrs Owen standing in the doorway of the hut. She had heard the commotion and come outside to investigate. One glance at her husband still whimpering on his knees told her that something awful had occurred. Even without William's demeanour, she could probably have guessed what it was. She looked briefly back inside to check that the children were still playing happily and then turned to me. There was a desperate, unspoken enquiry in her eye.

"He has sent a messenger to say we will be spared," I told her in answer.

"Halstead will be spared too – all us British will be safe," added William, his eye still glued to the glass. The roar of fighting from the capital was dying away now as the last Dutch resistance was quelled.

"Can we trust him?" Mrs Owen spoke quietly. Tears brimmed in her eyes, indicating that she already knew the answer to her own question. With her husband still ignoring us on his knees, to my surprise she stepped forward and threw her arms around me. She started to sob quietly into my shoulder. It was only then that I realised that she came a distant second in her husband's affections, behind the Almighty. I held her tight against me, briefly enjoying the feel of her breasts pressed into my chest. It was the simple comfort we both needed of holding another in a moment of crisis.

As I hugged her, another thought came to mind. "Oh God, I was supposed to be with them. Dingane told me to leave with the Boers, he wanted me dead among them."

"You are British too," Mrs Owen whispered, although I could not take a great deal of reassurance from that. Then I felt her stiffen and step back. She reached out and squeezed my arm in gratitude for our moment of mutual solidarity. Then taking a deep breath, she pulled herself together. In the blink of an eye she had forced herself back to the calm and resourceful woman I had admired. "Francis," she admonished, "get on your feet. There is nothing God can do for those poor souls now." He looked up, surprise showing in his features at her stern tone, but he did as he was bid. "We need to decide what we are going to do now," she continued. "We have the children to consider, we have to make plans to leave. I cannot continue to live at the whim of that… that monster."

"Yes, yes of course," agreed Owen, but then we all just stared at each other, lost for words, realising that we did indeed live at the whim of a monster. Moreover, none of us could easily see a way out. Then as the silence stretched between us, it was rent by a familiar, awful sound: the grim thudding of the execution drum.

William called out that a procession was coming out of the city gates. Children can be surprisingly callous about death and he was no exception. He related that the first few Dutch bodies carried towards the execution hill were dead already or at least unconscious as they were not moving. They were the lucky ones. The fight had not been entirely one-sided, though, for he shouted that at least two dozen black bodies were left in the courtyard, victims of the Boers' knives and dogs.

Soon another group of Zulus could be seen tearing out of the gates and heading to the Boer camp. The servants there had heard the screams from the city and were not about to wait around to be slaughtered like their masters. Some ran away on foot in panic, while the wiser ones grabbed saddles and made for the horses. The Zulu soldiers, all from the white shield regiment, covered the ground with surprising speed. There were no fighting sticks in their hands now; they held *assegais* aloft and spread out as they hunted down their prey. Those trying to flee on foot were doomed and a hail of spears soon made the going difficult for those around the horses. One servant gave up on a saddle and managed to mount bareback. He kicked back his heels and, holding on to the mane, got away. Another was struck in the

59

small of the back with a spear just as he got a foot in the stirrup. A third horse bolted from its rider when pierced in the rump. In all, only two servants managed to get astride and escape, and even they couldn't shake the Zulus running in pursuit.

By then the procession was well up the path to the hill opposite. The prone bodies made no fuss, but those further back were still very much alive. Some of the Boers fought fiercely as they were carried to their fate, even with warriors on each limb and fighting sticks wielded to subdue their victims. Others were yelling obscenities in Dutch as they were dragged along. Yet more, who must have guessed what was coming, cried and begged in vain for mercy. I distinctly remember a big Zulu carrying one of the boys on his shoulder. The lad was screaming and shouting in terror, probably for his father. That did it for me. I could not watch any more of this horror and retreated around the back of Owen's hut and some way down the slope. Even there the screams were audible, and followed by a steady succession of loud cracks as skulls were broken on the execution rock.

Above that hideous noise grew the sound of quavering voices singing hymns. The women had got the children in one of the huts and were doing their best to distract them from the slaughter outside. I looked up as I heard feet scrabbling over the rocks to join me and there was young William. Even he could not stand to watch any longer and I was surprised to see tears running down his cheeks.

"They are going to kill us all, aren't they?" he gasped between sobs.

I wanted to say something that would comfort us both, but the lad knew Dingane and the Zulus better than I. We were witnesses to his treachery and I doubted that the protection of King George, or King William as it had been when I left England, would last for long.

Chapter 7

We did not return to Owen's hut until we were sure that the killing had stopped. Its owner was prostrate on the ground outside, his body heaving with sobs. His wife was pulling on his shoulder, trying to get him back to his feet. William and I helped her get him inside. He ignored the curious stares of the children and threw himself down on his cot. I noticed his precious Bible lying face down in the dirt, where it had been thrown, by the look of it. I could hardly blame Owen for that; the events of the morning would have tested the faith of the Archbishop of Canterbury.

When I summoned the resolve to look across at the opposite hill, I saw the execution rock was now almost entirely buried under a pile of twisted and contorted bodies. The last of the Zulus were coming back down the path, one group holding aloft a lump of bloody offal as though it were a trophy. Already the boldest vultures had landed to begin their feasting, and at least a dozen more circled in the sky above. Turning my gaze to the city, I saw that the dead and wounded Zulus had been taken away, and the kraal was being filled again with soldiers. Even from that distance I could see from the blocks of shields of the same colour that their regiments were massing. They were not carrying fighting sticks now – this time the sun glinted off metal spearpoints. They were chanting again too, their cries punctuated by the thudding of weapon shafts on the sides of their shields.

Would they come for us next? I wondered. Several bands of the white shield warriors lingered around our hill, as they hunted down the last of the fleeing Boer servants. It was clear we could not hope to escape by running away. Instead, we would have to place our faith in 'King George' as our saviour. The thought of that fat, indolent – and deceased – monarch having any part to play in my security did not fill me with great hope. Yet we would not have to wait long to discover the strength of our royal protection: a party of Zulus was already on the path up to Owen's mission. There were half a dozen warriors, each carrying two throwing spears and a shield on one side of their body and their short stabbing spear held in their fist on the other. Had they come to dispatch us too? They probably thought six men was enough to deal with a middle-aged Englishman, a vicar and several women and children. On the other hand, it was not enough to drag us all up the execution hill. I took some comfort from that, as it was clearly where they preferred to do their killing. Then I saw that they had a royal messenger following on behind and I called for Owen to come out.

As I stood by the door to the hut, I could hear Mrs Owen urging her husband to pull himself together. Whatever she whispered must have worked, for a moment later Owen emerged, still wiping tears from his cheeks.

"I am sorry, Mr Flashman that you had to see me like that," he murmured. "You are a soldier. You have probably seen many such things before." He took a deep breath before adding, "Now I must beseech God to give me the strength to carry on, for his light shines brightest in the darkest hour."

I felt sorry for him. He might have been hopelessly naïve in accepting the challenge of his posting, but he meant well. He genuinely wanted to save souls and bring people to the grace of the church. Instead, he was now confronted with man's full savagery, red in tooth and claw, as the saying goes. The foundations of his faith and his understanding of humanity must have been rocked to the core by what he had seen. If he could conjure some divine purpose from that slaughter, he would be doing better than me, but then I had witnessed far too much over the years to keep searching for a meaning.

"Don't worry," I told him. "You never get used to sights like that." I nodded down the slope to the approaching delegation, "Let's hope that they come in peace." As my mind dwelt on the alternative I added, "I don't suppose you have any weapons in that hut, do you?" I had possessed a gun when I fell into the trap, but had not seen it since. Owen looked positively aghast at the idea that he might be tooled up with a brace of barkers. Yet before he could complain, the approaching messenger began to shout.

William appeared behind us and announced, "He says he is pleased to find us well." The emissary beamed at us in greeting, as though the pile of freshly slaughtered corpses visible just over his right shoulder did not exist. I don't think any of us gave William a reply, we just stared nervously at the grim-faced warriors and their sharp metal spear points. If they were minded to, they could butcher the whole hilltop settlement in a couple of minutes. Only talking could save us now, yet none of us could quite find the words. The messenger could not have failed to sense the fear and trepidation caused by his companions. He smiled again as he gestured to the soldiers behind him. "These men are for your protection," he declared before adding ominously, "the king wants to make sure that the subjects of King George are dealt with."

"Where is Mr Halstead?" Mrs Owen's voice came from the hut door. When I looked around, I saw Mrs Hulley standing anxiously at her shoulder. I had forgotten all about the translator; he had been among the Boers when they went down to the palace that final time. If Dingane had saved him, that would be some evidence of his wish to protect British subjects. The messenger hesitated a second too long after he had heard William's translation of the question before replying. "Mr Halstead is well and we will be with him shortly."

Mrs Hulley did not even wait for the translation of the obvious lie. She gave a little scream before asserting that they were bound to murder her Dick too. Had Halstead been alive he would surely have been sent back to us to prove it. If the poor devil had been among the Boers when the Zulus attacked, then he was almost certainly dead, for they were attacking every white man with a wild fury. Perhaps it was William's translation, but the messenger's strange words were not lost on me either: we 'would be with Halstead shortly.' Did that mean we would join his corpse on the hilltop? Owen must have thought the same, for I saw a fresh tear appear in his eye. He looked at his wife and started to usher us all back into the hut. Once inside he fell to his knees and started to recite what I later learned was the 91st Psalm. Most of the others joined him but, after palming a knife from the table, I stayed by the door watching our new sentries. I remember some of the words of the prayer were about the Lord being our refuge and fortress. I could not help but wonder if the Dutch had ever recited the same psalm in their churches. It had done them damn all good. I preferred to put my faith in sharp steel, not that I was likely to get much chance to use it against those long spears.

I glanced back into the hut and saw Mrs Owen gripping her husband's hand and briefly felt a pang of loss for Louisa. I imagined her at that moment in the Boer camp, awaiting in vain for my return with Retief. The way things were looking, I might never see her again. At least she had not chosen to come with the Dutch as I had feared. Seeing Louisa die too would make my own death infinitely worse. I pulled myself together as I spotted another messenger coming up the path. We were not dead yet and while we still breathed, there was still a chance we might somehow get away.

The new arrival was an older and far cannier bird than his predecessor. He was one of Dingane's advisors and stood watching our group closely as we emerged from the hut. He must have noticed the reddened eyes of the women and Owen struggling again to pull himself together to represent us. The courtier gestured for Owen and William to join him a distance from the others so that they could talk in private. With my neck also on the line, I strode forward, uninvited, to join them.

"The king guarantees your safety," the man announced through William, before immediately stating that Halstead had been sent to Port Natal to deliver a message to Gardiner. He was a far more convincing liar than his predecessor, but we were sure that the young man would have called in at the mission first to reassure us if he had lived. We did not reply, there was little point in arguing. The counsellor nodded at our apparent acquiescence. He went on to explain that Dingane had been forced to kill the Dutch as he had learned that they planned to attack and kill him in his palace. Quite how eighty unarmed Dutchmen were going to fight their way through three to four thousand Zulu soldiers he did not say. We greeted this ridiculous claim with more silence and for the first time the advisor looked uncomfortable. Possibly he was disappointed, perhaps he had expected protests and indignation that he could report to his master. A slight smile crossed his lips and then through William he asked, if we agreed that the king had done the right thing.

It was an obvious trap, but Owen could not bring himself to dissemble. "Tell him that we do *not* agree," he insisted. "Tell him that we could not possibly condone the murder of so many Christian souls that have done the king no harm." I saw that his knuckles were white as he gripped his restored Bible to his chest. He was working himself into a passion and so I swiftly interrupted.

"Shut up, you damn fool, or you will have us all killed," I hissed. "Do you want your wife and daughter dead because of your stupid pride?"

"No, Mr Flashman, of course not, but we cannot condone such an act. I would rather we enter heaven pure in faith, than sullied in hell for condoning such treachery." He turned to William, "Tell him exactly what I have said."

The boy looked at the clergyman and then at me. I was going to mutter another warning at him, but there was no time as he turned and immediately spoke to the counsellor. The man listened and frowned, looking again at Owen and then at the young boy before him, as though things did not add up. He did not hide his annoyance as he turned and started to stroll back down the hill to the palace.

"There," announced Owen, satisfied. "We have shown that we are men of faith and principle. We must pray to the Lord for our deliverance from such evil." With that he strolled back to the hut, his back stiffening slightly with pride and resolve.

"What did you really say to him?" I asked William quietly when Owen was out of earshot.

"I told him that we *did* approve," the boy whispered. "I said that we thought the king acted rightly as the Boers would otherwise have killed us as well as the king and his people."

"Well done," I told him. "That will make it harder for that bastard to cause trouble for us with the king, for I am sure that was his aim. Still, we will need to be on our guard and for heaven's sake, don't tell Owen the truth."

William grinned. "Don't worry, there is a lot that goes on around here that the reverend does not know about. I am going to talk to those guards to see if they know what's happening." A few minutes later the lad reported that the offal we had seen being brought down the hill was Retief's heart and liver. Dingane believed that if these were buried on the trail leading to the Boer encampments, that would stop the Boers seeking revenge. The lad also discovered that the justification that Dingane had given his warriors to kill the Dutchmen, was that they were all wizards. The guns the Boers had demonstrated must have looked a lot like magic to the warriors. They also knew the Matabele had been beaten with such weapons. Our guards thought that the king was wise to beat his enemy when their guns were still in their camp.

We watched some of the regiments head south in their loping run. I guessed that as well as burying Retief's organs, they would also guard their territory against any Boer retaliation. It was a relief to see that none were heading to Port Natal, which indicated that Dingane was leaving the British settlement alone. I dared to believe that we might be safe after all – we just had to keep Owen away from Dingane to avoid him making any rash statements. That simple hope, however, was dashed an hour later...

William spotted them first: sixty more warriors coming out of the capital and heading towards the path that led directly to our hilltop. He was convinced that we were done for. "Why would they send that many if they were not going to kill us?" he demanded. "We should warn the reverend so that he can do his prayers." His eyes started to water again as he added, "I should tell him what I really said, so that he does not think that it is his fault."

65

It was easy sometimes to forget the age of young William Woods. He was more worldly than Owen would ever be and our very lives depended on his choice of words. He had a cynical distrust of people that meant we had sometimes bonded like old comrades in the weeks I lived in that mission. Then suddenly you were reminded that he was a blubbing twelve-year-old boy, forced to live in a man's world and finding it frightening. I remembered my son at that age and put my arm around his shoulders. Even at this desperate hour, I had more in common with this child than the man in the hut behind me. While I could feel my guts churning anxiously, calming the boy helped to ease my nerves as well. I nodded to the eight guards we already had, who were watching us curiously, sensing our consternation. "Don't worry, they would be enough to kill us if the king wanted us dead," I tried to reassure him. "He would not send another sixty men to do the job, well, not unless he is worried about Mrs Owen chasing them down the hill armed with the skillet."

William laughed at that and wiped his eyes as I pointed out more happenings on the path below us. "Look, there is a man joining those soldiers leading a cow. If he is bringing that here, why on earth would Dingane give us a gift if he was planning to kill us?" As I spoke the words, I tried to convince myself that my argument was sound. Yet the revelations about Retief's liver had reminded me that I knew virtually nothing about Zulu beliefs. Perhaps you had to slaughter a cow before you murdered a holy man and all who lived with him.

As this party approached, our guards called out to them and hearing the commotion, Owen led the rest out of the hut to see what was happening. By then the man with the cow was calling out that we were not to worry, we would not be harmed. To the clergyman's complete bemusement, the messenger announced that the king was pleased with Owen and was sending this prized specimen to add to his herd of cattle. Then to my horror, the messenger announced that just Owen and William must accompany him back to the palace for an audience with Dingane. I could guess what had happened. The previous messenger must have reported to the king that he did not believe that Owen's reply to his question had been correctly translated. Dingane would interrogate the priest himself and those dark distrustful eyes would soon spot any treachery. Then we would be done for indeed. To make matters worse, Owen now believed he had just been rewarded for his honesty!

"I don't want to go to the palace," whined William, with what I thought was a well-justified fear that it would be a one-way trip that would end on the opposite hill.

Owen must have sensed the same, for his face was drained of colour as he took a final farewell hug from his wife. "We must go, William," he told the boy as he stepped forward and looped the lad's arm through his. "But we will go arm in arm with the Lord and he will guide our journey." I well remember the look of alarm that William shot me over his shoulder. It was clear that he did not find the addition of this spiritual companion any great comfort at all. Yet as the messenger's large escort closed about them, it was also obvious that Owen was right about one thing: they had no choice about going.

We waited three hours for them to return. I kept watching through the telescope, but they must have met the king in one of the huts, for I never once saw them. Instead I studied groups of soldiers and courtiers bustling about. A couple of times I heard horns being blown, but the sound I really feared – the steady beat of the execution drum – never came. Every time I tried to imagine Owen's conversation with the king, it ended badly. The damn fool, ignorant of the earlier lie, would probably be accusing Dingane of crimes that made Caligula look like a choirboy in comparison. I was sure that William would not be able to save us this time. I would have been even more apprehensive had I known that to avoid misinterpretations, Dingane had ordered Owen to answer by nodding or shaking his head.

We were all fearing the worst. Mrs Hulley, convinced that she was already a widow, had got herself into a near hysterical state. Mrs Owen, who doubtless also thought that widowhood – albeit for a brief duration – was imminent, was doing her best to comfort her. I stayed out of the way; my thoughts sunk into a trough of self-pity. Then to my astonishment, I saw two figures walking alone back up the path towards us. One only coming up to the other's shoulder, and both white. It had to be them and they were very much still alive!

Owen was met halfway up the hill by his wife, who had run down to greet him, weeping in relief. I was not far behind her, with Mrs Hulley and Jane close on my heels, for I too was desperate to know what had happened.

"He wanted to know if I was afraid," Owen explained. "But I had the Lord with me and so I shook my head."

"The king laughed and said he behaved well," added William.

67

"Then he asked if we wanted to go back to Port Natal," continued Owen, slightly irritated at the interruption. We all looked at him expectantly, hope suddenly soaring that instead of just surviving, we might actually get away. "I shook my head again," explained Owen, but he got no further before he faced a storm of protest.

"You bloody fool," I shouted at him. "We will be killed for certain if we stay here. Forget your wretched mission, we need to get away." Others were yelling in a similar vein and even his wife, loyally silent, looked shocked.

"You don't understand," Owen held up his hands to still the noise. "I know we want to go, I want to leave too, but he was testing our loyalty. If I had said yes, I am sure he would have viewed it as an act of betrayal. We would have been his enemies."

"He is right," added the little Jeremiah at his elbow. "I could hear them talking – they would have killed us for certain. You did well, sir," he added to the reverend.

"You did the right thing and I am proud of you," said Owen's wife, gripping her husband's arm. It was only then that I realised what an extraordinary event had just happened. For the clergyman, who had been ready to call the king out on his crimes, had now told a bald lie to keep us alive. For a practised dissembler like myself, this would be nothing, but for a man of high principle like Owen, it was a great thing indeed. The clergyman had one final bit of news, though, that soon dampened the mood; Thomas Halstead was dead. Despite his earlier assurances, Dingane now admitted what we had suspected, the British translator had been slaughtered with the rest of the Boers as he sat amongst them. The king had assured Owen that it was a mistake. He had not intended to kill the man who he had sent to ride among the Dutch.

It was nothing less than we had expected, but the news made our protection as subjects of King George seem even more fragile. I doubt many of us slept much that night. It had been a hot summer's day and the air in that hut was more fetid than usual. I had given up my cot to Mrs Hulley and her son, who did not want to sleep on their own. She spent most of the night weeping softly and I heard scant few snores from the others. I imagined that they lay like me: trying to get past the awful events of the day. Listening carefully, I could hear the distant snarl and bark of wild dogs fighting over their windfall of fresh flesh and bone. Yet if I started to drift off, I would hear the terrified screams and yells of the Boers on that hill, interspersed with that awful cracking sound of club on bone. The noise would not leave my head and even as I write this account, I can recall it clearly.

At my age it is not the details of battles that you remember most. At the time you are far too busy staying alive and it is often just moments of terror that stay vividly in the mind. You do not have the time to look around and note what more distant regiments are doing. Yet the aftermath is a different matter. The screams, yells and pleas for help from the wounded and dying, they are the sounds that haunt you. I occasionally had nightmares and those were the memories that would have me sitting bolt upright in bed, sweating in the darkness, particularly thoughts of Albuera where I had nearly died myself. Even then I knew that if I lived, the sound of the Boers being dragged up that hilltop would join those thoughts that could rip me from slumber.

We were tired and irritable as the first beams of sunlight came through the hut entrance. I got up to take a piss in the latrine ditch and found one of our Zulu guards there doing the same. Unable to speak a word to each other, we shared a common need and nodded companionably. It was strange how such a simple everyday act brought people together. I wondered if he lived in fear of his king too. But as he tucked himself back into his loin cloth and watched curiously as I buttoned my breeches, I was reminded that we were also vastly different. A glance across the valley confirmed that. The top of the execution hill was covered in flapping vultures and dogs that darted between them. Most of the corpses would have been torn open by now. Having been out in the sun for nearly a day, the stench of death and decay was very much on the wind. I shuddered at the thought of joining them and turned to look again at the guard, who was sauntering off to join his fellows. Perhaps he was wondering when the drum would beat and if he would be among those to drag me up the path.

With thoughts like that, breakfast was a sombre affair, at least until Mrs Hulley screamed. She looked like she had seen a ghost, and indeed we believed she had, for there in the doorway stood her husband. He was soon crying with relief too. He had seen all the bodies on the hilltop and had ridden hard for his hut. Seeing the warriors outside he had feared the worst, especially when he found his wife and son missing. Then he saw smoke coming from Owen's hut.

We had barely brought him up to date on events when guards appeared to take him to Dingane. He had been shocked to learn the fate of his fellow courier Halstead, whom he had known for a while, but he had no choice but to deliver his messages to the king. He kissed his weeping wife and hugged his son and must have wondered if he would see them again, for the news he carried was not good. Gardiner was still refusing to visit.

I remember sitting outside in the sunshine awaiting his return, feeling sorry for myself. I was still no closer to leaving while I remained under the heel of this petulant and brutal king. I stared out moodily into the countryside, where I spotted a handful of Zulus leading two of the Boer horses back to the city on long ropes. Half of the mounts had bolted when the camp had been attacked, the rest had been trapped in a cattle pen. Some of the animals had been caught and at least two had been killed by spears when the servants tried to escape on them. The warriors had little idea how to manage the horses and tried to treat them like cattle. I watched with amusement as one Zulu got knocked flying by a shod hoof in the chest. Two others were thrown off when they tried to ride them. That cheered me up a little. Then I saw Hulley making his way back up the hill with an escort of warriors. This time he did have news. Information that would shake me to my very core.

Chapter 8

I could tell the news would be bad as Hulley walked up the path towards us. He was more distracted than pleased at his wife's embrace and evident relief at his return, his frown only briefly turning into a smile. "Reverend, I think you and I should go for a walk." He turned to me, "You too, Mr Flashman, if you please." I felt my guts tighten in alarm as we strolled some distance from the huts, out of earshot of the others.

"What did he say?" demanded Owen impatiently.

"Well he did not believe me about Gardiner," started Hulley. "He must have sent his own spies out to see that the captain was well." The messenger lowered his voice conspiratorially and added, "He told me that he would serve Gardiner the same as he had done for the Dutch!"

"So much for the protection of King George," I exclaimed.

"And it shows his tales of wizardry and fearing a Boer attack were all lies too," added Owen.

"He also had no idea how many Boers were already in his lands," continued Hulley. "He thought that there was just one camp belonging to the people Retief brought with him. I think he has sent warriors to attack it, for he claimed that there were only thirty old men and boys to overcome."

"But there are far more than that, why have his spies not told him?"

Hulley shrugged, "Perhaps they were afraid to anger him, although he will be after them now. When I told him that there were Boer settlements stretching all the way from the Bushman's River to the Orange River, he was shocked. He kept asking if I was sure and when I told him I was, he got angry. He shouted that he had been lied to, but then he swore that he would destroy them all. He started raving about wanting no white people on his land as they all trick and deceive him."

"But my wife is still in one of those settlements," I gasped in horror. Then another thought occurred, "Oh Christ, I hope she is not waiting with Retief's people." My mind was reeling. Ever since the massacre I had been wallowing in my own plight, but now I knew that an army of murderous savages might be bearing down on Louisa. It was at that moment that I made a strange discovery. In my long inglorious career, I have lost count of the times I have quaked at the prospect of my own death. I have cared not a fig for others and aye, even speeded a few to their own end to preserve my own delicate thread of life. But that morning I discovered that there is something more frightening than my own demise, and that is the death of someone that I absolutely love. Oh I know I do not wax lyrical in these pages about my feelings. I have certainly not been the perfect husband and I suspect that she has not been the most faithful wife on occasions either. But we have known each other since childhood and been married for over thirty years. While we have spent long times apart, she was the one constant in my life and the thought of losing her was unbearable.

"We have to go back to the king and ask to leave," I insisted. "We need to get a warning to the Boers."

"Yes," agreed Hulley. "I am sure that if we stay here, he will kill us as well. We must get away."

Owen hesitated, "But what if he thinks we are betraying him too?"

"We have no choice," I said, gripping his shoulder. "We must ask now. I will come with you," I added, finding a reserve of courage I did not know existed. I had previously done everything I could to avoid meeting Dingane again. Now, it was far more important to ensure that the clergyman did not muff up the request and that we got away as quickly as we could.

Owen was still unsure of this decision by the time we returned to the huts, but his wife weighed in with her support for leaving. She also suggested that we take a gift to the king. After a rummage amongst their luggage, she brought out, of all things, an opulent opera cloak. Even at that desperate hour I could not help but ask what had possessed them to bring such an item to the depths of Africa.

"It was a gift," explained Owen huffily, as though there were still a chance of those fat mountains of blubber rousing themselves to the *Marriage of Figaro*. Still, I had to admit that it was impressive, a rich plum-coloured velvet lined with white satin. I was sure Dingane would be pleased with it.

As we made our way down the hillside with Hulley as interpreter, my sense of trepidation grew at the coming encounter, but my resolve to see it through did not weaken. To reach the gates of the capital we had to pass the remains of the Boer encampment, it was a vivid reminder of what might happen if we failed. We stared about us at the scattered belongings. Perhaps still believing the Dutch were wizards, the Zulus had left many of their possessions undisturbed. There were saddles, bridles, sacks of clothes, cooking pots and even a handful of muskets lay where they had been left. We had seen some Zulu soldiers exploring the camp before and they had even managed to fire some of the guns, although one of their number had been shot by accident in the process.

The guards let us through the gates and soon we were walking through the streets. This time we did get inquisitive glances. Everyone there knew what had happened to the Dutch and many stared at us, curious too, as to what our fate might be. As we approached the palace, we could hear singing warriors. Even though I did not understand the words, they sounded dark and sinister. When I looked at Hulley, who did understand them, I felt even more alarmed.

"What is it?" I asked. "Why do you look so worried?"

"I think we have come at the wrong time," he murmured. "That is one of their war songs. Dingane is probably sending more of his army to attack the Boers now he knows how many there are."

"Hell's teeth!" I exclaimed as we rounded a bend and stood before the open gates to the palace courtyard. The huge space was full of Zulu soldiers with their backs to us, arrayed for war. They stood in long straight lines facing the palace, kicking up the dust with their feet as they danced and sang. Then suddenly the song turned into a repetitive chant of "*Bulala!*" Each time thousands of their short stabbing spears would be punched in the air.

"Quickly," hissed Hulley grabbing my arm. He pushed Owen and I to duck down through the entrance of a nearby hut and out of sight. The two old ladies inside looked at us alarmed, but Hulley said something that produced a smile and then we were made welcome. "We cannot go to the palace now," Hulley insisted. "We must wait a while for those soldiers to leave."

"What were they chanting?" I asked, noting that the translator had gone pale and was licking his lips nervously.

"You don't want to know," he murmured and I saw now that he was really afraid. Owen and I glanced fearfully at each other and then expectantly back at Hulley. "They were chanting 'Kill, kill the whites'," he admitted.

We stayed in that hut for over an hour. The two old crones did not seem the slightest bit perturbed by having thousands of soldiers just beyond their grass walls calling for the death of their uninvited guests. They gave us stools to sit on and even poured us some of the local beer, which was a kind offering – not that we could relax.

"Will it be safe to go to the palace, even after they have gone?" asked Owen. "What if they attack the mission? Perhaps we should go back."

"No," I insisted firmly, finding some hidden courage. "If they attack the mission, we are all dead anyway. Our only hope is to leave and to do that we need the king's permission." I paused as my mind filled with the awful image of that bloodthirsty mass bearing down on whichever Boer camp Louisa was staying in. "We *have* to get away and warn the Dutch what is happening."

One of the old ladies ducked to go out of the hut doorway. I almost stopped her, fearing that she would alert the soldiers to our presence, but Hulley shook his head to stop me. "The guards at the city gates will have sent a runner to warn the king we are coming. He will know we are here soon if he does not already." He nodded at the doorway through which the woman had now left. "She will know that too, she doesn't need to warn anyone."

I did not find that news too comforting. I reached down, patting my pocket, to check the kitchen knife I had pilfered was still inside. At length we heard the soldiers moving. I half expected them to smash through the hut walls and lunge at us with their stabbing spears. Instead we saw hundreds of legs running past the low hut entrance, as their owners sang yet another of their bloodthirsty war songs. By then the old lady had returned with some fruit for us to eat. None of us was hungry, but Hulley warned it would be rude not to eat a little. Not wanting to offend our hosts, who had after all possibly saved our lives, we chewed down a little while waiting for the dust to settle from the running feet outside.

Hulley ducked through the doorway first and Owen and I listened for a commotion at his appearance or even a scream of agony as he was attacked. There was nothing and he called for us to join him. We stepped up to the inner gate and were allowed to enter, with the usual escort of guards just behind us. We stood silently in the hot sun just outside the palace entrance awaiting the king. Owen fidgeted and refolded the cloak we had brought as a gift while I stared around at the walls. There was no chance I was going to annoy the guards this time. I felt exposed and vulnerable, as though the hatred for my race that had recently filled this courtyard, was still present in the surrounding buildings and walls.

"Re-ver-end O-wen," Dingane had learned to say the name of one of his guests in English and his lips broke into a smile as he appeared. It was a grin that did not extend to his gaze, which still surveyed us with suspicion. His eyebrows rose in surprise at the sight of me and he spoke sharply to Hulley.

"He says he thought he had ordered you to leave with the Dutch," muttered the translator apologetically.

"Tell him I did not have the chance before he had them butchered," I replied, glancing to check that a guard was not approaching to make up for my tardiness. It was clear as day from the king's expression that he was deeply disappointed at my survival. Before Hulley could work out a reply, Owen stepped forward with his gift.

"Tell the king that we are giving him this as a token of our appreciation for his protection," soothed the clergyman diplomatically. Dingane snatched the cloth, his expression changing as he let the hem drop so that he could see what type of garment it was. He was ridiculously pleased with our offering, running his fingers over the ornate silver clasp before draping it over his shoulders and doing it up. Now the smile seemed rather more genuine and Owen decided to follow up his advantage. "Tell the king that while we are grateful for the guards he has sent to look after us, it looks certain that war will break out now with the, er…" Owen paused trying to think what term would least offend the king, "…Dutch invaders to his lands," he concluded. "While we are sure the king will be victorious, we must protect our families and we therefore beg leave to depart his capital and to return to Port Natal."

We waited while Hulley nervously finished the translation, fully expecting an eruption of anger. Instead, silence fell over the courtyard, while the king continued to run a finger over the satin lining of the cloak. Owen shuffled and coughed nervously, while I glanced once more at the guards behind us. Eventually, the king looked up and surveyed us once more. I felt a little like a bullock in front of the slaughter man, but Dingane simply nodded and spoke briefly to Hulley.

"He says we can go," announced the translator to immensely relieved smiles all round. In a moment we were bowing our thanks and backing out of the royal presence. We had got almost to the gate when the king called out something else, which slightly tempered our pleasure. "He says we can leave in the morning, but we must see him again before we go," Hulley informed us. "Apparently he has something to tell us that he cannot say to us now." I felt the hair on the back of my neck rise in alarm at that; I had no wish to enter this palace ever again.

We hurried back up the hill, Owen babbling his relief that the meeting had gone far better than he had expected. He was right about that, but strangely, the king's easy agreement to our request just made me more uncomfortable. He had not questioned why we thought we were in danger – there was little risk of the Boers fighting all the way to his capital – but nor had he tried to persuade us to stay. He might just be glad to see the back of us. Yet we had seen him act treacherously before and I did not trust the mercurial bastard one inch. What could he possibly have to tell us in the morning that he could not tell us now? I noticed that Hulley was quiet too and I suspected that he was thinking along similar lines. Still, we had no choice but to prepare for a prompt departure the next day. The women were delighted with our news and were soon packing possessions, while William greased the wheels on a wagon to carry them.

I was in a fever to get away to the Boers and Louisa. The Zulus still had plenty of Boer horses, but I was sure that they would not lend me one. Even if Dingane really was going to let us go, he would be wary of me warning the Boers – which of course was precisely what I wanted to do. The sight of the ox cart made me mad with frustration. It would probably be faster to walk. Owen was quick to allay my fears. We would head out to a church run by two American missionaries. He wanted to make sure that they were not abandoned and came with us, but more importantly from my point of view, they had horses. Given that I was on a mission to save Christian souls, Owen was certain that they would lend me one to speed me on my way.

The rest of the day was spent packing the wagon with food and supplies for the journey. The younger children ran around with excitement, while for us adults and William, the jollity was rather more forced. No one talked about what they would do when they reached Port Natal, for to do so felt like tempting fate that we would be allowed to leave at all. Owen had grown quiet ever since he described our meeting with the king to his wife. I suspected that she had cautioned him that Dingane might play us false. Certainly, by nightfall the reverend was beginning to fret that time might be running out for us all. He was not the only one. I stared across at the execution hill, where scavenging creatures were still feasting. I remained fearful at the prospect of ending up in the pile of rotting meat and bones, yet for once there was a greater terror within me than preserving my own skin. The thought of Louisa being impaled on those short stabbing spears terrified me. My terror was matched by a cold fury that the murderous despot in his palace below, could settle both of our accounts and there was damn all I could do about it.

76

Hulley spent the final evening with his family in their own hut. I was sitting outside watching the setting sun, trying to ignore the nagging doubt that I might not see such a thing again, when Owen sat down beside me. We silently watched the sky turn gold. I suspect that he was thinking along the same lines as I, for without a word, he reached out and gripped my hand.

"Whatever happens tomorrow, I pray we greet it with fortitude and courage," he stated at last.

"I would rather you pray that the murderous swine down there," I gestured towards the palace, "dies in his bed tonight, preferably painfully."

For once Owen did not reprimand my very unchristian sentiment. Instead he asked quietly, "What should we do tomorrow?"

"I don't really see that we have much choice," I replied gloomily. "There is only one track down this hillside for the wagon and that leads to the entrance of the capital. Even if we left the cart and tried to make a run for it on foot, well, we saw what happened to the Boer servants. We will just have to hope that King Bloody George gives us some protection after all." I gave a grunt of a laugh, "If he does, it will be the first time the fat fool has done something useful, even though he has been dead nigh on eight years."

I dozed on a chair outside that night, listening to the howl of the night creatures. Owen's hut was still humid from the summer heat and the couple lay whispering on their bed for what might be their final night together. I felt like an intruder if I lay close enough to listen. Instead outside, I was a few yards closer to Louisa and I tried to imagine what I would say to her if *we* were together for our last day. Strangely, it made me smile, for the only thing I could clearly imagine her saying was, "Buck up and fight on." By now she knew much of my adventures and was never surprised at my ability to wriggle out of any situation. I hoped to God that she was right this time, but more importantly that she might have the same skills herself.

Dawn came, as did roast chicken for breakfast. We could not take all the fowls with us and so feasted on some instead. Then having wiped the grease from our cheeks, we gathered around the wagon. Most of us looked at Owen expectantly and I thought he might launch the journey with yet another prayer, but for once words failed him. He stared down at his daughter and looked close to tears. "Let's go," he rasped hoarsely, unable to say any more.

It was Mrs Owen who tried to raise the mood. "The rougher the road, the sweeter the glory," she called and with that her husband's little mission started to make its way down the hill. Dingane must have been watching us through his telescope, for as we reached the bottom of the slope there were a hundred of his soldiers arrayed to meet us. They stood tightly packed in a curved formation, shields to the fore, spear tips glinting in the early morning sun. Jane gave a little scream of terror when she saw them, "Why are they so still and staring at us?" she asked.

"Just be glad they are not chanting," I told her, with the refrain of "Kill the whites" still very fresh in my memory.

One of the king's advisors stepped forward and gave a command. "He says that the men are to follow him to the palace," translated William. "The others are to stay here." Then he added, "I bloody knew it, we are done for now." He stepped forward to come with us, muttering more profanities under his breath, but Owen stopped him.

"Stay with the ladies and children, William. Mr Hulley can translate for us." It seemed an act of kindness, although the clergyman probably did not want the last words he heard on this earth to be a twelve-year-old boy yelling, "I told you so," as the spears closed in around us.

More than half of the reception party escorted us to the palace. As some cleared the street ahead of us, I noted that the city was strangely quiet. There was no laughter and chatter around cooking fires, no children playing. The few people we did see just watched us with silent curiosity. Perhaps they had heard what fate awaited us. I wondered, morbidly, if they were quiet too when the Boers made their final visit. We did not have to wait for Dingane when we arrived in the central courtyard. He was already pacing up and down outside his palace door, his new cloak flapping around him at every turn. Any hope that he would just wish us *bon voyage* and see us on our way were dashed instantly, for he had a face like thunder. A group of his advisers sat behind him against the palace wall and even they looked frightened. The king had evidently launched a tirade at them before we arrived and had now worked himself up into a proper temper.

"Why are you here?" he shouted at us as we approached. Hulley had barely finished translating before he went on. "Gardiner promised me a ship full of gifts and instead he sent you." He pointed at Owen, who had already turned ashen, and continued, "What use are you to me? What are you really doing here?"

I glanced over my shoulder and saw that our guards were now arrayed in a large semi-circle behind us. They seemed to be just waiting for the command to rush in and overwhelm us as they had the Boers. Beads of sweat had broken out on my brow that had nothing to do with the summer heat and my mouth was bone dry. Owen clearly felt the same terror, for he croaked the first words of his response, trying to explain that he had come at the king's invitation to teach Christianity.

Dingane impatiently interrupted the translation and pointed up the hill at the mission buildings. "I hear that you think I will have you killed," he announced, surveying us with those black, pitiless eyes. We stared at each other then, all at a loss for words. It was true, we did think that, but would he prove us right or wrong? Before we could ponder on it further he went on, "My people work for you and they have told me what you have said. They say that you speak evil of me. They say that when you praise your god you do so with hatred of me in your hearts. You and all who live with you tell lies about me – except the translator, Hulley." Hulley had the decency to look slightly embarrassed as he translated these final words, as though he were pronouncing a death sentence on the rest of us, but the king was not finished.

He shouted a command and two guards emerged from the palace, dragging a woman between them. Her face was contorted in terror and for a moment I did not recognise her. Only when Owen gasped her name did I see that she was one of the African servants who helped in the mission. The clergyman was shaking in terror now as Dingane pointed at him and continued, "This woman tells me what you really think. She has heard your wife and daughter call me a murderer and a rogue. She has heard you pray that your god will protect you from my rule and that he will punish me. She also tells me that you spy on me with your telescope. You think I have not seen that for myself with my own glass?" Owen's mouth was silently opening and closing like a gaffed trout, but he did not get the chance to respond before the king turned to his advisors. "Did you hear what they say about me?" he demanded. The men nodded anxiously, far too frightened to contradict their monarch, even if they wanted to. "You are traitors," Dingane roared at us and I flinched in terror, sure that the spears were about to rush in.

"But she does not understand English!" Owen was so frightened his voice had gone higher than William's, but now he knew he was arguing for his life and so went on. "She only knows a few words of English. She cannot possibly know what we are saying or praying about. She is simply trying to say what she thinks will please her king as she is one of your loyal subjects."

It was a masterstroke of an argument that also gave some protection to the girl, although for my money she understood a lot more English than Owen claimed. Everything she had reported was probably true, but to admit that would undoubtedly be fatal. Dingane looked down at the weeping servant with suspicion and then gestured for her to be taken away. He turned and walked back to his advisors, where the eldest of them hauled himself to his feet and began to talk nervously into his king's ear. I sensed he was the barrister for the defence in our trial and I silently wished him well.

Our man must have been persuasive, for despite several dark brooding glances in our direction, we remained alive. Eventually, Dingane barked another order and a table was carried out of the palace with some writing materials and a stool. Owen was ordered to sit down while Dingane began to dictate a message. Hulley stepped forward to help with the translation while I stayed where I was, wondering if this was a good sign. The letter would have to be delivered somewhere and Hulley was the obvious choice for that. The king would not need Owen alive after he had written the letter, unless he planned to keep him prisoner again to read any reply and draft further correspondence. As for me, he did not need me alive at all and had already expressed his disappointment that I was not already dead.

I drifted forward slightly to listen in. The letter was for Port Natal. Dingane was giving yet another excuse for killing the Boers. This time he claimed that they had kept the cattle he had sent them to recover. He also announced that he would not allow any other white people to live on his land. He then instructed Owen to confess in the letter that the clergyman had attempted to deceive him, although he did not specify what the deception was. He made his mark on the letter and handed it to Hulley. Suddenly, he was keen for us to leave. He smiled at us with absolutely no warmth at all and actually wished us a pleasant journey.

We bowed down, anxious not to cause any offence which could trigger another change in mood, and hastily made for the gate. I glanced back to see that our guards were no longer following us. Ominously, their commander had been beckoned by Dingane to receive new orders. Was he being instructed to murder us all – apart from the favoured messenger, Hulley – out on the road?

We hurried through the streets virtually at the run, anxious to get away as quickly as possible. As we emerged through the city gates, Mrs Hulley gave a scream of relief and swooned on the spot. We had no time for such dramatic displays. Her husband swept her up and deposited her in the wagon, while urging William to whip the oxen on their way. Mrs Owen, tears of joy on her cheeks, gripped her husband's arm and even I finally began to believe that we might escape. My belief was short-lived. We had only gone a hundred yards when our guards jogged out from the capital. I half expected a hail of spears to be thrown at us, but their weapons stayed in their hands. Their commander, though, was calling out to us, and even I could understand that we were being told to stop.

"We have to wait," announced Hulley. "The king might want to see us again."

Chapter 9

A hope dashed is always worse than no hope at all. We stood and stared in shock as our dream of escape crashed to pieces around us. What did the king want now?

"He is just bloody toying with us," I snarled. "The bastard will never let us go."

"Surely he wants his message delivered," said Owen, still trying to hang on to a shred of hope. "Perhaps he wants to add something to it."

I was tempted to snap back that he did not need us all for that, but bit down the retort. There was no need to upset everyone else any more than they already were. The women were weeping their frustration. Even the children sensed something was horribly wrong and looked down on us fearfully from the wagon. Some of the guards went on ahead to block the trail to Port Natal, not that we were likely to try and make a run for it with a hundred of them in pursuit. The rest stood by uncertainly for a while, but as no further messenger emerged from the palace, they went to sit in the shade. We had no choice but to wait too, unsure if the next royal courier would order our death, our release or something in between.

I paced about impatiently. An hour had passed since we had been told to stop and I was increasingly desperate to get away. Every minute wasted was one I could not use to get to Louisa. Unlike a British regiment, the Zulu impis I had seen had no carts or heavy guns to bring with them. They would cover the ground quickly and even if I were to get my hands on a horse, it would be a close-run thing who would reach the Boers first. It was maddening, for as we kicked our heels in the dust, I could see fifty horses in a guarded cattle pen nearby. The Boers' abandoned belongings nearby did not make us feel any more comfortable. There was a shaving mirror glinting in the morning sunlight where it had been hung from a nail on a tree. It might have been Halstead's, for most of the Dutch had beards. A few clothes flapped in the gentle breeze where they had been turned out of sacks. I drew a little closer as I saw something shiny on the ground. It was a crudely painted miniature portrait of a woman, doubtless now a widow or grieving mother.

Our guards had not stopped me from wandering about, even though there was a pile of muskets nearby. As I neared the centre of the old campsite, I had a better view of the pen containing the horses. It was made of shoulder-high thorn bush, but I could see the backs and heads of the animals above it as well as a few warriors. Some were trying to ride and finding out the hard way that horses were less patient than cattle. I saw one hoist himself onto the back of a mount and give a little cheer of triumph, before being bucked off into the dirt, to the laughter of his fellows. It was not surprising, really, for even at that distance I could see that they had the saddle on backwards and the bit of the bridle was pressing into the animal's nostrils. It was then that I had an idea.

"William," I called and gestured for the boy to join me in the Boer camp. He came warily, watching our guards to see if they would stop him.

When he got closer he called out, "It won't work, sir."

"What won't?" I asked, puzzled, for I had given no clue of my intentions. Indeed, as he approached, I had decided that I would keep it to myself. If the scheme did by some miracle work, then there could be unfortunate consequences for the rest of the mission group, including William. I felt a pang of guilt about that, for Owen and the others had been good to me. Yet at the end of the day, Louisa and I came first. For all we knew, Dingane was planning to kill most of us anyway.

"Grabbing some of them guns," replied the lad gesturing to the nearby pile of muskets.

"Heavens, boy, I am not planning to shoot my way past a hundred warriors with a single musket." I forced a laugh and was struck with another moment of inspiration. "No, I thought that if we make ourselves useful, then we might dissuade the king from dragging us up that damn execution hill."

"How would we do that?" he asked, his curiosity piqued.

"Call over to the men in that pen that I will help teach them how to ride."

A few minutes later and I was striding into the corral and already fearing I had just made a big mistake. For a start there were more Zulus there than I had thought. There were a dozen inside the pen and when we got round to it, we found a similar number by the entrance. The gate was made of two stout tree trunks leaning against the thorn bushes to make an 'x'. I climbed over and immediately noticed one horse lying dead by the fence with a deep, fresh wound in its neck. The other animals could smell the blood that was still soaking into the dry earth and were moving nervously up and down the far fence. In the centre of the space a tall Zulu was shouting at the others, while brandishing a bloodied spear.

"Be careful, sir," warned William. "That man with the fancy feather band on his head is Dickwa, the king's son. Judging from the way he was berating his fellows, he had inherited his father's temper. The dust, stuck to one side of his arm and chest, indicated that he was the one I had seen thrown from his horse earlier. The creature's corpse in the corner of the yard indicated that he also shared his pater's callous disregard for life. I realised that I would have to tread very carefully.

"Tell him that if he wishes, I can show him how to ride," I instructed William. The boy called out as requested. Dickwa turned and noticed us for the first time. His lip started to curl in contempt that he might need help from a white man and so I added urgently, "Tell him that a horse will make him the fastest Zulu there has ever been." His cronies laughed at this, keen to deflect his anger from them and were clearly encouraging him to give me a chance. He finally nodded his agreement and I felt a sense of relief. This might work after all.

"Tell him that learning to ride takes time," I instructed William. "He has to learn to trust the horse and the animal has to learn to trust him." As I spoke, I picked up another bridle from the pile of saddles and tack that the Zulus had brought into the pen. Then I walked slowly to the horses milling about on its far side. Talking quietly to them, I searched the herd for a suitable mount for the prince. There were some good horses here, powerful beasts full of stamina, but it was not those I sought. I found a nice docile mare, who stood calmly while I pulled the bridle over her head. I led her back to the group in the centre of the coral where Dickwa eyed both me and the animal suspiciously. I picked up a saddle and its cloth from the pile and soon had it secured. I had originally planned to leave the saddle loose so that the Zulu would not stay mounted for long, but realised now that this would not work with the prince. Instead I cinched the saddle tight and got one of his lackeys to crouch down so that Dickwa could tread on his shoulder to mount rather than use the stirrup. As I had hoped, the mare was as steady as a rock. With some difficulty William and I persuaded the prince to drop his bloodied spear and hold the reigns with both hands. Then I led the animal around in a wide circle, watching the new rider grin with pleasure as he felt the beast moving under him.

In no time at all I had got one of his warriors leading him around at the trot, with a pair on either side ready to catch their leader should he tumble from the saddle. He stayed aboard and was soon laughing with delight. My suggestion that we mount up a couple of his fellows was eagerly approved. I found livelier mounts for them and this time I did leave the saddle girths loose, slack enough to fit a hand in rather than a finger. Predictably, both new riders had fallen off their horses within the first couple of minutes, Dickwa howling with laughter at their fate. As I helped one back into the saddle, the rider noticed that the girth was loose, but instead of complaining he gave me a grin and whispered something to William.

"He says he thinks that you are trying to make him fall to keep the prince happy," the boy confided, also grinning at my apparent cunning.

"Tell him he is right," I confessed, "but if he sits up straight and does not lean to one side, he should stay on longer." Soon three riders were circling the corral, even if two were a little unsteady. We had already called some of the men watching at the gate to run alongside the new riders to help break their falls.

The prince was keen to control his own horse rather than be led. So, having earned his trust, I played my next card. "If I could be permitted to ride beside Your Majesty," I suggested, "then I could better show you how to ride." He agreed without hesitation. Even William showed no suspicion of my real motive when I went to make another selection from the herd. This time I chose one of the best animals and saddled it tightly with care. For the next few minutes I demonstrated using heels to spur the animal forward and how to use the reins. Dickwa managed reasonably well while the other riders each came off once, falling into the arms of other warriors at their sides.

I kept looking at the gate; the middle section was not that high. A horse trained for jumping would clear it easily. However, I knew nothing about my current mount and if it refused then I would be properly done for. I would have to risk it as a last resort, but for now I took a deep breath and turned to William, "If the prince would like to go faster, we could ride outside of the pen." The boy hesitated, for he must now have realised this had been my plan all along. He also must have considered what the consequences would be for him if I managed to escape. For a moment I thought he might refuse or betray my intentions in order to protect himself – as I might have done if someone had tried to leave *me* in the lurch. After a few seconds William called something to the prince as he trotted past. The man reined in hard, causing even his placid mount to protest slightly. Dickwa turned to stare at me and I half expected to be hauled off my saddle by nearby warriors. I was just preparing myself for a desperate run at the gate, when he shouted an order. Two of the soldiers still at the entrance threw the barrier down.

Freedom beckoned, but there was still a score of Zulus nearby, some with spears to hand, and so it seemed wise to continue the pretence a little longer. "Ask the prince to follow me," I told William and guided my mount forward.

I was barely halfway to the gate when the boy shouted Dickwa's reply, "The prince says *you* should follow *him*." There was a shout of delight from behind me and the prince came thundering past at the full gallop, still kicking at his animal's flanks. As I urged my horse to follow, I saw the prince yank hard on one of the reins. The mare I had chosen for him was an easy-going beast and she had put up with a lot that morning. Yet any animal has its limits and as it felt itself being directed at the thorn hedge, it clearly decided it had had enough. It skidded to a stop; its head went down, its rear went up and briefly Dickwa was indeed the fastest Zulu there had ever been. As he crashed down onto the top of the thorn hedge, screaming as the vicious barbs tore his flesh, I kicked my own mount into the gallop. No one paid me any attention as I went through the gate as all were running towards the hapless Dickwa. I was free at last and there was not a second to lose. I pointed my beast to the southeast and rode knowing that my life and that of Louisa's depended on it.

Chapter 10

It had taken them over a week to bring my feverish body from where it was found to the capital. I knew the Boer camps were around a hundred miles to the southwest and normally such a journey would mean two or three days of hard riding. To make that sort of time, though, I would need roads and reasonably flat terrain, something I certainly did not have. The only trails were those made by cattle herders and their beasts. I soon discovered that following those often led to pasture where the track simply disappeared. Instead, I had to use the sun for my bearings and fix a distant hill as a waypoint. There was certainly no shortage of hills and many were quite distinctive with rock peaks and steep summits. I kept a ready eye for a dust trail from running warriors, for I was sure that Dingane would send pursuers for someone who had duped his son. Yet I saw nothing. Mind you, the ground was criss-crossed with what the Indians call *nullahs*, ravines carved out by rivers. Most were dry now, but some were big enough to hide an army, certainly a Zulu impi, which you would only see if you stood at the edge. I approached each one with caution, yet only encountered a few animals searching for water. More often than not, I then had to dismount to lead the horse down the steep bank and then up the other side.

Even though I had not left Umgungundlovu before midday, I must have covered at least thirty miles before stopping for the night. The problem was that I was not travelling in a straight line. A frustrating part of my route was around hills and gullies. With no map and only the sun for a guide, I was not even sure I was on precisely the right heading. I was desperate to get on, but by then both man and beast were exhausted. With all the ravines it would have been near fatal to ride hard at night. I had chosen a good horse – it had done well. We camped near a river where we could both drink. Then I used the stolen kitchen knife to cut a strip from its blanket to hobble its front hooves so that it would stay near. While the horse grazed happily from the riverbank, I found very little to eat. There were all manner of strange plants yet I had no idea which were edible. Then I smelt onions near the river and eventually tracked down some wild garlic. I picked handfuls of the leaves. They were not much of a meal and my skin soon stank, but they were better than an empty stomach.

I slept a few hours but was woken by the horse, which was skittering nervously as far as its hobble would allow. I could hear the bark of some creature nearby in the darkness, whether it had come for water or was hunting us, I could not tell. What I was sure of was that if I lost my mount I was done for. I got up and gripped my knife, which I realised would be precious little use against a pack of tearing fangs. I started to shout, walking around the horse, picking up stones and hurling them in the direction the barking had come from. It seemed to do the trick well enough, and the barking subsided. Man and beast slept fitfully after that, but as the sun crept up over the horizon, we set off once more.

In all, that journey took us four days. I saw a Zulu impi on the third day, perhaps the one that we had seen chanting 'Death to the whites.' They were about five miles to the west of us. I watched from a hilltop as the line of tiny black figures crossed down and then up a ravine. It showed we were going in the right direction, but they must have had their own scouts around them and I was not getting any closer. We stopped that night in a small gulley, invisible to anyone unless they were about to fall in on top of us. By then I was weak from lack of food. Apart from the garlic and some sage I had found on our way, the only thing I had eaten was some half-rotten antelope from an abandoned kill. Judging from the horse's nervousness when we found it, its owner was not too far away. By then, however, I was so hungry I would have wrestled a lion for some meat. At least I had the blade to dig in and find some flesh that had not already been gnawed.

I struggled to wake the next morning from complete fatigue, with the horse faring little better. She at least had some grazing, while my stomach rumbled loudly and felt as though it was stuck to my backbone. Saddling up, I led her up the steep bank. I was sure I should have reached the Dutch by now. I was beginning to wonder if they had heard of the Zulu approach and moved on. Had this all been a wasted journey? Then as we toiled to the top of the next hill, I saw the distant smoke. There were three or four columns of it, several miles away, bigger than a campfire, I judged, but smaller than a whole settlement being burned. Then as I studied them, I heard a new sound; the distant crackle of muskets.

In an instant my tiredness left me and I overcame my natural instinct to ride *away* from the sound of guns. The Zulus must be attacking, I thought, and Louisa might be down there somewhere. This after all was why I had come. I mounted up and spurred the horse on towards the beacons of smoke. Perhaps sensing my urgency, the horse found some energy too and we galloped much of the next three miles. Then I saw the white woman.

At first, I thought she was dead. Perfectly still, wearing only a nightshirt, she was sitting against a tree. She was heavily pregnant and had some cuts on her arms from thorn bushes and her feet were bloody. I was just wondering what had killed her when she blinked.

"What has happened here?" I asked her. She just stared at me blankly and so I dismounted and grabbed her arm. "Do you know Louisa Flashman? Is she near here?" Still no sign of understanding – perhaps she did not understand English. "Have the Zulu been near here?" At this a tear fell down her cheek and she raised a hand pointing back over her shoulder.

Holding the reins of the horse I walked on, getting closer to the smoke. I reached for my knife, the only weapon I had. Then, deciding it would be useless against a well-armed Zulu, I picked up a broken branch of a tree instead. The shooting was still a mile or two distant, but was dying away. I silently prayed that this did not mean that the Boers were being overrun. At least there was no sound of fighting from whatever was burning ahead, in fact the surrounding bush was completely silent. I hefted my branch in my hand and cautiously climbed over some rocks.

I will never forget the scene that was revealed to me. There were three wagons, one blackened and smouldering. Then I saw a body lying in the centre of the clearing and for a moment my heart stopped. It was another woman, but what I spotted first was the shawl around her shoulders. Louisa had bought one just like it in Cape Town. I remember shouting out her name as I ran forward. I saw with horror that she had two spear wounds in her back, but then I noticed her boots. I could have wept with relief, for they were farmers' boots and not the fine-tooled leather ones that Louisa wore. Even so, to be certain, I gently lifted the body to see the face. A stranger's lifeless eyes stared back at me.

I was just about to relax when I caught a movement out of the corner of my eye. Whirling round with branch raised I found myself looking at a vulture. It was perched on the tailboard of one of the unburnt wagons. To my disgust I saw that it had been feasting on the corpse of a young boy, whose body was hanging over the side of the vehicle. "Get away!" I shouted, rising up and running at it, waving my stick in the air. The bird dropped down and with a couple of hopping steps launched itself lazily into the air.

I was close enough now to see inside the wagon and almost wished I couldn't. I climbed up hoping I was mistaken but no, there were three more dead children inside. The eldest, a girl of around eight, was still holding the hands of her younger siblings to comfort them as they died. They all had spear wounds to the chest, their nightshirts crimson with blood. I stood up on the side of the wagon and looked down at them, feeling a rage boil within me. What kind of animal could do that to children? Killing them in their beds. Then I remembered Dingane whipping up his soldiers with his shout of "Kill the whites," and my fury grew.

I cocked my ear as I heard a new burst of gunfire; the Boers were still putting up a fierce resistance somewhere nearby. From my higher vantage point on the wagon, I stared around in the direction of the shooting. There was no sight of any fighting through the scrub and undulating hills, not even wisps of gun smoke. Instead I tried to work out how these people had been attacked.

There were no Zulu or Boer men's corpses here, just dead women and children. Two of the big Boer dogs lay speared to the north of the wagons. They must have barked when they heard the Zulus approaching. It would have all happened the previous night as the children were wearing their nightclothes and had not been dead long. I could imagine the Boer men coming out to investigate and being met with a wall of Zulu charging out of the darkness, driving them back. The Boers would have fought hard, but their defenceless families would have stood little chance.

I got down and walked a little way to the south, finding first several Zulu bodies and then, against a small pile of rocks, the much-stabbed remains of three white men. This was where they had made their last stand. They had not sold their lives cheaply, for there were half a dozen dead warriors nearby. I was about to search them for a better weapon when I heard a gasp nearby. Stepping around a bush I finally found someone still alive. It was a Zulu with what looked like a gunshot wound to the guts. He looked blankly at me as I stared down at him with a bitter rage. His long throwing spear, his *assegai*, was lying in the dirt beside him. I picked it up and plunged the broad steel blade into his chest, taking grim satisfaction from his burbling squeal when I twisted the shaft.

The spear was better than my branch, but what I really wanted was a gun, or *Sanna*, as the Dutch called them. I searched around the rocks of the last stand. At last I noticed the sun glinting off the brass butt plate of a musket lying under a thorn bush. Using the spear, I managed to get it out without cutting myself to ribbons on those vicious barbs. A gun would allow me to fight the Zulu from a distance. I knew that if they got close enough to use those stabbing spears, I was done for. Next, I needed ammunition. I found a bloodied half-full powder flask on one of the Dutch corpses and in his pocket were a handful of the things they called *loopers* – four or five pieces of lead shot, each roughly the size of a pea, which were sown into a leather bag for easy loading. The Boers favoured these small pouches, rather than a single large musket ball as they dispersed shot over a wider area.

Suitably equipped, I loaded the gun and was preparing to leave when I remembered the pregnant woman I had passed. I could not just abandon her. The distant gunfire was continuing, which meant that the Boers must have a defensive line. If Louisa was behind it, she might be safe. If not… well I did not like to think about that. If the Dutch were saving my wife, then the least I could do was save one of theirs. I went back and found her exactly as I had left her. She ignored me to start with, seemingly content to just sit there and die. I pulled her to her feet, causing her to cry out in pain. She held on to me then, weeping quietly while I decided what to do next.

I remembered that Louisa had been told not to ride when she was pregnant with our daughter. Of course, she had a carriage as an alternative and in Leicestershire she was not being pursued by murderous spear-wielding African warriors. All things considered, I thought we could risk the girl in the saddle. I helped her mount up and as I put her bare feet in the stirrups, I removed a couple of thorns embedded deeply in them. She was crying again now, cradling her swollen belly and doubtless thinking about the father of the child. I took the reins and led the animal south around that gruesome clearing – she did not need to see that, although twenty minutes later we stumbled into another near identical grisly spectacle. Four wagons, none burning, but more than a score of bodies scattered about and that was without daring to look inside the vehicles. We went on without stopping, I was aiming for the land south of where the shooting was coming from. I wanted to give the site of the battle a wide berth; the last thing I needed was to stumble into the middle of it. Yet as we walked, the sound of gunfire was diminishing again, not growing louder.

Once when we passed a tall hillock, I left the horse tied to a bush and scrambled up to the top. I knew that there had to be thousands of

Zulus in the vicinity and with the scrub and trees, not to mention hills and gullies, they could be on top of you before you saw them coming. Crouching down near the crest, I peered cautiously over the top. There at last I did see some of the devils. They were a couple of miles off, a black crowd crossing a patch of clear land. To my relief they were moving north, back the way they had come. There had to be other regiments I could not see out there and I wondered if they were doing the same. Had the attack been beaten off? If it had, then the warriors were busy taking their spoils of war home, for when I craned around to look north, I saw large dust clouds. They had to be caused by cattle, several large herds that the Zulus had stolen from the Boers and which were now being driven north to Dingane.

I re-joined the pregnant woman. She had still not uttered a word and I wondered if she had lost her wits. It would hardly be surprising given the horrors she must have seen the night before. Yet as I led the horse south again, she began to sing. Her arms were wrapped around her unborn infant and while it was a Dutch song she sang, from the crooning tones, I guessed it was a lullaby. Just as we were circling around another burning camp a young Boer boy walked out of the bush in front of us. I tried to talk to him, but he ignored me and went to walk beside the woman, holding on to her ankle and joining in with her song. It was a bit like leading the Pied Piper, with her singing bringing forth children to walk with our party. At this rate I would be leading an assembled choir of lunatics when I finally arrived in the Boer camp. Then, belatedly, it occurred to me that if her singing was attracting children, it could also summon more unwelcome visitors.

"Be quiet," I whispered at the pair of them. They both ignored me and continued with their plaintive tune. I glanced nervously into the surrounding bush, which could be concealing all manner of horrors and shouted, "Will you shut the hell up!" They were quiet then, staring with hurt expressions as though I had just drowned a puppy in a pail in front of them. I opened my mouth to try and explain why it was important that we be as silent as possible, then my jaw clamped shut again. I remembered how the girl had reacted to the word 'Zulu' before. I led my now quiet band on, feeling their reproach burning into my back. I thought I would be damn glad when we found the Boers, but sometimes you should be careful what you wish for.

I heard the horses before I saw them. They had to be Dutch riders, I thought. The only Zulus I had seen mounted had been at Umgungundlovu and that had not ended well for them. "Over here," I shouted. There were some exclamations as they heard me and then four horsemen galloped from behind some bushes onto the ground in front of us. "By George, I am pleased to see you," I beamed at them in relief. "Tell me, do you know anything of Louisa Flashman? Is she safe?"

To my astonishment two of them levelled their muskets at me; their bearded scowls were far from friendly. "Are you one of those English bastards that was riding in with the Zulus?" one demanded.

I just stood and gaped at him for a moment. I was far beyond dumfounded and for a moment wondered if I had somehow misheard or if the man's English was not very good. "What the blue blazes are you talking about?" I exploded at last. "There are no Englishmen riding with the Zulus. Why in the name of holy hell would they do that?"

"Well I know there are," insisted the leader as he rode forward warily watching me and my little band. "I know because one of them has been seen and killed." He then gave an exclamation in Dutch and turned to one of his men and barked an order in the same language. The next moment my gun was being snatched away and, with two muskets still aimed at my chest, my hands were dragged behind my back

"What the hell is going on?" I demanded as I felt a rope being tied around my wrists.

The leader of the band looked down on me with hatred in his eyes. "If you are not with the Zulus," he demanded, "tell me how you are riding the horse of a friend of mine who went to see the Zulu king?"

Chapter 11

The man looked so furious I thought he might lynch me on the spot. If his family had been slaughtered like those we had seen, then he could be capable of anything. Yet the only story I had to get me out of this mess was the truth, which would include more bad news for my inquisitor.

I told my tale as quickly and simply as I could, giving them time to curse and swear when they learned of the fate of Retief and his men. I explained that we had feared suffering the same end. As I talked, I wondered if Owen and the others were still alive. Then I told of my escape before appealing to their common sense. "Why on earth, if I was fighting for the Zulus," I demanded, "would I rescue this lady and the lad and then call out when I heard you riding nearby?"

That convinced most of them, but the leader was reluctant to abandon the notion of the pernicious British being behind this latest atrocity. He went and spoke quietly to the woman, but whatever she told him backed up my story. Even then they would not untie my hands, but agreed to take me back to meet their leaders.

"Is Pieter Uys here? He will vouch for me," I told them. Uys had been the one Boer leader that D'Urban viewed as a friend. The governor had given me letters for him, but when I was last in the Boer camp, Uys was still on his way over the mountains. D'Urban had told me he was a brave and capable military commander. I hoped that Louisa had been staying in his camp, for I suspected that he would put up a strong defence.

"Uys has been and gone again," one of my Dutch guards told me before gesturing I should start walking.

After an hour or so we came across a camp where the Boers had been able to circle their wagons to form what they called a laager. This group must have heard other camps in front of them being attacked and had filled the spaces between the wagons and wheels with thorn bushes and other obstacles to create a solid defence. Judging from the bodies of several hundred Zulus lying around, it had worked well. A number of the wagons were painted light blue. In front of one of them a man was calmly giving orders, dispatching couriers and receiving reports. While others wept or raged, this fellow exuded a calm, intelligent authority. I felt a sense of relief, for surely he would see that an Englishman fighting with the Zulus was ludicrous. More importantly, such an organised character might know where Louisa was.

"Maritz," my captor called out to him. "I found this Englishman. He was riding Malan's horse. He says that Retief and his men have all been murdered."

There were several gasps of horror at this announcement. One lady screamed and began to wail, before being led away by other women. I guessed that she had just learned she was a widow. Others were exclaiming at Zulu treachery, but the man called Maritz did not seem the slightest bit surprised. "Of course they are dead," he snapped. "Do you think Dingane would have attacked us and left them alive?" He nodded at me and added, "Why is he bound?"

"I thought he might be another of those English bastards that fought with the black devils," replied my captor.

Maritz gave the man a withering look and ordered him to untie me. I was warming to this new leader. He had what Wellington would describe as "officer qualities". Another courier rode up and shouted excitedly to him in Dutch. Maritz simply nodded to acknowledge the message and then quietly issued a new order. He was, I judged, in his forties, but other older Boers obeyed him without question. Now he turned his blue eyes to me. "We will soon find out who this Englishman is that Vuuren claims he saw. I have sent him to find the body now the Zulus are retreating. He has taken with him Dick King, who has just ridden in from Port Natal. Now, sir, I know most of the Englishmen down by the coast, but I do not know you. What is your business here?"

I started to explain my story, how I had been sent here by D'Urban with messages for Uys. Then that I had been staying in the camp of a family called De Beer, when I had got lost on a hunting party. Sensing it was a long tale Maritz interrupted me, "Did you actually see Retief murdered?"

"No, I could not watch that," I admitted. "I saw them all being dragged up the hill, but then I went away. I still heard some of the killing. Afterwards, I saw them carry something down the hill, which the Zulus claimed was Retief's liver, so I am fairly sure he is dead."

We were interrupted by more horsemen arriving. I recognised Dick King among them. When there are only thirty white men in Port Natal, it is easy to remember the faces if not the names. I knew the white corpse tied over the saddle of a spare horse too; it was a young fellow called George Biggar. Louisa and I had stayed with his father

Alexander when we had first arrived in the territory. He had given us his sons' room. I remembered watching George and his brother Robert clear out some of their possessions to give us more space. Others knew George too and that it was preposterous to believe he had been leading a Zulu attack. The fellow who had boasted of shooting him was now protesting that it had been dark. He insisted that he was not to know that George was fleeing the Zulus, rather than leading them.

At least I was no longer under any suspicion. I asked Maritz if he knew anything of my wife or the band led by De Beer.

"They were further north," he said quietly. I felt my blood suddenly chill and whirled around to stare back the way I had come, where pillars of smoke still marked where some of the camps had been attacked. "There are lots of survivors," Maritz added. "Several hundred of them. I have sent them south to a bigger camp at Doornkop."

Only my empty stomach stopped me being sick. My mind was filled with the image of the woman I had briefly thought was Louisa. It wasn't her, I was sure of that, but was my wife lying out there in another camp, spear wounds in her back and the ground underneath black with her blood. Maritz was still talking but I was only half paying attention. They were about to ride north to pursue the Zulus and search the camps. Suddenly I noticed that he was looking at me expectantly. I realised that he was asking if I wanted to join them on their raid or go on to Doornkop.

"I will go on to Doornkop, if you don't mind," I told him politely, as though I were refusing an extra slice of cake. I could not think of her being dead, my mind refused to accept the idea. I would go on to this larger camp and there I would find her, alive and well.

I joined a band of other survivors on the journey, including the pregnant woman and the boy. At first I was in a fever to go faster, but as we progressed our group got larger as others joined us along the way. I soon found myself searching the countryside for any sign of a familiar face. Many of my companions were still in their night clothes, often with bare feet and several had bandaged cuts and wounds. Many, like the lady who had just discovered she was a widow, were weeping, but others like the pregnant woman, were in a silent state of shock. There was one moment of alarm when black faces emerged from behind some rocks. I swung my returned musket up to cover them, but they called out and several of the Boers answered and beckoned them forward. They were some African servants to the Dutch. The Zulus had been as enthusiastic in killing them as they had been in slaughtering the whites.

There were nearly eighty wagons in the Doornkop laager, which included those of Retief and his followers. That afternoon several of their wives and sons came up to me to ask how their menfolk had died. I simply told them that they had been killed quickly; there was no point in recounting the screams as they were dragged up that hill. In any case I was too busy searching for Louisa to waste time on the details. There must have been some two hundred refugees in the camp when we arrived, many wounded, all distraught and some verging on madness. They were scattered all over the camp, some taken into wagons or tents and others like me hunting desperately for their loved ones. I must have tried to search every inch of that laager. Some of the carts and shelters had become impromptu dressing stations, filled mostly with women. Their matrons would often not let me enter, but I would only move on if they could assure me that they knew everyone inside. There was no sign of Louisa anywhere or anyone who knew of her whereabouts. As hope began to diminish a new cart would appear with more wounded and dozens of us would surge forward, desperate to find our kin.

As dusk fell, I found myself sitting by a fire suffering an internal torment. My brain told me the probability was that my wife was dead. I had only found one survivor of the DeBeer camp, a gravely wounded woman called Elizabeth. Her child had been stabbed to death in her arms and she only lived as the Zulus had thought she too was dead. She was barely coherent with grief, but I managed to grasp she had no idea what had happened to Louisa. I had seen their forward camps – they would have stood no chance at all against thousands of vengeful Zulu soldiers. Yet while I accepted that logical sense, my heart could not comprehend that she had gone. It was simply impossible. Tomorrow I decided, I would borrow a horse and ride out to join the search. She had to be out there somewhere.

I spent three days riding with the Boers looking for survivors. We found over a score of them, but none were Louisa. Half of those we rescued were so gravely injured, they died on the way back to Doornkop. Most we came across, though, were already dead. I forced myself to look at every woman's body. Some faces had been mutilated by Zulus or animals and were barely recognisable, but I looked for marks to make certain that they were strangers. Soon we had carts full of bodies. These grisly cargos would be hauled south while we followed the circling vultures in the hunt for the living and the dead.

Many of the men I was searching with were also grieving the loss of their own families and friends. I well remember one of them when we came across a wounded Zulu who had crawled to a river for a drink. The Boer dismounted, his face a mask of hatred. He had his musket but did not shoot. Instead he swung the musket butt with all his might into the warrior's back. The Zulu screamed, but he was shown no mercy. The Dutchman kept swinging that gun butt down with all of his strength, perhaps thirty or forty times. His victim had probably died with the third or fourth blow and was beaten into a bloody pulp, the river crimson around him. None of us tried to stop the Boer and I admit that I might have done the same if we had found Louisa's body among the dead. Eventually, the man dropped his bloodied weapon, sank to his knees and began to sob.

I'll own that I had a tear or two myself when we got back to Doornkop. Partly it was self-pity, but it was also one of the saddest sights I ever did see. The bodies had been laid out for identification in long rows. It was the first time some of the men had seen their wives and children since the attack if they had been riding out driving the Zulu north. They were a close-knit community who travelled in large bands and would wander up and down the rows looking for friends, relatives and faithful retainers.

The servants had been more numerous than the Boers in the camps and some two hundred and fifty of them had been killed in the attack. There were five rows of them, some partly covered with bits of thorn bush to keep the vultures off. There was another line of fifty Boer men and a slightly longer line of women. Yet it was the next four lines that took your heart away. I have seen some bloody sites in my time: the aftermath of battles, massacres and sieges, but nowhere I think have there been so many children deliberately killed. One hundred and eighty-five of them had been slaughtered. Most had been asleep in their beds when the attacks started and had stood little chance. There were over a dozen tiny babes still wrapped in bloody blankets and others of all ages. Some, like the boy I had seen half hanging over the side of the wagon, were never recovered. His body must have been snatched by some creature, dragged off and devoured.

I must have gone up and down the row of white women half a dozen times. The bodies had started to swell in the heat and while the thorns had kept the vultures away, they could do nothing about the flies or the growing stench of decay. I had also been around the wagons again as other bands had found and returned more wounded, but there was still no sign of my wife. Not knowing her fate for certain was driving me mad, although it fed a tiny sliver of hope. Yet I knew that the overwhelming likelihood was that the woman who had shared my bed these many years was now lying dead, abandoned in the dirt.

The funerals started the next day. Everyone lent a hand in digging the long trenches that would serve as graves. There was not enough material for shrouds. Most of the children were buried wrapped in the bloodied bedclothes they had died in. Some siblings were interred together in bundles. To save cloth, the same was done for some of the adults too and yet more were buried with just a neckerchief covering their faces. Presiding over it all was their minister, a man called Smit. He was a sickly squint-eyed preacher, who I had seen pulling on a bottle a few times around the camp as though his life depended on it. Mind you, I did not blame the fellow for that, as he threw all his energy into tending his grieving flock. He expounded over the graves with a demonic passion, spittle flying from his lips as he kept waving at the heavens. I could not understand a word as it was all in Dutch, but it comforted those who did.

That was the day that I started to accept that Louisa was gone. I don't really remember much of the next week or two. I know I wandered around in a state of despair, like many in that camp of sorrow. I could not get over the injustice of it all. My beautiful wife, not to mention all those children, all blameless and innocent and yet murdered for no good cause. God knows what Reverend Smit had told the Boers, but if that was all part of God's plan, then I despised religion. It might sound strange coming from a man who had a stately pile in Leicestershire and another house in London, but in an odd way I felt homeless. Buildings are just wood and stone; it is people that make homes. I realised that Louisa had been the one constant in my life. My mother had died when I was young and my father had been dead for years too. Louisa and I had played together as children and while we had spent years apart, I always knew she was there.

Uys arrived around then. He welcomed me and invited me to stay in his camp. He did what he could to comfort me, but he had many other grieving friends among the Boers too. We heard that the Zulu army had returned to their capital and so there was no immediate danger. Messages were sent to Port Natal to see if they had been attacked and if not, to discuss what to do to meet the Zulu threat.

My next really clear memory must have taken place in early March. I had been sitting with my back against a tree, feeling sorry for myself, when a man threw himself down on the ground beside me, careless of the broken thorns often in the dirt. He had a bottle in his hand, gin from the look of it, which he offered me. I refused. I have never liked the stuff.

At first, he spoke to me in Dutch, but when I told him in English that I did not understand, he switched to that language. "You lost people too?" he slurred.

"My wife," I admitted. I had wanted to be on my own but had found that grieving men often wanted to sit together, often in silence, as though they took some comfort from sharing their fate. This fellow, though, evidently wanted to talk.

"I lost my wife and four sons," he blurted out. "My four beautiful boys all dead." He started to sob then. I was trying to think of some excuse to leave him, when he looked at me through tear-filled eyes and added, "Do you know, that is not the worst of it."

I was surprised, "What is worse than losing your wife and children?"

"I was there," he whispered, ashamed. "I was there when it happened. I was fighting those devils, killing them, but they drove me back. I could not save them. A man should save his family, not be alive while they are dead." He took another pull from his bottle and then looked up into the sky and implored, "God, why did you not kill me too?"

"If you had been killed too," I told him, trying to provide some comfort, "you would not be able to avenge them."

"Avenge them?" I watched his glazed eyes comprehend the thought. "Avenge them," he repeated and before my eyes he started to transform. The bottle slipped from his fingers, his back straightened and his slack jaw came up in a determined air. My new friend was having a moment of revelation of the type that Reverend Owen must have dreamed about. But while the cleric wanted conversions to Christianity, I had created one for vengeance and killing. "You are right, brother," the man's voice was getting stronger now. "I will avenge them. I will make those demons pay for what they have done." With that he got up and strode away. I confess that at the time I thought little more of the conversation. I was just glad to have got rid of the fellow and to be left on my own again. Yet as the days passed, my own advice began to play on my mind.

If you have read my previous memoirs, you will know that I am not one to charge off into the maw of death without a bloody good reason. Decades of fervent poltroonery are embedded deep in my soul. Yet as time passed my despair slowly turned to anger. It had happened to me before when I had lost friends and comrades in battle; grief at their loss had sometimes prompted me into reckless actions. This time, though, the urge was far more intense. My anger grew into a white-hot fury that began to consume me. For once I cared not a fig for my personal safety, all I wanted was Zulu blood. In particular, I wanted that tyrant Dingane dead. He had terrified me when we had met and he had ordered the attack which had killed Louisa. He had her death on his hands and I yearned to pay him back. I would sit and daydream about killing him even though he was much bigger and stronger than I was. I would imagine having my old sword, still hanging in my study at home, in my hand. I wanted its razor-sharp blade cutting him again and again until he begged for quarter. I wouldn't kill him quickly, no, he would be made to suffer in terror like all those dead children. I would sit and smile as I pictured him suffering the most gruesome death imaginable. When Uys told me about the messenger from Port Natal, I already knew what I had to do.

Chapter 12

I was not the only one to go on an emotional journey in the weeks after the attack. At first the camp was rocked by rumours that the Zulus were returning, but patrols quickly despatched discovered no sign of them. It was enough for many families, though: their dreams of a 'promised land' had been dashed and this new territory had proved a far more dangerous Garden of Eden than they had expected. They packed their remaining possessions and with sad farewells, headed southeast over the mountains, back the way they had come. Yet on the way they must have passed other bands, like those led by Uys, coming to support the new venture, so overall the numbers in the Doornkop laager did not change greatly.

While some families had retreated, others were determined to stay. Men are usually seen as the more warlike of the sexes, largely because we do most of the fighting. (Mind you, I have known some fearsome fighting females in my time.) Yet men often go to war because they are goaded to by women and so it was now. Some, like the man who had sat beside me under the tree, would have undoubtedly fought anyway, but Boer womanhood in that camp made their demands clear. Perhaps it was the sight of so many dead children that made them pugnacious, but they were determined that the fruits of their wombs would not have died in vain. So it was that a resolve to fight the Zulu grew. The Boers had already beaten back the Matabele, but Dingane's kingdom was a far greater challenge.

Messages had passed between the Boers and Port Natal. I learned that Owen and his party had finally made it there and confirmed the fate of Retief. With war imminent, the thirty traders and hunters there would not stand a chance if Dingane's army tried to drive them into the sea. Yet the settlement had always been a refuge for those Zulus trying to escape the king's justice, even if some were returned when he demanded. The whites were not the only ones to sense war was coming. Some of Dingane's own subjects saw this as an opportunity to rid themselves of the tyrant. Many may have already been fugitives of his army, but now they flooded down to the coast in droves. The British reported that they had over a thousand warriors ready to fight alongside them.

Plans were laid for a co-ordinated joint attack that would divide the Zulu army. The Boers almost came to blows amongst themselves over who was to command the venture. Their wagon trains were fiercely independent and with Retief, their former leader, dead, there was no agreement on who should replace him. Maritz thought it should be him as he had led the defence, but others such as Uys also pressed to be considered. As he campaigned for the leadership, Uys suggested that I return to Port Natal to fight among the British instead of for the Boers as originally planned. I suspect that having a friend of the unpopular D'Urban in his camp did not add to his appeal among the suspicious Boers. I was happy to go, for I thought it was time I went back to my own people. Dick King, who had been riding back and forth as a courier, offered to guide me to ensure I did not get lost.

I well remember my next sight of Port Natal. When I had last seen it the white settlement, a selection of run-down shacks, was roughly the same size as the collection of African huts that had built up around it. Now the original part of the town looked like one of those parasite-eating birds perched on the arse of a rhino. There was a huge new settlement right alongside, stretching for half a mile or so inland. For a moment I started in alarm, wondering if Dingane had already captured the place as the town now much resembled Umgungundlovu in appearance, albeit a little smaller. There were scores of the dome-shaped Zulu homes already standing and from the wooden frames I could see being built, the place was still growing. Interspersed with them were cattle pens of braying beasts and hundreds of people moving about.

"Changed a bit, hasn't it?" Dick grinned at my obvious astonishment.

"Where the hell have they all come from?" I asked.

"Some are survivors of the village that refused to kill Retief," he explained. "Others have had family members executed and want revenge or fear that Dingane will turn on them next. You have been in his palace, you probably know more about his enemies than me."

"He certainly topped a fair few," I admitted. There had been executions most days and Dingane had been on his throne for ten years. He must have accrued a lot of enemies in that time. Yet I also remembered the fear that the king instilled in his subjects, which prompted my next question. "But are we sure they will fight?"

"Christ yes," he chuckled. "They are fair champing at the bit to get going. I am surprised that they have not already gone without us."

One of the first people I saw when I walked down the main street was Reverend Owen. I half expected him to be furious with me – after all I had run out on them and my departure must have put his family in more danger. Instead, he greeted me like the long-lost cousin I had once pretended to be. "Mr Flashman, what a relief it is to see you. We feared the worst when we saw that horse bolting with you aboard. I had worried that history would repeat itself and your journey would end in mishap."

He must have remembered that I had ridden my mount into a trap before we first met and clearly thought that I was a useless muff of a horseman. I was quick to grasp the excuse he offered, "Yes, the ruddy thing took off like a rocket and I could not control it. I think it was trying to get back to the Boers and luckily it took me in that direction."

"And have you been reunited with your dear wife?" he continued, but immediately recognised the stricken look that must have crossed my features at the mention of her. He reached out and put a hand on my arm, "Oh I am so sorry. We had heard that there had been much slaughter among some of the Dutch camps. If you would like to pray…"

"No," I cut him off. "I know you mean well, but I am struggling to accept any god that would allow her to die like that. I don't want to pray; I want to kill as many of those murderous bastards as I can."

"But think of your immortal soul, Flashman," he started.

I just laughed bitterly, "I fear that has been destined for the fiery pit for a long time now. Good day to you, Reverend."

There were other familiar faces in the little settlement. Young William was there, now reunited with his parents and an uncle. He insisted on introducing me to his family. They all lived in a two-room cabin, scraping by with odd jobs. They had obviously heard tales of me from their son and were embarrassed at what a friend of the governor would think of them lending their son to a murderous tyrant. Like most of the other English, they had come to Africa in the 1820s, tempted by promises of rich lands and an easy life. The reality had been far different. Having lost their farm in Xhosa raids in the south, they had come north to Port Natal and had been there for six years. Life was still tough and so when Dingane learned of their son's linguistic abilities and offered him a comfortable life in the palace, they had no choice but to consider it. It seemed the elusive Captain Gardiner persuaded them to agree, probably because he feared offending the king with a refusal.

I had been looking forward to catching up with the naval man whose scheming had brought me here, but I was destined to be disappointed. He was still living on his farmstead some miles away.

Another familiar face who was in town, though, was Alexander Biggar. He had let Louisa and I stay with him before and he was pleased to put me up again. We had our grief in common and that first night we opened a bottle to console ourselves. He was unaware that the Boers had shot his son by mistake. He thought the Zulus had killed the boy and I did not correct him. They had, in a way; if they had not been attacking the Boers, he would not have got in the middle of the fight. I had just got to the mellow stage of sobriety when there was a knock at the door. To my surprise, there was Mrs Owen standing in the street, asking to talk to me.

"Let's go for a walk," she suggested, taking my arm, "and don't worry, I am not going to pray with you." Exchanging a puzzled glance with Alexander, I allowed her to lead me off. Soon we were strolling around the outskirts of the African part of town. Cooking smells from countless fires wafted in the air around us, along with shouts and laughter as people settled down for the night. "Francis told me what happened to your wife and your determination to fight," she said quietly. "I can only imagine your grief, but do you think that is what Louisa would have wanted, you getting yourself killed?" I did not reply and so she went on, "You told me once you have a son and daughter. Do you not want to stay alive for them?"

"My son is in his twenties now. He will be fine…" I started. Then my voice trailed away. I realised with a sudden shock that I had not been thinking about coming back or surviving at all. It had not been a conscious decision, but in my grief-filled state, going into battle and dying in a, for once deserved, blaze of glory had felt an easier option than living on without my wife. For a coward like myself, facing that thought was a bit like an abstaining Methodist waking up with a hangover and a satisfied trollop in each arm.

"You have so much to live for, Thomas," she whispered, watching the comprehension cross my features. "Don't throw your life away."

"I won't," I replied, still confused. Then she reached forward and hugged me. The feeling of another human body against my own, that basic bond of humanity, broke my reserve then. My old schoolmasters would have been appalled for I confess that I sobbed on her shoulder for quite a while. I remember holding her tight against me as though I could absorb her strength. There was no lust in that embrace, not for that saintly woman, for she had done more for me than a string of harlots before or since: she had restored my sense of self-preservation.

I did not need to thank her, for she knew what she had done. I walked her back to where she was staying. Before she went in, she kissed me on the cheek and wished me well. As she went inside I could see, over her shoulder, that Owen was on his knees praying. I smiled as the door closed behind her. His wife understood far more about the human spirit than he would ever know.

I had a reassuring feeling of apprehension as I woke the next morning. It was the day the forces of Port Natal were due to begin their attack on Dingane. You might wonder if after the revelations of the previous night, whether I still wanted to take part. Well I did. I still had a burning desire to avenge Louisa and kill as many of Dingane's murderous soldiers as possible. It was just that now I was sure I wanted to survive the encounter. In any event there was little choice. The Zulu king certainly did not respect timidity and we had no means of escape if his army tried to sweep us into the sea. Our best chance lay with acting in concert with the Boers and their assault was due to begin at roughly the same time.

The history books will tell you that this march was led by a man called John Crane. He was a loud and eccentric fellow who wore an ostrich feather in his hat and carried a huge elephant gun in a leopard skin holster on his horse. He had his own band of Zulu followers as did another man called Ogle. Yet neither had the first idea how to command a Zulu impi or an army that had now grown to some fifteen hundred warriors. The thirty of us Europeans were outnumbered fifty to one in that army. An old Zulu general called Umfazi was the one who was really in charge. He was a grizzled grey-haired veteran who had lived in exile for years. I was pleased to see that he knew his business too. He sent out many scouts ahead of us, for this was ideal ambush country.

We had set off on the seventeenth of March 1838. I remember the date well as a man called O'Malley told everyone it was St Patrick's day. The Zulus had spent part of the morning doing some kind of dance, which reminded me of the ones I had seen at the palace. In fact, for a man who had recently developed a virulent hatred of all things Zulu, my allies did not make me feel that comfortable. Apart from white armbands that they wore to distinguish themselves from the enemy, they looked exactly like the men who must have slaughtered Louisa. A few had muskets, but the rest had the same shields, the same weapons and spoke the same guttural language. I had to remind myself that when I had fought the Ashanti it had often been hard to

106

distinguish friend from foe. It was even the same in North America when opposing militia troops or when Iroquois war bands met. Still, I wasn't sure I trusted them above half, and I was not alone.

"Yer have to wonder if they have changed sides once, would they be doin' it again?" suggested O'Malley as I rode alongside him. "I know one thing for sure and certain: I'll not be gettin' in the middle of them when we attack. Stabbin' spears comin' at me from all directions that would be. I'll be stayin' back with me gun here," he patted the butt of his musket, "blasting anyone who does not have a bit o' sailcloth tied to their arm."

That sounded very sensible to me although Robert Biggar, Alexander's other son, was sure that our allies would stay loyal. "They will fight to the death," he assured me. "They know that Dingane will kill them anyway if they are taken prisoner." I agreed that Dingane had never struck me as the forgiving sort. "Umfazi says," he continued, "that if we can inflict some defeats then there is a good chance the king will be overthrown. He has many enemies who will take advantage of any weakness."

"Well let's hope their main army goes for the Dutch, then," I stated with feeling. "For with our numbers, we will struggle to beat much more than a single one of his impis." The Dutch had experience of defeating other African kingdoms when they fought the Matabele. Their guns and horses gave them the ability to meet the enemy on their terms. Our contingent only had thirty mounted Europeans and the rest of our force had no tactical advantage over Dingane's soldiers – or so I thought.

Our army had set off into the countryside at a cracking pace, with the Zulus covering long distances at a steady run rather than a march. I was damn glad to have the horse to stay with them. Despite his age, Umfazi kept up on foot with the vanguard and was continually receiving reports back from his scouts and sending other men racing ahead. A couple of the horsemen had offered to gallop forward to do reconnaissance too, but the general declined. He thought that the riders would be spotted by our enemies before we had a chance to see them. At the end of the first day, one of Dingane's outposts had been found, a mere score of men, who were to report if anyone approached Umgungundlovu from Port Natal. Again, the general declined offers of help. During the night a selected band of our Zulus made their way to surround the unsuspecting warriors.

Umfazi signalled that we should start our march just after dawn the next day and two hours later I rode past the first of Dingane's soldiers. They were all dead, their stomachs torn open to release their spirits. We had not lost a single man in the attack, as we'd caught them completely by surprise. We pressed on, still at some pace, for there was a large Zulu town ahead and the general wanted to capture it before they had any chance to report our advance. Our Zulu soldiers chanted to themselves as they jogged on. It felt more like we were part of one of their armies than these native allies were part of a British one. Consequently, I began to harbour a nagging doubt that Umfazi might actually be loyal to Dingane. I thought he might suddenly have his men turn on the Europeans before delivering us to his master. That concern only grew as I saw how he planned the assault on the town.

Zulus attack in a tightly packed mass, but they do not use ranks or columns. Instead their formation resembles a bull, looked down on from above. The men in the 'horns' sweep around their enemy to encircle it, while those in the 'body' move in to provide the killer blow. It was a technique their great king Shaka devised and it is invariably successful. Umfazi organised John Crane and his band of warriors to be one horn. Ogle and his men would be the other, while he would lead the main force. There was no place in a normal Zulu attack for mounted soldiers, but our general wanted to ensure that no one escaped the town to warn Dingane of our presence. The rest of us were given fifty guides and told to follow a series of ravines and river valleys to stay out of sight until we came up on the Umgungundlovu side of our quarry. There we were to shoot anyone who managed to slip through the horns. This made good sense, for once the king learned we were there he would send vastly bigger numbers against us. Yet for all that, as we went down one twisting gulley after another, I soon lost my bearings and my suspicions returned. Why had most of the Europeans been separated and why did we need so many men as guides? On we rode for three or four hours. Just when I had convinced myself that we would finally emerge outside the gates of Umgungundlovu itself, we rounded a bend to find a shallow valley with fifty cattle grazing, along with a similar number of sheep and goats.

We reined up and when I reached for my gun a black hand came up and grabbed my wrist.

"No," said the leader of our escort, smiling. The man had been jogging alongside us for most of that day and had barely broken into a sweat. He gave me a gap-toothed grin and then ordered thirty of his men forward. They advanced at an ambling run, spears and shields in their hands and still chanting one of their songs. As the animals began to part around them, I saw now that there were half a dozen boys among them who had been guarding the herds. They watched the approaching men with curiosity, but no sign of alarm. The soldiers must have looked like any other of Dingane's patrols, although I noticed the young shepherds glancing occasionally in our direction, clearly wondering what a group of white men were doing in their valley. They were still unsuspecting when the soldiers reached them. With a shouted command the men attacked. Short stabbing spears flashed out and in a few seconds the lads were all dead on the ground.

I did not know whether to be sickened or relieved. Having seen recently so many dead Boer children, killing those trusting boys made me realise how similar our allies were to our enemies. On the other hand, I consoled myself with the thought that they would not have slaughtered their own if they were really loyal to Dingane. As my suspicions began to abate, there was a shout of warning. Halfway up the valley side another boy had been dozing. Having witnessed what had just happened to his fellows he now broke cover, sprinting away up the hillside to raise the alarm. In a flash a dozen Zulus were in pursuit, spreading out so that whichever direction their prey took over the rough ground would bring him closer to one of them. It reminded me of a pack of hyenas that Louisa and I had seen hunting when we had first arrived in Africa. They had spread out after a young gazelle. Then as now, I found myself urging on the hunted rather than the hunters. The boy was darting left and right, but as he neared the crest the ground became steeper and covered in loose rock. Twice throwing spears had clattered harmlessly into the rocks around him. Then just as he got purchase on a rock a few feet from the summit, an *assegai* was hurled into the small of his back. With a little wail he tumbled back down the slope towards his pursuers. An *iklwa* stabbing spear rose and fell to finish the boy off. The hunters sang some sort of chant around the body, perhaps as a mark of respect for his courage. Then our escort regrouped, and we continued on our way.

It was perhaps half an hour later that we heard the first sign of the main attack. There was a small crackle of gunfire and then a piercing shriek carried on the wind. I was not even certain the sound was human and looked to O'Malley at my side to see if he had heard it too.

"They've started, then," he called. "Now we will see what they've got about them." With that he spurred his mount forward up the slope to join our escorts, who were already sprinting up the hillside to join the fray. I was not sure what to expect when I crested the rise, but around half a mile in front of me was a Zulu town. There must have been well over a hundred of their domed huts behind a tall thorn bush rampart. From the screams that were now much clearer, I deduced that our soldiers had already tricked their way in through one of the gates. A stream of terrified men, women and children was pouring out of the gate on my side…straight into the waiting 'horns' of men commanded by Crane and Ogle.

At first I thought we would get no trade at all, but the locals knew the terrain better than the attackers. Some had used a nullah to escape the trap, unfortunately for them it ended just in front of us. Twenty of them suddenly appeared fifty yards ahead, then, seeing us waiting, scattered in all directions. One warrior, holding his shield in front of him, charged straight towards me, his *iklwa* outstretched to gut my horse if he got close enough. A woman followed close behind him, squealing fit to burst. O'Malley rode for her while I smiled in delight. The warrior seemed to think that his shield would stop a musket ball and I was happy to demonstrate otherwise. He would be the first to pay for Louisa. I pulled my musket from over my shoulder and took careful aim. I let him get quite close, judging where his moving body was behind the shield, I did not want to miss. The familiar crash of a musket butt into my shoulder and then he was down, sprawled in the dirt. Looking around, I saw that the other fugitives were all dead or captured. O'Malley was binding the still screaming woman with a strip of leather and cackling with delight.

"This one will warm my bed tonight," he crowed. "We'll see if she is still screaming then." I turned away in disgust. This was supposed to be a military invasion, not a Viking raid. I dismounted and reloaded my musket as a precaution, although the only living Zulus I could see now were either being bound or had the white cloth strips around their arms. I used the muzzle of my gun to lift the shield off my victim and was surprised to find that the corpse was as old as I was. Grey hair and a beard had been hidden behind the cowhide as he had charged. Mind you, his *iklwa* looked well used. He may have been a formidable warrior in his day, but I doubted he had been used to attack the Boers. The poor bastard had probably been trying to protect his daughter, who even now was being thrown over O'Malley's saddle.

I could take little satisfaction from my vengeance so far and that feeling only deepened when I reached the town. Most of the bodies there were old men and boys; the younger men would be away fighting in their regiments elsewhere. I fervently hoped that they were fully occupied with the Boers rather than approaching us, as our force was descending into chaos. Crane and Ogle's contingents were brawling and stick fighting over the ownership of a pen of cattle. The only casualty we took in the whole battle was when Crane shot one of Ogle's warriors to settle the dispute.

Over five hundred women and children had been captured. Many of the warriors and some of the whites such as O'Malley, were determined to keep them as wives and concubines. I was dismayed to see that any thought of inflicting a military defeat on Dingane had been replaced by a simple greed for loot. Later I found the humiliated Ogle with some of his men holding a captured elderly chief's feet over the flames of a fire. They were trying to persuade the wailing man to reveal where a cache of ivory tusks was buried.

We were still in the captured town that evening and I anxiously searched the horizon for the dust of marching impis. The general had sent out scouts to warn of approaching enemy forces, but I doubted we would be in any state to mount a defence. The night was filled with the screams of women and the cries of children as men took the spoils of war. Ogle had found his tusks but, before he had died, the chief had warned him that we would pay a terrible price for what we had done to his village. I had a nasty feeling that the old man was right.

I thought Umfazi might be disgusted by the collapse of his army, but he looked inscrutable. The Zulus had a long tradition of stealing the cattle of their enemies. The only reason they had not attacked the Boers again was because they were too busy driving captured herds back north to their king.

Perhaps Umfazi did know how to motivate his men, for the next morning he announced that there was another town half a day's march away with even more cattle. He claimed it was also occupied by only old men and women. A cheer rose up and most of our force were ready to march on. Around a hundred were left to guard what we had already taken and the rest of us pressed on into the countryside. This time there was no great effort at ambush and concealment. We must have been spotted early in our march, for when we got to the new town, which was even bigger than the last, it was deserted. The huts might have been empty of humans, but the pens were still full of cattle and more

111

roamed along the nearby riverbank. We now had several thousand of the animals to herd and it was clear to all that our invasion was over. We could not guard that number of beasts and still fight the enemy. On top of that there was a new brooding conflict between Ogle and Crane's men, with the latter thinking that the looted tusks should be shared between them.

Umfazi put the towns to the torch. High thorn fences are a formidable obstacle if you want to capture a Zulu town intact, but in that dry summer heat they burned like kindling. The straw roofs of the huts also blazed fiercely sending dark columns of smoke high up into the sky. If he did not know we were there before, Dingane would now. The only saving grace of our slow withdrawal was that the huge dust cloud kicked up by the animals hid just how few in number we were in comparison to the king's army.

Chapter 13

I will confess to feeling a huge sense of relief when I clapped eyes on Port Natal again. For despite the expedition having every appearance of a disaster waiting to happen, in many ways it had been a success. We had returned with five hundred prisoners and around seven thousand head of cattle. In this endeavour we had only lost two men, one of those shot by our own side and the other to a snake bite. I had assumed that our good fortune was due to Dingane's forces being fully occupied in seeing off the Boer attack. Yet when we got into town, we discovered that the Dutch assault had not yet even started. To my astonishment we learned that they were still bickering over who should command. Uys and another leader called Potgieter had refused to serve under Maritz, but nor would they serve under each other. How we had been able to march into Dingane's territory and steal so much from him without him retaliating was nothing short of a mystery.

There was another pleasant surprise awaiting us two days after we returned, for into Port Natal bay came a small sailing ship called the *Comet*. It was a trader, buying ivory and hides and bringing supplies such as gunpowder and ammunition. Its arrival caused fresh division among the white settlers. Some, such as the Owens, wanted to leave straight away as they would never feel safe in Natal again. Others, though, had been living in the territory for ten years and had made a living from it. They did not relish starting afresh somewhere else and the Boers' victories over the Matabele gave hope that the Zulus too could be driven back. There were also a few like Alexander Biggar and myself who wanted to stay to avenge the loss of loved ones. We were all agreed, however, that the vessel would provide a last refuge that the Zulus could not reach if things went against us. Nobody wanted the ship to sail until matters had been resolved one way or another and so the captain was persuaded to stay in port for a month.

Dick King rode again to the Boer camp and plans were reorganised for another joint attack. This meant that the army of Port Natal would have to march again – and if I was to be among it, we would have to be much more professional. I was not alone in that opinion; when we learned of the Dutch delay, I think most realised that we had been miraculously fortunate to survive our first expedition. A council of war was held and changes made. Ogle was dismissed and Robert Biggar was appointed joint commander with John Crane. Umfazi looked amused as these announcements were made – he knew that the white leaders were largely irrelevant as he commanded the vast majority of the army. Yet, surprisingly, when it was put to him that all would forgo taking any more cattle, women or other loot until the Zulus had been defeated, he readily agreed. I had taken young William to the meeting as an interpreter. He told me that the old general had announced that, "Until Dingane is defeated, any loot taken is only borrowed." Furthermore, he wanted to train his Zulu warriors as he did not think they fought well, although they had looked damned handy to me. The old general had then glared at John Crane and suggested that he might want to exercise his men too. Now we had more ammunition from the *Comet*, Robert Biggar insisted that all Europeans drill with weapons. He said we had to be more soldierly and I was entirely in agreement.

One elderly Zulu was not enough to avenge Louisa, but if I was to fight again, I wanted the best men around me I could get. I was determined to be alive and aboard the *Comet* when she sailed. I had already met her captain and discovered that he had a chest of thirty muskets aboard. I bought the lot. The white militia of the town were already armed as were around thirty of their African servants. There must have been around a hundred Zulus who had acquired muskets too. Yet despite Robert's best efforts, I suspected that they would remain an undisciplined lot. Years before, in Brazil, I had trained former slaves to be marines and now I decided that I would train some more Zulus with firearms. I had seen them fight; they were fit, brave and brought up to obey orders. I had also learned a trick or two from the Dutch that I thought would be useful. With my own band of well-armed Zulus about me, I believed I would be as safe as possible on our next expedition.

I took William with me to put the idea to Umfazi. I thought he would be impressed with a man of my military experience offering to help, but if he was, he hid it well. He did, however, agree to give me thirty warriors to form my little band. Next, I went to the town blacksmith. While the British army fired a single musket ball, approximately two-thirds of an inch in diameter, I had been impressed with the effectiveness of the Dutch *looper*, which exploded out from the muzzle of the gun to hit more than one enemy from a single discharge. I gave the smith a handful of musket balls. He flattened them out a little before cutting each into five or six chunks. Armed with these and a musket I then went to stand behind Biggar's warehouse to carry out some experiments. I wrapped half a dozen lead

114

fragments in a piece of leather, loaded it, and fired at the planking side of the building from a hundred paces. Alexander did not come out to complain, but then I could not find any of the pieces of lead embedded in his wall either. I tried again at fifty paces and three struck home, one too high to do any damage to a man. Thirty paces gave better results: five lumps of lead in the planking, deep enough for me to have to use a knife to get them out. I looked back at where I had fired from – it was a perilously short distance. If we let an impi get that close, they would be seconds away from coming at us with those stabbing spears. I tried one final shot at twenty paces. This time Alexander did come out to complain, as one fragment had punched its way clean through the inch-thick planks.

Young William was invaluable over the next two weeks while I trained up my small company. He helped me explain that we would need to let the enemy get close so that each shot would kill or wound several of Dingane's soldiers. I drilled them to fight in two ranks so that the first could retire behind the second to reload, although whether they would be given the time in the heat of battle was debatable. I had insisted that my men abandon all their shields and spears. It would be impossible for them to fight with those as well as a musket. That was when I faced my first mutiny. Their leader was a man called Bafana and he absolutely refused to give up their traditional weapons. In the end we reached a compromise where they would keep the *iklwa*, the short stabbing spear. As we had no bayonets, they would be useful if we were reduced to hand-to-hand fighting, something I was determined to avoid. For my part, I had acquired a seaman's cutlass. It was the only sword I could find. The blade was shorter than a sabre, but I had fought with one before.

I thought the training went well and William was greatly impressed with my military prowess. With practice the men could reload fast enough to fire two shots a minute – not as fast as British infantry, but the redcoats sometimes drilled for months before the movements came without the need to think. His father and uncle turned up to watch one morning and although interested in the *looper* idea, still preferred to use the larger single ball as it gave them a longer range and more chance of a solid kill. They also used them for hunting. The Boers, though, were convinced that their ammunition was better. Given the huge disparity in numbers between us and the Zulus, I wanted every advantage I could get. We were not short of leather or women who could sew. Soon we all had cords around our necks with a score of the little leather bags tied to them with thread. These were easy to break off and drop down the muzzle. I was so pleased I invited Umfazi for a demonstration. He watched impassively as, through William, I explained that when we fired at thirty paces the pellets would spread out to hit several men at once. Between them, my two ranks then fired off four volleys in a minute. I awaited his congratulations. Instead, he borrowed an *assegai* and strolled out in front of my men. He must have been close to fifty paces in front of us when he turned, and with a grunt of effort, launched the throwing spear high into the air. Its point landed in the dirt just a yard from my boot. He muttered something to William and then strode off shaking his head.

"What did he say?" I asked.

The boy gave me a disappointed look as he explained, "He said that without shields, your men will not live long enough to fire their first shot."

After that, my men resumed their shields as well as the muskets. Bafana suggested that the rear rank could then shelter themselves as well as the men in front with their shields as they prepared to fire. I had to admit that it was a sensible solution. Unfortunately, my military preparations suffered another setback that very evening.

The Owens had invited me for dinner. The Hulleys and young William were there as well. It was a jolly reunion, without the fear of having our brains dashed out hanging over us. I was just explaining how I was training my company of men, when Mrs Owen asked how I would give orders when we were on the march.

"Well, I will use William, of course," I replied, thinking it obvious.

"You are not taking a twelve-year-old boy to war," she replied firmly.

"Nonsense. I have known drummer boys much younger than William in the army and as powder monkeys and even midshipmen giving orders in the navy."

"I don't care what you have seen before. His parents would never permit it and I would speak to them if they did. You must know that if your army is overrun, he will not stand a chance."

I turned to the object of our discussion and gave the lad an encouraging smile. "Well, William, you should have a say in this. Do you want to stay here with your mother or come on an adventure with me?"

The boy considered for a moment, ignoring the stern glare from our hosts, and then announced, "Nah, I will stay here. I have seen your men and I have seen the king's army. I think you're gonna get beat."

"Well, thank you for that," I replied grumpily. "I had forgotten what a ray of sunshine you are."

As I walked back to Biggar's house that evening, I had to concede that the lad had a point. Dingane's army would outnumber the Port Natal force by ten to one. Even if the Dutch were able to destroy a good part of it, the odds would still be against us. As I stared out in the bay, I could see the lights on the *Comet* and part of me wished I was safely aboard. Yet everyone knew that I was D'Urban's representative and a military man. When I had first arrived back in the settlement, I had sworn fervently to all who would listen that I would kill every one of Dingane's men that I could get my hands on. I could hardly slink back on the ship now. I still *did* want to punish those Zulu soldiers who had killed my wife. They had turned my soulmate into a piece of butchered meat, carrion for wild animals, and I so dearly wanted them to pay for that. A fire for vengeance still burned within me and it would take a lot more than the body of an old man to extinguish it... just as long as I could get back in one piece.

I was not the only one with an eye for survival this time. No one was setting foot on the trail back into Dingane's territory until we knew for certain that the Boers had also started their attack. With luck they would vanquish the Zulu king's army first and we would face a reduced, perhaps already retreating force. There were even bold plans for joining up with the Dutch and advancing with them together to Umgungundlovu. Personally, I thought that was the wildest optimism. If I could sate my bloodlust and feel that they had paid a price for Louisa, not to mention all those children, then I could retire satisfied and still be able to look myself in the eye in a mirror.

Finally, in the middle of April we got the news we had been waiting for. Dick King rode into town to say that the Boers had settled their differences and had set off, riding into the Zulu heartland. Even then we left it a couple of days before we started out. I was hoping Dingane would hear first of the Dutch advance into his lands. He could send his whole army against it before he learned of ours. We might then have a chance of defeating whatever force he had kept in reserve.

A drummer beat the step and a banner, stating we fought for justice, flapped at the head of our column. Robert Biggar and John Crane rode behind the colour party, the nominal leaders of our band. Some distance behind, at the head of his warriors strode the real leader. Umfazi's features were as expressionless as ever, as he gambled once more on beating his old master. Without Ogle and his supporters, there were fifteen Englishmen and around twelve hundred Zulus as we set out this time. It was a pitifully small force compared to that of our enemy. I remember looking down from the crest of a hill for a final look at Port Natal. I stared beyond the hundreds of native huts, the buildings of the main street and out into the bay. I had a sudden feeling that Mrs Owen was right. Louisa might have preferred me to be standing on the deck of the *Comet* at that moment, but it was too late now.

Chapter 14

For the first four days our second expedition was much like the first: we saw no sign of Dingane's army. Dick King was sure that they must be engaged with the Dutch by now. He rode out southwest for a day, searching for our hopefully victorious allies. O'Malley was full of tales of how the Boers had beaten armies of thousands of Matabele. He was confident that they would make short work of the Zulus too, but I was not so sure. True, I had only seen our enemy stick fighting and dancing, but they had looked as tough as Spartans. While they had been unable to vanquish the Matabele, they had conquered many other kingdoms. I was not convinced that the near two hundred muskets we had between us would make that much of a difference.

At noon on the fourth day our scouts reported a hundred and fifty Zulus resting around campfires in the distance. They had clearly strengthened the size of their outposts since the previous month. The broad Tugela River lay beyond and Umfazi wanted to know if they protected a Zulu force that waited by the water. John Crane led most of our horsemen down a valley around the outpost. The enemy sentries were clearly on their guard, for the riders were soon spotted. Robert Biggar, watching through a glass his father used for hunting, reported that the Zulus were running even though they outnumbered the riders more than ten to one. When we reached their hilltop, we found that they had abandoned some spears and shields as well as bundles of possessions in their desperation to get away. Cane went in pursuit, shooting several of them before they reached the river and fled across. I had been surprised at how easily Dingane's soldiers had been driven off. Perhaps some of them had seen the demonstrations of Retief and his men at Umgungundlovu. Whatever the cause, they had certainly developed a healthy respect for armed horsemen.

We camped by the Tugela River that night. It gave us some protection, but we could see no enemy forces on the far bank. The next morning, we pushed through the reeds on the shore and I waded my horse across. The water was no more than waist deep for my company, who held their muskets and powder flasks high out of the gentle current. A short distance from the other bank we found another village. Dingane's men had spent the night there and, perhaps exhausted from the previous day, had been slow to rise. Crane's troop had already ridden around to cover the far gate in the thorn barricade, while my party and others advanced to press them at the nearer one. We had the bastards trapped and outnumbered – just how I like my enemies – and now we would make them pay.

At first a few of them appeared at the nearby entrance to the village. A fusillade of musket shots left three on the ground and the rest pulled back. It was those firing solid ball who had opened fire as they had a longer effective range. I pushed my men on to get closer. In the narrow gaps between the huts of the village, their spraying fire would give them the advantage. As we passed through the gate, an *assegai* whooshed over my head while I heard another thud into a shield to my left. I caught a glimpse of four of Dingane's warriors standing just inside of the thorn barricade. Half a dozen of my men fired, sending a hail of jagged lead in their direction. We pressed on through the smoke to see that the four enemy soldiers had all been hit, but only one was dead. It did not matter, for seconds later all had been stabbed and despatched with *iklwa* spears. We started to fan out between the huts, more of our own Zulu warriors joining us.

There was screaming, shooting and shouting coming from all around the compound now as the defenders were hunted down. I caught a glimpse of movement out of the corner of my eye and quickly swung my own weapon to bear. I had nearly pulled the trigger before I noticed the strip of white cloth on his arm. The man grinned at me, unaware how close he had come to being killed and pointed to a high-sided cattle pen. He jumped up on the side, raising an *assegai* that he hurled down on someone hiding on the other side. In a moment a second man was bounding up over the fence, just yards in front of my muzzle. I fired and had the satisfaction of seeing him blasted back into the enclosure. My new companion was already dropping down beside him, his *iklwa* raised to finish them both off.

I quickly reloaded and pressed on. In the middle of the village was a central space much as there had been in Umgungundlovu. Similarly, next to it was a large hut that must have belonged to the chief. That was where a number of the defenders had chosen to make a last stand. The entrance, like most Zulu huts was low, waist height. As I arrived the body of a warrior with a white strip around his arm was being dragged out of the doorway. Dingane's men must have been standing on either side with spears for anyone trying to get in. Two of my men aimed their guns through and fired, but it was hard to see anything in the darkness. A couple more were ready to try and charge in with their *iklwas*, but I pulled them back. We had no idea how many were inside and anyway, I had a much better idea of how to get them out. I stepped up to the side of the hut and reached into my pocket for my tinder box. In a moment I could see the first wisps of smoke curling out from the thatch.

We might not have spoken the same language, but we understood we had the enemy exactly where we wanted them. Men grinned in delight and then started to spread out around the hut in case some tried to break out through the walls, which were only made from grass and saplings. The central space was soon half full of my men and other Zulus, all hefting their weapons expectantly.

For a while nothing happened, although we could still hear fighting from elsewhere in the compound as the last of the other defenders were rooted out. Flames were soon flickering up one side of the roof and smoke began to drift out of the door. Those inside must have realised that crawling out of the entrance would be fatal. We watched as part of the wall a distance away from the flames started to shake as the occupants desperately pulled at the supports to give themselves a new way out. Several of my men opened fire at the movement. There were screams from inside. Then a hole was ripped open in the thatch and they started to emerge. Never be the first into a breach: that first warrior was struck by so many *assegais* he resembled a porcupine before he fell to one side. There was a rush out then, of at least half a dozen, one I remember had smoke coming from his hair where it had caught alight. I fired into the mass with the rest and watched them tumble. More shooting came from round the back of the hut where they must have staged another breakout. The devils stood no more chance than rats surrounded by terriers. The hut partially collapsed then with a roar of flame and a column of cinders going up into the sky. If any more were inside they were no longer in a state to come out. I looked down at the pile of corpses in front of me and felt a grim satisfaction; the ledger was slowly being balanced.

I was feeling pretty pleased with myself as I walked out of that Zulu village. My men had acquitted themselves well, we had no casualties and we must have settled at least a score of Dingane's soldiers. I had saved the lives of other warriors too by burning out their enemies. Already the cinders had spread to other huts and soon the whole town would be aflame. A couple of old men had been spared and a few prisoners taken, including three women who had been found among the huts. I found O'Malley helping himself to one of them, binding her wrists to a rope looped over the pommel of his saddle.

"Hey, no booty, remember?" I called to him.

"What the hell," he protested. "What am I supposed to do? Kill a prime piece like this or leave her for some other devil to enjoy? No, this beauty is comin' home with me." I did not really care what happened to the woman and went on, looking for where I had tied my horse. I found the mare halfway to the river, where Cane was questioning another prisoner with a Zulu interpreter. The Englishman had the muzzle of his elephant gun pressed into the captive's genitals, making it clear what would happen if he did not get answers. Others were still running about, shouting excitedly to each other about their part in the attack.

I noticed Umfazi because he was not moving: he was stood stock still, staring fixedly to the west. I glanced in that direction and had already turned away again before something made me look back. There was dust coming up on the side of a distant hill. I felt a sudden chill on that warm summer's day. It could be a herd of cattle, I thought, or some other wild beasts, but I had a nasty feeling it wasn't. Umfazi saw me watching. He glared at me and, pointing at the thick column of smoke rising above the burning village, grumbled something in his language. Of course, I did not understand, but from the look of disapproval on his face, he was probably reprimanding the bloody fool who had just lit a beacon to summon the enemy.

I called Cane and Robert Biggar over and together we all stared west. The dust was three miles off. Umfazi suddenly pointed his *iklwa* to a nearer hill, where a handful of Zulus had suddenly appeared on its summit. There was no doubt now, Dingane's men were coming and thanks to me, they knew precisely where we were. We had no idea how many were in that dust cloud but I guessed it had to be at least an impi – a thousand men. That would give us a slight advantage in numbers, yet if it was any more we would be in trouble. Well, my lad, I thought to myself, you wanted vengeance and here it is. I was already vowing to be much more careful in what I wished for.

A line was quickly organised to face the enemy, our left flank up against the river for protection and our right closer to the village. I immediately took my men to the left flank. Revenge was all very well, but if things got hot we would need to escape over the river. I did not want to be cut off from the water. I tied my horse to a bush twenty yards back so that it would be handy if a fast retreat was required and then turned my attention to my men. Most still had at least a dozen of the *looper* bags of ammunition hanging around their necks. They were calm but could not help but stare at the dust cloud that was coming ever closer. They weren't the only ones; there was chatter and pointing all down the line. Dingane's men were making use of the ground to keep their true numbers hidden. I just hoped that meant that there were not that many of them.

Umfazi had been roaming up and down our formation with Robert Biggar and John Crane to ensure that we were all prepared. With my muskets on the left flank, most of the other Europeans and men with guns had placed themselves either in the centre or right flank to balance things out. O'Malley, though, sat on his horse nearby, his captive still snuffling in the dirt beside him. Our general suddenly appeared before me with a couple of his warriors in tow. He glared at me and then at my men and the river before giving a heavy sigh. Then he turned to one of his warriors and took from him a shield, which he thrust at me. He did not worry about O'Malley having no protection and so I wondered why he was so keen on my safety. He started to draw in the dirt with the point of an *assegai*. First he drew the river, pointing at the water to show what it was. Then he drew a line that represented my men. Finally, he drew a large arrow aimed at the corner of the two lines and pointed to where Dingane's men were gathering. It was obvious that he expected the enemy to try and drive us from the river, to cut us off and encircle us with their horn formation. He slammed the *assegai* into the dirt at the junction of the lines, making it clear that we had to stop them.

I understood now why he thought it important I stay alive. He had been less than impressed with my experience gained from years of service in the British army. I had got the distinct impression that I would not have cut the mustard with the Zulu equivalent of Horseguards. Yet here I was now commanding a critical point of his defence. I was just about to try and explain that I understood, when a horn blew from the direction of the enemy. We all looked up and I felt my stomach lurch in alarm.

As though it were a single creature, a vast snake of shields had appeared on the crest of a slope some five hundred yards in front of us. It started by the river and circled us at least as far as the village. There was not just a single line of heads behind the shields either – there were at least two or three.

"Christ, there are bloody thousands of them," I muttered, horrified. I turned back to Umfazi only to find that he was already strolling back to the centre of his command. I was left standing there alone, with a spear embedded in the dirt at my feet. I dropped the shield and picked up the *assegai*, idly turning it over in my hands. Heaven knew what I was supposed to do with that, for it took skill and practice to throw them well. Dingane's men knew how to handle their spears, though, and they started to beat them against their shields. The thuds against the cow hides were rhythmic like a heartbeat and then they began to sing. Thousands of voices chanted out their challenge in a song. I had heard similar at Umgungundlovu but not on this scale, and not when all those spears were about to be flying in my direction.

Umfazi's commander of the men to our right in the line started up his own song. His men began to beat their shields in return. Several of my soldiers looked back at their officer. Did they expect me to lead them in a rousing chorus of *Mother Kelly's Daughter*? I doubted that would help but I suddenly knew what would. I walked through the middle of their rank and began to pace out thirty steps towards the enemy. Then I pushed the *assegai* firmly into the ground. A few of my men grinned, they knew the spear was a firing marker. I tried to look unconcerned as the beating and chanting continued behind my back, but my throat had already gone dry. The leader next to me was howling at his men and waving his arms about to whip them up for the attack. I had nothing. I could not even speak to my command without William. I thought of all the commanders I had known before, who would give rousing speeches before a battle. Napoleon had whipped his men up before Waterloo; Cochrane had stirred his crew to incredible feats; even that blowhard Travis had talked men into dying with him. Words to stir the soul, that was what I needed. Something to show that years of education at Rugby in classics and literature had not been wasted. Instead, the only thing that came to mind was what I had seen an Ashanti do before the attack on Cape Coast Castle. I undid my trousers and bared my arse at the enemy.

I doubt it was the sight of my buttocks that prompted them, but a few moments later, to a deafening roar, the enemy started to move forward. I retreated hastily back behind my men and glanced along our line to check that it was standing firm. I had barely got into place when Dingane's soldiers stopped again to resume their singing and bang their shields. They had only advanced a hundred yards. Then suddenly they moved forward once more. Again they stopped, still more than two hundred yards away. They were giving a deep chanting roar now, their line still ruler straight, with gaps between the front rank and the ones behind. I guessed that the sporadic moves forward were to break our nerve. Well they nearly worked with me. I remember staring around to ensure that my horse still waited patiently. I doubted it would be long before I was running to its saddle. I stood my ground, though, for I knew that if the line broke now it would probably be fatal to all of us. Fortunately, everyone else seemed to know that too, and not a single man moved. There was a handful of shots from further along our formation, but unless his elephant gun was rifled, even John Crane could not hit a target at that distance. I picked up my shield, loosened the cutlass in my belt and ran my fingers over the stock of the musket hanging from my shoulder. I had wanted the chance to kill Dingane's men. Now, for better or worse, I was going to get it.

The enemy line surged forward once more. This time I knew it would not stop, for it would have halted in the range of many of our guns. They did not yell a guttural roar as we would have done. Instead it was a protracted "Oooh" sound; the noise a couple of maiden aunts would make when exclaiming over a pretty frock. By Christ they did not look like maiden aunts, though, black faces grimacing in hate over the top of the waving wall of shields. They kept in a solid line, too, with good discipline. I heard a few more of our guns fire further down the line, but the range was still long and they were likely wasting their shots. My beauties, though, stayed still and quiet, not one even raised their gun, their eyes fixed on the *assegai* stuck in the turf before them. One hundred yards, seventy, sixty then I saw the running men start to raise their throwing spears and turn side on to launch them.

"Shields up," I shouted, raising mine, but my boys had anticipated the order for they knew better than me what was to come. They say the sky was black with English arrows at Agincourt, well it was not that bad, but the spears were bigger and heavier. I felt one thud into my shield and when I looked, saw the point protruding a couple of inches through the thick hide. One of my men screamed as he was struck in the shoulder and he staggered back from the line. Through the gap I could see that Dingane's men were nearly up to my *assegai*.

The first rank fired. I heard a slight whistle as the shards of lead were blasted through the air and then the enemy were tumbling down. The whole front line of their charge opposite us had been hit, all apart from one man who had miraculously survived unscathed. He must have run on ten yards before he realised he was alone. I remember seeing the sudden confusion on his face as he staggered to a stop in front of the two ranks of men that were changing positions. I was about to raise my gun to finish him off when O'Malley called out, "He's mine!" The Irishman was still mounted on his horse and fired his single musket ball over the heads of my men. The lone warrior crumpled to the ground like a puppet who had just had his strings cut. Already the next line of Zulus was clambering over the fallen bodies of their comrades, but my second rank was readying to fire. Another "Oooh" as the enemy tried to charge again and was met with a further withering volley. This time none of them was left standing and already the warriors beyond them were edging back the way they had come.

There was no time to celebrate our victory, for Umfazi's men to our right were not faring as well. Weight of numbers meant that the battle between the traditionally armed Zulus was not going our way. Their line was being pushed back, but this meant that the sides and back of their opponents was slowly being exposed to us. I fired my musket into their flank from just ten yards away. Two men fell and another staggered away a bloody mess. Then more guns crashed out. My first rank finished reloading and soon a hail of shot was pouring into the enemy. Attacked from two sides, they did not stand for long. A horn blew from somewhere in the distance and suddenly the whole enemy line was running back.

There was no triumphant cheer from our side, however, for when we looked, the enemy line looked no smaller than it had at the start of the battle. More men had appeared from somewhere to replace those we had killed and the singing and shield beating merely started again. Mercifully, my company had only suffered one casualty, the man struck by the *assegai*, and he would live from that wound. The warriors to our right had fared worse; a score of corpses and a similar number of wounded were being laid out behind them. Biggar and Crane were already shouting orders to close up the gaps and shorten their end of the line.

"That was probably just a probin' attack," declared O'Malley. "There is plenty more of the buggers over yon hill. They want to see what we are made off. Will ye quieten down, you damn bitch, you're not dead yet, are ye?"

This last was directed at the blubbing captive, still tied to his saddle. It looked like she might be free again soon, for when I stared further along our line I was appalled. "We only just beat that lot back," I protested, pointing at the stream of bodies. "At this rate we will be whittled down to nothing."

"Nonsense," asserted O'Malley. "You show them a firm defence and they will back off and leave us alone." I doubted that the Irishman had met Dingane. If he had, he could well have imagined the fate of a

Zulu general under the stern glare of those black eyes declaring, "Sorry, Your Majesty, things got a bit tough and so we let them go."

There was a shout from my men as one of the apparent 'corpses' in the mound ahead of them suddenly got to his feet and sprinted for his life, an arm hanging loose at his side. A couple of guns fired but he was already too far away. Without any bidding from me, a dozen of my company went forward with muskets and *iklwas* to ensure that there would be no further 'resurrections'. Like many a battle I have been in, there was now a lull in hostilities. The enemy continued their singing, but I could see warriors moving up and down their line behind the wall of shields that faced us. Having tested us out, I suspected that they were planning something different.

I watched the *iklwas* rise and fall over the wounded with a growing sense of apprehension. Would that be my fate too? Still, it paid to be as prepared as possible and as my men started to return, I went out and stopped them. We still could not talk to each other but by gesture and mime, I got one to help me pick up a corpse and put it five paces back from my *assegai*, which still stood stuck in the ground. Then we picked up another body and laid it on top. I got them to understand that they were to build a rampart of the dead to obstruct the next charge. I also put some more *assegais* into the ground five paces on our side of this new barricade. I wanted my men to shoot only when the first of the enemy had climbed over, to create an even bigger obstruction.

The work had taken over half an hour and while I kept nervously looking at the enemy, they showed no sign of moving. My men had just finished the barricade when two of them came over, jabbering at me excitedly in their strange language. They were quite worked up about something, but I could make no sense of it. I cursed the cowardly William for leaving me in the lurch. His father and uncle were further up our line, but I knew that they spoke little more Zulu than I did. Frustrated at my lack of comprehension, one of the men grabbed me by the arm and dragged me closer to the river. He was still raving about something and now he was pointing at the reeds. At first I saw nothing, just the heads of the long grasses moving in the gentle breeze. Then I spotted what he saw; some of the movement was not so gentle. As I watched, some of the stems and seed heads were snapped and fell out of sight.

Hellfire, the Zulus had been quiet because the cunning bastards had sent warriors to creep up on us and burst out on our flank. I knew where they would come out, for we had flattened a great clump of reeds when our army had crossed the river, but how to give orders to get my little band waiting for them? I gestured for the rest of my command to join us and had them stand by our new rampart as though it were to be our new defensive line. As I did so excited chattering spread through the ranks with many eyes darting across to the moving reeds. I did not want to alert the enemy that we had rumbled their plan too soon and so I kept them in a line facing the wall of distant shields. I also wanted to check that they were all loaded and ostentatiously used my own ramrod to check that there was a charge in my gun. Then I used the rod to check some of their weapons, causing a few to hurriedly reload. While I worked, I kept glancing at the reeds, measuring the progress of Dingane's men by the slowly breaking stems. Several of my men were watching me and grinning. They guessed what was going to happen next and were telling the others, who chuckled darkly at thwarting the enemy's plan.

It all happened suddenly. As I glanced furtively at the river, a black face suddenly appeared through the grasses. He must have been trying to check on their progress but gazed out at precisely the moment I looked in that direction. Our eyes briefly met and then the head disappeared. I heard a shout of alarm from among the tall grasses.

In a perfect world I would have been able to get my rank to wheel to their left and start an ordered volley fire into the reeds. Instead I shouted, "*Bulala!*" the Zulu word for 'kill' was one of the very few I knew. My men might have lacked the regimentation of Napoleon's Old Guard, but they had been eagerly awaiting the order and they knew what to do. In a moment they were lining the bank and firing into the unseen enemy. I pulled one man back who looked set to charge in after them and led by example, quickly reloading my gun to fire again. A couple of *assegais* flew out of the reeds, but they went high over our heads as they had been aimed blind. Then half a dozen of the enemy Zulus started to push their way out of the reeds towards us. At least two were already wounded but even the others found the thick riverbank mud and rocks slippery. They had no chance to reach us before the muskets were ready to fire again. We all fired once more, mostly guided in our aim by the screams and yells of our enemy. As more reeds were cut by flailing lead, we were able to catch a glimpse of some of them and it was clear that their attack was over. Those that could were wading back the way they had come. Others lay still, the water darkening about them.

I glanced back at the shield wall on the hill. It had not moved to help the attack, but we were still desperately vulnerable, scattered out before them. We had done enough to thwart their ambush and so I shouted and gestured for my men to return to join the line of our army.

A few minutes later we were back in place. I strolled to the river end of our ranks to look upstream, but there was no sign of the enemy now. That is until I looked down into the water. Pieces of broken reed flecked the surface, but far more telling was the colour of the stream flowing past me. The water was pink with blood. As I turned away, I saw the first corpse float past. It was face down, leaving its own gory trail in the current.

Dingane's men appeared to be waiting for something and whatever it was, I did not think it would bode well for us. Then at last they began to change their positioning. Instead of a straight line, the middle bowed forward as more men joined there. It was to be one of their bull's head formation attacks. Umfazi strengthened our middle too and I watched John Crane and Robert Biggar join them with some more of the Europeans. That would be where the next battle would be won or lost. I thanked my stars that we were only up against the thinner horns. Not only that, we were also on the river side of the line for a fast escape if necessary. Once more I glanced back at my horse, which was still grazing the grass. It was increasingly likely that the animal would be essential to my survival, as I did not fancy our chances above half. We had ridden our luck so far. I had not lost a single man and even my wounded soldier was bandaged and back in the line. The mound of bodies to our front, not to mention those drifting past in the stream, was a testament to our success. I had made them pay for Louisa, but now the words of Mrs Owen were ringing in my ears: the vengeance would be lost if I were to be killed too.

The next attack started much like the first. Their line charged and those opposite us launched their spears on the far side of the barricade of bodies. I had my shield up quickly, but this time it was not hit. There was plenty of time to ready our muskets as with more "Oooh's" our enemy scrambled towards us. First one volley and then the next. The ground was carpeted with their dead and wounded, but still they came on. There were more of them this time and we would not get time to reload. My men were grabbing their *iklwas* and bracing themselves with their shields, while their valiant commander was stepping back, bowels churning and preparing to run. Then I saw him, a big fellow with a feather in his headdress, who seemed to be one of their leaders. Yet it was not his size or feather that seized my attention, but what was tied to the top of his shield. It was a long tress of hair, human hair, hair that was exactly the colour of Louisa's.

Suddenly I had the clearest vision of the man standing over my wife. He was pulling a great spear out of her back and then bending down to wrench out his trophy. There was a roar of rage nearby, which I suddenly realised was coming from me. I don't remember dropping my musket or pulling out the cutlass from my belt, yet my next clear memory is sticking the blade in the side of a man wrestling with one of my soldiers. My eyes were locked on that shield and yet as I pushed through the throng, I sensed another warrior coming at my right-hand side. As I should know, fear or fury gives a man extraordinary vigour in a moment of crisis. Now, almost without thought, I shoved his spear away as I slashed the cutlass across his throat. I was pushed forward by a man behind and blood from my victim gushed all over my chest, but I did not care. Another Zulu got in my way and I hacked at him too and then the shield was in front of me. Its owner was trying to stab down on one of my men. He did not even notice me until I tore the cowhide out of my way. I rammed the cutlass up into his chest, right under the ribs to the hilt and then found the strength to twist the broad blade in his guts. I remember screaming at him in my rage. No coherent words, just an animal roar. I wrenched the blade out and turned looking for someone else to kill. A black body raised a spear at my elbow, but just in time I noticed the white armband. As suddenly as it started, our part of the battle was over. Dingane's men were falling back, their leader mewing his death throes at my feet.

I stood there, covered in blood, surrounded by dying bodies I had slain. For me it was a unique experience. Some of my men were staring at their leader in surprise while others, distracted by things elsewhere, were backing away. For a moment I was shocked at what I had done, it was almost as though I had been possessed. Then I remembered what had provoked me and I looked back down at the shield. Those flowing, familiar locks were now spattered with blood and so it did not really matter that I used my gory blade to cut them free. I raised the tresses to my face, yet there was no familiar smell. For a moment I was lost in my memories, but then a scream nearby reminded me that I was still standing in the middle of a battlefield. I pushed the hair into my shirt and stared around me as though waking from a dream… and swiftly realised that it was turning into a nightmare.

Our line was being broken apart in its middle. The huge 'head' of the Zulu formation had driven a wedge through our forces, dividing them in two. Anyone on the far side was already trapped and lost. Some of Umfazi's men on my side of the wedge were still trying to contain it but others were running. I saw two of my men fleeing for the river, tearing the white cloth off their arms. Then my eyes caught a new movement on the other side of the water. Coming down the far bank towards us, no more than a quarter of a mile away, was yet another Zulu impi. That must have been what the others had been waiting for. They were coming at the run to spring the trap to catch us all. There was not a second to lose and I began to push my way through the men fleeing in panic to reach my horse. I thanked my stars that no Zulu knew how to ride or it would not have still been there, but when the crowds parted I felt my heart lurch with despair. The mount had not been taken, but the mare was of little use now. She was lying on her side, her legs flailing weakly in a pool of blood with a hurled *assegai* in her neck.

There was nothing for it but to plunge into the water after the others. There were screams and shouts of panic all around me now. Everyone could see the force we were racing with to the far bank and knew our fate if we failed. I was quickly up to my waist in the river, pushing away a corpse that was floating downstream. It was quicker to wade than to swim, but only just. I pressed on, my feet sometimes slipping in the mud and my legs burning from the exertion. The impi was only a few hundred yards away now, I could hear their strange war cry as they watched their victims floundering before them. Suddenly the water became shallower and I picked up speed. I would make it to the bank in time but what then? The river was littered with scraps of floating white cloth, and some of my former comrades had even retained spears and shields. They would easily be able to blend in with our attackers, but that was not an option for me. I splashed my way up onto the shore a marked man, who would soon have hundreds of the devils on his heels. I plunged into the nearby undergrowth, my imagination filled with images of stabbing *iklwas* being thrust into my body and ripping my guts open. Christ I was done for. I ran on as fast as I could, twisting and turning through the bushes, my legs totally sapped of strength.

I heard screams behind me as the first of the impi came up on those still trying to cross the water. It would only be moments before the murderous horde were spreading out in my direction too. I hurtled on in gut-searing panic and yet suddenly, into my mind came a memory of Mrs Owen and her warning me not to get myself killed. She had promised to pray for me. Well, if she had, I could attest that her God works in wonderous ways, for as I rounded another thicket, in a small clearing ahead, I saw my hope of salvation.

O'Malley was sitting on his horse with his back to me, sawing furiously with his knife at a rope tied to his saddle. He must have tried to escape with his captive hanging over the pommel, but even the amorous Irishman must have realised that this would not serve. The girl was now in the dust, still bound by the other end of the cord he was cutting. The last strands parted as I started towards him. He was about to ride away again as I called out, "O'Malley, wait!"

The fool should have ridden away then when he had the chance, but instead he hesitated and called back, "Stay away, Flashman." He even brandished the knife, "We will not make it with two of us aboard."

He was right there. I had to get closer. "Wait, I'm done for," I gasped, exhausted. "Just take this gold ring back to Port Natal for my son." I held up my left hand where I now wore a signet ring on my little finger.

O'Malley saw the precious metal glinting in the sunlight and then looked at its wearer. I was covered in blood from my head to my wet waist where it had been washed away. He must have assumed that a good amount of it was mine. The exhausted gasping as I continued up to him was certainly genuine. "Quickly, then," he urged, holding out his hand for the gold and taking a quick glance over his other shoulder, for the shouts from the river were getting louder.

That was all the chance I needed, for there was not a second to spare. I grabbed his left boot and pushed up with every last ounce of strength I possessed. The Irishman gave a shout of alarm as he felt himself falling down the other side of his horse, his knife flashing futilely over my head. I had his boot out of the stirrup as I pushed and had already grabbed the rein from his flailing hand. My boot was in the iron as he hit the dirt and in the blink of an eye I was in the saddle, kicking his remaining boot out of the other stirrup as the horse whirled about in confusion at the change of riders.

"Sorry, old man," I called down at him as I spurred the mount on. "It was you or me." I doubt he heard me over the thudding hooves. He was rolling around onto his back, his dusty face already red with fury and fear.

"Flashman, you bastard!" he roared. I dare say there would have been more invective, but at that moment there was an "Oooh" from behind him. The first of the shields appeared between the bushes beyond.

I had apologised almost automatically, for I was not sorry at all. One of us was done for and it was not going to be me. However, even with the horse I was not safe. More men were spilling out on my right. I urged the mount even faster and had to lay low to avoid an *assegai* hurled just over the saddle. Guiding us more to the left, I risked a look back. Where O'Malley and his woman had been sprawled, there were now a crowd of Zulus, their spears rising and falling

Chapter 15

I did not care in which direction I rode off, as long as it took me away from those devils behind me. Yet when I reached the top of a hill, I could make out the trail our army had left on its way to the river. A force of over a thousand men leaves a path a child could follow. This one would take me back to Port Natal and safety. I knew I was not out of danger yet and when I stared back the way I had come, I glimpsed half a dozen Zulus coming after me. They were a mile behind, their shields dancing as they ran over the rough ground. I knew the distances they could cover from stories I had heard at Umgungundlovu. They could keep going for hours without stopping. I urged the horse on towards the trail, trying to keep her at a steady pace that would slowly stretch our lead without wearing her out. My pursuers could follow the trail too, but I dared not strike out on my own. I did not know the country and could easily get lost or trapped in some blocked valley.

By late afternoon those hunting me were out of sight, but I did not doubt that they were still on my scent. As night fell, I was exhausted, but I dared not stop. Equally I could not risk the horse getting injured stumbling over some rock in the dark. Dismounting, I led her on by foot, making our way by the dim light of a few stars. It must have been well into the small hours when we stumbled across another river. Man and beast both needed to drink. I finally allowed us to rest on the far side, confident that I would hear anyone trying to splash across behind us.

I jerked awake with a start to the sound of a whinny. The mount was pulling against the reins I had tied to a tree and stamping its feet in alarm. The horse had woken me, but what had woken the horse? I jumped up and whispered to soothe it as I stroked its neck, my ears straining for the sound of splashing in the water. I had not meant to fall asleep and wondered how long I had been dozing. Light was just starting to appear in the eastern sky. I whirled round as I heard a deep growl from nearby. The horse was rearing now. I did not blame it, for the noise terrified me too. It sounded like a big cat – a leopard or a lion. There was still blood on my clothes; perhaps it had smelt that or the horse, thinking we were an easy meal. The creature certainly did not seem deterred by my presence. I reached up to try and calm my mount again and this time felt for the pistol O'Malley had kept in a holster on his saddle. I had checked it was loaded during our pursuit and now I slowly aimed it where the noise had come from.

Should I fire to frighten away the cat or save the shot for when it charged? To be killed by the Zulus would be bad enough, but to be devoured by wild animals would be even worse. I had been extraordinarily fortunate to kill a tiger in India when it had charged me. I doubted that I would be that lucky again. In the dark, I would probably not see the creature until it was too late. I still had my cutlass as a last resort and so I took a deep breath and fired. There was another snarl and then the sound of something moving through the bush, away from me, I hoped.

Having been startled by the gunfire, the horse now began to calm down as I hurriedly searched O'Malley's saddlebags for powder and ball to reload the pistol. Despite a chill in the night air, I wondered if I should immerse myself in the water to wash away some of the blood, which might attract further predators. I had taken several steps down the bank to do just that before some other thought occurred: crocodiles. I had not seen any in South Africa, but if they had hippos then they probably had those scaly devils too. If they were nearby, they too would get the scent of blood in the water. Perhaps we were in danger even near the bank. Our pursuers would certainly have heard my shot if they were nearby. They too might be getting closer.

My mind was filled suddenly with all sorts of horrors. I hurriedly untied the horse and led her off into the night, loaded pistol in hand. As we made our way carefully in the darkness, I remember reaching into my shirt and feeling Louisa's hair. I talked to her, it helped calm me down to imagine her spirit beside me. I told her that I had avenged her and that I was now going home. I promised that I would look after the estate in Leicestershire that she loved and vowed to myself, not for the first time, that I would never leave England again. With part of her pressed against my chest, I felt close to her again. Tears ran down my cheeks as the sun crept slowly up on the horizon.

As light spread across the landscape, there was no sign of any Zulus on the trail behind me or lions and leopards nearby. Just some antelope grazing on a hillside. I breathed a sigh of relief and mounted up to press on to the coast. I half dozed in the saddle, mind and body exhausted. I might have felt that the forces of Dingane had been punished for killing Louisa, but it had come at a terrible cost. No one in England has ever heard of the Army of Natal. It was not an official British army, nor a Zulu or a Boer one. It was a force of men fighting

135

for their own survival. Of the seventeen Englishmen that rode with it, only four of us finally made it back. Dick King was another; he managed to hide in the riverbank until dark and slowly made his way back on foot. Of our Zulu comrades, the vast majority were killed too, including Umfazi. But by removing those strips of white cloth and disguising themselves among their enemy, several hundred did survive. They made it back to their families, although for them the dangers were not yet over, as we will see.

I slept that night in a sheltered gully. Using some powder and the flint from the gun, I started a fire to keep prowling teeth and claws at bay. There was grazing nearby for the horse, which I had hobbled and at last I began to feel a little safer. By noon the next day I had crested a hill and there before me lay Port Natal. More importantly, just beyond was its bay of glistening sea and in the middle of that was the safe refuge of the *Comet*.

Somehow one of the other survivors had got there before me. As soon as I appeared in the town, I was surrounded by those seeking news of my former comrades. William's mother was distraught over her husband and his brother, who I had not seen among those trying to escape. I could not give her much hope.

Also in town was a messenger from the Boers, whose army had also been defeated by Dingane's men. Their divided command had fought separately. My friend Dirk Uys' force had been ambushed and his fellow commander, Potgieter, had refused to go to his aid. Uys and several others had been killed, including his fifteen-year-old son, who had refused to abandon his wounded father. Our efforts to divide the enemy forces had failed miserably; the Zulu army had first defeated the Dutch and then turned its might on us. I could easily imagine those black eyes glittering with delight in Umgungundlovu. He had vanquished both forces sent against him. The question now was: What would he do next?

The answer came over the next two days from a stream of returning Zulu survivors of the Army of Natal. It was also confirmed when Dick King staggered in. Dingane's entire military host was on their tail, marching to drive the settlement of Port Natal into the sea. They were only a day or two behind and lookouts were posted to give us warning of when they were close. In the meantime, pits were quickly dug in the cattle pens to bury valuables and surplus stores. The animals were then driven around the enclosures numerous times to hide any sign of the excavations.

As we awaited the annihilation of the settlement, some, like Mrs Wood, kept their eyes fixed to the horizon for sight of more survivors. Her husband and his brother were still missing, but Dick King was the last white man to reach us. There was no panic, at least among the Europeans and their handful of black servants, for we knew we would retreat to the safety of the *Comet*. But there was no room in the small vessel for all the Zulu families, nor supplies to feed them. Groups of them began to move out in all directions, planning to lose themselves in the countryside and escape the coming onslaught. Some tried to take their herds of cattle with them, while others abandoned their beasts to make faster progress. Despite the danger, however, a good number stayed. There was still a trickle of Zulu survivors coming into town, which gave hope amongst those waiting that more might follow.

At noon the next day we heard a couple of shots from the hills. A while later a small cannon boomed out on the ship when its lookout spotted a dark shadow of men pouring over a valley pass. We still had at least a couple of hours until they reached Port Natal and so made our way down to the little wooden jetty. A number were aboard all ready and it only took three boat trips for the rest of us. We were all on deck within the hour. Despite the approaching danger, none of the Zulus tried to join us – most found the idea of going out to sea almost as frightening as Dingane's coming invasion.

Even though we were safe, it was a tense and apprehensive group on those planks: the Owens, Jane their servant, the Hulleys, the fortunate Mr Ogle, who had been thrown out of the army and around twenty others. It was the first time I saw Captain Gardiner and his wife, although they spent most of their time below in a cabin. Mrs Wood and William both stayed on deck, still staring anxiously ashore. Alexander Biggar too watched in vain, grief-stricken at losing two sons in as many months. For those who needed it, we were not short of spiritual guidance, for as well as Owen, there were also the two American missionaries on board. They did what they could for the newly grieving, of which there were many. The white settlers of Port Natal were an isolated, tight-knit community and they had just lost nearly half of their number.

But if we thought that the horrors were over, we were to be disappointed. Late that afternoon we watched as Dingane's vast army approached the town, spreading out into its feared bull's head formation. The commander of our vessel, Captain Rodham, was observing through his glass and reported that he could see dozens, perhaps hundreds of our Zulus still in the settlement. They had left it too long waiting for their loved ones to return. As we looked on, some made a desperate effort to run out to the surrounding hills, but the 'horns' of the bull were now extending and certain to wrap around them. Others fled along the coastline in both directions while yet more, apparently resigned to their fate, waited in their part of the settlement. At the last minute, some fifty of them changed their minds about sea travel and headed down to the jetty. They shouted and yelled, waving their arms and imploring us to send the boat back to save them. Our deck had largely been silent as we had watched the horror unfold, but now as the desperate screams from those on the dock carried across the water, a heated debate broke out.

"We must do something," Mrs Owen insisted. "We can't just leave them there to be slaughtered." Her husband and the other missionaries agreed. Rodham hesitated, unsure what to do, and asked if there were any volunteers in his crew to row the boat. None were forthcoming and I did not blame them. Even if they set off straight away, it would be a close-run thing and they might not reach the shore before Dingane's men got onto the beach. Some of the passengers had offered to row instead when another voice called out across the deck. It was Captain Gardiner.

"It is no use," he explained. "The boat will only take at most twenty with the six oarsmen and then it would be low in the water and slow to get away. If you row it to shore those desperate people will rush it. You will be swamped and sunk. Even if you did manage to stay afloat by fighting some off, you would soon have *assegais* raining down about you." He gave a heavy sigh and concluded, "There is nothing we can do." The calm authority of this experienced naval man carried the day. Even the missionaries lost their ardour for a rescue after that description of their fate. Gardiner went alone to the quarterdeck. He leant on the rail and stared back at the country he had staked his future on. He had been given a tract of land bigger than Yorkshire and now he had lost it. Worse, his scheming to convince D'Urban that the land was ripe for British colonisation had brought others here like the Owens and I, who had paid a terrible price for his deception. Part of me wanted to tip the swine overboard, but that would have been too little and too late. Perhaps I was exhausted or maybe my need for vengeance was fully sated, but I just could not summon the strength to hate Gardiner. He had not set out to kill anyone; he had just hopelessly underestimated Dingane's ruthlessness.

138

Others who had made that mistake were on the jetty, still shouting in vain for help as the king's soldiers ran through the town behind them. No Port Natal resident still on shore was spared. We watched in horror as some were stabbed on the beach. Others waded into the water, but they were pursued until they were either stabbed or drowned, for they were not able to swim. All along the shore and up towards the hills, the horns of the pursuing army spread out to ensure none escaped the king's retribution.

Soon fires were blazing among the Zulu huts, while in the white settlement everything left unburied of value was either stolen or smashed. Captain Rodham, watching through his glass, reported that some of Dingane's warriors were cavorting about wearing women's dresses and bonnets. They found a barrel of brandy but instead of drinking it, they smashed it. The liquor soaked into the wood of a store house floor, which blazed fiercely when later put to the torch. I recall Reverend Owen insisting that the souls of Dingane and his soldiers could not be saved and that they were all consigned to hell. That first night as we stood on deck watching the devils dancing in front of the flames, it looked as though many were already there.

The next morning a heavy rain shower doused the fires, making the land look grey and forbidding. Most of us wanted to weigh anchor and sail away, but incredibly, there was a handful that wanted to stay in this benighted country. Amongst them were Mrs Wood and her son William. They were still hopeful that at least one of the Wood brothers would somehow make it back. Dick King and I did our best to explain that this was unlikely, but they were adamant that they would be waiting for them if it did. There were a few others who wanted to try and retrieve possessions, including Ogle, who was keen to recover his captured elephant ivory that he had buried for safekeeping. So, for them we stayed.

Messengers must have been going back and forth to the king seeking instruction. Some of the Zulus had shouted at us from the jetty and once we lowered a boat with William aboard to see what they wanted. Keeping well out of *assegai* range, we discovered that they were demanding Ogle. They had learned how he had tortured their chief. Hand him over, they promised, and they would leave and we would be safe. Ogle had been in the boat with William and instructed the boy to tell them to go to hell.

We began to think that they would never depart, but after they had occupied the town for a week, the first impis began to head home. The next day the rest left, yet we stayed aboard another day fearing a trap. When we finally lowered the boat for the shore, six Zulus did appear on the beach, but William discovered that they were refugees from our army who had returned too late to rescue their families. They had taken their revenge the previous nights, stealing through the settlement to kill lone Zulus with their *iklwas*, then returning to cover by dawn. We found the bodies of their victims in the town, two still dressed in women's clothes but that was nothing to the slaughter we found in the Zulu settlement.

We had heard the screams that first night and watched the vultures circling the next day. Dingane must have ordered the death of all those who had rejected his rule, but even though we expected it, the sight was still sickening. Most of the bodies lay in blackened circles that had once been their huts. Their limbs had twisted and contorted as their muscles had contracted in the heat. Charred skulls were thrown back with gaping mouths, capturing their final screams of agony for eternity. Some huts must have been packed before they were torched as these demonic figures were entangled together two or three high in a ghastly pyramid. Others, perhaps those who had tried to escape this death, had been wrapped individually in thatch and burnt. Still more had simply been stabbed with spears and it was these that the vultures and wild dogs had feasted on. Hardly any of the bodies were complete; many had been torn apart, with abandoned half-eaten limbs covered in flies scattered around.

The stench alone from this death and decay was appalling. Once again we tried to persuade the Woods and others to leave on the *Comet* with us, but they would not be moved. On seeing that some of his warehouse still stood, Alexander Biggar decided to stay too. He had now lost both of his sons. He was content to die on the same soil that had taken them. We kept a ready eye on the horizon for the return of any of Dingane's men while we did our best to salvage planks and restore a handful of buildings to usable shelters. Some loose horses were recovered, bodies were dragged off the streets and scattered possessions reclaimed.

By then I was in a fever to get away from this accursed shore. I breathed a sigh of relief when Ogle and some men marched in with their tusks, for at last we were ready to depart. I wished Alexander well and, with Mrs Owen, attempted in vain once more to persuade the Woods to leave. Then we made our way down to the boat. The salty sea air made a refreshing change from the reek of rotting bodies and I helped pull on an oar to speed us on our way. We were just weighing anchor when there was a shout from a man aloft unfurling one of the sails. He had spotted a horseman riding along the shore towards us, a white man, waving his hat in the air to get our attention.

The captain ordered the sail reefed and the anchor dropped again, while I swore in frustration.

"Christ on a stick," I fumed, "those bloody Boers will be wanting us to fight with them again, as if we have not done enough. They started this bloody war. If they had just stayed in British territory none of this would have happened."

"Dingane started the war," Captain Gardiner corrected me, "and I think we should listen to what they have to say." The others agreed and while I seethed and paced up and down the deck impatiently, a boat was lowered. I watched irritably as it beached and the Dutchman climbed aboard to be rowed back to the ship. He was a young man, still covered in the dust of a hard ride as he was helped to climb up the side of the vessel. He finally stood unsteadily on the deck, holding on to the rail and staring about him. It was clearly the first time he had been on a ship.

"Who are you and what can we do for you?" asked Gardiner to remind the man of his business.

"Oh, I am Henrik, Maritz sent me," he began. "We have heard of your defeat by Dingane and that you have suffered many dead. I have been sent to ask if any of you know what happened to a man called Thomas Flashman?"

Heads turned in my direction as my jaw dropped in astonishment. "*I* am Thomas Flashman," I stated.

The boy beamed in delight before announcing, "Then, sir, I am pleased to tell you that your wife has been found alive."

Chapter 16

That moment will be etched on my memory to my dying day. Reverend Owen dropped to his knees, beseeching all to join him in thanking the Lord for his mercy. His wife ignored him and threw her arms around my neck, leaving tears of joy wet on my cheeks. Or perhaps the tears came from me, as I stood there stunned and shocked. As I recall, my overriding emotion at that moment was fear, which might sound strange. But suddenly I was frightened to believe Louisa was alive, for I knew that if the news turned out to be false or she died before I could reach her, the despair would undoubtedly send me mad. I could not go through that grief again.

I remember gasping, "But how?" Henrik explained that she had been stabbed in the leg in the Zulu assault but had escaped by stumbling out into the night. She had been found unconscious two days later, covered in cuts and even claw marks, by another family of Boer survivors. They were terrified of more attacks and so did not join the laager at Doornkop, instead heading south over the mountains. They nursed Louisa as they went. Her wound became infected and she had been delirious with fever. Eventually, she was well enough to talk and explained who she was and that she had to return. When her hosts passed a wagon heading north, her stretcher was carried over and another family brought her back.

I should have asked how badly she had been hurt, but instead I found myself asking, "Does she still have her hair?" Henrik looked somewhat surprised at this enquiry as did others, but he confirmed her long locks were intact. I reached inside my shirt for the tresses I still had pressed to my skin and held them out in the sunlight. I had been sure they were hers, but now I knew some other woman had suffered the fate I imagined for Louisa. I looked at the shore, remembering the sights and smells of death, and gently dropped the bundle over the side of the ship. The sea felt a more peaceful place.

When she reached Doornkop Louisa discovered that I had been part of the defeated Army of Natal. After all that she had suffered, it appeared she was too late and that I had been killed. Maritz told me later that she had been distraught at the news, but that he had wanted to be absolutely certain that there were no survivors. That was why he sent the messenger, who, thank God, had arrived in the nick of time.

As Henrick and I reached the laager, he rode on ahead shouting, "Mr Flashman's alive!" at the top of his voice. Heads turned and people came out of wagons to see the commotion. After so much tragedy they grinned at the good news. Many knew our story. They would have remembered me searching for Louisa when I was there before. I had visited every wagon more than once. They had got to know Louisa by then too. As I galloped into the circle of carts there was cheering and people slapped me on the back as I dismounted. Others tried to shake my hand and congratulate me on my survival, but I did not care a jot about that. All I wanted was the blessed sight of my wife.

My paltry pen and ink cannot come close to describing the joy at seeing Louisa again. The crowds parted and then there she was, on her feet, although supported by two others at the elbow. Her cheeks were sunken and her dress hung loose on her frame. Ironically, the hair I had remembered was now much greyer as a result of her ordeal. My eyes noticed all these things, but my heart just saw the pretty young woman I had married over thirty years before. In a moment we were in each other's arms and I don't recall us saying anything for quite a while. We just held on to each other, scarcely able to believe that we were both still alive.

After a while we were shown into a wagon where we could sit in some privacy. She had some brandy tucked away and we shared it, while grinning like idiots at the sheer joy of being together. Then she insisted that I tell her my tale and exclaimed in horror when she heard the risks I had taken avenging her. She tried to tell me of her adventures, but mercifully, she had been delirious for much of the worst of it. She showed me the three deep cuts on her arm that seemed to have been made by the claws of a big cat and the gnarled scar on her leg made by a spear. Some brute had stabbed her with an *iklwa* before he was shot by a Boer. She had limped off into the dark night, no idea where she was going, only that she had to get away from those murderous spears. The next think she remembered clearly was waking up in a wagon.

She was still as weak as a kitten and soon tired from our talking. I left her asleep on a cot and went to find Maritz. "I have to get her away," I told him. "We need to get back to Cape Town so that she can recover her strength before we get a ship to England."

"Is the *Comet* still at Port Natal?"

"No. I saw it sail away while I was riding here."

Maritz gave a heavy sigh and I saw that he was not well himself. His hands were swollen and he had sat down heavily after greeting me.

"Then you will have to wait for another ship. You cannot cross the mountains now. Your wife is too ill to stay long on a horse and winter is coming. Wagons will not get through now. The roads will be thick with mud; there will be snow on the peaks and soon the rains will turn the rivers into raging torrents." He smiled and added, "It will be a tough season, my friend. We do not have much, but we will share it. Yet I doubt you will mind the hardships if you have your woman by your side."

"You are right," I agreed. "Sometimes I have to pinch myself to believe it, especially when I think back to all those graves we dug." A thought suddenly occurred, "If you are short of supplies, I know that there are some at Port Natal. We buried powder, ball and sacks of mealie before Dingane's men arrived. It was not dug up again before the *Comet* sailed and the few that stayed there will not need it all."

The situation was so desperate that Maritz set off for Port Natal the next morning. The rivers were already rising and they wanted to take a number of wagons with them and get them back before the water was impassable. They returned with three cart loads of provisions, which were shared out among the camps. The Boers had declared Port Natal part of their new land and offered the few people left in the settlement their protection.

It was a tough winter, even with the extra supplies. Food was rationed and even grazing became scarce for the animals with the ground often waterlogged. Latrine ditches became flooded and people were getting sick. Some groups went off to set up new laagers elsewhere, Maritz and his family were one of them. They settled near to where the Zulus had attacked before, but I was not risking that. We stayed with the biggest group, which moved to a place called Gatsrand. There were nearly three hundred wagons there and somehow they had also acquired two small cannon. There was a river protecting one side of this new laager but no one was taking chances with its defence. We set up a central ring of carts and the remaining wagons formed a wider perimeter, some two deep. All the vehicles were chained together and any openings were packed with thorn bushes. Then the men started to dig a huge protective ditch around the laager.

Louisa and I had been given a wagon and we had the same rations as the rest. It was more than enough to keep us going, but there was not a lot of meat to help regain lost strength. Louisa remained thin and while the Boers were reluctant to slaughter too many of their remaining cattle, I would join some of the men in hunting expeditions to add more sustenance to the communal pots. I also took my turn at the digging, working on the stretch of ditch outside our wagon. By June the rivers were thought to be too high for the Zulus to cross and the defensive trench was half flooded too. Yet no one knew what the future would hold.

The weather began to dry up in July and it became possible to reach Port Natal again. At least once a week a rider would travel between the port and the Gatsrand laager. I must have asked every one of them about news of another ship. It seemed the British had forgotten about the outpost. There were so few of us left there now that trading vessels did not think it was worth their while. We had heard that Ben D'Urban had been replaced as governor by a man called Napier. He clearly did not care what had happened to his predecessor's envoy to this remote wilderness. I hoped that the Owens would get a message to Ben that we were alive and needed help, but heaven knew what influence he still had in the colony.

Each day I would take Louisa for a walk to help her strengthen her leg. To start with she could only manage a few paces, but most days we went a little further than before. She leaned on a stick and eventually we made it to the little plank bridge that led over the ditch and into the country beyond the laager. It was good to get her in some fresh air, for despite orders not to, some of our group had begun to use the defensive ditch as a place to empty their chamber pots. The place reeked.

We spent many an hour talking about what we would do when we got home to England. It was over three years since we had been there, and the last letters we had received from our children were a year old. The court case that had driven us from England had to have been resolved by now and I would curse daily the spiteful villain that had instigated it. I counted down the number of days before we could leave. Even if no ship appeared, come the spring we would join a wagon heading south. It would be a longer, more arduous journey, but every step would take us closer to comfort and a ship to London.

We were not the only ones thinking of getting away. Several families had become disillusioned with this land over the winter. The new life had been much more dangerous than they had anticipated. Some had lost nearly everything and saw little prospect of rebuilding their fortunes in Natal. News of their predicament had been taken back over the mountains to the Dutch trekkers still to make the journey, but support had been less than forthcoming. Some in the laager wondered if more would join them in the spring, while others felt that they had little choice but to swallow their pride and head back.

We were all so wrapped up in planning our own futures that we did not sense the coming danger. As the river levels began to recede, we were not the only ones planning a journey.

Chapter 17

It was the middle of August when it happened. Many of the rivers were now fordable but the mountain passes were still not suitable for wagons. A couple of horseback riders had made it through over the huge Drakensburg range. Even they had struggled, but they brought news that many more settlers were planning to follow them as soon as the route was clear. I remember the mood in the camp lifting. Perhaps more might have opportunities there after all. Then almost without any warning, suddenly the whole future of the Boer existence was hanging precariously in the balance.

A single Zulu had been seen the previous day. One of the men guarding cattle had fired on him to drive him off. There was no great alarm as several had been spotted roaming around the nearby veldt over recent weeks. Most assumed they were thieves trying to grab a stray head of cattle or two. That suspicion seemed confirmed when a man rode in to announce that a band of Zulus had driven off two men herding livestock a few miles away from the laager. A band of thirty horsemen was quickly organised to drive off the intruders and bring the cattle back. I watched them go, and remained unconcerned. As the days were getting longer the hens were laying more and as I recall, I was far more interested in fresh eggs for breakfast. We had barely finished our meal when one of the riders came hurtling back towards us at the gallop, waving his hat in the air and shouting something. He had got himself out of breath and no one could understand what he was yelling. It was only when he had finally raced through the gap in the wagons and reined his mount hard to a stop, that he was finally able to gasp out his message.

I did not understand the Dutch, but that was not necessary to grasp that something catastrophic was occurring. In a moment the women were screaming and gathering up their children, while others ran for their wagons. The men left in the camp stared at each other with fear in their faces and then went for their guns. Throughout all this pandemonium Louisa and I stood by our wagon, wondering what the hell was going on. I felt a sick apprehension coursing through my veins and squeezed my wife's hand, as much to comfort myself as her. While we did not know precisely what was happening, there was one word we could understand all too clearly from the shouts about us: Zulu. Having by some miracle both survived our earlier encounters with Dingane's soldiers and spent weeks since then talking of going home, we felt numb with shock at the thought of facing them again.

After everything we had been through, I was even more fearful of Louisa being killed than of dying myself. I know Louisa felt the same about me. The women and children were already gathering for protection in the smaller circle of wagons at the centre of the laager, but she refused to go. "I am not leaving you," she insisted. "If we die now, we die together. Anyway, you will need someone to load for you."

By then the rest of the mounted Boer patrol were coming back, splashing through the river that protected our defences from the north. They soon started rounding up the loose horses and driving them through the gate into the laager. There were hundreds of heads of cattle and sheep in sight, but not enough room for them inside the circle of wagons. We were pitifully few to face even a single impi. There were only around a hundred and twenty men in our little settlement. Another thirty were tending cattle nearer the mountains, but they were too far away to come to our aid. As soon as the last of our little garrison was inside, a wagon was pushed into the gateway and chained to the ones on either side of it. More thorn bush was pushed with poles to fill the gaps. With its trench outside, and vicious two-inch thorns on foliage all around, the laager would make a formidable obstacle for any attacker, especially one that did not have cannon or firearms. Yet it was an awfully long perimeter to protect with our meagre number of defenders. Our barriers also meant that there would be no retreat if our line was breached. The chains, ditches and thorns intended to keep the Zulus out, would also keep us trapped inside if the enemy broke through. There would be no escape this time if we failed. We would either fight with the Boers and win, or we would all die together.

I still had my musket from Port Natal and now some of the Dutch went around the wagons handing out powder and ammunition. I received two large powder flasks and a pail of their *loopers* ammunition. Louisa was not the only woman who stayed in the outer circle of wagons; the grizzled old farmer in the wagon next to ours had his wife with him too. She was soon loading a collection of weapons. Their son was one of those away near the mountains. When the farmer saw I only had one gun he went and fetched me a double-barrelled shotgun to add to my armoury. He had been our neighbour for a while, although we had spoken rarely as he did not understand much English.

148

He had always seemed rather severe and I suspected that he disliked the British from his time in the colony. Yet now as he handed over his weapon, he gave me a comradely grip on the shoulder. If we were to fight and possibly die alongside each other, then, he seemed to be saying, he deemed the Flashmans acceptable companions.

I was still unsure how many of Dingane's men we faced. Many of the patrol who had ridden in were now standing on some of the wagons on the eastern side of the circle and staring out in that direction, keeping watch. I gave a small sigh of relief, for our wagon was on the western side. For a long time there was no sign of any Zulus and I began to wonder if it had all been a false alarm. Then there was a cheer as distant horsemen were seen galloping towards us. It looked like reinforcements were on their way, although if it was the men from the mountains they were coming from the wrong direction. Brows creased in puzzlement as the horses got closer. There were around fifty of them, far more than there had been at Port Natal. Then as one of the riders changed direction the mystery was solved. "They are bloody Zulus," I called out, "and they have guns on their backs, too!"

"How they ride?" growled my neighbour and I did not think it was timely to admit that I had helped teach them. Perhaps Dickwa had got all those thorns out of his arse and climbed back in the saddle. A mounted column of men with guns was the type of force that Dingane would have wanted, having seen Retief's demonstrations. They would hope to beat the Dutch on their own terms. Fortunately, I had not taught them musketry. The Zulu horsemen opened fire on us at a range of at least two hundred yards. Their shot fell harmlessly short while they wheeled away to reload.

"Well, if that is all of them, we will see them off with no bother," I stated confidently. I waved a gun at the old man and then pointed at the distant riders, "They cannot shoot," I called at him, and grinned. "I am surprised we have gone to all this trouble," I called to Louisa as I continued to study the horsemen. They were taking an age to reload too.

"Thomas…" she started.

"We would be better sending our own riders out to deal with them than hiding in here," I continued. "The Dutch riders should be able to see them off in no time, I will—"

"Thomas!" Louisa's call was more insistent and when I looked down at her she had gone pale and was staring to the west. "Look," she said, pointing.

"Holy fucking Christ!" I stared in horror as hundreds of Zulus were quietly climbing out of a gulley that had hidden their approach, to stand some five hundred yards away. No, there weren't hundreds, there were bloody thousands of them. The silence of their arrival only made them more threatening somehow. I was certain then that I was looking at our death. I pulled Louisa towards me and hugged her as tightly as I could. I was not the only one sensing doom; I noticed the old couple in the next wagon fall to their knees in prayer.

There was shouting in the laager now and soon the rumble of wheels as a dozen men dragged the two cannon from the eastern side across to us on the west. Why the hell did our wagon have to be on this side of the laager? I cursed our luck. Men were now running from other wagons to join us. One climbed up over our tailgate. He had to be short-sighted, for he was grinning cheerfully as though he could not see all the impis readying to attack.

"Mr Flashman," he nodded to me as he shrugged off a pair of guns, two powder flasks and a heavy satchel of ammunition. Then he raised his hat and gave Louisa a little bow, "Mrs Flashman, charmed to meet you."

The whole situation was becoming surreal. "You have looked out there, have you?" I asked gesturing to the other side of the canvas wall of the wagon. Perhaps he had come from the eastern side and not yet noticed what we were up against.

He grinned again and patted one of his guns, "Yes, do not worry, we will keep them at bay."

It is just my luck to get saddled with the camp idiot, I thought as I turned away. When I looked back, another man was also joining the old couple and two more men were now in the wagon on our other side. I climbed over the back of the driver's seat to stand on the footboard and discovered yet another Boer setting himself up between our wagon and that of the old couple. He too nodded companionably in greeting as he loaded his guns. I almost did not dare look back at the Zulus in case they had grown hugely in number. When I did, my worst fears were confirmed. There had to be getting on for ten thousand of them, against around a hundred and twenty of us. As I watched them slowly forming up in their bull's head formation, I came damn close to spewing my recently eaten egg over the side of the cart.

150

Our wagon would be facing the middle of the left horn. Staring along our line, I could see the cannon being set up to meet its head. There were just a handful of men guarding the other sides of the laager now. In contrast there were two or three between each wagon facing the head and doubtless many more hidden by their canvas sides. Even so, the five thousand men in the centre of the Zulu formation faced no more than sixty Boers and two cannon. The odds were impossible. I stole a glance at Louisa, which calmed me somehow. At least we were together and if we were to die in each other's arms, well that was not a bad way to go. There was no choice but to embrace the insanity of the moment and prepare to fight. I crouched down on the footboard and rested the muzzle of my shotgun on the side of the seat.

"No, Mr Flashman, come inside." The idiot was gesturing for me to come back inside the wagon, from where I could not see the enemy. "You stand here," he announced, placing me halfway between the end of the vehicle and the iron hoop that held up the middle of the roof. Then his knife flashed out and he slashed a six-inch cut in the canvas just below my eyeline. "Shoot through here," he told me. "The cloth will protect you from the *assegais*." I nodded in understanding. He might not have been such an idiot after all.

"What is your name?" I asked.

"Pieter," he grinned as though he knew I was reappraising him. "Do not worry. As long as we keep on shooting, they will not get through."

"I have found these," Louisa had been rummaging about in the trunks on the cart. Now she held up two carving knives and a small hatchet for kindling. "I thought that they might be useful if they get in here." She looked at me and added, "For hand-to-hand fighting." Pieter and I exchanged a glance; we both knew that if we were reduced to these we would be done for. He already had a knife, but I took one of the blades and tucked it into my belt.

"Thanks," I gave her arm an encouraging squeeze. "Let's hope we don't need it."

I thought that the Zulus would do some of their chanting and dancing before they attacked, as they had against the Army of Natal. This time, however, they stayed ominously quiet as they formed up. Then one of their generals stepped forward and he shouted just one word: "*Bulala!*"

151

Chapter 18

The warriors roared the word back at him, but from ten thousand throats the Zulu for 'kill' came out as an incoherent roar. Then, as I squinted at them through my slit in the canvas, they launched themselves forward. "They are coming!" I called to Louisa.

The colour had drained from her features and her lips had shrunk a little from her teeth in her fear. She was terrified, but she slung one of the powder flasks around her neck and promised me quietly that she would not let me down. I don't think I ever loved her more than at that moment. Yet there was no time to respond, for the Zulus were closing fast, already no more than three hundred yards away. I tried to count the heads behind the swaying wall of shields in the horn coming our way and guessed that they must be ten deep. There were four or five times as many in the centre of their attack and now our two cannon fired into the mass. They had used solid shot. I saw one of the balls plough through the crowd until the sheer weight of bodies brought the iron to a stop. It left a furrow of fallen in its wake, with dying screams, shields and spears tossed into the air. Just a moment later this groove had disappeared as the running men came on, regardless of the dead and wounded that they must have trampled underfoot.

I glanced back into the laager and gave a groan of despair. "Christ, one of the cannon has overturned, we are down to one gun."

"Don't worry," replied Pieter. "It always does that. The barrel is too long for the carriage. They will soon roll it onto its wheels again." He was right; already its crew were man-handling the little cannon back into its place. "Now, don't fire too soon," the lad shouted over the growing roar of men still bellowing for our deaths.

"I have been shooting people since long before you were born," I retorted irritably, pulling back the hammers on the shotgun. That was when the *assegais* struck. Louisa gave a little scream as the first of them thudded into the canvas. Two pierced the cloth in front of us, but the weight of the shafts pulled them back out. There were thuds as more hit the wooden sides of the wagon and I saw one embedded in the driver's seat. I heard whinnies from the horses in the laager and guessed that some had been struck by spears hurled over the top of the wagons. I pushed the shotgun through my slash in the side, relieved that the wide double barrel kept the cloth well apart to give me a good view. Damn, they were close already. I needed every pellet to strike home and aimed for a spot just ten yards beyond the ditch. I had barely lined the barrel up when the first man crossed my sight. I waited a second or two more until there were half a dozen bodies to strike and then pulled the trigger. Pieter fired at the same moment and then I eased my gun a little to the left and fired the second barrel.

As I passed the still smoking gun to Louisa and picked up my musket, we were rewarded with the sounds of screaming outside. The yells of agony, however, were quickly drowned out by the shouts of "*Bulala!*" As I squinted through the cloth once more, I saw the ditch full of struggling bodies. They were no more than ten feet away, virtually point-blank range. I fired into the mass and saw several thrown back, their heads and chests covered in blood. Two more *assegais* struck the canvas while others tried to smash down the thorn bushes with their *iklwas*. There was not a moment to lose, but when I reached again for the shotgun, I found Louisa sobbing as she fumbled with the ramrod and dropped it.

"I'm sorry," she wailed. Her hands were shaking and she had knocked over a flask, spilling powder on the cart floor.

"Don't worry, take your time," I soothed picking up the fallen flask and refilling my musket. I went through the actions of reloading the gun without having to think about it. I had done it so many times over the years. Strangely, the sight of Louisa's terror overrode any fear that I might have felt myself. I could only imagine the half-forgotten nightmares that this experience was bringing back. It seemed certain that the Zulus would break through and this time the spears would finish what they had started before.

I pointed the gun out once more. There was a man who had got a spear wedged under a thorn bush, which he was trying to tug away. I knew that there were ropes holding the bushes in place, but I was not taking any chances: I shot him in the chest. He flew backwards, as did the men on either side of him. By the time I had pulled the musket back Louisa had the shotgun ready. I gave her a moment to reload before firing again, stealing a glance along the line of wagons. The cannon were firing once more, despite Zulus hurling *assegais* in their direction. One of the gunners lay with a spear in his leg, but already his fellows were hauling their gun back on its wheels. I saw the old man in the next wagon lean out to shoot down between our vehicles. His appearance prompted two spears to fly in his direction, but he managed to retreat safely back behind the canvas. The man shooting from between our two wagons, however, was not so fortunate. Blood poured from a wound on his head but despite his injury he crouched

153

behind the old man's cart and continued to reload. We all knew that this was a fight to the death – there could be no retreat.

The whole line of wagons was now wreathed in powder smoke. I looked to where the old man had shot to find the ditch full of Zulus pulling furiously at the thorn bushes. I gave them both barrels and glimpsed half a dozen being hurled away before I ducked back into cover. The war cries from just a few feet away were deafening. Time and again I fired through that rip in the canvas and with each shot I must have hit three or four men as they were so tightly packed. In return, all we received were a few *assegais*, which fell harmlessly away. The two cannon must have been inflicting terrible casualties, as each time they fired it was into a huge mass of bodies. I began to wonder how much more of this punishment they could take.

Louisa and I were nearly halfway down our pail of *loopers* and the gun barrels were now too hot to touch. I was just poking the reloaded shotgun out of the wagon when I heard her scream. I whirled round to see her fall to her knees. For a moment I thought she had been wounded, but then she picked up the hatchet and raised it above her head. I just had time to glimpse the black hand; it was feeling for some kind of purchase to pull its owner up, when the steel flashed down. There was a scream of agony from outside and the severed limb fell to the wooden floor. Its fingers still twitched as the tendons relaxed, like a crab lying on its back. The hatchet was still embedded in the wood, such was the force of her strike, and Louisa stared in horror at what she had done.

"Well done, old girl," I called as I twisted the canvas back for a better view of her assailant. The devils had somehow managed to prop one of their corpses up over the thorns. The one-handed man had fallen away, but two others had replaced him. One barrel took care of them and knocked the corpse off the thorns. The other shot blasted into three or four others waiting to take their turn. By the time I had pulled the gun back in, Louisa was on her feet and trying to reload the musket, although her hands were shaking worse than ever. Her eyes kept darting back to the severed hand as though it might somehow spring back into life. I picked it up and tossed it outside. "You are doing well," I encouraged as she fumbled another *looper* to the floor. I would have dearly liked to take her into my arms, for tears were now streaming down her face, but there was no time for that. The air under the cloth was thick with the smoke from our priming pans, but Pieter was still reloading and firing with calm efficiency. We could not

154

afford to stop. I gave her a quick hug of encouragement and then started to reload the shotgun.

That first attack ended as quickly as it had begun. A horn blew and suddenly all the Zulus that were capable, were pulling back out of range. "They are giving up!" I shouted scarcely able to believe it. I turned to embrace Louisa, but she had already slumped down on a chest, exhaustion etched in her features.

"You did a good job," Pieter congratulated her. He peered around the side of the wagon and gave a low whistle. "We all did well. Look at the bodies out there."

I looked, and I was stunned. While the wounded emitted a cacophony of wails, in comparison it was eerily quiet now without all the war cries. The gunpowder smoke slowly drifted away to reveal a scene of utter devastation. There must have been close to a hundred dead or dying men in front of our wagon alone, lying several deep in the ditch. In front of the cannon it was far worse, with long lines of men marking where the balls had torn through the enemy ranks. The ground was carpeted in bodies for around a hundred yards.

Some were trying to haul themselves off or hobble away. One, his arm hanging limply at his side, shouted something as he went. Pieter raised his gun again, but I told him to stop. "Let him go. He will not be able to fight us and we might need that ammunition. Do you know if there is more of it?"

He went off with an empty pail to find out. I was grateful that we were left alone for a while in that moment of calm. I sat beside Louisa and put my arm around her, feeling her thin shoulders tremble under my hand. "You really did do well," I told her. "I could not have fought like that without your help."

"They were so close," her voice quavered slightly. "And that hand... I thought it was going to be like it was before." She shuddered at the thought and I wondered if this experience had brought back other memories she had been trying to forget. Then she tensed again and demanded more urgently, "Will they come back?"

"I don't know," I answered honestly. "They have passed other smaller laagers such as Maritz's to get to us. They will have known the smaller ones were there – we have been seeing their scouts for a week or more. Dingane seems to have sent his whole army to destroy the largest laager the Dutch have. It is another attempt to drive them from his lands. Perhaps he thinks the others will go if we are beaten."

"Or his men will slaughter the others after they have killed us," suggested Louisa gloomily.

"Nonsense," I forced myself to sound cheerful about our chances. "There have to be at least a thousand dead out there, possibly two. We have hardly taken any casualties at all. They cannot keep attacks like that up. They may well give up and go home." Even to me, that final prediction felt more than a little optimistic.

Louisa looked up, caught my eye and grinned. She knew what I was up to and even if she did not believe it either, she was grateful to me for trying. "Thank you." Then in a stronger voice she added, "Now go and look outside. I know you are itching to see what is happening. I will be fine resting here."

I got up and went to stand on the driver's footboard. The Zulus had retreated at least five hundred yards away. Many were down by the river drinking or washing wounds and it did not look like they would be attacking again any time soon. Yet neither were any crossing the river and showing signs of retreating further. I could see at least a hundred of their wounded dragging themselves away, and hear a steady drone of gasps and wails from the wounded unable to move in the ditch or beyond. I wrenched out the *assegai* stuck in the footboard and found six more embedded in the wooden side of the cart. Turning my gaze inside the laager, I saw several dead horses with spears in their sides. The rest were milling around on the far edge of the circle, away from the recent sound of shooting. Most of the women had come out of their central shelter now and were tending the wounded, which amounted to about a dozen. One man was lying still, covered in a blanket. There was a bloody handprint on the side of the old man's wagon – most likely from the man who had fought beside us. I hoped he was getting treated and was not the one under the blanket.

The old farmer appeared around the side of his wagon holding a hoe, it seemed a strange time to start gardening. He saw me watching him and gave a grim nod of approval, before gesturing at the carnage outside. "Good," he announced. Then he raised his hoe and began to push his thorn bushes back into place. When he finished, I gestured to borrow the hoe to do the same. He grabbed my hand and gave a grunt of amusement at my soft palms before holding up his own calloused mitts. Clearly, I was not to be trusted to use his hoe correctly and he strolled off to work on the bushes beside my wagon too.

The sun was getting high in the sky by then, and it was turning out to be a warm day. Some of the women walked around the laager with water and others even began to cook. There was no sign that the Zulus wanted to restart the battle and that was just as well, as we were running short of ammunition. Pieter had returned with just half a pail of *loopers*, but he had also brought half a bucket of round lead musket balls. He sat himself down with a hammer and rock to try and flatten some, to make some more *loopers* of his own. We left him to it, sat down by our wagon and managed to eat some food.

"Why have they stopped attacking?" asked Louisa

"There are often lulls in battles to allow each side to lick their wounds," I told her. "Their general will have seen that they are not making progress, so he has called his men back."

"Is there really any chance that they will just give up or go away, or attack one of the other laagers instead?" she asked hopefully.

"I think not," I admitted, "or they would have crossed back over the river by now. No, we will need to be on our guard for whatever they do next. I fear it will be different to their first attack." What that new approach was we did not see until late afternoon. By then the wounded had been bandaged up and all but one of them was back in the wagons, ready to fight once more.

"They are getting ready again," called Pieter, who had been watching the enemy through the bushes while he beat at his rock anvil. I got up to see for myself; my God but he was right. They were still three hundred yards off, but I could make out lines of Zulus forming before us, this time well-spaced out with a couple of yards between each man. All had brown and white shields and so must have been from the same regiment. Behind that first impi another formed up, fifty yards beyond them. "What do you think they are up to?" asked Pieter.

"Maybe they heard you hammering away," I told him. "It looks to me like they think we are running low on ammunition. Before, we were hitting three or four with every shot. If they attack like that, we will only be able to hit one at a time."

"So they are sacrificing their own men?" he queried. "We will kill everyone when they get close."

"If we do not run out of ammunition first," I corrected him. "Now, you better save me the roundest of those musket balls, as I have a feeling I might need them."

Louisa had fallen into an exhausted sleep and I regretted having to wake her. I tried again to get her to stay in the central redoubt but, as I suspected, she would not hear of it. Soon the three of us were back in our wagon with Pieter and I peering through the cuts in the canvas.

The first rank was now slowly advancing. They kept glancing nervously at each other, clearly anxious about what was to come. I had chosen my musket and loaded it with a solid ball. This was the gun and ammunition I was used to and with one man to aim at, I planned to kill him further out. Our cannon did not fire this time as they were worse than a handgun against a single man.

When the Zulus were a hundred yards off they broke into a run, but they did not come straight at us. Anticipating our volleys, they darted left and right and began their "*Bulala!*" war cry. It sounded much less formidable this time, perhaps those shouting it knew that the odds were that *they* would be the ones killed.

I watched one coming directly for me and called out to Pieter that he was mine. He jinked left and right as I settled my cheek against the wooden stock of the gun and squinted down the sight.

"Come on, lad, don't keep me waiting," I muttered, for I saw now that the warrior was much younger than the men we had been killing that morning. Seventy yards, sixty – it was hard to get a clear line on his torso behind that shield as he darted about. I had to hit him with one shot. Fifty yards and then I saw him turn his body side on as he prepared to launch his *assegai*. As the spear left his fingers, he was square on to me and I was ready, gun aimed for the middle of his chest. I don't know where his *assegai* went, but I know my ball hit him exactly where I intended, sending him sprawling back, dead in the dirt.

"Well done," called Pieter. "I'll bet you cannot do that again."

"Watch me and you will see how a British soldier shoots," I replied, selecting another round ball and reloading. Shots were ringing out now all along the line of the laager and I doubt any of the Zulus got as far as the ditch. The second rank of Zulus was already advancing when I pushed the musket through the canvas again. I did not envy my man, who had just seen what had happened to his predecessor. This one ducked about even more but it did him no good, for sooner or later he would throw that spear and then I would have him. A minute later and my gun crashed out again. A second Zulu lay dead, almost on top of the first.

The third rank came forward. Their shouts of "*Bulala!*" were even more hesitant than the ones before as they surveyed the scene before them. As I lined up on my next target, I could see the poor devil's eyes fixed on the small pile of corpses in front of him. He must have doubted that he would live through the next minute. Just then, a horn rang out. Their general must have decided that this new tactic was simply executing his men rather than wasting our ammunition. The man in front of me darted away, his heart no doubt singing with relief.

Chapter 19

We waited for the rest of that afternoon and evening for them to try
something else. While Louisa slept once more, Pieter and I watched as
the Zulus milled about, their commanders unsure what to attempt next.
I began to hope that they would simply give up and go away, but there
was no sign of that happening. A group of twenty-five Boers mounted
up and rode out, attempting to drive the enemy further away but I
knew they could make little impression against such a vast force. The
warriors used cattle as shields as they hurled *assegais* whenever the
Dutch were close enough to shoot.

A hostile stalemate settled between us. We could not force
Dingane's men to withdraw but equally they could not breach our
defences – at least in daylight. As night fell, I became convinced that
they would try to attack again under the cover of darkness. I was not
alone in my concern. We tied lanterns to the big rawhide cattle whips,
which were lashed to wagons so that they illuminated the ditches and a
pathetically small patch of land beyond. The laager was soon
surrounded by a circle of lights, moving gently in the wind. By then,
cooking fires were burning in the Zulu camp and we could see bodies
darting about in front of them. They were slaughtering cattle too; we
could hear the bellow of the beasts as they were slain.

"We are more likely to hear them before we see them," I told Pieter.
I insisted that we slept on the ground under the wagon where it was
dark, therefore preserving our night vision and affording us a good
view through the thorn bushes. Despite my urging, the old couple next
door refused to leave their wagon. The man who had fought between
our vehicles was resting elsewhere. I watched our neighbour, clearly
illuminated as he sat by his lantern, squinting out into the night. If
Dickwa knew what he was about, he would ride in and pick off such
men with impunity.

Pieter and I took turns keeping watch. Louisa did a spell too,
refreshed from her earlier sleep. There were several false alarms as the
dogs picked up scents on the breeze and a couple of times a flurry of
shots was fired into the night. As the dawn light crept into the eastern
sky, revealing a low fog over the river, it was the Dutch who went on
the offensive. Another mounted patrol went out and when several
hundred Zulus chased them away, they ended up in front of one of our
cannon. The blast of the big gun must have killed or wounded at least
a dozen. We were back in our wagon by then, for the cry of *"Bulala!"*

160

was building once more from the Zulu camp, which was still hidden by the mist. I blew out the lantern as it would just guide the enemy towards us. We could see barely a hundred yards into the early morning gloom and I cursed the riders for not letting the Zulus sleep in peace.

"Here they come!" called out Pieter. I thrust my musket through the rip in the canvas and saw a line of sinister black shadows coming towards us through the haze. They had an almost ethereal glow to them.

"Will it be like before?" Louisa asked, standing beside me with my loaded shotgun ready in her hand.

"Yes, but don't worry, they won't get through." I gave her a reassuring hug. She smiled back but as she turned away, I saw her glance down at our ammunition pail. Yesterday Pieter and I had started with a bucketful each, but now, even with replenishments, our buckets were only half full. I was comforted somewhat by the fact that at least we had plenty of powder – four large flasks between us.

Once more I picked out my man. He almost stumbled over the corpses on the ground in front of him and I shot him as he launched his spear. I heard the *assegai* bounce harmlessly off the canvas as I reached to take the shotgun.

As I pushed the muzzle of the gun back out, I heard Pieter grunt in surprise. "They look like the imps of Satan," he murmured. Squinting down the barrels, I could see what he meant. It seemed a trick of the light, but there was a ghostly glow to the second line of warriors as they came on. The shotgun was loaded with *loopers* and so I would have to let my next mark get closer before I killed him, and, with luck, the ones on either side too, as this line was much thicker. I watched as they ran on full tilt towards us. They vaulted triumphantly over the corpses of the earlier lines and then, as one, their shields moved away as they prepared to throw their weapons. We gasped in alarm: their secret was now revealed. They had 'glowed' because nearly all the throwing spears they had hidden behind their shields had a tuft of burning grass tied to the end...

Like a scene from ancient times, the air was suddenly filled with flaming arrows, only now they did not land so harmlessly. I heard one thud into the canvas roof of our own wagon. Its point had pierced the cloth and I could see an orange glow beyond. I tried to push it back out, but the spear fell on its side, touching its flaming end to the roof and almost immediately the cloth started to burn.

161

"Pull it through!" shouted Pieter as he fired into the line that was now almost upon us. Grabbing the steel tip, I did as he suggested and threw the spear away, but the cloth was still smouldering about my head.

"Leave it to me," yelled Louisa. "Quick, they will soon break through." She was right. I pushed the muzzle back out, I saw several Zulus already in the ditch, one using a cord made from grass stems to try and pull free a thorn bush. I quickly gave them a barrelful of lead, which stopped that endeavour. Leaning briefly out of the end of the wagon, I fired the other barrel at several men in the ditch between us and the old couple. Our neighbour's canvas was already alight in two places and I could see more warriors coming towards us with the same unearthly glow. There was not a second to spare. As I reached for my musket, I felt water splash my face as Louisa used a pitcher to soak the canvas above our heads.

Half a dozen more warriors with flaming spears readied themselves to launch them towards us. One fell to my musket and I think Pieter got another. At least four spears flew through the air, one thudding into the wooden side of the cart and another high over the top. Two hit the canvas but one bounced harmlessly away. Louisa grabbed the point of the other and yanked on it, stamping out the flaming straw that fell about us.

"Careful," I warned, "there is spilt powder on the floor." As Louisa splashed more water about, I hurriedly reloaded the shotgun. The ditch was full of warriors once more and there were yells of agony as I blasted metal fragments into two points along it. As I swapped weapons, I heard a piercing scream from our left. Spinning round I saw the old lady staggering about in their cart with her clothes aflame. Her husband was desperately trying to beat them out with those calloused hands. I turned to look at Louisa and my fears were confirmed: there were dirty grey marks all down her clothes. "Take off your skirt," I ordered.

"What?" she gasped. Clearly this was not the moment for amorous intentions. Seeing I was deadly serious, she bent for one of the knives and was soon sawing at a tape that held the garment around her waist.

"It is covered in powder from all the reloading, just like the old lady's," I explained, already raising my musket and looking for a new target. The canvas cover of the old couple's wagon was now burning fiercely, revealing the occupants inside. They were still beating at the flames as more scraps of burning cloth fell about them.

"We must help them," urged Louisa.

"I will," I replied. A Zulu was running in close to their wagon with a clear target to aim at. I waited for him to slow his pace as he brought his throwing arm back and then I fired. He tumbled away, still holding his *assegai*. I poured another measure of powder down the barrel and dropped a ball after it. There was no time for the ramrod so I slammed the butt on the floor of the wagon to settle the contents of the barrel at its bottom and hoisted the gun once more. It had only taken a few seconds, but even that had been too long. When I looked up again the old man had lifted his still smouldering wife in his arms and was carrying her to the footboard to get her out of the wagon. Just at that moment, a spear flew by, and struck him deep between the shoulder blades. The couple sprawled back into the wagon among the flames. As their assailant shrieked in triumph, my next ball made sure it was the last sound he made.

Louisa was sobbing, but did not stop reloading. As I turned, catching a glimpse of her now in her petticoats, she handed me the shotgun and took the musket. Some Boers from elsewhere in the laager had run forward and were carrying the bodies of the old couple out of the wagon. The vehicle was now well ablaze. The cut thorn bush branches would catch light and burn as well and soon we would have a breach in our defences. The Zulus knew this and more came running in our direction, waiting for the flames to do their work. I fired the shotgun into the growing mass of the enemy and noticed that those who had rescued the couple were now doing the same. One was shouting something and gesticulating wildly, and I recognised the word 'cannon'. A gun crew trundled one of the big weapons over. It seemed that the battle was just about to reach its climax, when suddenly the familiar horn sounded and the Zulus began to withdraw once more.

"What the devil!" I exclaimed as I watched them running back. "Why are they retreating when they have just got a breach in our lines?"

"Those fiends will be up to something," gasped Pieter, "you can count on that." As he turned, I saw that he had a deep cut in his right arm that was bleeding badly.

"You're injured!" exclaimed Louisa and she bent down and tore a strip from her petticoat to make a bandage.

"One of them got me with a spear when I fired from the back of the wagon," he explained. Remarkably, he was still in good spirits. He had

163

another cut on his head and chuckled when I protested that he was trying to leave my wife naked as she supplied another dressing.

I still did not understand why the Zulus had pulled back. They would certainly have lost a lot of men rushing the breach in our lines, for we would have poured fire into them, yet there were thousands more of Dingane's men than us, so I knew that ultimately they would have been bound to get many of them through. Now, though, their opportunity was lost.

With no spears to worry about, Dutch men laden with pails of water extinguished the flames in the neighbouring wagon. We all got down to help. The old man was dead and his wife, severely burned, looked like she would not be far behind him. They were both taken back to the central circle where others were being treated for wounds. At least half of the defenders were now sporting bandages. As Louisa rummaged among the trunk of clothes she had been given for another skirt, I went to see if there was more ammunition: we were now perilously low. One more sustained attack and we would be reduced to throwing their spears back at them. But to my alarm, there was not a spare musket ball to be had. I even found one Boer with an armful of twenty *assegais* he had gathered as a last resort.

Things were desperate and the Zulus were showing no sign of retreating. Indeed, a call went out to warn us that they were spreading out for an attack once more. As Louisa and I were about to climb back into the wagon, she threw her arms about me and clung tightly. She did not need to ask about our chances, for she could see our fate as well as I. There was no need for words, for we knew each other so well. It was like a final act of communion. I think we both felt sure that we would die together on that cart.

"They might run away again..." I started, feeling almost obliged to give her some comfort, but she put a finger to my lips.

"I don't want your last words to me to be a silly lie," she whispered. "Tell me that you love me."

So I did and we embraced again. I will admit there were tears on both our cheeks as we climbed once more into that wretched wagon. Pieter was already there, flexing his injured arm and counting the *loopers* he had left. "They are not hiding their burning spears this time," he announced, gesturing out beyond the laager. I looked and saw a long line of warriors, spreading halfway around the circle of wagons, holding their blazing spears aloft. A horn sounded and I took a final glance at Louisa. She smiled back in a radiant way that made

164

my heart sing. Then I turned back to the enemy, cocking my musket as I did so.

"What are they doing?" asked Pieter, puzzled.

Instead of running towards us, the line of warriors remained where they were, their flaming spears lowered. Then I saw the first wisps of smoke rising in front of them. "The bastards, they are going to burn us out!" Damn, it all made sense now. Their general must have seen how easily our wagons had burned and decided to let wind and fire do his work for him. Already the first flickers of flame had reached the long dry grass. Further along the line, the smoke was drifting slowly in our direction.

"We must make a..." Pieter then said a word in Dutch I did not understand.

"What?" I asked, puzzled.

"We must burn the grass near the wagons ourselves and then put the flames out before they get out of control. Then there will be nothing left to burn when their flames reach us."

"He means make a fire break," explained Louisa.

"But that means going outside the laager," I protested. I did not like the idea of a swarm of Zulus coming out of the smoke when we were scattered beyond our defences, but the line of Zulus had already disappeared behind a growing blaze.

"We have no choice," urged Pieter. "Come on." With that he jumped down and shouted instructions in Dutch to the men about us. In no time one of the thorn bushes had been pulled out of the way and Boers were streaming over the corpse-filled ditch. I tore Louisa's discarded skirt into strips and tied them around the end of two spears I pulled from the side of our cart. They burned fiercely when lit and so, carrying our torches, we followed the others out.

I soon handed over my torch to Pieter; for every person lighting the flames we needed at least two people beating them out. Otherwise we would have done the Zulus' work for them and burned down our own camp. Some went ten paces out and lit more fires and then left them. The rest of us started smaller fires along the edge of the ditch, stamping them out as soon as the grass was black. Abandoned Zulu shields proved to be particularly effective at beating out the flames. A few of the wounded warriors still lying in our defensive trench cried out and wailed, perhaps they thought we were planning to burn them to death. One even managed to get up onto his hands and knees, his face and chest covered in blood as he waved his *iklwa* and shouted something in his tongue. It did him no good; someone shot him back down again for his trouble. The smoke was getting thick by then, carried on the wind from both the Zulu fires and our own. Our eyes were stinging and our throats raw, yet there were others who were suffering more.

The long grass that the Zulus were burning was still strewn with the bodies of their own comrades. Many were only wounded, not dead, and those poor devils screamed as the flames got closer. Most lay opposite where the cannon had been placed and some now emerged through the smoke, crawling or limping for their lives. They were shown little mercy, though, for we were still working desperately to save ourselves. A few guns fired but with ammunition so low, the Boers used knives and even spears to dispatch them. One of the Zulus came staggering out of the smoke near me. He had a stomach wound and held his guts in with one blood-soaked arm. He was yelling something as he staggered over the line of fire that Pieter had just finished lighting. The Dutchman simply turned and plunged the point of the burning spear into the side of the man's chest. As the Zulu sank down to his knees his blood flowed down the shaft of the torch to put out the flames. All life was extinguished in him too, for he then pitched forward, dead, into the already smouldering grass.

Louisa and I eventually found ourselves down on our hands and knees where the smoke was thinner. By then we both had Zulu shields and were frantically using them to press out the flames as soon as the ground was blackened and burnt. The heat was incredibly intense and I could barely see a yard or two ahead of me due to the thick fumes. It was relentless work; you would beat out the flames in one patch and turn to deal with another, only to find that the first had started to smoulder again. It took only a moment for the wind to whip up a ripple of orange fire or carry a burning piece of grass that could start a fresh conflagration. We worked together, but always with one ready eye on the space between us and the ditch to ensure we were not cut off.

Above the roar of the fire, we could hear the Zulus singing and it was getting closer. They must have been following their own line of the blaze and delighting in the destruction they believed it was causing. Soon we could see the orange glow of their flames coming towards us through the smoke. There was now a broad blackened strip in front of them: I just hoped it would be enough. As I beat out a final wisp of smoke, I felt a hand on my shoulder.

"Come on," shouted a man, gesturing for us to get up. He had a neckerchief over his mouth, but I recognised Pieter's now soot-stained face. "We have done all we can. If it works, we have a chance." He led the way to the gap in our defences but even back inside the laager the smoke was still thick. There was also now a strong smell of roasting meat in the air as the flames cooked the bodies left in the grass. As the last of the Boers returned, the thorn bushes were pushed back into place. We climbed back into our wagon to await events. The old couple's vehicle had been turned on its side while we had been gone. Someone had built a fire step behind it from planks and barrels for men to fight from. The Zulus knew that they had created a breach here. They would consider it our weak spot if they attacked again. Well they would be in for a shock if they did. A loaded cannon – the one that stayed upright on its wheels – waited for them next to the upturned wagon.

We coughed and spluttered and squinted into the smoke for the next half an hour. The canvas side gave some protection from the heat, although the cloth got so hot that we had to splash it with water to stop it from burning too. The flames from the Zulu fires were now as tall as a man, like a fiery army marching towards us. It seemed almost impossible that a black strip of earth just ten paces wide would stop it. Occasionally, through gaps in the smoke, I would spot little patches of unburnt ground in our firebreak strip that we had missed. Would that be enough to carry the fire on?

By the time the Zulu fires reached the scorched ground we could barely see or breathe. All around us people were coughing and gasping. But then someone managed to croak that the flames were diminishing. I did not believe it at first but, gradually, gaps began to appear in the flickering orange ranks. A few tendrils made inroads into the blackened strip but they were soon starved of fuel. There was now more danger from the wind blowing embers of grass against wagons or over them into the ground beyond, but we could quickly extinguish them as soon as they settled. Slowly the smoke began to thin out so that we could see the outline of the men beyond. The Zulus would have been watching us too. Instead of a cluster of blazing wagons, they saw a defensive line that had now stood firm for a day and a half.

The Boer in charge decided to show them that we were still resolute in our defence. He ordered the cannon to fire a solid shot right into the thickest part of the enemy line, which was now almost opposite where we were standing. The gun crashed out and I remember seeing the

167

smoke twist where the ball passed. We could not see its impact, but we heard the screams it caused and knew it must have done terrible damage amongst the crowded men. We did not know it then, but later we learned that it killed one of their generals.

Dingane's army had been fighting us since the morning of the previous day and had lost well over a thousand men, perhaps two or three times that number. They had just listened to the screams of their wounded as they were burnt to death and stepped around their charred corpses. They had expected the flames to bring about our ruin, which would have justified this sacrifice. Instead, they found the laager almost as strong as it had been at the start. They were not to know that we were now measuring ammunition by the cup instead of the bucket. They may have guessed that we were tired and exhausted from two days of vigilance and fighting, but their men must have been fatigued too. Yet for all their effort, they had nothing to show for it. The Boers in the circle of wagons appeared to be just as untouchable as when the impis had first arrived.

They had tried all they could think of to beat us and had been defeated at every turn. It must have looked like there was little point in continuing the same failed tactics. As we watched, slowly the band of warriors began to disappear with the smoke.

Chapter 20

It took several hours for us to realise that our peril was over. The Zulus still milled around, and for good reason. Whoever was in charge did not relish telling Dingane that his army had failed in its mission. To soothe the temper of their monarch, they resolved to return with every head of cattle and sheep they could find. A mounted patrol of Boers rode out to try and save some of the beasts, but they were hopelessly outnumbered by Zulus.

Many, including me, were convinced that the withdrawal might be a trick to get us to lower our guard. That night lanterns were lit around the laager once more and tired men searched the darkness with reddened eyes for any sign of their return. A dawn patrol brought the news that the Zulu army continued to retreat. It was now moving its herds north ten miles away. Only then did I begin to relax.

The ordeal had hit Louisa hard. She had been weak before it started and must have used every last ounce of her strength to stand at my side for so long. As soon as she knew we were safe, she slept for a whole day, barely taking any of the food and drink I brought her. After two days and nights of hardly any sleep I was exhausted too. How others found the strength to start to clear the battlefield of corpses was beyond me. The land to the west of the laager looked like a scene from hell, with blackened and twisted bodies visible for several hundred yards. More of their dead had been left where they had camped, while the ditch around the wagons was full of their corpses. That first night after the Zulus left, we could still hear the occasional wail of a wounded man, either in the ditch or beyond. None of us had the strength or inclination to investigate. By dawn, however, the wailing had stopped and we were woken by the growl of wild dogs fighting over the bodies and countering barks from the Boers' own hounds. Vultures too were eating their fill.

The next day men from Maritz's laager arrived to offer their help. While graves were dug and a funeral held for the few dead we had suffered, Boers with ropes and horses started to drag the Zulu bodies to a small ravine. Several days later and the job was still only half done, while the stench of decay was nearly unbearable. Some thought that the putrefaction in the ravine would infect our water supply. A decision was made to move the laager closer to Maritz's. With nearly all of the Gatsrand cattle driven off by the Zulus, the Dutch leader leant some of his own beasts to pull our wagons towards his camp. I

169

paid little attention to all of this, for Louisa was not getting much better. She had relapsed into a fever and had barely been out of bed since the attack had ended. The camp doctor visited and prescribed complete rest, although as he had long since run out of any medicines, he had nothing else to offer anyway. One of the women gave me a flask of a strong beef broth and I would do my best to ensure that Louisa drank at least a cupful every day.

It took us nearly a week to travel the thirty odd miles to Maritz's camp. The cattle were not quick, and often we had to carry Louisa on a stretcher to avoid her being bounced around as the cart rolled up and down rocky gullies. By the time we arrived she was well enough to sit up in a chair and was eating meat again, yet she was still very weak. It was September by then. The rivers were dropping and the mud in the passes was drying up. This was when I had expected us to be travelling south over the mountains back to the colony and Cape Town. Now that arduous journey was out of the question until Louisa was much stronger. What we really needed was a ship to carry us away in comfort. When we reached his camp, I was frustrated to find that Maritz had already left to visit Port Natal as such a vessel had just docked. It was called the *Mary* and carried fresh supplies, including powder and ammunition, which would enable the Boers to resist any future attack by Dingane.

The Dutch leader had already been gone a week. It was another sixty miles to the coast and over rough terrain. I did not dare rush Louisa on another journey before she had recovered from the first. I persuaded Pieter to ride to the coast for me and offer the captain whatever it took to stay in port to wait for us. I told him I could pay as soon as we reached Cape Town; D'Urban would have seen to that. We waited in Maritz's camp to give Louisa a chance to rest for the journey, but my plans were thwarted. Three days after he set off, Pieter was back with the news I had feared most. By the time he had reached Port Natal the harbour was empty: the *Mary* had already sailed.

A wagon train piled high with all sorts of supplies came in over the next week or so. There were medicines now, although Louisa was gaining strength without need of them. Some wagons had barrels full of powder and others were loaded with musket balls. People began to feel more secure again. They soon looked better, too; until then, some had been dressed in little more than rags or garments that appeared to be made up solely of patches. Now bolts of cloth and donated clothes were distributed, which greatly improved morale in the camp. As people preened about in their new finery and Reverend Smit insisted on more prayers for our deliverance, thoughts once again began to turn to building a future in this new land.

As well as supplies, the wagoneers carried news brought to them by the crew of the *Mary*. The Boers back in the colony had heard of the treacherous murder of Retief's party and the massacre of children when the wagons had been scattered. They had also learned of the successful defence of the laagers that had stopped the massacre spreading. Passions were inflamed and many were planning on coming over the mountains to join the Boers in Natal. These supporters had also paid for the *Mary's* cargo. They had been forced to move quickly as Napier, the new British governor, was determined to stop any further exodus from his colony. He had tried to seize the *Mary* and her cargo to stop it reaching Port Natal. Without means to defend themselves, he thought the settlers would be forced to return. The new governor had been furious to learn that the Boers had declared their part of Natal independent. He insisted that they were still British citizens and subject to British law. Napier had vowed to do everything he could to prevent the Boers from succeeding in their venture.

We were warned that a man called Joubert was coming, who would try to persuade all the African servants to return to the colony. The apprenticeship of these former slaves would soon come to an end, leaving them free to choose their own futures. While many had been killed in the massacre, around a hundred were left. Napier was determined to ensure that these people would get their full freedom, even if they had been taken out of British territory. The servants would be required to sign a paper in front of Joubert to confirm that they wanted to stay in Natal, otherwise he would take them back to the colony.

Maritz arrived back in his laager the same week that Louisa started to walk again. I was shocked to discover that he was far closer to death than she was. When they carried him out of the wagon on a stretcher, I could see that his body was grotesquely swollen. He had dropsy, a grim disease, and it was clear to all that he would not be with us for much longer. We all took time to pay him our last respects while we still could. I remember that when Louisa and I stood in front of him, his eyes still glittered with amusement under the swollen lids.

"You were at Gatsrand, weren't you?" he asked. Without waiting for a reply he continued, "You are riding your luck hard, *mijnheer* Flashman. You should take that woman home."

171

"Without you, my friend, I might never have found her again," I told him. "Trust me, I am trying my hardest to do exactly that."

He died four days later. He was only in his early forties, although you would never have guessed it if you had seen him at the end. The Boer community reeled about rudderless. They had lost four leaders in under a year: Potgieter had returned to the colony accused of cowardice, while Uys, Retief and now Maritz were dead. After the funeral it was decided that they would rename the place the laager stood on as Pietermaritzburg.

As the Dutch discussed who their new leader should be, I heard for the first time the name Pretorius, who was on his way over the mountains. His backers indicated that he was a religious firebrand who would knock the Zulus into the middle of next week. Certainly, the severe Reverend Smit was a keen supporter, which almost certainly meant we would not get on. He sounded like the kind of zealot who insisted on a cold bath each morning and put more faith in prayer than musket drill. Well good luck to him in that case, for Johnny Zulu would make no allowance for piety, especially with Dingane giving the orders. They could have chosen the Archbishop of Canterbury for all I cared, as I was not staying. As soon as Louisa was well enough to travel, we were going to Port Natal. There had to be another ship soon. When it appeared, we would be sticking to it like a treacle-coated barnacle until it reached Cape Town.

It was well into October before I laid eyes on that familiar bay again. The sparkling sea was disappointingly empty, although the settlement on the shore was recovering since I had last been there. A handful of houses had been rebuilt and at least a dozen Zulu round huts too. Louisa had been looking forward to meeting young William, having heard plenty about my time in Umgungundlovu, but we discovered he had already left with his mother. They had finally given up hope of the Woods brothers surviving the battle and had taken a long and arduous route down the coast back to the colony. Ogle was still there, though, and I was pleased to see Alexander Biggar too. Once more he offered to put us up in his now repaired house. He warned us that with the governor trying to block supplies reaching the Boers, it might be a while before another ship arrived.

Despite his own grief, Alexander Biggar was a tower of strength in those days. His store was now well stocked again thanks to the *Mary*. I had been worried about another visit from Dingane's men. With no ship to retreat to we would not have stood a chance of survival, but he

172

reassured me that there was no cause for alarm. Around fifty of Umfazi's old warriors had returned and they now looked on Biggar as their chief. Some farmed small plots of land while others would patrol the hills, hunting for the pot and ensuring no enemies approached. When they came across other Zulus, they would try to gather intelligence on what was happening in Dingane's territory. We heard from several sources that the king had dismissed his soldiers and allowed them to go back to their families and villages until they were needed again. That made sense, for he could not keep them standing indefinitely.

"We will hear if they come our way," claimed Alexander confidently. "But there is damn all left for them to destroy now."

"But what if they *do* come?" I insisted. "Hell, if Dingane hears I am here then he may want to settle the score. I injured his son and stole from him. If your Zulus are getting information from his people, perhaps they are giving information on who is here in return."

Alexander grinned. "They would not betray you. I would trust them with my life. But if you are still worried, come with me." He led us down to the shore. There, at the top of the beach, was a mound covered in sail cloth. He pulled the canvas back to reveal a small jolly boat, big enough for at least six people. "I bought it from the *Mary*, he explained. I use it for fishing most of the time but if we need to, we can row out into the bay and stay out of reach of any attacker."

It was barely bigger than a craft you would find on a boating lake, but it soothed my fears. I felt far more comfortable staying with Alexander knowing it was there. He and I took to going out in it fishing in the evenings when the day was cooler and he was sure that the fish were more likely to bite. I remember one time trying to persuade him to join us when we eventually departed. "There is nothing left for you here," I cajoled. "All this place has is bad memories. Even if you build it again, Dingane could come back and burn it down. You would do better to come with us on the next ship. When we get to Cape Town, I can speak to D'Urban to get you a position there. Or come back to England with us. Do you still have people in the old country?"

He stared wistfully back at the shore. For a moment I thought he was considering the proposal, but then he shook his head. "You can only say such a thing because you have your Louisa back." He held up a hand to forestall my protest. "I know you mean well, and I am

173

delighted that you are reunited. But out there," he pointed to the shore, "what's left of my two boys lies in the dirt."

"But I was prepared to leave here when I thought Louisa was dead. You know that. You were with me on the deck of the *Comet*."

"Aye, but I know why you marched with the Army of Natal too." He gave a heavy sigh. "If I had come with you and stood alongside my Rob, at least I would be at peace now." He was silent for a moment and then continued, "If I left now I would go insane, knowing that devil is still on his throne. I lie awake sometimes and imagine killing him. Not quickly – he does not deserve that. A slow tortured death where he has time to beg forgiveness for every single person he has killed. My boys, Umfazi's people, those children you told me about in the Boer camps, even the hundreds of his own people that the reverend described being dragged up that hill near his palace. I want him to scream in agony for them all."

His voice had dropped to little more than a whisper. As he poured out his feelings, he sounded more than a little mad in his grief, and yet I understood him. In the past I had imagined the death of the tyrant myself. I too had wanted to avenge Louisa and had taken appalling risks to do so. "My African lads are the same," he continued, pointing at the cluster of Zulu huts that had been rebuilt on the edge of town. "Most of them have lost everything, including wives and children. Some have seen their whole villages destroyed. We will all keep fighting until that cold-hearted bastard is dead."

October turned into November and the weather got steadily hotter. Each morning I would walk to the top of a nearby hill and squint into the eastern sky to check the sea horizon. Each day it remained disappointingly empty. The days were getting easier, though, for little by little Louisa was getting stronger. There was plentiful meat and vegetables and using a cane, she would walk a few yards further each day. By the end of the month, if I went at a slower pace, she would join me on my ascent up the hillside.

While she recuperated, things were happening elsewhere. Joubert visited the newly named Pietermaritzburg and left with half of the apprentices, the rest electing to stay. Yet this drop in the population was more than replaced by Boers coming over the mountains, including their new leader Pretorius. This fresh commander wasted no time in sending out proclamations calling for every Christian soul to join him in a march to crush their heathen enemies. He made it sound like a crusade, though he had some damn strange ideas on how to run an army. To my dismay, Biggar was thinking of joining and taking his Zulu warriors with him.

"You must be mad," I protested, waving the latest dispatch we had received from him. "He has never even seen a Zulu before, never mind fought one. He probably thinks he can destroy them by calling down fire and brimstone from his travelling pulpit. It says here he demands an oath of obedience and a vow to build a church if they are successful. The fool is even planning twice daily prayer meetings. He will be more concerned about the number of Bibles in his army than guns and ammunition. It's nonsense," I declared, dropping the paper on the table. "All this rushed talk about teaching the Zulu a lesson and avenging those massacred. Well, we have heard that before from Uys and even your Rob. We know how that ends, although this army might die on its knees if ambushed while they are still communing with the Almighty."

Biggar laughed, "I'll own he has some strange ideas," he admitted. "But the last Boer force was defeated because it had a divided command, so he is making sure that will not happen to him. And from what I hear, not all his ideas come from the Bible. He has brought a new cannon with him so that they now have three. He may not have fought the Zulu, but he has learned from those that have. He is taking a load of wagons with him and they will laager the carts like a mobile fort when the enemy is near. You know better than I how well that works."

That, I had to concede, did sound like a sensible strategy, as long as they were not caught unawares. The country was ideal for ambushes and if they were cut off from water in the hot summer they would not last long. Alexander was sure that his Zulus and other scouts would spot the enemy's approach, giving them time to build a good defensive position. I just had to hope for his sake that he was right. Yet it was only as he mentioned that his Zulus were going with him, that I realised that Louisa and I would be left virtually alone on this hostile shore.

"But what about us?" I protested. "With you and your warriors gone, we will be defenceless if Dingane sends some warriors here."

"You will be safe," insisted Biggar. "Dingane will gather his army and march it against the Dutch when he hears what is happening. There is no cause for him to come here. Anyway, Ogle is staying and a handful of the older Zulus and the women. They will look after you." There was a fire in his eyes now as he anticipated the opportunity to fight his nemesis again. I knew there was no point in trying to dissuade him. He was right that we would be safer in Port Natal than with the Boers. This new Boer force would probably be facing odds of twenty to one and I did not fancy their chances. Once Dingane had beaten this new enemy, he would undoubtedly turn his attention to the remaining Boer laagers, which by then would only contain women and children. He would want to rid himself of the Dutch threat to his territory once and for all. Perhaps after that, he would look again at the last remaining white men clinging on at the edge of his kingdom. I prayed fervently that we would be long gone by then.

"But what do we do if another ship does not come?" I pressed.

"They are bound to come sooner or later. Ogle has more ivory to sell for a start." He grinned, "At least now if Dingane does come, you will all be able to fit comfortably in the boat."

That was little comfort. I did not trust Ogle any more than a bankrupt cracksman. If his ivory was at risk, he would probably make off in the boat with it and leave us ashore. I resolved to go heeled with a pistol in future. Yet it still felt safer than joining Biggar. This Pretorius sounded like he would be as much use in battle as Reverend Owen.

It seemed, however, that the new Dutch leader was a capable organiser. Over the next couple of weeks he amassed a force of four hundred and sixty men. They were joined by sixty servants and around a thousand oxen and horses to pull fifty-four wagons and ride patrols around them. It was a formidable venture, but I knew it would still be hugely outnumbered by Dingane's forces. It also left the remaining Boer camps virtually defenceless. If Pretorius failed, all would be lost. Yet with regular prayer meetings communing with his 'higher command', this young man was not wasting time. They had to make the most of the summer months before the rivers became impassable again.

Biggar set off with his warriors at the end of November. Before he left, we held a farewell feast for him. It was a strange affair, with forced *bonhomie* that sometimes faltered and left us staring awkwardly at each other. I was sure that I would never see him again and I think that he felt the same. The odd thing was he seemed resigned to it. He was content to fight his enemy once more and if he failed, he was sure his sons would be waiting for him.

We watched them set off the next morning, his band of warriors looked indistinguishable to me from the enemy that they would be fighting. Some of the remaining Zulu women and children disappeared off into the bush later that day. They clearly did not fancy their chances of surviving here if things went wrong. I did not blame them. Port Natal had never been an impressive settlement. I doubted Ben D'Urban would have been pleased with it had he seen it when we first arrived. He would certainly be appalled to have the place as his namesake now. Half of the main street was still a burned-out ruin and just a handful of habitable buildings remained. There was only one made from stone; the rest were constructed from salvaged timber and new green wood that was now shrinking in the heat. Come the rains, most of the roofs would leak like sieves. Apart from Louisa and I, there were only four other white people, with Ogle the unofficial leader now that Alexander had gone. That first evening I noticed that he had taken the boat out into the bay as if to fish. It was more likely that he was staking his ownership of the craft, making it clear that he would decide who got a berth if its use became necessary.

Ogle was a cunning weasel of a man, vicious, too – I could never forget him torturing that Zulu chief over the fire. His weakness was greed. Most of the others in town were his cronies and while they would expect a seat, I was sure I could bribe our way to a pair of berths in that precious boat if necessary. He knew we were friends with the governor and while most of our belongings had now long gone, he would remember the piles of luggage we arrived with. I am not above toadying to some villain when it serves my purposes. I prepared to start greasing the way for our escape if required. Fortunately, I had not even begun when it proved unnecessary, for at long last a new sail appeared on the horizon.

Chapter 21

It was a big ship and Ogle swore that he did not recognise it. "That is no coastal trader," he declared. "It has not been here before. I reckon it is Portuguese, perhaps putting in here on its way to their settlement up the coast." The Portuguese town of Lourenço Marques was around four hundred miles north, well beyond Zulu territory. I knew of it as some of the Boers had visited the place, but the journey had been so arduous that many had died on the way.

Whoever commanded the ship knew about the sandbar outside the bay. They understood that a vessel that size would need to wait for high tide to get into the anchorage. We sat for most of the morning squinting into the sun, trying to make out the colours of its flag, which flapped briefly from behind a staysail. Ogle was sure he could see the red and green of Portugal, while a young African boy insisted that he could see the British flag. I did not care either way; I sat there holding Louisa's hand with a ridiculous grin spread across my face. Whoever it was, they were sure to give us passage and wherever they were bound, it was almost certain to be better than here. With luck they would take us to a British port and from there we could start our journey home.

By noon, the tide was high enough for the ship to edge its way into the bay, I could just make out a man in the bow chains dropping a lead to measure the depth. A mainsail obscured the flag, but then as the ship reached the centre of the bay, we heard the rattle of the anchor chain and the vessel slowly swung on its new mooring. There, resplendent in the early afternoon sun were the British colours. I remember Louisa laughing with delight beside me: we were on our way home for certain. Then things got even better. Side on to the vessel we could see a lot of people on deck, far more than a normal crew. Unless my eyes were deceiving me, many of them were wearing red coats. I hardly dared believe that they were soldiers, for it would mean we were absolutely safe now. As they began to climb down into the boats, there was no doubt about it. "They are wearing kilts," I announced unnecessarily as we could all see the fact for ourselves. "They must be a regiment of Highlanders."

"But what are they doing here?" asked Louisa. "Do you think Ben has sent them to find us?"

"He has taken his sweet time if he has!" I exclaimed. "There seems to be just a single company of men, perhaps eighty of them. That is too few to fight anyone, but more than you would need to escort us back to the ship." We would not have long to find out as their commander was already pulling towards us in the lead boat. He stood in the stern staring over the heads of the oarsmen towards us waiting near the jetty. Not one of us was armed, but he evidently thought five men and a woman standing on the shore necessitated the unfurling of colours. Soon a large Union Jack was flapping from a flagstaff in the boat, as if there was any doubt as to the identity of the kilted men in red jackets.

"Welcome to the town of Port Natal," I called out as they came within earshot. "Or D'Urban as it has now been named," I continued. All I got for my courteous greeting was a grim glare from the man, whose uniform showed that he was a major. From his expression you would have thought I had just goosed his mother.

"Stand aside!" he roared back, as though the six of us were likely to resist the arrival of the thirty soldiers in the longboat. "I intend to land," he added pompously.

"And there was me thinking he was just taking a ha'penny tour around the bay," chuckled Ogle. We all duly stepped back. The man was clearly full of his own importance, but as I needed him to give us passage, it would not do to antagonise him before he had even stepped ashore. The bow of the boat dug into the sand and the first of the soldiers jumped over the side. Their officer nearly stumbled as he ran down the thwarts of the boat to join them, snatching up the flag on the way. Splashing down onto the wet sand, he advanced halfway towards us, holding the staff in front of him as though it would frighten us away. The rest of his men tumbled out behind him and I groaned as I saw their piper begin to inflate his instrument. The peaceful morning was about to be ruined by that awful racket. Then, like Captain Cook claiming Australia, the officer plunged the pole into the dirt and began to shout "I claim this land…" He got no further before his voice was drowned out by that rising drone of a set of pipes beginning to play. Irritably, he turned on the miscreant with the instrument and barked, "Stop that damned noise!" I felt a moment of affinity with the major before he turned and glared at us again, before declaring loudly, "I claim this land for Her Majesty the Queen."

It would have been more impressive if the flag had stayed upright. Instead he struck rock two inches down and the thing began to topple. He was forced to grab the staff again as he hissed at his sergeant, "Fraser, get some rocks to prop this up." His sergeant dutifully rushed forward to pile some rocks about its base as did several of the other men.

"Well, now we have that out of the way," I said in a voice dripping with sarcasm as the flag was finally freestanding, "perhaps I could ask you for a passage back to Cape Town in that ship."

"Never mind that," interrupted Louisa, "Who is this queen you are claiming the land for? What has happened to King Billy?"

I did not think it possible, but the officer managed to draw himself up even more as he glared down his nose at us. "His Majesty King William died in June last year. He has been succeeded by his niece, Her Majesty Queen Victoria." His lip curled in contempt as he added, "I take it you are Boers to treat our monarchs with such disrespect."

"Do I sound Dutch?" I retorted in my crispest English accent. "My wife and I were asked to visit here by the previous British governor and have since faced all manner of trials. Until now we have been unable to leave, but I am sure the current governor would be obliged if you would give us passage."

"We have also met King Billy on a number of occasions," added Louisa, grinning. She was clearly enjoying bringing this ass down a peg or two as she continued, "Unlike you, he was very keen on informality."

"But the governor has been informed that the Boers have claimed this land for themselves," the major protested. He was staring about, as though he expected a horde of angry Dutchmen to appear and try to tear down his colours

"They have," I confirmed, "But that does not matter a damn. Nor will you claiming it for our new queen make a jot of difference. Is that what you have come for, to claim this territory back for the governor?

"Partly," the officer admitted, but then he added something that left us all dumbfounded. "My orders are also to protect the Zulu from Boer aggression."

We stood and gaped at him in astonishment. My mind could barely believe what my ears had just heard. "But… but what kind of half-witted, poxed imbecile could possibly think that the Zulus need protecting? Or that a single company of British infantry would be sufficient if they did?"

The major looked furious at the criticism. "Civilians cannot be expected to understand military matters or affairs of state. My orders come directly from the governor and are in accordance with the wishes of Her Majesty's colonial office in London." He gestured at the men behind him and those still rowing ashore, "We might be few, but the governor does not believe that the Boers would dare fire on British soldiers. We will give them a hot reception if they do."

Ogle laughed in scorn. "You bloody fool," he scoffed. "It is not the Boers you need to worry about. The Zulus don't need your protection – they will slaughter you for breakfast."

"My men are from the 72nd Highlanders," the major retorted indignantly. "One of the finest regiments in the British army. You have clearly never seen the Highlanders charge their enemy, sir."

Ogle looked set to yell more insults, but I held out a hand to stay him. At this rate we would be left on the beach out of spite when the ship sailed away. Speaking quietly to calm the situation, I tried to put the young fool in his place, "As it happens, I do know a *little* about military affairs myself. I have also seen the Highlanders charge their enemy. In fact, I had the honour to command a company of the 74th Highlanders while serving in India with the Duke of Wellington."

The major's eyes narrowed in suspicion, "What is your name, sir?"

"Flashman, Major Thomas Flashman." I noticed the sergeant look up at that. I continued, "I also served with the duke in Portugal, Spain and at Waterloo."

"Mmm," muttered the major, looking unconvinced. "This all sounds very convenient. From what I have heard, if all the men who claimed to be at Waterloo were actually there, you would have beaten the French by noon."

"How dare you…" I began and I could sense Louisa bridling beside me. This jackanapes had just suggested to my face that I was a liar. I was damned if I would duel the villain over the insult, though, and I was just trying to work out what I could do, when the sergeant stepped forward.

"With respect, sir," he tugged on his officer's sleeve, "but I think I have heard of an officer called Flashman serving in the 74th."

"Are you sure, Fraser?" The major still looked dubious.

"Yes sir," persisted the soldier. "It is an unusual name and this officer had quite a reputation." I felt myself grow an inch taller. It was immensely gratifying to be remembered in this manner after over thirty years. Yet it was nothing less than I deserved, for I had – albeit inadvertently – saved the regiment when I had managed to open the rear gate of the fortress at Gawilghur.

"A reputation?" repeated the major as I beamed in satisfaction.

181

"Yes sir. My first sergeant served with him in the 74th." Fraser glared at me and then continued in a scandalised tone, "He told how this officer once forced the entire regiment to *bathe* in a river."

"Really?" There was a hint of interest now in the major's voice. His nose twitched in distaste, perhaps at the proximity of his sergeant, who must have smelt ripe after days in the close confines of a ship in the summer heat. He gave me a reappraising look and then could not help but glance back at the calm sea behind him. It was obvious what he was thinking and several of his command were already looking alarmed.

"It gets worse, sir," Fraser continued. Pointing an accusing finger, he added, "This officer burned the regimental pipes." There was an audible gasp of horror from the nearby piper, who suddenly clutched his instrument to his bosom as though it were a babe and he was in the presence of Herod.

"Is that it?" I demanded, furious that these were the episodes that had passed into regimental legend. "What about me saving the regiment at Gawilghur, or warning them of the charge of the Rajputs?"

"Or the Persian commander you killed in single combat," added Louisa. "You still have his sword at home."

"Er, yes that too," I agreed hesitantly, for I had not been entirely honest with Louisa about how I had beaten the Persian. "What is the name of this fellow with a very jaundiced memory of my service?" I demanded.

"Sergeant McTavish, sir."

"Well I have never heard of the villain," I insisted. "He has probably made it all up and was not even there."

"Oh, but he was, sir," Insisted Fraser. "He was attacked by a crocodile when you made them bathe. He wore a tooth from the beast around his neck, I have seen it myself."

"Wee Jock!" I gasped in surprise. My mind filled with the memory of the scrawny young drummer boy trying to drag his 'big lizard' out of the water.

"Yes, I remember him," added Louisa, "such a sweet child." Fraser frowned, puzzled, clearly struggling to equate the man he remembered with that description.

There was no point denying things now. "So Jock made it to sergeant," I confirmed. "Is he still alive?"

"No sir," replied Fraser. "He died five years back of fever, but he held you in high regard," the man finally conceded.

182

"I apologise, sir," the major drew himself up to attention. "Please forgive my bad manners, it was inexcusable to doubt you." He held out his hand, "I am Major Charters."

I grudgingly took the proffered paw, "Well if you arrange passage for my wife and I on that ship, we will say no more about it."

"That is very generous of you, sir," replied a chastened Charters. "Would you mind if I ask, were you also at Assaye, sir?"

"Yes, I was at Assaye," I admitted. That day was the most famous of the regiment's battle honours and one Wellington considered his finest victory: a beleaguered line of redcoats advancing into the maw of fifty cannon and then routing an army several times their size. There was no need to tell him that I had watched most of the action from a rooftop in the village behind the Mahratta lines.

Having established my military experience, I gestured up the beach, "Perhaps, Major, we could have a word in private?" We strolled a few yards along the sand while Louisa stayed back with the others. "What exactly are your orders?" I asked.

"I have a proclamation signed by the governor to claim this town and surrounding land for the Queen. I am also to remind the Boers that they are still seen as British citizens and subject to British law. As you are a friend of the former governor, you will recall that the colonial office forced him to give back land he had taken from the Xhosa. Now London is concerned that the Boers are seizing land from another African kingdom, with no justification other than force of arms."

"And London wants the Boers to move back into the colony, to help build its prosperity and pay taxes to the Crown?" I suggested.

"You surely do not support the brutal suppression of the native people, sir?" queried Charters. "It is our duty to protect them from Boer aggression." We had reached the top of the beach now and the major caught sight of some of the older Zulus moving in their huts on the other side of the settlement. "I say, do you think one of those men could carry a message to the Zulu capital to let them know that we are here to aid them?"

I shook my head in despair at his ignorance before replying. "I have met Dingane, the Zulu king. He might be a treacherous tyrant, but he is no fool. He knows damn well that once white farmers get a foothold on his rich, fertile kingdom, they will want more of it. He does not want any whites in his kingdom at all. That is why he slaughtered Retief and his followers"

"But surely he has heard that the British government tries to deal fairly with African kingdoms," Charters queried. "He cannot equate us with these rapacious farmers."

"Earlier this year, the British settlers here led an army of over a thousand men against Dingane in a combined attack with the Dutch. I am one of just a handful of survivors. Dingane's army then burned this town to the ground, slaughtering everyone they could find. The best thing you can do is put us all on that ship and take us back to Cape Town."

"I can't do that. I have orders to stop the Boers from attacking the Zulus."

"Well you are too late. Pretorius and his army have already set off and nothing you can say will stop them. They are all fired up with religious fervour. I rather suspect that the Zulus will not need your help to defeat them. Not only that, once they discover you are here, they are likely to send an army to attack you too."

The fool actually laughed at that. "I am sure that a volley and our bayonets will see them off."

"You have no idea what you are up against, do you?" I asked with growing anger.

"As well as my Highlanders," he boasted, "I have three field pieces back on the ship and ten gunners from the Royal Artillery. I am sure that they will be enough to see off a rabble of tribesmen armed with spears."

"There will probably be at least ten thousand of them when they come," I told him quietly, taking a grim satisfaction from the growing look of shock on his features. "Some will be mounted and with captured guns, but it is not those you need to worry about. The main force will attack in a formation resembling a bull's head. You can form up and fire into the centre, but the horns will curve round and take you in the rear. Your guns may well take a few hundred down, but that will not stop them. When they get fifty yards off, the sky will be filled with their throwing spears. Those that survive that onslaught will have to face waves of them running in with shields and short stabbing spears. A skilled man with a bayonet might beat one or two, but not with a third Zulu shoving a spear into his back. Remember, I have seen both a Highland charge and a Zulu attack. Trust me when I tell you that you should not let that ship depart while your men are still ashore. Without it to escape to, you will not stand a chance."

184

"But then how do the Boers beat them?" he asked. I explained that in the open the Dutch were beaten too and how it was only when they were in their laagers, which gave them protection from the spears, that they could keep the Zulus at bay. "If you want to stay here, you need to build a stone castle with its own water supply, similar to those they had in medieval times," I told him. We both knew that he did not have the manpower for that.

"Well even if it is too late, I am still duty bound to send to Pretorius the governor's order not to attack the Zulus." He patted a pocket, which must have contained the governor's demand. "If he presses on regardless, he will have to answer for his actions afterwards. The governor has also instructed that any gunpowder here is seized and any further deliveries of Boer powder to the port are confiscated.

"I suspect the governor will be the least of Pretorius' concerns," I replied. "We heard this morning that Dingane has learned of the Dutch preparations and has gathered a huge army to confront them – up to fifteen thousand men, commanded by some of their best generals." I pointed to the camp of our friendly Zulus and suggested, "They can carry your message to the Dutch camp, who will be able to direct them on to Pretorius. But include a note to the camp to let them know that you are here with a ship."

"Why should I do that?" asked Charters puzzled.

"Because this Pretorius seems far more concerned with God-bothering than fighting. If he is defeated, there will be hundreds of defenceless women and children in desperate need of a safe haven."

"But my orders are to protect the Zulu, not their enemies." Charters sounded uncertain, still trying to match instructions from London and Cape Town with the realities he now faced.

I had a sudden memory of the long lines of tiny wrapped corpses after the massacre and was determined it would not happen again. But Charters was clearly anxious to please his superiors and so was easy to manipulate. "The governor will win support from all the Dutch remaining in the colony by saving as many of them as we can," I told him. Then I looked him in the eye, "Can you imagine what they would say in London, or indeed in this new queen's court, if they learned that you sailed away from here, leaving hundreds of defenceless women and children screaming for help on the beach to be massacred?" He blanched at that. 'Obeying orders' would be no defence for such an action. He would be pilloried in the press and shunned by society.

185

"No, no, of course not. You are right, but we will need to load additional food and provisions onto the ship for these extra passengers."

For the next few days Port Natal was a hive of activity. Messengers were duly dispatched, guns brought ashore and sacks of mealie and dried meat loaded onto the ship. Charters must have reflected on my words, for he also seized a warehouse owned by a man called Maynard, which was the only stone building in the town. In it was stored nearly a ton of Boer gunpowder, which was likewise confiscated. The major used the warehouse as the centre of a defensive bastion that he now had his men set about constructing. He appropriated another wooden building nearby as a barracks for his men and instructed some to dig a well for fresh water. The rest of his command was employed cutting wood for timber, making bricks from river mud and building a palisade around the seized buildings. He called the place Fort Victoria after our new monarch, although I doubt she would have felt any more flattered if she had seen it, than D'Urban if he had inspected what was left of his town.

It took two weeks to build the basic structure and while construction had kept the Highlanders occupied, I seethed with frustration. I did not want Charters preparing to stay on this wretched shore; I wanted him planning to leave. The sooner Louisa and I got our boots on the deck of the ship in the bay the better. The major had ordered more supplies loaded aboard and its master estimated that for a short trip down the coast we could load at least another two hundred souls aboard. I did not relish that embarkation. Memories came back of those pitiful Zulus on the beach screaming for help when I was on the *Comet* with the Owens and Captain Gardiner. This time I thought that the ship would be full to the gunwales, with possibly the ship's boats in tow loaded with women and children. Even then, there might be some left behind on the shore. The bay of Port Natal was wide and protected by promontories on either side and a sand bar out to sea. The waters were calm here, but out in the ocean there were often huge waves from the southern seas, not to mention man-eating sharks. I doubted any towed and heavily loaded boats would survive the journey. Having been lost at sea in such a craft before, I would make damn sure that Louisa and I travelled on the ship.

"Well it is no Tower of London, but I think Fort Victoria might make a Zulu chief think twice before attacking us." Charters and I stood on top of the stone warehouse as he proudly surveyed his

186

defences. He pointed at the guns that had been brought ashore and now rested in new emplacements. "We have explosive shells for those; neither the Boers nor the Zulus will have ever faced anything like them. They could kill hundreds as they approach, and from quite a range too." He sighed contentedly before adding, "There may be less than a hundred of us, but with cannon, musket and bayonet I think we could certainly see off a thousand, possibly two."

I did not want the fool getting any ideas of staying and so I was quick to puncture his dreams. "And what if ten thousand attack at night? Your vaunted cannon will be of little use then. The first you will know that they are here will be when they are swarming over your walls, more numerous than ants." I pointed out to the distant hills. "We have to rely on our scouts to warn us of the enemy approach and their numbers. You can stay here if you want, but at the first sign of those devils coming this way, my wife and I are being rowed to the ship." There were definitely advantages to being a civilian, I thought. Not only was it permissible to retire at the sight of the enemy, you could even boast of it.

"Well, let's see what numbers they send against us first," insisted Charters. "It might just be a delegation of their chiefs, for I still cannot believe that this Dingane fellow would dare to take on the might of Britain."

"That is probably what the poor devils who died in those blackened circles thought too," I said, pointing to where the local Zulus had been burnt to death in their own huts. "They thought that they were under British protection."

"There was no British flag or force of arms here then," insisted Charters pointing to the colour flapping from his newly installed flagpole. "I dare say that this Dingane thought that they were rebels to his own rule. That is quite different to being soldiers of the Queen." I had to grudgingly admit he had a point and I stayed silent. Emboldened, he continued, "The artillerymen were asking again if they could test fire their guns. It would help them put in range markers."

"That is out of the question," I insisted. "They would hear such gunfire at least ten miles away, twenty with the wind blowing in the right direction." To the best of our knowledge, news of the ship and soldiers at Port Natal had not yet reached Umgungundlovu, although we were overlooked by a range of hills, which concealed our activity. It was only a matter of time before some unwelcome eye peered in our direction. "We need to give ourselves as long as we can," I continued, "so that we have time to react once we get news of Pretorius…" I was interrupted by an unwelcome droning sound, "Never mind the noise of shellfire," I grumbled. "It's bad enough that the bloody piper is sounding off morning, noon and night. I glared at the offending man and added, "If you had ever heard what the Zulus call music, you would know that this din is just awful enough to attract them."

"Did you really burn their pipes?" asked Charters, chuckling, and with, I thought, a note of envy in his voice.

"Yes, but they were more the tattered remains of the instrument left after Assaye." I smiled, "But feel free to follow my example."

The following morning our messengers returned from the Boer camp. Despite their white flags, they had been captured and held for several days and their messages confiscated. It was unclear then if the letters for Pretorius had been sent on to the intended recipient, for the Boers in the camp had decided to respond on his behalf. Their reply, signed by several claiming to be 'representatives of the people', demanded Charters restore the gunpowder to them. They insisted that they must be able to defend themselves in what they described as 'their perilous situation'.

Quite how *perilous* that was, began to come to light two days later, when a pair of our Zulu scouts encountered one of Dingane's messengers. Before he died, the man revealed that the whole Zulu army was closing in on the Boer force, who were unaware of their presence. Already the king was planning a celebration in anticipation of his victory. This was just what I had feared. I had never met this Pretorius, but nothing I had heard about him indicated any military experience. I doubted he knew an *enfilade* from an *enchilada* dish I had once enjoyed in Mexico. By all accounts, he put far more faith in his gospels than his guns. It seemed only a matter of time before his force was destroyed.

Over the next five days I rode twice down the trail to the south, half expecting to see a column of dishevelled refugees hurrying in our direction. Each time the path was empty but when I returned to Port Natal the second time, I spotted someone approaching the town from the west. It was a lone runner and while I did not recognise him, some of the Zulus in the camp did, for they rushed out to help him into town. It was one of Biggar's warriors and the news he carried was astonishing.

188

God knows how far he had run without stopping, for it took him a full minute to get his breath. As he gasped, he reached into a pouch around his waist and handed me a scrap of paper. On it was scrawled: *Zulus beaten and routed. Now marching on palace – AB.* Alexander Biggar was clearly a man of few words, but his news was scarcely credible. They would have been fighting deep inside Zulu territory. Just five hundred of them defending their laager against over fifteen thousand Zulu would be quite an achievement. When I had been part of a defence against ten thousand, we had only just held our line. Yet if Biggar was to be believed, Pretorius had not just fended off his enemy, his men had sent them fleeing from the field. As I passed the paper to Charters, the runner was getting his wind back and gasping out more astounding details.

"He says there so many Zulu dead that they blocked a river and turned the water red," translated Ogle. "There are gullies full of bodies and those that were left were chased off by Boers on horseback."

"How many Boers were killed?" I asked.

Ogle asked the man and then challenged him on the answer, but the runner was insistent. "He says none of the Boers were killed," Ogle gasped. "I can't believe it, but he says that just three men were wounded, including Pretorius, who was speared in the hand." Slowly we gathered more details. The Boers had seen the Zulu in time and built their laager next to a river containing a hippo pool. This meant that the Zulu could only attack on three sides. The Dutch goaded their enemy to make assaults in huge waves so that their muskets and cannon could take a terrible toll. Boers also rode out on horseback to attack the flanks of the charging impis so that they were assailed on three sides. According to the runner, they fought for most of the day like that. Despite having their leading generals present, the Zulus did not vary their tactics or try to burn the laager as they had with us before. They just kept repeating the same kind of attack and getting the same result. Eventually, more Boer horsemen rode out and drove them away entirely.

If we had any remaining doubts over the Boer victory, these were resolved by new visitors. The first was a Dutchman who had ridden from their camp to ensure we had news of their triumph. He claimed that there were at least three thousand Zulu dead. He also told us that the battle had taken place just thirty miles from Umgungundlovu. Already Pretorius and his army were advancing on the capital in the

189

hope of bringing Dingane to justice for the murder of Retief and his men, as well as the massacres amongst their laagers.

The next day six Zulu deserters jogged into the camp. They had been at the battle but did not want to be near Dingane when he learned that his army had been beaten. One of them had relations among the Zulus living with us and wanted to join our community. Given that just a few months before, the Zulu army had burned the settlement and slaughtered everyone they could find, I was surprised that these men were welcomed so easily among their people. They insisted that Dingane was the villain. His soldiers had to obey his commands, or they too would be killed. Yet they assured us that the king's days were coming to an end. They explained that two of Dingane's half-brothers had been killed in the battle with the Boer force, which had heavily impacted the morale of the Zulu army. It would also greatly increase the king's fury at their defeat. Having been bloodily repulsed at the laager, they had no confidence that Dingane could defend his capital. Like countless deserters before them, they insisted that they were not alone and whole impis had fled to escape the wrath of their king.

It was hard to judge how much of their tale was true. I am certainly not one to condemn a man for running away from battle. Yet I could well imagine that morale in the Zulu army must have suffered. This had been the climactic clash between the best of the Zulu kingdom and the largest Boer force. The Africans had been soundly beaten. Much as I begrudged giving Pretorius the credit, the better weaponry and tactics he had employed had won the day. I was also pleased to know that he had not spent too much time on his knees afterwards giving thanks for his triumph. I did not doubt that some Bible-thumping had taken place, but he clearly had not lost the momentum of his victory. If the Zulu army was deserting *en masse*, then catching Dingane defenceless in his capital would be the sweetest end to the campaign. I chuckled at the thought, for it meant that we would soon be going home.

For Charters and the new British governor, however, news of the Boer victory was nothing short of a disaster. With their territory in Natal now secure, even more Boers were likely to come over the mountains to join families already here. That meant the British colony would be losing more of its most experienced and hard-working farmers. I doubted that the governor would let them go that easily, but if the Crown wanted to reclaim Port Natal, it would now take a lot more than a company of Highlanders. I tried to persuade Charters that the game was up: the Boers had won and there was no point in trying to protect the Zulu now. If he were to march his men between the opposing forces, he was likely to be attacked by both sides.

"The best thing to do is sail back to Cape Town," I told him, with not a little self-interest. "Take the seized powder with you if you want. The confidence of our Dutch friends will be high now and there is a good chance that hundreds of them will soon turn up here demanding it back. You will be hard pressed to refuse them. No one will thank you for starting another war."

"This is Crown land now," he protested. "I could not abandon it even if I wanted to." He paused, frowning. "Anyway, their victory sounds suspiciously one-sided to me. Have you ever heard of such an imbalance in casualties?"

I had to admit that I had not.

"We only have their word for their success," continued Charters. "That note from your friend Biggar could have been a forgery. It was extraordinarily brief; you would think that they would want to boast of the details."

"Possibly, yet the runner who brought the message sounded convincing. In any event the other Zulus here believed him. And what about those deserters?"

"They could have been coached. Even if the Boers really have won, they may have taken heavy casualties, which they would want to hide from us so that they appear stronger than they really are."

I thought that Charters was clutching at straws, not wanting to believe unfavourable news. Yet he was adamant that he wanted more proof before he would believe the scale of the Dutch victory.

As things turned out, I did not have to wait long to receive another example of Alexander Biggar's handwriting addressed to me. It came the next morning and read: *"Palace captured, defenders put to flight. Can you come, need to know where Retief and men are buried."* The runner confirmed the contents of the note and explained that the Zulu army had disbanded. He had passed dozens of them on the way to the coast, all returning to their villages.

"That is all very well," I grumbled, "but the Four Horsemen of the Apocalypse could not drag me back to that hell hole again. I will draw them a map and they can find things from that."

To my surprise, an objection came from the last person I would have expected. "You cannot let Alexander down," insisted Louisa. "He has been so good to us and those men deserve a Christian burial."

"He can find the bones from a map," I countered. "Anyway, I thought the last thing that you would want is for us to be separated again."

"We would *not* be separated, for I will come with you," she replied. Patting her scarred leg, she continued, "I am bored staying here. I want to see where the man who caused my limp and so much pain lived. If he is dead or a captive, so much the better."

While Louisa was now largely recovered from her wounds, I would not hear of it. I was adamant that a map was the best solution, that is until Charters came to talk to me. "If you were to go to their capital," he mused, "then you would be ideally placed to confirm the remaining strength of the Boer force and whether or not the Zulus have truly been beaten. You have friends amongst them; they will trust you with the truth."

"And what if the Zulus have not been beaten?" I pressed, "I could be right in the soup again. Not that I care for myself, you understand," I lied, "but my wife would insist on coming with me."

"They must have been pushed back well beyond their capital or they would have defended it," he reasoned. "You would need to go no further than that." He gave me a shrewd, calculating look and added, "Of course, if the Zulus are beaten, then I would have no reason to keep the ship in the bay. It would be safe to let it return to Cape Town for more supplies and to take any passengers with it."

So there we had it, a naked bribe: do as Charters asked and then, at long last, start the journey home. Given that I had argued against releasing the ship while there was a chance the Zulus could attack, I could hardly change my tune now. Yet it was a hundred and fifty miles to Umgungundlovu, much of it over rough terrain. The few older Zulus we had in camp would struggle to keep up with horses, never mind scout ahead for danger. The idea that Louisa and I could ride all that distance alone was preposterous. Even if I took both the shotgun and musket I had kept from the battle at Gatsrand, we would still be horribly vulnerable. We did not know the trail and there were all manner of ravines and gorges to get lost in. There were lions and a menagerie of other wild animals that could do us harm. It would be just my luck for us to be charged by another wild elephant.

Even if we escaped everything that Mother Nature could throw at us, we knew that Zulu deserters were roaming the same territory. Many would have lost comrades in the recent battle. Two white people, neither in the first flush of youth, would prove a tempting target for vengeance. It was a preposterous notion and I did not waste a moment in rejecting the idea. I listed all my objections to Charters until even he was at a loss as to why anyone would risk such an ordeal, especially with their wife in tow. It was decided that the truth of the Boer claims would be revealed in due course. We would just have to wait.

Fate can be a capricious mistress when she is trying to tempt your plums over the flames of danger once more. Having resolutely made my decision, I was making my second attempt at a reasonably accurate map, when I heard riders galloping up and being challenged by the sentries outside. I pricked up my ears when I heard them announce they came from Pretorius. I watched from the window of my quarters as they were granted access to Fort Victoria. Covered in dust from their journey, their beards made their grim scowls look even more forbidding. They stared about them at the gun emplacements and soldiers, muttering angrily between themselves. They looked as bitter about what they saw as a dairy maid finding a drowned rat in the cream bowl. Charters came out to meet them and I made sure that I was close enough to eavesdrop.

"We heard that you have seized our gunpowder," their leader stated, coming straight to the point. "You have no right to take it. The powder is our property, and we want it back."

"And you can have it back," agreed the major amiably, before his voice hardened. "As soon as you give me an undertaking that all Boer forces will return south of the Tugela River and stay there." This would restore to Dingane all the territory he had just lost and give him the opportunity to regroup. Most importantly, it would also enable Charters to claim that he had protected the Zulus as ordered. He also doubtless imagined that their king would feel indebted to him. Yet he must also have known that the Boers would never agree. They stood and glowered silently at him for several seconds, but surrounded by curious Highlanders, there was little that they could do. They turned to leave but Charters followed them to the gap in the new palisade. They were nearly there when the leader stopped and turned to Charters again. I did not catch it all, but I distinctly heard the word 'Flashman'.

A minute later and a kilted redcoat found me in my quarters drawing a picture of the execution hill and escorted me out to join the gathering. I had already guessed what they wanted. The Boer leader, reluctant to return empty-handed, must have known about the request for me to join them to help find Retief. Now he and his men were offering to give me an armed escort back to Umgungundlovu. I had little excuse to refuse now and Charters nodded encouragingly as the proposal was made. At first, they objected to taking Louisa too – it was no place for a woman, they told me. I wholeheartedly agreed and offered to return to my cartography but then I noticed one of the riders whisper in their leader's ear. The man nodded his assent and so it was that we found ourselves heading once more into the Zulu kingdom.

Chapter 22

It was a surprisingly pleasant journey, particularly once our escort knew that we had fought with them at Gatsrand. I happily agreed with their leader that Charters was a pompous prick, who had no idea what he was doing if he thought he was protecting the Zulus. Once that was established, we got on famously. They were considerate of Louisa, checking regularly if she needed to stop and they certainly knew their business crossing Zulu territory. They had a scout ride ahead and two more on the flanks, who would communicate with hand signals when on high ground. There was antelope for the pot and each evening we would camp in some sheltered spot, with sentries posted. As we ate, they would ask me about my time in the capital, how I came to be there and about my meetings with Dingane. One evening they asked about Retief. I told them about his conversations with Owen and how his men thought that they could trust the king once the treaty had been signed. I also recounted the final farewell ceremony, where dancing turned in the blink of an eye to an unprovoked attack.

"Is that how they died?" asked one of the riders.

"Some did," I conceded, but I did not want to say any more. It was not simply that I wanted to spare Louisa the horror; the tale had aroused memories that I had long tried to forget. It is the only place I have been where a sound rather than a sight dominates my memory: the screams and that awful knocking sound as brains were dashed out. The next day the leader and I rode out of earshot of the others and he asked me about it again. He explained that his wife had a relative amongst the party whom she had been very fond of. "Then trust me," I told him, "you really do not want to hear the details of how they were killed."

Despite their care, we were both exhausted from several days of hard riding when we finally reached Umgungundlovu. As we crested the last rise, it was immediately clear that the place was vastly different to how I remembered it. The huge city of tightly packed huts made from grass and thatch had largely disappeared. Dingane had tried to burn his capital when he was forced to abandon it. The buildings must have been tinder dry and had burned fiercely, cinders igniting everything downwind. Instead of concentric rings of domed structures visible over the thorn bush walls and pens full of cattle, there was now just a vast charred black smear of ash where much of the city had been. Only a small section remained, which must have been upwind of where the fires had started. The cattle pens were empty and where once thousands had lived, now not a soul was to be seen.

Ironically, the Dutch had made their camp in roughly the same place that Retief had made his. I was taken immediately to see their leader. Andries Pretorius was around forty, younger than I had expected. He had dark hair, a beard and no obvious military demeanour. On the table in his tent was a large Bible lying on top of a map, and that seemed to sum the man up. He greeted me warmly.

He rose and held out his good hand – the other was still heavily bandaged. "I am sorry to bring you all this way, Mr Flashman," he gestured to the city behind him. "But I believe that your assistance will be essential in enabling us to put tortured souls to rest." I had a horrible feeling he was just about to start preaching at me when his eye caught sight of Louisa coming up behind me. His jaw gaped open in surprise. "Your wife, I presume." He recovered himself and gallantly kissed her hand. "Mr Biggar told me of the trials you have both suffered in these lands. I fear this may not be a place for a woman. You must be the first white lady these hills have seen."

"No," I corrected him. "Reverend Owen, who lived here, brought his wife, daughter and a maid servant with him. But are you saying that this area is not safe? Are there still Zulu armies in the vicinity?"

"Oh no," Pretorius reassured me. "They have been driven far to the north. I simply meant that we cannot offer much in the way of womanly comforts."

"Oh, I am sure I will manage," confirmed Louisa breezily. "As long as Thomas and I are together, we will cope." She smiled brightly but I saw her rub her wounded leg and knew that she was trying to hide her fatigue. Pretorius noticed as well and immediately ushered her to the only chair and called for refreshments. Giving her a chance to rest in private, he led me outside.

"We have found hundreds of bodies up there," he pointed to the execution hill. "Lying halfway down the side of the slope were two skeletons, still clothed, we think they are from Retief's delegation. The rest on that hill all seem to be Zulus. Are our comrades buried somewhere else?

I thought back and shuddered slightly at the horrors hidden on that summit. "No, they are all up there, apart from Retief's liver, which was buried somewhere on the trail you came in on."

"So why can't we find them?" demanded Pretorius.

"When I was here before," I told him, "Dingane would execute one or two people every day, sometimes more. Retief and his men were killed nearly a year ago, which means that there must be hundreds of bodies now on top of them. They are definitely there. I saw the bodies after they had been killed.

Pretorius muttered something in Dutch, possibly a prayer, and gazed to the heavens. Then he turned to me. "It will be grim work for the living, but we must do honour to the dead." He had evidently been hoping that most had been buried somewhere else. Now there was no alternative but to start a gruesome excavation.

I largely left them to it. I only went up that hillside once as it held too many awful memories for me. Hesitantly, I walked along the path that I had seen so many condemned take as a final journey. The place was a living nightmare. Closer to the summit the ground was scattered with bones. The summer heat had blackened any skin that remained on the bodies so that it was impossible to tell their race. Vultures, wild dogs and other devourers of carrion had taken most of the flesh, breaking bodies apart and mixing some remains into an impossible tangle. The Boers had fared better than most of the local victims as their clothes had kept most of the bones together, although very few bodies were completely intact. I nearly stumbled over a discarded leather boot, only to find that the bones of a foot were still inside it.

By the time I reached the summit they were starting to uncover more of the Boer bodies. I recall two men raging with grief when they discovered what they thought was the body of Retief's twelve-year-old son. I remembered seeing the boy when he was alive. He had made me smile as he was wearing men's clothes that were far too big for him. The big red shirt still had its sleeves rolled up but now instead of an arm, two bones missing the hand protruded from it. The checked pattern on the front was black with dried blood and part of the garment was torn to shreds from beaks and claws. Much of what those animals had left behind had subsequently been consumed by grubs and insects, so that now there was little more than mummified skin and bone. The cause of death was clear, though, as it was for all the victims; the skull had been shattered.

The leader of the band who had brought us here came to stand beside me as I looked down at the boy. "Tell me," he whispered with tears in his eyes, "did they kill them quickly in the palace and then bring the bodies up here?"

For a moment I was tempted to lie, but instead told him the truth. "A few died in the palace, yes, but most were brought up here to be killed on that rock," I pointed at the boulder on the summit. He looked at the stone and then at the long path we had all come up that stretched away to what was left of the capital. He looked a tough man, but his bottom lip trembled slightly as he imagined that last awful journey, perhaps picturing his wife's relative struggling with his captors.

I put a hand on his shoulder, "Don't tell your family," I advised. "They don't need to know."

I stayed up there for the afternoon and it was awful work. Swarms of flies rose up every time a body was disturbed, revealing maggots and increasing the stench of decay. We soon all had neckerchiefs tied around our faces and while they helped keep the flies out of our mouths, they did little to counter the stink of death. As I helped lift one body, a rat jumped out of its jacket, causing me to yelp in surprise. By the time I came down the hillside again we had accounted for a score of bodies, around a quarter of the total. Pockets were searched for clues to their identity, but the Boers were only able to name half a dozen of them.

The next day while others continued the macabre hunt for old friends, I took Louisa, Pretorius and a few other Boers on a tour of what was left of Umgungundlovu. We passed through some avenues of intact huts near the main gate before we started to walk on ash. I saw metal pots, farming implements and spear points among the cinders. The residents had clearly not been given long to evacuate if they were leaving useful items like those behind. One of the Dutch found a small silver cup. They had already excavated some ivory from a pit that had been poorly hidden outside the city boundary. We reached the central courtyard and saw that the palace complex had been burned to the ground. Several fires had been started there and barely a stick still stood. Pretorius asked where Retief and his men had been attacked. I pointed out the area in the courtyard and he immediately fell to his knees to start praying. Several of the others joined him, but Louisa and I strolled over the remains of the palace looking for anything that might have been left behind in the embers. All we found for our trouble was the blade of a small knife, its handle long since incinerated.

It was two days before Christmas when the Dutch found the remains of Retief and with them an extraordinary present. While the body had been badly butchered by the Zulus when they took his liver,

Retief's leather satchel was still over his shoulder. It contained various of his papers and astonishingly, still readable inside, was the agreement on the extra land signed by both him and Dingane.

I was summoned by Pretorius to view the treaty, which was then in his tent. He wanted me to see it still existed so that I could detail the terms to Charters when I returned to Port Natal.

"Are you satisfied that it is genuine?" he demanded.

"I am sure it is," I confirmed. "I was living with the man who drafted it when it was written. I recognise his hand and he told me what was in it." I paused looking at the names of the rivers that marked out the boundaries of Retief's grant and then at the map still lying under the Bible of the Dutch commander's table. "But do you still need this?" I queried. "You have already taken far more land than Dingane granted to Retief. Where do you plan to stop driving the Zulus north?"

"Who are you to ask such a question?" demanded a grim-faced Boer. "Will you take our answers back to the British governor as an English spy?"

I opened my mouth to protest but Biggar got in first, "Damn you," he shouted. "How dare you insult my friend. He fought against the Zulu with my son and he fought against them with your people at Gatsrand. He nearly lost his wife to those devils. Do you really think he is with those fools who want to protect them?"

My accuser had the grace to look slightly shamefaced at this defence, but before he could apologise, Pretorius spoke up. "Do not forget that Mr Flashman is a guest here at my invitation." He turned to me, "To answer your question, we will drive them north until we are satisfied that they will never be a threat to us again." He gestured at the treaty on the table and continued, "I want to break the power of this treacherous king."

The following afternoon a burial service was held for all the Boer bodies and pieces such as the full boot I had found. A trench had been dug near the bottom of the execution hill and the remains of Retief and his comrades were laid inside. Not everyone was accounted for and there was a trail of bone fragments down the path to the pit, but most were there. Broken skulls stared sightlessly at men who stepped forward to eulogise on the jumble of bones before us. Much of it was in Dutch, so I could not understand it and the now much disturbed remains still reeked to make your eyes water. There was a sense of relief when men stepped forward with spades to finally cover the harrowing spectacle. When that was done, the mass grave was marked with a pile of stones.

I spent Christmas day 1838 in exactly the same place I had spent it in 1837: Owen's hut. On its own hillside, it had been spared the conflagration of the capital and was much as I had remembered it. No one had lived in it since the reverend's family. The bedframes were still there although the straw mattresses had been gnawed through by rats, which we could still hear scurrying about in the thatch. Yet the place gave Louisa some privacy from the Boers and I found comfort in the symmetry of staying there again. Mercifully, the prevailing wind blew the stench from the execution hill opposite, away from us. We invited Biggar and the two other Englishmen with Pretorius to join us for a Christmas lunch of roast antelope haunch. It saved them from a morning of listening to preaching and sermonising from their leader, most of which was incomprehensible to them. Biggar brought a small bottle of brandy with him that he had saved especially for that day. We all toasted the season and looked forward to a much happier future.

I had done my duty to Pretorius, Retief had been found and buried and the contract recovered. With the festive celebrations out of the way, we would be provided an escort back to Port Natal. When we got there, I would do my duty to Charters too. Everyone I spoke to, including Biggar, who I trusted implicitly, confirmed that the Boers had only suffered three wounded in their climactic battle with Dingane's soldiers. While there were always some out on patrol, the Boer force was still some five hundred men. Furthermore, the Zulu had been forced to flee from their capital and were a beaten and broken force, offering no further resistance. That information had to be worth an immediate passage home as it would be safe now to let the ship sail south. As the shared Christmas spirit warmed my innards, the thought of Louisa and I finally going home warmed my soul.

Alexander left us in the afternoon as it was his turn to join a patrol. He was back by the evening and the information he brought with him sounded like the icing on our Christmas cake. They had captured some prisoners and one had revealed that the last vestiges of the Zulu army still loyal to Dingane, just a few hundred men, were hiding in a river valley to the north. They were guarding the royal cattle, a herd of several thousand, many of which had been stolen from the Boers during their earlier raids. There were even rumours that the king himself could be among them.

After days spent in their gruesome excavations of Dingane's butchery, the prospect of capturing the king and bringing the war to an end proved irresistible to the Boer army. Even Louisa and I were happy to delay our departure to see how things unfolded. To be able to announce the king was dead, or at least a prisoner, would add great value to my report to Charters. Yet it was more personal than that, for both of us. We had separately come as close to death as at any time in our lives due to this man. He had given me nightmares that had left me sitting up sweating in the middle of the night and I know Louisa had suffered the same. We would both sleep more comfortably knowing he was in hell where he belonged.

We were not disappointed when Pretorius told us that he could not yet spare men to escort us back to Port Natal. His entire army wanted to be part of this final adventure and receive a share of the sizeable herd they would capture. We were given the option of staying in Umgungundlovu, where we would have just the dead for company, or accompanying them. Staying did not appeal. Alone in what was left of the empty enemy capital, there was always the risk that some of its former residents could appear. It felt far safer to stay with the Boer army. The place where the cattle had been found was only a day's ride north after all.

Chapter 23

We set off early on the 26th of December, Boxing Day. The Boers had quickly packed away their possessions into their long line of wagons and then mounted up, eager to be on their way. The wagon drivers had their horses tied to the back of their vehicles and I persuaded Louisa to travel in one of the carts with her mount tethered alongside its wagoneer's. I was not sorry to leave Umgungundlovu; it had always appeared dark and ominous, like its former occupant. Yet as the big leather whips cracked and lumbering oxen finally got the wheels rolling, I felt a sudden sense of unease. Something just did not feel right about this venture. In a calamitous career packed with all manner of perils, I have developed a finely tuned sense for danger, which I have learned not to ignore. Yet I could not put a finger on the problem this time. All I knew was that if Pretorius had unexpectedly offered an escort to the coast, I would have taken it.

I wondered if my disquiet was down to the weather. The summer sun had been blocked out by a huge bank of brooding clouds that came in from the east. I tried to lose the sense of doom by convincing myself that we were far better off with the army than alone in the capital with just a mountain of decomposing corpses for company. This column had beaten off a force of fifteen thousand Zulus without loss. Dingane's army was broken and scattered, with perhaps only five hundred left. The informant who had brought this information had been thoroughly interrogated, his face bore the bruises to prove it. He was mounted on a horse with those in front to guide the way. Although even now they were taking no chances and his hands were tightly bound behind his back. Pretorius was alive to the dangers of deception and traps. He had a score of scouts riding ahead and along the flanks of our march to ensure that there were no surprises. Even if by some miracle the Zulu army had regrouped, we would have plenty of time to circle the wagons and prepare a defence.

I could not think what other precautions he could take, but the feeling of foreboding would not go away. Like my mood, the clouds got steadily darker as the day progressed. Then, late afternoon, I nearly fell from the saddle in surprise when there was a huge crash of thunder from directly overhead. Oxen bellowed in fear, horses reared in panic and a couple of riders did tumble to the ground, yet none were hurt. In the time it took to get the column moving again, a light rain had begun, which reduced visibility. Pretorius sent out yet more scouts and passed word down the line that we would soon be at our destination.

We came to a halt on the top of an escarpment that overlooked a huge plain below. That at least is what we were told, as Pretorius did not want too many looking over the edge in case we alerted the Zulus to our presence. Biggar *had* looked over and confirmed that it was a steep climb down to flat land below. He had spotted a river with a few cattle grazing at the bottom of the cliffs, but the continuing rain stopped him seeing further. His warriors had told him that the place below was the Ulundi Plain and the river was the White Umfolozi. At least the top of the escarpment was reasonably flat and scouts who had explored all around it reported it empty of the enemy. Still we took no chances; we formed the wagons up into a laager, protected on one side by the cliffs and placed sentries out to warn of anyone approaching from other directions.

During the day Louisa and I had chatted to Pieter, with whom we had shared the wagon fighting at Gatsrand. We had no wagon of our own to use and so he invited us to sleep in his.

"It will be like old times," he boasted as we all settled down for the night. He had set up a blanket screen halfway down to give us some privacy, but his voice chuckled through it. "We will fight them as we did before, but this time I doubt that they will put up much resistance."

"I am not sure I am going down onto that plain in the morning," I told him. "I have been feeling uneasy about this all day. There is something not right, I can feel it in my bones."

"It will be fine," he reassured me. "You have not seen them run like I have. They are broken and defeated." He laughed again and added, "and with this rain they cannot burn us out, either."

He was soon snoring and a while later I was the only one still awake in the wagon. I lay there unable to find a rational explanation for my fears. I began to wonder if I was being unduly cautious. The patter of rain on the canvas roof gradually died away and, still unable to sleep, I carefully eased myself out from under the blankets. Quietly putting on my boots, I dropped to the ground outside. The mud was soft underfoot and the low clouds blotted out any starlight. I squinted out into the surrounding countryside and saw only pitch darkness. Inside the laager, light flickered from three campfires, sending shadows dancing around the space between the wagons. I walked towards the flames, noticing a couple of Boer sentries half asleep by the one entrance that had been left between the carts. My heart hammered as a Zulu appeared behind them. I opened my mouth to shout some alarm but stopped just as he nodded companionably to the guards. I cursed my foolishness; the man had neither shield nor spears with him. It must have been one of the Port Natal contingent who had gone outside to relieve himself. I followed the man to one of the fires where half a dozen other Zulus sat talking quietly with a white man.

"Can't you sleep?" called Alexander Biggar, looking up.

"No," I shuddered in the cold. "I can't shake the thought that we are walking into a trap. Don't you think the story that prisoner told was just a bit too convenient?"

Biggar thought for a moment, "Maybe," he admitted. "But if they were going to ambush us, I think they would have chosen a better place. I could not see far earlier with all the rain, but some of my boys know this place well. They tell me that there is nowhere down there for an army to hide. Now, do you want a nip of the last of the Christmas brandy?"

I sat with him for a while and we talked about what we would do when we finally got back to Port Natal. Beside us, his Zulus chatted among themselves in their strange tongue, laughing and telling stories. They certainly did not seem to have any concerns about what the next day would bring.

The sun was well up over the horizon when I awoke the following morning. Louisa and Pieter were already up and by the time I emerged from the wagon, a hot cup of coffee was waiting. It was another dull, grey day, but there was no rain and visibility was better.

"Do you want to see over the edge?" asked Pieter, grinning. He gestured to the end of the escarpment. "I have already looked. Go on, it will stop you worrying." I nodded and he led the way out of the laager to where a dozen men were on their hands and knees in the wet grass, peering down into the valley beyond. "Keep down," my companion called as we got close. "We don't want them to see us and know we are coming."

Finishing my coffee, I put the cup on a rock and crawled forward. As I reached the edge, I felt a weight lift from my shoulders. Far down below us the river twisted and turned through a shallow valley. There were no deep ravines or gullies, and the sparsely spread scrub was barely sufficient to hide a man, never mind an army. At first the only living things I could see down there were cattle. They were grazing on the grass of the riverbank, and a few had waded into the water for a drink. Then, some distance upstream, I saw smoke drifting up into the morning sky from a fire. Half a dozen men sat around the flames, one feeding them with more wood. They were making their breakfast, oblivious of us watching them from above.

"There are thousands of them," breathed Pieter. Confused at first, I followed his gaze to the flat featureless Ulundi Plain on the other side of the river. A farmer at heart, his attention had been drawn by the livestock. I grinned, for while there were a few hundred beasts on this side of the river, on the other bank they dotted the pasture for as far as the eye could see.

"It must be the royal treasury," I told him, for we both knew that the Zulu valued wealth in terms of cattle. The informer was right, this vast herd would be worth a fortune to Dingane. With little to reward his remaining supporters, he would be even weaker when the Boers took them south. "How will we get them up here?" I asked, puzzled. Peering down I could see a narrow path zig-zagging down the escarpment. It would be fine for men and horses in single file or possibly two abreast, but you could never drive a large herd of animals up it.

"The slope is shallower a mile or two to the west," Pieter explained. "We camped on the cliff for safety, but we can drive the cattle over the river and then to the west. It might take a day or two to round up them all, but we can do it."

Pretorius must have been thinking along the same lines, for he was soon issuing orders. Three hundred Boer riders under a man called Landsman along with Biggar and his fifty Port Natal Zulus were ordered to prepare for the descent. Our general was not leading the attack personally, using his injured hand as an excuse, which was still in a makeshift sling. The rest of us were to guard the laager and I was one of the few happy to be left behind. The rest were vociferous in their protests: they had travelled hundreds of miles, fought battles and now they wanted to play their part in what they were sure was the final act of the war. With no need for stealth now, we all stood on the edge of the escarpment to watch the raiding party descend. Biggar's Zulus led the way, jogging easily down the steep path. The horsemen moved more cautiously, a few dismounting from nervous mounts when some of the loose stones on the narrow path started to move under their hooves.

They must have been halfway down when the Zulu herdsmen finally spotted them approaching. They pointed, shouted and jabbered about for a moment, before grabbing their belongings and running off to the east, still yelling their heads off.

"I wonder who they are shouting to?" mused Pieter beside me. "More drovers down the valley? Or perhaps Dingane is hiding in a cave in the cliff?" Landsman must have been wondering the same, for he shouted for Biggar to follow them along the riverbank. Behind us, the complaints of those ordered to stay behind were finally bearing fruit. They had pointed out to Pretorius that the plateau on which the laager stood was empty for miles around, with no cover to hide an enemy nearby. If Zulus were to appear on the horizon, then they could simply ride along the riverbank to the west and come up the shallower path. Many insisted that if he allowed them to join the raid, then they could return to their places within a quarter of an hour if necessary. Eventually, our commander relented. Anyone who wished could join the raid, but they were to return immediately if they heard a signal cannon fired and bring the rest with them.

Louisa and I were content to remain with Pretorius and around a dozen other Boers who, due to wounds or sickness, were staying with the laager. Pieter, however, had other ideas. "Come on," he cajoled me, holding out my double-barrelled shotgun and my musket, along with a satchel of ammunition. "You don't want to miss the end of Dingane if we find him." Our Bible-thumping general had insisted that if the king were found he was to be taken prisoner, "to face God's justice in a court of law." Yet with emotions still raw after the burial of Retief's party, I would not have given two pins for his chances of surviving the day.

"Go on," Louisa encouraged. "I will be safe up here and I will not get any rest with you pacing back and forth to the edge to see what is happening below." I hesitated – that nagging worry from the previous day remained at the back of my mind. I climbed up on the side of the nearest wagon and had one final look around at the plateau surrounding the laager. It was as empty as a pauper's purse, but I still felt uneasy leaving my wife with just a dozen incapacitated Boers to defend her. "Just go," she insisted, "I will be fine."

"All right," I agreed reluctantly, "but I want you to have this." I handed her the musket and a handful of cartridges from the satchel.

She laughed. "Do you think I am going to fight off a Zulu impi with this?"

I kissed her and smiled, "No, but I feel happier if you have some means to defend yourself. We should be back before any Zulus, but you never know, there could be a wild animal, a lion even." I was sure that Pretorius and the others would take care of such a threat if it appeared, but I just felt more comfortable knowing she had a weapon to hand. I slung the satchel over my head and picked up the shotgun before turning to follow Pieter.

By the time we were mounted up and on the trail down the escarpment, most of the others were ahead of us. A man called De Lange led our party, while Landsman's group were all down on the riverbank and trotting their horses east. Suddenly there was a flurry of shots from up ahead of them. As we whirled around to look, several hundred Zulus appeared on the trail ahead. They must have pressed themselves against the escarpment further along to avoid being spotted from above. Now they could see the Boers approaching they broke cover. Yet instead of attacking most were fleeing east, yelling their heads off as they went. This must have been the rump of their army that the informant had told us was here. The horsemen behind were urging me on; everyone wanted to be in on this final pursuit. My mount followed those in front with little guidance needed from me as I stared after the fast retreating warriors. Some were holding their shields high in the air and I wondered if that was because they were protecting a particularly tall man in their midst. I grinned; the corpulent king would not be able to keep that pace up for long. They would either have to make a stand or abandon the bastard to what little mercy he could expect from us.

A score of Zulus had sacrificed themselves by trying to block the path of the pursuit to give their comrades more time. *Assegais* flew at Landsman's men, but a flurry of shots took the warriors down with the horsemen barely breaking stride. More of an obstruction was caused by panicked cattle, which had fled the emerging Zulus only to be frightened again by the gunfire. They put their heads down and barrelled down the path towards us before splashing across the river. We were down on the riverbank now and at last it was safe to spur my horse on into a gallop to follow the men in front. I glanced back up at the top of the escarpment. Louisa was easy to spot amongst the Boers, who stared down to see what was happening. She must have been watching me, for she waved, content to see her man charge into action, safely at the rear.

The river meandered into a huge S-shaped curve further ahead. If the Zulus followed the path they would be cut off and so they had no choice but to splash through the waist-deep water. It slowed them down, giving their pursuers the chance to catch them. More guns fired as the Boers approached the crossing point. Those in the middle of the stream as they arrived stood little chance and I saw several throw up their arms and fall back into the water. We were catching the front party too. Pieter was alongside me and I saw him staring over the river to our left. "That's odd," he commented, "most of the white cattle are in front of us and most of the black behind."

I ignored him. I was half standing in my stirrups to see over the men in front. There *was* a big warrior in the group we were chasing, although I was not sure he was fat enough to be Dingane. I was just wondering if the king could have lost some weight when what Pieter had said finally registered. Cattle hides of the same colour...that rang a bell in my memory, and I frowned as I tried to cudgel it out of my wits. Then with the speed of a viper strike the thought occurred – and it was just as welcome.

My head whipped around to stare at the distant white cattle. "By Christ, it *is* a trap," I gasped, but I was too late.

Chapter 24

A horn sounded from a ledge high up the escarpment to our right and a distant voice shouted a command in Zulu. Before my eyes the white lumps on the plain began to break apart. The nearest had been several hundred yards away and I swear you would not have given it a second glance. It was just a white cow resting on the ground after the rain, surrounded by plenty of beasts that were very real. Yet now as I watched, the white hide began to separate into five shield shapes. Behind them Zulus rose from where they had lain on the ground, raising spears triumphantly and shouting. The sound was indistinguishable at first, but then I recognised it as they settled into a chant: *Bulala*. Kill.

With a great sense of trepidation, I looked back the way we had come. The black cows behind us, which had also been indistinguishable from real beasts from the top of the escarpment, were also transforming into well over a thousand warriors. All across the plain, the huge herd that had attracted the greed of the Boers, was rising to trap them. Real cattle amongst them bolted in panic as the shouting began, although most of those had been placed near the river to aid the deception.

"There are bloody thousands of them," I whispered, almost in awe as I stared across the river. My thoughts were interrupted by the sound of shooting ahead. The informant, still with his hands bound behind his back, had spurred his horse into a gallop and was charging through the river towards his comrades. A volley of shots from the betrayed Dutch followed him, but none struck home.

Like me, the Boers were staring about them in bewilderment at the sudden change in their circumstances. I like to think that a lifetime of unpleasant surprises caused me to recover first. "We have to go back!" I shouted at the men about me. "We can't be trapped down here."

"It's too late," replied Pieter, twisting around in his saddle. "They are already at the bottom of the escarpment." He was right; a hundred Zulus already blocked the route back up but many hundreds more were running in from the west. I swore vehemently. I had been dismissive of the Zulu generals, who had found no way to break a laager, but the swine who had planned this ambush was an evil genius. The informant had played his part well, luring us in with tales of the 'royal herd'. And once we were down the slope the deception continued, with cattle herders and the supposed rump of Dingane's army drawing us east, away from the 'cattle' who would shut the door of the trap behind us. Riding back up that steep path to the top of the escarpment would be a slow and precarious business. With *assegais* hurled at man and beast, we would be like ducks in a shooting gallery. A wounded horse could easily knock half a dozen down the cliff. Pieter was right; I could see that it was too late, but as I looked at Zulus rushing in from all directions screaming for our deaths, I could see no escape at all.

I felt that all too familiar sense of rising panic. Staring up at the top of the bluff to our right, I could still make out a tiny figure in a dress standing with Pretorius and the others. Was she going to watch her husband torn to pieces before her very eyes? It seemed inevitable. We had a cliff to our right, thousands of Zulus boring in over the river to our left and at least a thousand more blocking the only way out behind. In front the five hundred Zulus who had already crossed the bottom of the meandering 'S' curve in the river, were defending the far bank, more confident now that reinforcements were streaming in.

"We have to go on," shouted Pieter above the rising noise of war cries and shooting. "If we can get past them and onto the plain, our horses can outrun them." There was a bloody big 'if' in that sentence, but he was right, it was our only hope. Landsman, commanding the front of the column must have reached the same conclusion. He was now leading his men into the water in front, while more Boers gave withering supporting fire from our bank. I felt bile burn the back of my throat and I tasted coffee again at the thought of fighting through that lot. "Come on!" called Pieter, urging his horse forward with the others.

Landsman was already halfway across, his horse rearing as an *assegai* shaft struck the creature on the head. Incredibly, the Zulu on the far side were falling back as they were assailed by a hail of lead from our bank. More Boers pushed their horses into the water and soon the first were climbing the far shore. I was happy to let them spearhead our retreat, for I have never found being in the front a healthy place to be. Yet as I glanced over my shoulder, my stomach spasmed once more at the sight of hundreds of the murderous bastards now charging down the bank behind us. I remember muttering a prayer and making fervent promises to the Almighty if only He would let me live. "I will never leave the shores of England again," I vowed, as I coaxed my mount down the bank and into the water.

Several Zulus were floating face down and a horse was lying on its side in the shallows, its legs thrashing wildly, unable to get up. The noise was deafening: the crash of guns, thousands of angry voices calling for our death, the screams of men and animals, much of it echoed off the cliff face to our right so that it seemed we were surrounded. By the time I was halfway across the river there must have been two hundred Boers milling about on the far shore, shooting and shouting, driving the enemy back. We were in a desperate plight and this was the time for clear and decisive leadership, yet inexplicably this was the very moment that the Boer force broke in two.

Landsman led his advance party to the right, splashing over another curve of the river towards the bottom of the cliff. He must have been hoping that there would be a path along the bank that would enable him to skirt the attack. De Lange led the second group to the left, the route that led directly up onto the plain and the space to escape. Both leaders were yelling at the Boers to follow them and I saw several men change from one group to the other. Confusion was now added to my terror, for they were all bellowing in Dutch and I could not understand a bloody word. To dither would prove fatal and so I went left with De Lange, largely because that was where Pieter and the men around me headed.

We had only gone a few yards when I swiftly realised that I had made a mistake. We were on the Zulu side of the river now and the white-shielded warriors began to run in amongst us. De Lange organised his riders into a broad front of around sixty, who began to fire into the throng. As they did so they turned back to reload leaving those behind to take their place. Suddenly, to my horror, I found myself on the front line, with a pall of musket smoke from their earlier volley obscuring my view of the yelling fiends in front.

"Push forward!" yelled Pieter beside me, urging his mount on so that he could see what he was firing at. The last thing I wanted to do was ride closer to the enemy, but I had the sense to know that I would be even more vulnerable if they charged through the smoke with their spears. Our only hope was to keep them at bay with our guns. If we were reduced to hand-to-hand fighting, the huge imbalance in numbers would ensure we were overwhelmed. I kicked my heels back in the nick of time for they were nearly on us. Bringing the shotgun up, I blasted two with one barrel, watching as they both tumbled away. I just had time to swing the gun round and blast another with the second shot. Then I was turning back myself as replacements pressed forward into the line. My hands were shaking so badly that I spilt powder as I tried to reload. Fumbling, I managed to get *loopers* down each barrel. There was no time for ramrods so I did what I saw the others doing, knocking the butt on the saddle pommel to shake the charges home. There was barely a chance to put powder in the priming pans before I found myself in front again.

This time I did not charge forward; our line was moving back, and it was not hard to see why. There must have been at least a thousand of the white shields in front of us. They had coalesced into a solid line. We heard a steady thud as their short stabbing spears beat against the white leather hides, interspersed by shouts of "*Bulala!*" It was the most sinister rhythm I have ever heard. I ducked as an *assegai* flew over my head. There were far fewer of the throwing spears than I expected. They must have used most of them in their earlier battles with the Boers and had not been able to make many more. One man stepped out from the line and, turning his back on me, began to rail at his fellows. He was clearly exhorting them to some new mischief. There is only one way to deal with rabble rousers like that: I raised my gun and fired, just as he punched his spear into the air. Metal fragments in the *looper* flayed his back open and pitched him into the shields beyond. There was a roar of outrage from their owners who began to move forward as one.

"Oh Christ!" I yelled as I wheeled my horse away in panic. I was immediately impeded by a line of mounted Boers preparing to fire. "Get out of the damn way!" I shrieked at them while they cursed me in turn for blocking their shot. As my horse started to push its way through, one of them fired a musket almost next to my head. I felt the heat of the muzzle flash on my cheek and my ear was ringing from the noise of the discharge. Disorientated, I pushed on; there was no way that they were stopping that lot. My mind had gone blank apart from a sheer, naked terror as I stared about and saw enemies on all sides. Men were swinging musket butts down on Zulus all around them. I remember hearing a high-pitched scream over the din and looked up to see a Boer with an *iklwa* point buried deep in his belly. The Zulu wrenched his spear free and turned, hunting for another victim. He was just yards away and looked at me, a mad rage in his eyes. He had already taken two paces forward when I got the gun up. For an awful second I could not remember which barrel I had fired. I cocked the left and breathed a sigh of relief as the butt slammed into my shoulder from the recoil. The Zulu was dead, and I suspected the Boer he had struck would not be long after him. He swayed in the saddle, holding his guts but another rider helped steady him and lead his horse away. I did not see any more after that, for I was in a headlong retreat. For once I was not alone. I looked about me to see that the whole Boer line was now galloping back alongside.

De Lange shouted something, but again in bloody Dutch! For a moment I had no idea where we were going, but then I realised we had little choice: we had to ride after Landsman's party and hope they were making better progress. We splashed once more through the river, the middle of the 'S' this time, heading towards the escarpment and the sound of new gun fire. Suddenly, there were more Zulus in front of us, but they were facing the other way. Then they heard the thunder of hooves behind them and turned in alarm, fear on their faces as they found themselves trapped between the two Boer groups. There was no choice but to charge straight through them. Hardly any of us were loaded. I changed my grip on the shotgun to hold it by the hot barrels, swinging it like a club beside me. One of the first to retreat, I found myself in the front line of horsemen. I watched as a Zulu in front of me whirled round, raising his shield and drawing back his stabbing arm. There was little I could do to avoid him. I was hemmed in by more horsemen on either side and further ranks of them behind. I swung the shotgun butt and may have even closed my eyes, for all I remember is feeling the wooden stock make solid contact with something. Then I was through, man and mount mercifully unscathed. Yet any relief was short-lived, for we had just jumped from the frying pan into the fire.

I stared ahead in horror, for Landsman had brought his men up a path that just led to the blank wall of the escarpment. It was in every sense of the phrase, a 'dead end'. They had dismounted, forming a laager with just their horses, and had been firing over their saddles. As I pulled up and glanced nervously behind at the white shields still on our tails, De Lange swept past and started yelling at Landsman. I did not need a translator, for he was pointing east and looked furious. Landsman's followers were doomed if they stayed in their laager. There was no escape up the cliff. They could only fight until they ran out of ammunition and then they would be overwhelmed. As I stared at that escarpment, I had white shields running up behind and at least a thousand black shields still charging in from our right. Our only hope now was to go left, to the east, over the top curve of the 'S' in the river. There were still Zulus coming in from that direction, but we just had to pray that our combined force could punch its way through. I hurriedly reached into my satchel to reload the shotgun while Landsman's party remounted. I saw Biggar pointing and the Port Natal Zulus ran forward to lead the new advance. They began to spread out to drive off the nearby enemy, but we did not wait for them, or at least I didn't. I knew instinctively that this was a race – we had to break out before Zulu reinforcements, running in from across the Ulundi Plain, could trap us for good. The sight of Zulus fighting against Dingane's forces enraged the enemy and many of the fiends came running for them, howling blue murder. Four warriors charged one of Biggar's lads to my left, yelling their heads off. They had foolishly run forward in a tight group and so I took aim and gave them the contents of a barrel. There was a bang, a puff of smoke and the thud of the butt once more against my shoulder and then the odds were evened. The survivor of the group still standing looked bloody and I doubted he would put up much resistance. My Zulu comrade shouted something in thanks and raced forward to finish him off.

More enemies were lining the far bank of the river and I fired the remaining barrel at them and hurriedly reloaded while I waited for the rest to catch up. I was not foolish enough to try and cross by myself.

Suddenly, Biggar appeared. "Wait for the others," he shouted unnecessarily as he reached into his satchel for another cartridge.

"Do you think we will make it?" I shouted back at him. As I did so I glanced over to our left. The white shields had guessed our intentions and the first of them were already splashing through the water further upstream to cut us off.

"We will be in good company if we don't," Biggar replied enigmatically. I assumed he was referring to his sons, but did not have time to ask, for a growing thunder of hooves heralded the arrival of the entire Boer force. For the first time they rode in a block of over five hundred horsemen. It was a formidable sight. The Zulus on the far riverbank started to edge back. Those that did not move quickly were blasted by a flurry of fire as De Lange led the Boers without hesitation into the water. They were soon up the far bank too, shooting lead into anyone who got in their way. It happened so quickly that I began to believe we might have a chance after all. I splashed once more into that dammed river in their wake. The far bank was littered with the bodies of the dead and dying, but they were all Zulu and I galloped on until I was safely in the rear of the Boer formation. Biggar and his warriors were now running along behind. To my surprise, most of the Port Natal force had survived.

There was more gunfire coming from my left now. The white shields were trying to attack the flank of the horsemen. De Lange was organising his men to fire volleys to keep them back, but this only slowed us up. As our retreat suddenly stalled, it allowed more of the white shields to cross the river and join their comrades in the struggle. Large rocks and thorn bushes growing near the river also got in the way and soon the riders were milling about in confusion. If you expected your correspondent to join this desperate effort, well, you really don't know me at all. There was only one tactic that would serve here: panic-stricken flight and leave the devil to take the hindmost… which was certainly not going to be me.

I galloped past, yelling at them to ride on. "Come on!" I implored. "We have to outpace them, or we will all die!" While they spoke Dutch among themselves, most understood English and they could also comprehend the sense in what I was saying. The Boer I had seen stabbed earlier was still on his horse, held there by men riding on either side and they were the first to turn and join me. Yet others were hesitating. I watched as an unintelligible debate broke out among the mass of riders. Some were pointing at me and to the now near empty plain to the north and others gesturing at the gunfire currently keeping the white shields at bay. I might not have understood a word of what was being said, but it was clear I was winning the argument. More horsemen turned to join me and so I urged my mount on, up the slope onto the plain. It was a relief to see the riders behind me as I had not fancied crossing the vast expanse on my own. It was still pock-marked with scattered groups of Zulus that had made up the more distant 'cattle', running in to join their brothers. I stared around again to see that the trickle of riders had become a flood. De Lange must have realised what was happening and given up on the fight, for now the whole Boer force was riding as one in my wake.

The white shields were still on our heels, though, and beginning to catch Biggar and his Zulus who were falling behind. Landsman yelled something and around fifty Boers broke away and looped back to fire a volley into the front of the enemy force to slow them down. As they returned up onto the plain I breathed a sigh of relief: we had made it. The few Zulus we could see were scattering away from us. None of them fancied taking on five hundred horsemen. Then as I looked back to confirm that Biggar's warriors were managing to maintain a distance from their pursuers, I saw the escarpment beyond and felt another pang of alarm. Despite my best endeavours, Louisa and I were separated again. This time there were several thousand murderous Zulus between us, and she only had a dozen old or wounded Boers for protection. They all had horses, though, and I tried to comfort myself with the thought that having seen the battle from above, they would ride away at the first sign of Zulus approaching the laager.

We kept up a steady pace across that plain for two hours. At first every few minutes a group would wheel back and fire into the white shields, but they gradually fell further back. Biggar and his warriors fell back too, but not by as much. Our only casualty during that time was a horse. It had a deep spear wound in its side and finally stumbled and fell, unable to get up. Its rider put it out of its misery and climbed up to share another's mount. The horses had fared worse than the men, for there were at least half a dozen with a double burden on their backs. The other mounts had been lost at the river crossings.

Eventually, we judged it was safe to stop for a while. Men and animals needed time to recover from the shock of the Zulu attack. Several of the Boers were sporting wounds, some of which were quite deep cuts that needed quickly bandaging. To my astonishment, every single man who had set off down the escarpment was still with us. The one I had seen stabbed in the guts had the worst injury by far. His clothes were soaked in blood and it would probably have been a kindness to leave him to die in peace. We left him to rest in the grass while we drank from water bottles and argued over what we should do next.

Most were convinced that having driven us off, the Zulus would now climb the escarpment and burn the laager. They swore and cursed at that possibility, many having got themselves into debt to buy their wagons in the first place. I privately hoped that they did burn the wagons, for it would force Pretorius and more importantly, Louisa, to withdraw. My fear was that they would stay there until nightfall and find that the Zulus had encircled them in the dark. When I expressed this concern, De Lange was insistent that we would be back in the laager by dusk.

"How the hell will we manage that?" I queried and others nodded in agreement. I was not alone in thinking this was impossible.

"Well we cannot keep riding north when everything we have is to the south," he started. "We cannot go up the escarpment on the same path we came down, it is too slow and narrow. But we can ride to the west, out of sight of the Zulus across the top of the plain. Then we will ride south again, cross the river and go up the shallower path that we were going to drive the cattle up."

"That is too obvious, they will be expecting us to do that," protested another Boer called Potgieter. "We must abandon the laager and ride

216

further to the west. That way we can avoid the Zulu army entirely." I was not sure if this was the same Potgieter who had abandoned Uys to his fate, but he certainly divided his audience. Some shouted their agreement while others, some hoping to keep their wagons, shouted him down. It sounded a far more sensible approach to me, and if it were not for the fact that Louisa was in the laager that he was so casually dismissing, then I would have been all for his scheme. Thankfully, the majority, including Landsman and his followers, agreed with De Lange. We would try to make it back to the wagons and there, hopefully, I would be reunited with Louisa. All were sure that if we could reach it, we would be able to fight off this Zulu army from within the safety of the laager. It was a much smaller force than they had beaten before from within the circle of wagons. That was all very well, but I had a nasty feeling that the Zulu general, who had the cunning to come up with this ambush, would not be so obliging as to let us get back to the plateau unopposed.

Chapter 25

It must have taken us at least three hours to ride along the northern edge of the Ulundi Plain, travelling from east to west. This time we did not rush; the horses were tired and we knew our lives would depend on them later. The man I had seen stabbed in the guts earlier, was one of the few who stayed in his saddle. His hands were pressed into his gore-stained bandage and he was moaning softly. Given the blood he must have lost, I was amazed he had not toppled off his mount miles back. The rest of us took the time to dismount and let the animals recover from the exertions of the morning, particularly those that had two riders aboard.

Potgieter still bleated that we were making a mistake, as if we did not know that the hardest challenge lay ahead. The white shields who had been trailing us had long since fallen back. Now none of the enemy could be seen, and it looked as if we had the plain to ourselves. Yet I was very conscious that while we could not see them, it was almost certain that the Zulus would have a man watching us from near the top of the escarpment. As we had spotted all the dots of supposed cattle from that same vantage point early that morning, so they would see the dark shadow of the Boer force moving steadily across the plain.

The Zulu general would know that the Dutch would desperately want to get inside their wagon circle from where they could fight with virtual impunity. I half expected a column of dark smoke to rise in the afternoon as the laager was attacked and put to the torch, but there was nothing. I could not help but wonder if Louisa was still up there, perhaps also watching us move across the plain and worrying that she would never see me again. It was odd that the carts had not been burned, for the Zulus would have seen the Boers ride away from them and know that they were now virtually defenceless. Then I realised that the only explanation was that the wily Zulu commander was using them as bait. If he destroyed the laager then many more, including me, would see the sense in Potgieter's argument and try to avoid a battle entirely. Instead, the thought of regaining their protection was drawing us back. They would know better than us that there was only one shallow slope we could charge up to reach the plateau. As we finally turned south again, my guts were churning with anxiety, for I was now certain that a new trap was being laid.

Our goal was not hard to spot: there was a clear V-shaped gap in the escarpment marking the more gradual climb up to the heights. We walked straight towards it seeing as there was little point in trying to hide our destination as we crossed the featureless plain. If we were not back at the laager by nightfall, the chances were that all would be lost. I was already bone tired and my feet ached in my boots, yet I knew that fatigue would soon be the least of my worries. Sure enough, when we got to within around two miles of the river the wounded Boer still on his horse gasped something in Dutch. Whatever it was, it had the others shouting in alarm and swinging back into their saddles. I put my foot up into the stirrup with a sense of fear and trepidation, a feeling that was fully realised a moment later when I looked to the south.

Along both banks of the river a black mass was moving, like two sinister snakes, heading directly towards our crossing point. "There are bloody thousands of them," I gasped. It was hard to make out individuals at that distance, it was just a solid, undulating block of bodies and shields. I guessed that there had to be at least two thousand on each bank. They were running, we could tell that much and the force on the far bank was further ahead.

"Come on," shouted De Lange, in English this time so that I and the other three of my countrymen in the group could understand. "We must get to the crossing before them."

"You will never make it," shouted Potgieter and I had a horrible feeling he was right. There followed a furious exchange between Potgieter, De Lang and Landsman but I did not understand a word of their Dutch. It was clear, though, that Potgieter still intended to take his followers further west, to try to outrun the Zulus and escape without fighting them. "Who else is with me?" he shouted in English, staring at me, Biggar and the others.

"Damn coward," Biggar muttered in response, but I confess I was sorely tempted. Looking forward at the twin fingers of doom spreading out before me, I did not fancy our chances at all. Then I looked at the top of the escarpment and considered Louisa's prospects if we did not manage to fight our way through. She was virtually alone and defenceless, a hundred miles within Zulu territory: there was no choice for me, I had to go on with the others.

As Potgieter cantered off with his sixty followers, the rest of us urged our tired horses into a gallop. As we did so, the Zulus on our side of the water started to spread out away from the river. As we raced on, they began to form an odd hook formation that would wrap around our rear. I had not seen anything like it until I realised that it was half of their traditional bull's head, with the horn as the hook. We gathered speed and I was sure that we would reach the riverbank before them, but the first of the Zulus on the far side of the river were already nearly at the crossing point.

There was another shout of alarm and I saw horsemen riding towards us. For a moment I thought it was Potgieter coming back but then I realised that the riders were Zulus. There were fifty of them with muskets and, bizarrely, some were also trying to ride with shields.

A command went out in Dutch, which was then repeated by someone in English. "Solid ball only, shoot the riders, we want some of those horses." It had to be Dickwa's cavalry, I thought, and sure enough I spotted his feathered headband among the lead riders. Their horsemanship had got little better since I had last seen them. One rider tumbled from his mount as they began the charge and they came as a herd rather than line abreast. The Boers waited patiently for them to approach as we kept up our own steady gallop. They were still two hundred yards away when Dickwa's cavalry started to shoot. Those with shields fired their guns with just one hand and the shots went wild. One horse tumbled down, possibly hit by a stray shot fired from within the group.

What followed next was chaos. Most of the Zulu riders were struggling to wheel their horses away to reload. I saw one tugging furiously on his animal's ear in an effort to turn his head and change direction. Not surprisingly, some of their horses were whinnying in alarm at this treatment and their herd instinct must have been pulling them to join the larger Boer formation. Other riders were content to charge at the Boers even though they were now hopelessly outnumbered. I saw Dickwa still at the front of his men, his gaze searching the cavalry ahead of him. For a moment our eyes met, a split second of mutual recognition in the turmoil around us. He clearly remembered me, for a look of fury crossed his features and he swung his musket to his shoulder. He had saved his shot, but now wasted it, still at the gallop seventy-five yards off. Heaven knows where the ball went, but it was nowhere near me. I cocked a barrel of the shotgun – never mind his damn horse, if he came near me I would blast the fool off his saddle. I did not need to bother, though, for now the Boers were reining their mounts to a stop and their muskets began to crack out. They could not miss at that range. At least two balls struck Dickwa in the chest and he tumbled lifeless from the saddle. His mount trotted on without him to pull up alongside the men who had relieved it of its rider. Other Boers were grabbing loose horses and in a moment those who had been sharing a ride were up in often bloodstained saddles of their own.

There was not a second to lose, for the Zulus coming up on our left flank had seen the slaughter before them. They began to yell their *"Bulala!"* war cry to show that they intended to avenge their fallen comrades. My heels were back and we were galloping on before the last man had remounted. Already others were ahead of me; it was just a few hundred yards to the river now and we would surely get to it before the Zulus on this side of the water. The far bank was a different story, however, and already a hundred or more warriors were waiting for us there as at least a thousand more rushed to join them. I thought the first Boers to the river would charge across before the opposition got any heavier, but to my surprise they turned in confusion, pointing and shouting in Dutch. A moment later and I was beside them, sharing their horror as they stared aghast at the scene before them.

Evidently, the Ulundi Plain was not completely flat – the western end was at least three yards higher than where we had crossed before. For that was the distance of the drop down to the water and there was a similarly steep climb up on the far side too. The higher land had constricted the flow of the water. Instead of a gentle current there was now a fast-flowing torrent to negotiate, interspersed with rocks and boulders.

"We will never get our horses across that," one of the Boers shouted at me. "We will have to leave them here and cross on foot."

"We won't stand a chance of getting up the escarpment on foot," protested his fellow. I barely paid any attention, for I was paralysed with fear, which did not alleviate any as I stared about me. Behind us, the Zulus on our bank were closing in and I could hear our rear-guard open fire to keep them at bay. We could not stay here, that was for certain. Our only chance – a paper-thin one at that – was to cross. Yet even while my comrades debated our options and others newly arrived on the scene exclaimed their dismay, another hundred warriors had joined the reception committee waiting for us on the far side.

Alexander Biggar pulled up alongside. He was clearly made of sterner stuff than me, for he instantly saw what had to be done. "Come on!" he yelled to those about him. "Death or victory!" Without a moment's hesitation, he launched his horse down the slope. I half expected him to topple in, but the animal kept its footing and launched itself into the water. Biggar pointed its nose up stream, knowing that the current would take them back. The first of the Port Natal Zulus splashed in after him, while Dingane's warriors roared with delight that we were finally heading their way. Now De Lange arrived and started shouting orders. He was speaking in Dutch and so I ignored him. The first Boers started to slide down into the water after Biggar and I was content to let them. There was no way that I wanted to be among the first up the far bank.

The man at my side pulled on my sleeve. He gestured at De Lange, who was still yelling and trying to organise the Boers into a rank facing across the river. "He says you with shotguns should be the first across. They will be better at blasting a space at short range." He grinned and held up his musket, "These are more suited to giving you covering fire from here." I stared appalled at the double-barrelled weapon in my hand. Why on earth had I given Louisa the musket? I opened my mouth, searching for an excuse, anything to delay getting into that water, but it was too late. "Go!" my smug companion shouted. With that he reached forward and with a short whip gave my mount a sharp clip on the rump. Both rider and animal screamed simultaneously in protest, yet my horse was already moving forward, hooves clattering on rocks as we slid precariously down into the water. I just had time to drop the shotgun into the saddle holster, for I would need both hands just to stay aboard. With a final leap we splashed in. The river came up to my boots and like Biggar I pointed us up stream to fight the current.

The world suddenly became a narrow strip of water and two steep banks – that was all I could see. It was quieter, too, as the noise of the battle with the Zulus on the northern shore behind us was lost in the splash of the rushing stream. So low down, I could only see the heads and shoulders of the Zulus on the opposite shore and soon not even them. Now the sense of De Lange's scheme came clear. With the river so much lower, he could safely fire over the heads of those crossing to help clear the far bank. The range was such that muskets and the few rifles that the Boers had, would be deadly accurate. Yet equally, the Zulus only had to drop back behind the crest of the far shore to be safe and I knew they would not be far away when we crossed.

Biggar and his warriors were now almost halfway across. I held back nervously, there were at least a dozen Boer riders in front of me, but more were still slithering down the slope behind. There must have been at least fifty of us riders in the stream, a few remounting after

222

coming off on the way down and almost that number of our Zulus around Alexander. We were beginning to make progress across, but then one of the Port Natal boys had to open his damn trap and yell an insult at his countrymen waiting to slaughter us. God knows what he shouted, perhaps he accused Dingane of being a goat fornicator, for there was a howl of outrage from the far shore. Then, like treacle pouring out of a cup, hundreds of warriors came streaming down the far bank, shields and spears in the air, screaming for vengeance.

They reached Biggar and his men first. The river around them was soon a boiling frenzy of stabbing and splashing as rebel and loyalist fought furiously to the death. The water was already turning red. Boers with muskets behind us must have killed at least a score of the attackers as they ran down the far shore. The marksmen picked off more as the Zulus fought and waded across the river. They were coming for us now, like a black murderous tide. The air was full of noise: screams, shouts, gunfire, an Englishman muttering prayers and the whinnies of panicked horses. Mine was struggling against the current and only the sight of more Zulus getting into the water downstream deterred me from fleeing in that direction.

I glanced back at Biggar and his Port Natal warriors, it was obvious that even with the supporting fire from the bank behind, they were losing, and badly. Several times I saw our boys hold up their left arms, brandishing the white strips of cloth to show they were on our side. Yet in the fight it was hard to see them in all the splashing and I suspect that a number were killed by Boer fire. Many dead and wounded, with and without armbands, were floating away in the fast-flowing stream. I was incredulous. Despite the fusillade poured into them, Dingane's men were still advancing across the water.

Several wounded Port Natal warriors were wading back to join us. I pulled out the shotgun and blasted a warrior without an armband who was in pursuit. "Come back!" I yelled at Biggar. He was getting cut off from the rest of us. I dared not shoot in support, for the spray of shot at that distance was just as likely to hit friend as foe. He glanced up at me and gave a slight nod of recognition but made no effort to break away. He swung his gun butt down on his right just as a spear plunged up into the left side of his back. His body arched in agony and then countless black hands reached up to pull him from the saddle. I remember shouting in anguish as he was dragged several feet upstream, *iklwas* rising and falling until he stopped moving altogether. I was shouting as much for myself as for him, as his death seemed to foretell what was in store for the rest of us. I doubted that there were any loyal Zulus left alive in that group now, but I did not care; we would probably all be dead in a minute or two. I gave the murderers my remaining barrel of shot and took satisfaction from seeing several staggering away, bloody and wailing. I was not the only one shooting. There was a deafening roar of gunfire from behind me and soon no one was moving in that patch of water.

Despite the carnage, still more Boers were sliding their horses down the bank into the water. By now there must have been around a hundred riders in the river. Most had stayed in a rough line under the bank to allow those shooting from the grass above them a clear shot. There were still three hundred Boers on the ground behind me, too, desperately trying to fight off Zulus to their rear and to their front.

As I watched, more of Dingane's men splashed down into the river to join their comrades. It felt inevitable now that we would be killed in their trap. They were chanting something as they came, moving in unison as though instead of individuals they were some vast predatory creature. I would go down fighting anyway, I thought. I had a satchel full of ammunition and there was no shortage of targets now. I blasted both barrels of lead across the water into the nearest Zulus, who were only ten yards away.

Still they came on, many holding their cattle hide shields in front of them as though they would offer some protection, but the dried skins held by the front ranks were torn to shreds by our furious fire. A hundred shotguns were now blasting from close range, with at least as many muskets firing from above and picking out their targets. As I knocked the gun butt against the pommel of the saddle again to shake down the *loopers*, I noticed that the Zulus were no closer than before. Squinting through the growing mist of gun smoke that covered our side of the river, I shot down at least two of the Zulus opposite, only to see them instantly replaced. A few had tried to rush our line, but being waist-deep in water meant they could not move quickly and consequently, all had been felled by a hail of lead.

The noise of chanting and gunfire was making the horses nervous. I could not blame them, as I was terrified myself. My mouth was dry and I had to force my hands to stay steady as I reloaded to avoid fumbling charges into the water. My horse skittered sideways against the rider to my left as I took my next shot and the man beside me cursed at my inept riding skills. But these were not cavalry horses trained for battle and, looking along the line, I saw that more than a few were jumping about.

As I reached again into the satchel, a mount several to my right screamed. It reared up, its rider only just staying in the saddle. Whether it had been struck by a stray shot, a thrown spear or a creature under the water, we will never know. But for its unfortunate rider, it then chose to plunge forward into the waiting ranks opposite. I watched in horror as it briefly ploughed a path through the shield wall, its rearing hooves lashing out at the men blocking its way. Then there were more screams, both human and animal, as the spears lashed out.

That rogue charge had created a dent in the Zulu line; men had their backs to us as they looked to blood their spears on their enemy. I heard shouting in Dutch and saw that De Lange was now in the water and he was pushing forward to try and extend the space.

"Follow him!" shouted the man to my right. "We have to get across." I had given up all thought of the far bank, but clearly others hadn't. De Lange was leading a tightly packed wedge of men and they were blasting down all about them at point blank range. To my astonishment, the great mass of Zulus started to divide. It was like Moses parting the Red Sea, and frankly, not much less of a miracle. We pressed forward and the Zulus fell back. The man next to me and I took turns reloading, so one of us was always ready to fire. We could not miss at a ten-yard range; equally, it would take the Zulus several seconds to wade that distance and they knew they would not make it. As we moved away from the northern bank I could hear more horsemen were splashing down into the river behind us. Yet I could see no reinforcements joining the Zulu in the water.

Slowly, we began to make progress. Even then, every inch was hard won. One Boer's horse got its foot stuck in the mud and rocks. As the animal stamped and tried to free itself the Zulus sensed weakness and surged forward again. A flurry of shots forced them back but even so, they hit their mark and we saw the rider hunched over, a deep spear wound in his chest. He toppled, lifeless, from his mount landing face down in the water and started to drift away in the current. One of the Boers dismounted and splashed after him but shook his head after a brief inspection of the body. He was beyond help and the corpse was left to float on; we had to concentrate on saving the living.

By now De Lange was halfway across and as their aim was now blocked, even more Boers came down from the bank to join us in the river. Increasingly outnumbered, the Zulus were pulling back. Many went downstream, a few swimming or using their shields to capture the current to pull them along. Others tried to climb back up the far bank, but hardly any made it. As I got closer to the middle of the throng, the noise of the battle behind us grew louder. The Boers in our rear-guard were still firing volleys at the Zulus that encircled them. I just hoped they could hold them off long enough for us to try and climb out of the other side of the river. There was no time to lose and yet all around us were reminders of our fate should we fail.

The water was thick with bodies, nearly all Zulu. Most were dead but some still flailed weakly, grabbing at the legs of horses as they passed. I saw one shot with a musket when he tried to raise his spear for a final thrust, but most were long past fighting. In between gunfire you could hear wails of agony and gurgling and spluttering as the warriors drowned about us. I confess I did not care a fig about them. They would all have killed me given the chance and as far as I was concerned, had got their just desserts. I was far more worried about the Zulus waiting unseen behind the opposite bank; from the chanting, they sounded very much alive. As we approached the far shore, the noise became a deafening roar, drowning out even the shooting on the bank behind us. It sounded like there were thousands up there waiting for us – and there probably were. They were not visible to us as they had learned to stay out of sight of the guns. Instead they were content for us to try and climb to them. The riverbank was a formidable obstacle. At its base, it seemed even steeper than the one we had slithered down, although it was roughly the same height: three yards of sloping mud and stone, now strewn with dead or dying Zulus and their blood and gore. Even De Lange looked hesitant at leading his men over such a barrier. There were a few seconds where every man looked at each other, hoping that the other would go first. I knew damn well I was not going to be in the 'spearhead', for that was almost certainly what they would get in the chest for their trouble. Eventually, some young blood jumped down from his horse. He yelled something in Dutch and slung his gun strap over his shoulder. Then he put his foot on the nearest rock, grabbing at tufts of grass for handholds. It was clear that no horse would make it up the slope with its rider and so the rest of us began to dismount too.

The boy started to climb, little more than eighteen and full of the certainty of youth that he could not be killed. Two others scrambled up just behind him, both with shotguns at the ready. I watched, transfixed, with a deep sense of foreboding. I remembered the companies of young men known as 'forlorn hopes' sent first into fortification breaches during the Peninsular War – they rarely ended well. With a sudden thrust the lad leapt up to stand on the top of the bank, but his victory was all too brief. Almost immediately he gave a scream and toppled forward and out of sight. The sound was drowned out by a huge roar of acclaim from the waiting Zulus, which was partly interrupted by the two Boers near the top firing their guns blindly over the summit. As they hurriedly reloaded, we all stared up expectantly, unsure what to do next.

"Go on!" shouted someone from the relative safety of the river. "Get up the bank!" The words had barely left his lips when there was a flurry of shots, picking off Zulus as they appeared fleetingly on the shore above us. Then a dark shadow flew over my head and something heavy splashed down nearby. It was the lifeless body of the boy, thrown down by our reception committee. I could see at least four or five wounds and the water around the corpse immediately turned red. What little zeal anyone had for the climb had now disappeared, although we all knew we had no choice. De Lange put it succinctly, speaking for once in English: "We climb up, or we die here." Then he hefted his own double-barrelled weapon and called out, "Shotguns up first!"

I feigned a limp as I reluctantly stumbled forward. I hoped someone else would take my gun up for me, but no bastard did. Many looked at their own musket with relief as they trained them at the top of the bank, ready to take down any Zulus who appeared. The two Boers already near the summit fired again and moments later they were joined by six more. By the time I scrambled within reach of the top there were already a dozen firing and taking no harm in return. They were stretching up to take aim now rather than firing blind and I steeled myself to do the same.

With my eyeline just over the edge of the bank, my worst fears were confirmed: there were at least another thousand, probably more, to fight our way through. Thank God few if any had their *assegai* or throwing spears left, for all those I could see only held their short stabbing weapons. The ground in front of me was already carpeted with their dead and dying. Those still alive were crouched down and pulling back to escape the lethal hail of metal scraps coming from our guns. I took aim and encouraged some more on their way although I did not doubt that they would rush us when they saw the opportunity.

De Lange was still shouting and I heard more men scrambling up behind me. A quick glance showed that the bank was now packed with Boers ready to make the next assault. I hurriedly reloaded and had just finished priming when he gave the order. Oh Christ, I thought, this is it. With men behind pushing me on, there was no choice but to scramble up over the lip of the bank. This was the moment the Zulus had been waiting for: when we were few and vulnerable and standing in the way of guns that had given us covering fire. With a mighty roar they rose and bore in on us. I thought we stood as much chance of stopping them as King Canute did in stopping the tide. For a moment I was frozen in horror but then as the guns around me started to fire, I quickly came to my senses. Raising the barrels to the horizontal, I watched as Zulus began to stumble over bodies shot down before them. Then I fired, watching the impact of each barrel scythe down its own victims.

There was no time to reload. Looking up my eyes met those of a huge warrior running straight towards me. He grinned as he must have seen the fear in my face. The man was six foot tall, broad and well-muscled. He was probably in his mid-twenties, whereas I was well past my prime. All I had going for me was a lifetime's experience of frantic struggles in desperate situations. As he drew back his *iklwa* to tear it through my guts, I knew I had only one chance. To turn or run would be fatal; I had to get inside his attack. I watched surprise cross his features as I lunged towards him. I could not reverse the gun in time and so I slammed the hot muzzles hard into his face, catching him on the bridge of the nose.

He howled in pain as his momentum carried him into me. I only just stayed on my feet and could smell his musky sweat as his chest pressed against mine. His eyes were streaming with tears, but he would blink them away in a moment and then I would be in trouble once more. His right arm had wrapped around my shoulders and I caught a glimpse of the *iklwa* in his fist. Dropping the gun, I seized the shaft and in a single movement I wrenched it from his hand. With all my strength, I plunged the long point up into his side. More bodies knocked into us and as his knees buckled, we went down together. There was a rasping wheeze as he hit the ground, but he fought on. I felt his fingers scrabbling for me. His thumb found my eye socket and I twisted desperately away before he could gouge down. Then his hands were around my neck and I knew what would follow. He must have known his wound was fatal, but he was determined to take me to hell with him. His power was immense; I could not tear those fingers away. As I gasped and gagged, trying to breathe, I grabbed hold of the *iklwa* shaft again and wrenched it up and down to tear his innards. Incredibly, he was still squeezing, and I knew I would black out in a second or two. Somehow, I found the reserves to give the blade one final shove and then slumped across his chest, fully expecting his gurgling growl to be the last thing I heard.

I am not sure if I lost consciousness, but I do know that the sensation that brought me back to the living was the stamp of a boot on my back. For a moment I relished the realisation that I was still alive. Then I remembered that while the Zulu and I had been fighting the most personal of combats, there was still a battle going on all around me. I thought of the boot. I knew it was definitely a boot, for I could still feel the nail marks in my back. The Zulus fought with bare feet. Slowly I raised my head off my victim's chest and looked about. To my left a white face stared back at me. I started to croak at him before realising that the eyes were lifeless and there was a spear wound in his neck that had half decapitated him. My hearing was coming back, and the noise of fighting about me grew much louder. Another booted foot kicked my side and now I realised that I lay among a forest of moving legs, all belonging to trousered Boers. They were surging forward, which meant that somehow, we were winning.

I reached out and grabbed a passing ankle. Its owner shook me off and then looked down. He said something in Dutch and then tried English, "Hey, are you alive?"

"No," I rasped, "I am a bloody angel, will you help me up?" He chuckled at that and I felt strong arms reach me under the shoulders and haul me up on my feet.

"Here," called one of my rescuers and he pulled my arm around over his shoulder to help me stay up.

"What are you doing?" I asked, pulling my arm back.

"You're wounded," he replied, pointing at a bloodstain on my shirt.

"That is from him," I gestured down at the body at my feet. Virtually the whole blade of the *iklwa*, nearly a foot of flattened metal, was inside the man's chest.

"In that case, you will want this." My shotgun, its muzzle still covered in gore was thrust back into my hands and with that, my rescuer disappeared back into the crowd about us. I staggered on in his wake, still trying to work out what was happening. I heard shooting ahead and automatically I reloaded my gun as I looked about. There must have been at least two hundred Boers now on the southern shore of the river and when I looked behind me, I saw that the horses were being driven up the bank now too. De Lange had organised the men to fire rolling volleys and as I moved forward, I suddenly found myself in the front rank. I fired my gun almost blindly into a cluster of Zulus ahead of us who were retreating, before turning to reload.

As I worked my way back into the throng, I found a group of Boers each holding the reins of three or four horses. One saw the blood on my shirt and made the same assumption as before that it was mine. "Here," he passed me some reins. I did not correct him. Heaven knew how many horses had survived and I was not going to pass up on the chance of getting on one early. Gratefully, I swung myself up into the saddle and only then did I get a better idea of what was happening. In front of us the Zulu were falling back on either side and only a few hundred stood between us and the path onto the plateau. The patch of river I could see was half full of horses, but these were now being driven up in numbers onto the southern shore to join at least three hundred Boers that now surrounded me. The remainder of the rear-guard was pulling back over the river.

Over the next few minutes the number of Zulus in front of us dwindled further. At the same time the rest of the Boers and their horses joined us on the southern shore and soon all were mounted up once more. De Lange led a charge to sweep away the last of the Zulu blocking the route to the plateau and we all followed on behind. In truth it was the slowest charge I have ever seen. Men and horses were down to their last ounces of strength, but it served its purpose. The Zulus had long since learned that shotguns and muskets could kill at a far longer range than they could attack. I followed on behind, warily watching for any last-minute attack on our flanks, but most of Dingane's soldiers had finally given up on stopping us.

As I galloped the last few yards up to the higher ground, my thoughts turned to the laager. I half expected the Zulus to have attacked and destroyed that as well. It was what I would have done in their shoes. Yet as we gained height, we soon spotted it in the distance. I desperately wanted to know if Louisa was still there and safe, but my exhausted screw could barely manage more than a walk. I urged it on into a trot when I could and gradually the specks of wagons grew bigger until I could see for sure that they had not been burned. Horses with more stamina outpaced mine and I watched anxiously as they approached the circle of carts. I assumed it had been abandoned by those we had left behind, but as the first riders approached, a man with a bandaged hand stepped out to welcome them.

Chapter 26

I could not remember when I had been so fatigued. It was not at all surprising as we had been in and out of the saddle for ten hours. Much of that time was in a funk of terror, which can be a damned exhausting business. Yet when I spotted a figure in a dress searching the riders for a sight of me, I felt the weariness melt away. Even the horse stumbled into a gallop to cover the last few hundred yards.

To this day I don't quite understand how we made it all the way around the Ulundi Plain and back to that precious laager. Of course, not everyone did. Six Boer riders were dead as were nearly all the Zulus from Port Natal. Around a hundred were wounded, some badly. Louisa wept when she heard of Alexander Biggar; he had been so good to us during our time in Port Natal. I could not forget that last look he gave me. He could have tried to cut back to join the rest of the Boers, but he made no attempt to come our way. Perhaps he thought the day was lost and was content to follow his sons.

There was no thought of breaking camp that evening as hardly anyone was in a fit state to ride another mile. Pretorius would stride to the edge of the escarpment and while he could see a few Zulus moving around below us, there was no sign of their army. He loudly proclaimed that it would be better if the Zulus did attack the laager that night, for our garrison would be able to destroy them from their mobile fort. A few weary heads nodded in agreement, but most I suspect thought like me: there is a man who has not spent all day fighting already. Instead of letting his command rest, he insisted on a prayer meeting to give thanks for our deliverance. I excused myself and lay down in a wagon. My last memory was hearing him fulminating over Potgieter and at those who had ridden off.

The Zulus could have attacked that night and I am quite sure that I would have slept through the entire battle if they did. Instead, they stayed away, but around eleven o'clock a few of Potgieter's group finally made it back. The rest were making their own way south, no doubt to avoid their leader's wrath. The Zulus did not attack the next day either, much to the frustration of Pretorius. Indeed, their army had disappeared, but most of us were grateful for a period of rest. The following day, the 29th of December, the laager finally started to make its way south once more. I saw Umgungundlovu for the final time on the very last day of the year. It was not a place I was going to miss.

There this story might have ended. When we returned to England, Louisa and I both swore that we would never leave these shores again. We go down to London for the season but spend most of our time in Leicestershire. Louisa's health fully recovered apart from the limp and I resolved that my adventuring days were over. All was well apart from one nagging irritation: Dingane. He had been overthrown by his half-brother, Mpande, whose forces had chased the old king out of the Zulu kingdom. A treaty was then agreed with the Boers, who were granted even more land than had been offered to Retief. Natal looked set for a period of peace and prosperity.

Two years after we left Africa, the British and Boers were still arguing over who should rule in Natal, but everyone had forgotten about the vicious tyrant who had caused so much suffering. I often remembered that conversation with Alexander Biggar when he had talked about how dearly he would have liked to make Dingane pay for his crimes. How I wished he could have had the chance, rather than dying in that river. The only news I had heard of the old king was that he was now a guest of another African monarch in a neighbouring land. He still had some supporters and people seemed content to let him live out his days in peace. That thought burned in my craw, confirming my suspicions that the devil looks after his own. That is until I returned from walking my dog one summer afternoon.

I had been out with my new Irish wolfhound – I had been fond of the breed since my time in Spain. This one was named O'Malley, in honour of the man who had unwittingly saved my life. The animal was bounding about chasing pigeons when we came up to the house and a maid called that a package had been delivered for me. I went inside to find a box marked from the Colonial Office. I cut the string securing it and inside found a brown paper parcel and a letter addressed to me from Ben D'Urban:

Dear Thomas,

I trust you and Louisa are fully recovered now from your time in Africa. I can only apologise again for the trials and tribulations you suffered in my service. Your continued friendship is much more than I deserve. Yet I wonder if I might call on you for one further favour.

We have received a report that Dingane has been murdered by agents of his brother and the enclosed has been sent as proof of his demise. I have shown this to Reverend and Mrs Owen, who now believe that the villain is dead. Yet Mrs Owen suggested that I send this to you. She thought that you would wish to see it and could send your own confirmation. I look forward to hearing from you.

Ben

I stared at the little parcel, intrigued. What on earth could be in it that would enable me to confirm the death of a king some five thousand miles away? It was far too small for his head and I doubted that even that would be recognisable after three months' knocking around in the hold of a ship. I tore open the paper to find a ten-inch square of cloth. It looked as though it had originally been white, but now most of it was covered with a deep russet stain, which I took to be dried blood. Certainly, someone or even some creature had seeped gore into it, but I could not see how the deuce I was supposed to know who that was. I touched a corner that was still a grubby grey; the weave was tight and smooth, certainly not African cloth. It could belong to anyone, I thought. Then I noticed that there was a seam along one edge, attaching it to more fabric underneath.

I turned it over. The underside was stiff like board with congealed blood. It was a much thicker cloth that had acted like blotting paper and was a similar brown colour to the reverse. Then I saw it and I am certain that a slow grin of satisfaction must have spread across my features. There in the corner was an inch or two of the original colour. I took the parcel out into the sunlight to be sure, but there was no doubt. The cloth was a rich shade of plum, one that I had last seen over two years before on an opera cloak.

Historical Notes

As usual I am indebted to a range of sources to confirm the information provided in Flashman's account. These include the senior librarian at the South African Heritage Foundation, who recommended a range of histories such as by George McCall Theal and especially, *The Great Trek* by Robin Binckes. This more recent publication brings together a wide range of contemporary sources. Of particular help, especially for the first half of the book, were accounts written by those who were there with Flashman: Francis Owen and William Woods.

The Reverend Francis Owen

Owen published the journal he wrote while he was in Umgungundlovu, a copy of which is available in the British Library. It records the arrival of an unnamed white stranger in December 1837 and the forced use on him of the king's often lethal physic. The man survives although the date he left Owen's mission is not recorded. Owen also describes the trials of his journey overland to Natal with his wife, family and servants. They are briefly held hostage by one African chief, as well as being robbed and abandoned by their guide. Their wagons were bogged down in mud or capsized in rivers, and they were treated as strange curiosities by virtually all they met. You can easily imagine them regretting leaving their safe lives in Yorkshire, however, they persevered. While Owen goes into some detail on the spiritual challenges he faces, there is extraordinarily little on how the more practical obstacles were overcome. As their guide abandoned them on the journey, it seems likely that someone else, possibly his wife, took the lead here.

Owen also describes his struggles as he tried to convert the Zulus to Christianity. He quotes many of the same examples of preaching and lessons that Flashman mentions and the arguments and misunderstandings that result. A sense of frustration is clear in his writing. Dingane seems to have tested his faith to the limits, with long interrogations and by sending inquisitive boys to his school. The two got along better when the king asked Owen to help him read and write.

Those in Owen's mission were the only surviving white witnesses to Dingane's discussions with Retief and the subsequent murder of the Boers. In his journal Owen explains that despite the danger, he thought it was his duty to remonstrate with Dingane over the death of Retief and his men. When he wrote the account, he still believed he had done so. However, in a diary published by William Woods many years later, he admits to changing Owen's words to imply that the Reverend reluctantly thought that such an act was necessary. This may explain why Owen, his family and others in his household were able to escape with their lives. It was, however, a close-run thing, and involved various threats and interviews with Dingane, as described by Flashman. Some of the quotes recorded by Flashman are also included in Owen's journal, such as Mrs Owen's brave call of, "The rougher the road, the sweeter the glory," as they thought they were about to face death.

Owen left the Church Missionary Society and returned to England in 1841. In 1844 he became the second vicar of St Thomas' Crookes church in Sheffield. He served there for nearly ten years before deciding to take a tour of the Holy Land. Sadly as he embarked for home he caught 'Syrian fever' and died in Alexandria on 14th November 1854, aged 52. In 1857 his wife, Sarah Pennington Owen, remarried another clergyman, John Livesey. She died in 1863, aged 54.

Influenced by his personal circumstances, Flashman may have been rather too disparaging of Owen's mentor, Captain Allen Francis Gardiner. After his exploits in Natal, Gardiner went on to found a South American Missionary Society. He died with other missionaries of starvation on the southern tip of the continent in 1851.

Dingane

Flashman's description of Dingane and his capital Umgungundlovu largely matches contemporary accounts. Physically, he was a tall and powerful man, who had murdered his brother Shaka to seize the throne. By the time Flashman met him, he was around forty-two years old and had been ruling his kingdom for nearly ten years. The execution hill, known to the Zulus as KwaMatiwane, was used as Flashman described for both the death of Retief and his followers, but also for many Zulus who had incurred the king's wrath. This included many of the followers of the chief that Dingane ordered to murder Retief's party following their first visit. Like Owen, Flashman gives the name of this chief as Isiguabani – presumably as he heard the story from Owen, but other accounts use different spellings, the most common being Silwebana.

After his overthrow by his half-brother Mpande, Dingane went into exile and was murdered in 1840.

The Massacre of the Boers

This event is now known as the Weenen Massacre and took place around the present town of Weenen, which is the Dutch word for 'wept'. Many of the forward Boer camps were caught completely unawares, with most of the occupants slaughtered. Only when those further back had a chance to form a laager, were the Dutch able to put up an effective defence. The casualty numbers were as described by Flashman, with many children among the dead. George Biggar was killed when he and Dick King rode to warn the Dutch of the attack.

The Army of Natal

The few accounts of this army detail it being led by white settlers, based at Port Natal. However, it was overwhelmingly made up of rebel Zulu warriors, who would have had their own leaders. It launched two invasions into Dingane's territory. The first deteriorated into a looting expedition and returned unscathed with a large quantity of cattle and prisoners. The second invasion, with Robert Biggar one of its leaders, had the misfortune to face several thousand of the Zulu army. It encountered Dingane's forces, who had just defeated a divided Dutch force that had tried to fight them on open ground. The Army of Natal was caught in a classic Zulu bull's head attack that broke apart their line and virtually annihilated the force. As Flashman describes, apart from himself, only three other white settlers made it back to Port Natal, the most well-known being Dick King, who hid in the riverbank until nightfall and then escaped under cover of darkness.

Battle at Gatsrand

This attack took place on the thirteenth and fourteenth of August 1838. There are fewer accounts of this encounter than of the more decisive battle at Blood River. Estimates for the number of Boer fighters taking part varies from seventy-five to a hundred and fifty. The action took place largely as described by Flashman with the Zulus initially assaulting the western side of the laager and later using flaming *assegais* and grass fires to try and break down defences. They also had warriors riding horses and shooting firearms, although these were not used effectively. At least one account suggests that the Boers fought the Zulus on foot from outside the wagon circle. However, it is hard to imagine how possibly as few as seventy-five men could see off ten thousand Zulus in this manner. Flashman's assertion that they fought from inside the laager as normal, seems more likely.

Blood River
This is by far the most famous engagement between the Boers and the Zulu with a large iron replica of the laager now standing as a memorial on the battle site. The astonishing disparity in casualties: three wounded on the Boer side and approximately three thousand Zulu dead is confirmed by most accounts. The Zulu generals did not vary their tactics as they had at Gatsrand and threw away any advantage of surprise. The Boers fought from within their laager with virtual impunity and then sent out mounted patrols to attack the Zulu flanks until they were forced to withdraw. Three British men fought with the Dutch, including Alexander Biggar.

Battles around the White Umfolozi River
There are few records of the White Umfolozi River engagement, where the Zulus achieved an extraordinary deception and ambush. Reading the accounts, it seems astonishing that the Dutch/British casualties were as low as they were, but a shortage of throwing spears seems to have played a part in their good fortune. Alexander Biggar is reported as the first of the party killed, during the final river crossing. Some accounts say he could have survived if he had abandoned his Port Natal Zulus, but he chose to stay and fight with them. The Ulundi Plain is now better known as the site of a battle between the British and the Zulus, where the forces of King Cetschwayo were finally defeated after the engagements at Isandlwana and Rorke's Drift in 1879.

Natal after Flashman
Major Charters was replaced by a Captain Jervis as commander of the Durban garrison at Fort Victoria in January 1839. With the support of the governor, he endeavoured to be more constructive, organising a meeting between the Boers and the Zulu to agree a peace treaty. Dingane was not present, but his advisers agreed new boundaries and to pay nearly twenty thousand cattle by way of compensation. Reluctantly, Jervis also returned the Boer gunpowder. Dingane only paid a fraction of the agreed compensation. He also suffered a defeat against a nearby African kingdom when he tried to seize some of their territory to replace the land he had conceded. By then he had lost much

credibility with his own people and his half-brother Mpande launched a coup against him. Mpande agreed a peace treaty with the Boers and together they agreed to fight the forces of Dingane. However, in the subsequent war it was Mpande's army, not the Boers, that defeated that of his half-brother.

Captain Jervis and his garrison left Port Natal at the end of 1839, leaving the Boers finally free from British interference – although the governor still insisted that they remained British citizens. Left on their own, friction grew between the Boer leaders, particularly Pretorius and a son of Maritz. The Boers also tried to impose their will on neighbouring African kingdoms, who complained to the British. In 1842 British troops returned to Natal, marching in force from the colony. The Boers, led by Pretorius, resisted the incursion and after several skirmishes they besieged the British force then camped near Durban. After twenty-six days a larger British force and a warship arrived to lift the siege and drive the Boer forces off. The subsequent peace treaty required the Boers to accept the authority of the British government in the region. With reluctance, Pretorius persuaded the Boers that signing the treaty was in their best interests. The residual Boer resentment was one of the factors behind the later Anglo–Boer Wars in the 1880s and 1900s.

Thank you for reading this book and I hoped you enjoyed it. If so I would be grateful for any positive reviews on websites that you use to choose books. As there is no major publisher promoting this book, any recommendations to friends and family that you think would enjoy it would also be appreciated.

There is now a Thomas Flashman Books Facebook page and the www.robertbrightwell.com website to keep you updated on future books in the series. They also include portraits, pictures and further information on characters and events featured in the books.

Also by this author

Flashman and the Seawolf

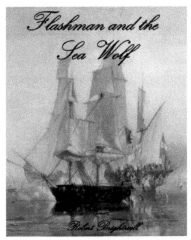

This first book in the Thomas
Flashman series covers his
adventures with Thomas Cochrane,
one of the most extraordinary naval
commanders of all time.
From the brothels and gambling
dens of London, through political
intrigues and espionage, the action
moves to the Mediterranean and the
real life character of Thomas Cochrane. This book covers the start of
Cochrane's career including the most astounding single ship action of
the Napoleonic war.

Thomas Flashman provides a unique insight as danger stalks him like
a persistent bailiff through a series of adventures that prove history
really is stranger than fiction.

Flashman and the Cobra

This book takes Thomas to territory familiar to readers of his nephew's adventures, India, during the second Mahratta war. It also includes an illuminating visit to Paris during the Peace of Amiens in 1802.

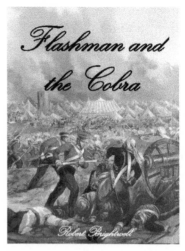

As you might expect Flashman is embroiled in treachery and scandal from the outset and, despite his very best endeavours, is often in the thick of the action. He intrigues with generals, warlords, fearless warriors, nomadic bandit tribes, highland soldiers and not least a four-foot-tall former nautch dancer, who led the only Mahratta troops to leave the battlefield of Assaye in good order.

Flashman gives an illuminating account with a unique perspective. It details feats of incredible courage (not his, obviously) reckless folly and sheer good luck that were to change the future of India and the career of a general who would later win a war in Europe.

Flashman in the Peninsula

While many people have written books
and novels on the Peninsular War,
Flashman's memoirs offer a unique
perspective. They include new
accounts of famous battles, but also
incredible incidents and characters
almost forgotten by history.

Flashman is revealed as the catalyst to
one of the greatest royal scandals of
the nineteenth century which disgraced
a prince and ultimately produced one
of our greatest novelists. In Spain and Portugal he witnesses
catastrophic incompetence and incredible courage in equal measure.
He is present at an extraordinary action where a small group of men
stopped the army of a French marshal in its tracks. His flatulent horse
may well have routed a Spanish regiment, while his cowardice and
poltroonery certainly saved the British army from a French trap.

Accompanied by Lord Byron's dog, Flashman faces death from Polish
lancers and a vengeful Spanish midget, not to mention finding time to
perform a blasphemous act with the famous Maid of Zaragoza. This is
an account made more astonishing as the key facts are confirmed by
various historical sources.

Flashman's Escape

This book covers the second half of
Thomas Flashman's experiences in the
Peninsular War and follows on from
Flashman in the Peninsula.

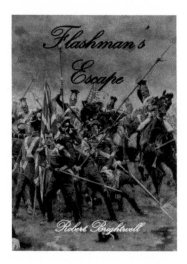

Having lost his role as a staff officer,
Flashman finds himself commanding a
company in an infantry battalion. In
between cuckolding his soldiers and
annoying his superiors, he finds himself at
the heart of the two bloodiest actions of
the war. With drama and disaster in equal
measure, he provides a first-hand account of not only the horror of
battle but also the bloody aftermath.

Hopes for a quieter life backfire horribly when he is sent behind
enemy lines to help recover an important British prisoner, who also
happens to be a hated rival. His adventures take him the length of
Spain and all the way to Paris on one of the most audacious wartime
journeys ever undertaken.

With the future of the French empire briefly placed in his quaking
hands, Flashman dodges lovers, angry fathers, conspirators and
ministers of state in a desperate effort to keep his cowardly carcass in
one piece. It is a historical roller-coaster ride that brings together
various extraordinary events, while also giving a disturbing insight
into the creation of a French literary classic!

Flashman and Madison's War

This book finds Thomas, a British army officer, landing on the shores of the United States at the worst possible moment – just when the United States has declared war with Britain! Having already endured enough with his earlier adventures, he desperately wants to go home but finds himself drawn inexorably into this new conflict. He is soon dodging musket balls, arrows and tomahawks as he desperately tries to keep his scalp intact and on his head.

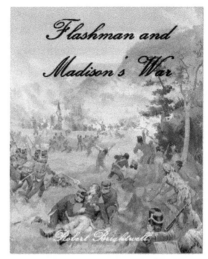

It is an extraordinary tale of an almost forgotten war, with inspiring leaders, incompetent commanders, a future American president, terrifying warriors (and their equally intimidating women), brave sailors, trigger-happy madams and a girl in a wet dress who could have brought a city to a standstill. Flashman plays a central role and reveals that he was responsible for the disgrace of one British general, the capture of another and for one of the biggest debacles in British military history.

Flashman's Waterloo

The first six months of 1815 were a pivotal time in European history. As a result, countless books have been written by men who were there and by those who studied it afterwards. But despite this wealth of material there are still many unanswered questions including:

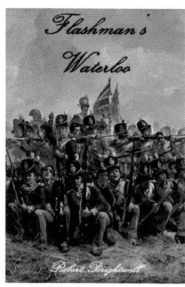

-Why did the man who promised to bring Napoleon back in an iron cage, instead join his old commander?

-Why was Wellington so convinced that the French would not attack when they did?

-Why was the French emperor ill during the height of the battle, leaving its management to the hot-headed Marshal Ney?

-What possessed Ney to launch a huge and disastrous cavalry charge in the middle of the battle?

-Why did the British Head of Intelligence always walk with a limp after the conflict?

The answer to all these questions in full or in part can be summed up in one word: Flashman.

This extraordinary tale is aligned with other historical accounts of the Waterloo campaign and reveals how Flashman's attempt to embrace the quiet diplomatic life backfires spectacularly. The memoir provides a unique insight into how Napoleon returned to power, the treachery and intrigues around his hundred-day rule and how ultimately he was robbed of victory. It includes the return of old friends and enemies from both sides of the conflict and is a fitting climax to Thomas Flashman's Napoleonic adventures.

Flashman and the Emperor

This seventh instalment in the memoirs of the Georgian rogue Thomas Flashman reveals that, despite his suffering through the Napoleonic Wars, he did not get to enjoy a quiet retirement. Indeed, middle age finds him acting just as disgracefully as in his youth, as old friends pull him unwittingly back into the fray.

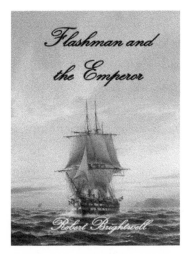

He re-joins his former comrade in arms, Thomas Cochrane, in what is intended to be a peaceful and profitable sojourn in South America. Instead, he finds himself enjoying drug-fuelled orgies in Rio, trying his hand at silver smuggling and escaping earthquakes in Chile before being reluctantly shanghaied into the Brazilian navy.

Sailing with Cochrane again, he joins the admiral in what must be one of the most extraordinary periods of his already legendary career. With a crew more interested in fighting each other than the enemy, they use Cochrane's courage, Flashman's cunning and an outrageous bluff to carve out nothing less than an empire which will stand the test of time.

Flashman and the Golden Sword

Of all the enemies that our hero has shrunk away from, there was one he feared above them all. By his own admission they gave him nightmares into his dotage. It was not the French, the Spanish, the Americans or the Mexicans. It was not even the more exotic adversaries such as the Iroquois, Mahratta or Zulus. While they could all make his guts churn anxiously, the foe that really put him off his lunch were the Ashanti.

"You could not see them coming," he complained. "They were well armed, fought with cunning and above all, there were bloody thousands of the bastards."

This eighth packet in the Thomas Flashman memoirs details his misadventures on the Gold Coast in Africa. It was a time when the British lion discovered that instead of being the king of the jungle, it was in fact a crumb on the lip of a far more ferocious beast. Our 'hero' is at the heart of this revelation after he is shipwrecked on that hostile shore. While waiting for passage home, he is soon embroiled in the plans of a naïve British governor who has hopelessly underestimated his foe. When he is not impersonating a missionary or chasing the local women, Flashman finds himself being trapped by enemy armies, risking execution and the worst kind of 'dismemberment,' not to mention escaping prisons, spies, snakes, water horses (hippopotamus) and crocodiles.

It is another rip-roaring Thomas Flashman adventure, which tells the true story of an extraordinary time in Africa that is now almost entirely forgotten.

Flashman at the Alamo

When other men might be looking forward to a well-earned retirement to enjoy their ill-gotten gains, Flashman finds himself once more facing overwhelming odds and ruthless enemies, while standing (reluctantly) shoulder to shoulder with some of America's greatest heroes.

A trip abroad to avoid a scandal at home leaves him bored and restless. They say 'the devil makes work for idle hands' and Lucifer surpassed himself this time as Thomas is persuaded to visit the newly independent country of Texas. Little does he realise that this fledgling state is about to face its biggest challenge – one that will threaten its very existence.

Flashman joins the desperate fight of a new nation against a pitiless tyrant, who gives no quarter to those who stand against him.

Drunkards, hunters, farmers, lawyers, adventurers and one English coward all come together to fight and win their liberty.

Lightning Source UK Ltd.
Milton Keynes UK
UKHW010649151020
371631UK00001B/41